HAT'S ENTERTAINMENT!

HAT TRICK

HAT'S ENTERTAINMENT!

LUKE CHMILENKO
AND
G. D. PENMAN

Podium

Cover design by Mansik Yang and STK Kreations

ISBN: 978-1-0394-5418-7

Published in 2024 by Podium Publishing
www.podiumaudio.com

HAT'S ENTERTAINMENT!

CONCERNING THE BADLANDS

Every great tale has a beginning, middle, and end. My tale, nay, my quest, nay, my legend is now coming to its middle.

But before we can look to the events that took place deep beneath the surface of the world, we must consider that which has already passed. We must think back to where we began.

Mainly because I do not trust any of you to have an attention span better than Ig's, and thus I imagine everything that occurred in the previous tome has already been lost to your memory.

So allow me to reintroduce myself. I am Absalom Scryne, the greatest wizard that the world has ever known. Learned in the arcane arts, puissant in the wielding of power, Archmage of Arpanpholigon and number one on *Wizards! Magazine*'s Top 10 to Watch Under 1000. I am, in the realm of the mystical and arcane, something of a big deal. Which is why my murder came as such a surprise.

The last thing that I remember, I was in my tower in the Invisible College of Arpanpholigon, diligently developing dweomers, and the next my physical body had been destroyed and my spirit transubstantiated into the nearest object that had been sufficiently doused in magic to retain it. In this case, my hat.

My murder should have been an impossibility. Each day I woke and layered protective spells upon myself, not to mention the various enchantments woven into the chambers in which I dwelled and the tower in which I worked. Anything with hostile intent should have been rendered down to its component atoms long before taking a shot at me, which suggests that my slayer was a sorcerer of considerable capability. To match and overpower my defenses would have required utter genius. And having spent many decades, nay, centuries in the company of my coworkers, who were, despite their deficiencies, considered to be among the most capable arcane academics in all of creation, I knew that not a one of them had either the competence or the drive to defeat me. It was a mystery. And given that as a wizard, my entire purpose is to delve into mysteries, tear them apart and release them as carefully structured, peer-reviewed spells, solving this mystery drove me as surely as my desire to find the person who had killed me and turn them into something unpleasant, then turn them inside out.

As a hat, the full suite of human senses was denied to me, and for a time I had no awareness of what was going on around me. Days, months, or years may have passed while I was lost in the endless night of senselessness. When awareness did finally return to me, I was in what I can only describe as the worst place imaginable.

To wit, I was atop the head of a kobold.

Imagine, if you can, the worst smell that you have ever smelled. As though excrement and decay had a baby and decided to baptize it in sewage. Then imagine that the worst smell imaginable had a physical form. That physical form was Ig.

The kobold in question was one of the most intellectually stunted creatures I had ever had the misfortune of crossing paths with. As such, it was rather easy to convince him to undertake the journey back to Arpanpholigon on my behalf, so that I might discover who had murdered me and seek vengeance. On the downside, his fundamental lack of focus meant that as I attempted to teach him magic—so that the most harmless resident of the Badlands might traverse them without becoming prey to one of the many more fearsome monsters that dominate those wild lands—he struggled somewhat. And by struggling somewhat, I of course mean that he utterly failed every time he attempted to cast a spell.

Within moments of meeting him, he was almost consumed by a fish. Not a fish monster, not a dragon-fish, just a fish. Kobolds are not particularly resilient. In fact, I'm fairly confident that the only reason they have not gone extinct is because of the comedic potential of their ongoing survival while other, far more competent creatures are wiped away in the sands of time.

After the fish, there were some other wild animals, some mild starvation, an ogre artist that wanted to cut off his ears, and then it was all downhill from there.

I would go so far as to say that a great deal of shenanigans ensued, in fact.

Against my advice, we teamed up with a group of adventurers, most of whom have since expired in tragic and heroic ways. Ig was extremely sad about this turn of events; I considered dead to be the natural state of being for adventurers. And death by violence to be natural causes.

Through no fault of mine, we came into conflict with a village of werewolves who were having their humanity held ransom by a traveling bard during our journey, culminating in Ig throwing a stick and distracting them.

Next we encountered a city of allegedly civilized ogres, which we may have inadvertently set on fire, resulting in yet more vengeance being sworn against us. Though I must say their leader seemed to have a personal grudge with Ig even outside of the whole inferno situation. A grudge that was later resolved through decapitation, thankfully. His, not ours.

We also picked up a necromancer who had once been a friend of one of the adventurers in his edgy youth, a penis-obsessed man who later betrayed us before dying in a hilariously catastrophic way: exploding into a fountain of bunnies while being chewed on by werewolves.

In short, he died as he lived: exploding while being done-in doggy style.

We fled into a dwarven mine to escape the ravaging were-beasts once the necromancer popped and were all set to travel underground to our destination, avoiding all of civilization, where we would be subject to judgment and possible extermination as a result of outstanding bounties on Ig's adventurer chum and the nature of the kobold atop which I was perched.

Kobolds are considered vermin at best in most civilized lands.

All of which, I believe, more or less catches us up to the present.

Ig was feeling confident for the first time in his entire life and elected to cast a ball of heckfire to seal the tunnel behind us.

Despite successfully casting a spell for the first time ever, he overdid it a bit and blew us all in different directions. Resulting in me, a hat, being blown off his head and down another tunnel from him entirely as the entrance to the mines collapsed.

Much to my immense irritation.

Without a head to ride upon, I would have sat for all eternity in the dark of the collapsed tunnel. Devoid of senses or awareness of the passage of time. The worst heck that I could conceive of being banished to. Endless darkness and nothingness.

Approximately thirty minutes after the explosion, someone came to investigate the tunnel collapse and put me on. Thus beginning the second phase of my grand adventure, and the gradual realization that there were in fact worse fates than being placed upon the head of a kobold.

CHAPTER ONE

CONCERNING DWARVES

It should have come as no surprise that I was retrieved from the rubble by a dwarf. I was in a dwarven mine, and even were it not, there are very few creatures that happily go wandering around in dark tunnels beneath the earth that are not dwarves. At least none that have heads that I would fit on.

"Fitting" was perhaps a little generous of a description. Just as the kobold has an unusually small head, to account for its unusually small brain, so too does the dwarf have a particularly broad one. This is not, as one might have hoped, because they have a brain of unusually large proportions, but rather because nature has equipped them with a skull thick enough to survive constantly banging on the tops of their mine shafts, and the occasional tunnel collapse. They are born with a built-in helmet, which serves them well throughout life, as one of the most bullheaded species in the world.

So I was perched atop the head of this dwarf rather than surrounding it.

One might have assumed that there was some enchantment that I had woven that encouraged strangers to put me on their heads when they discovered me inert, but in fact, that is simply the natural response of all sapient creatures upon discovering something hat-shaped. Admittedly, I am a particularly attractive hat, what with the perfect point, beautiful felting, and elaborate embroidery, but were I a simple bowl, more likely than not I would have found myself dropped onto just as many heads.

The person within that head adjusted me once or twice as I struggled to stay silent, then my own impetuousness overtook me.

Greetings, friend dwarf. I am Absalom Scryne, Archmage of Arpanpholigon and currently, hat.

Or rather that is what I would have said. I made it as far as *Gr*—before I was yanked off the dwarf's head with force.

Dimly I could feel the tight grip on my rim distorting its shape through the eternal shroud of nothingness to which I'd been condemned. Then after what seemed an age, I was returned to the dwarf's scalp.

"You talking to me, hat?"

I am indeed.

"Thought so." I was pulled off the dwarf's head yet again.

Oh come on.

It was difficult not to feel a little frustrated, being blinked in and out of existence repeatedly. Particularly when there was little to nothing I could do to control my situation. I was powerless without a body, and while it was possible I might have seized control of the dwarf before being yanked off again, if I failed, that would have been the end of my hopes. Better to let the dwarf come to me in her own time and develop some degree of trust rather than snapping a trap shut on her finger.

Ah, yes, you may have noticed that I refer to the dwarf using feminine pronouns. This may be something of a surprise to those of you who have seen a dwarf with their beard and gruffness but have not been educated in their nature. You see, gender is not something that is particularly relevant to a dwarf. Strictly speaking, all of them are female, except for a few specially bred males that hang around the king to inseminate her when it is required. I believe that they are raised on a diet of slightly different mead as babies to initiate the sex change. Regardless, they typically adapt the masculine naming structures of other species as they have discovered that it results in them being taken more seriously. Even though, strictly speaking, the worker or drone dwarves are all female, and their king is, strictly speaking, a queen, they will all be referred to as his sons.

If this confuses you, do not be alarmed; it confuses most people that learn about hive-based species and attempt to apply what we know of our own structures to them. The fact that dwarves look like smaller, more hirsute, versions of humans probably exacerbates this confusion, but in terms of social structure, they more closely resemble bees, ants, and mole rats.

As such, I shall attempt to refer to the dwarves we encounter as masculine, despite my superior knowledge of their biology and social structure driving me to do otherwise, as the goal of communication is for us to be understood, even if we do have to dumb things down a little.

Anyway, the dwarf put me back on *his* head, immediately asking, "How can you talk?"

I am not, in fact, a hat.

I was ripped off, examined, and then returned to the dwarf's head. "Yes, you are."

I am not only *a hat, I am also a wizard, who has been trapped within said hat.*

The dwarf did not immediately remove me again. This was progress. Of course, that did not mean that the conversation was in any way going my way. "That's not a thing."

I can assure you, it is. There is a great deal of historical precedent for the creation of magical items in such a manner, for instance . . .

The dwarf grumbled. "Stop talking."

As you wish.

We trudged along for a while without further communication. The dwarf's incredible eyes were able to pick out the flat surfaces of this shadowy underworld without any sort of light at all. I'd have put it down to the dwarf's photographic memory if I weren't experiencing it for myself. Seeing without light.

"Why did that tunnel fall down?"

I gave no answer, as requested.

"You may speak now."

As you wish.

"The tunnel, collapsed. Why?"

Idiocy, mostly.

"Speak sense, you . . ." He called me something that does not translate into the common tongue and would be too filthy to be translated even if it could have been.

I would assume it was because of the catastrophic explosion of heckfire that was being used to seal the mine entrance and prevent the ingress of a horde of ravenous werewolves. Also, please do not refer to me in such a manner. I have never performed an act like that in my life.

"Suppose it's hard to," the dwarf conceded. "When you're a hat."

It's fairly hard when you're a wizard too.

"So you blew the tunnel?"

Not I. My companion, Ig.

"What sort of . . ." Another fairly horrific word of Dwarvish came here that translates loosely as "an animal in the middle of making love" but more directly translates into something so grotesque that it cannot be put into words. ". . . name is Ig?"

A kobold name.

"You brought kobolds down our mine?!"

I came into your mine atop a kobold, singular. In the company of a swordsman who was meant to guide us back to the city of Arpanpholigon, where I might be restored to my human state.

The dwarf's thoughts were not the fleeting, sharp little things that I had experienced atop Ig's skull. Rather, they were more akin to the shifting of tectonic plates. There was definitely movement going on down there, but it was so far down and so massive that it appeared that nothing was happening at all. At least until a little volcanic eruption of words came up. "King isn't going to like it."

Kings rarely like anything.

"Going to have to turn you in." That particular turn of phrase made me a little concerned. Either I was being treated as a criminal or as contraband.

Neither of which were treated particularly well in the carefully structured society of a dwarf hive.

Faintly, I mumbled, *I would prefer if you wouldn't.*

The dwarf nodded, then picked up the pace of their progress. "Going to take you to the king; he can decide what to do with you."

I wasn't quite at the stage of pleading yet, but some mild wheedling was certainly within my remit. *It might be more advantageous if you were to simply reunite me with my friends and we can get out of your way.*

The dwarf grumbled. "Already brought down a vital tunnel."

I'm fairly certain that you didn't want werewolves flooding your mine, so . . . you're welcome. Also, I am dubious as to how vital the tunnel was, given that it had gone unused for years.

"It was a . . ." This time the word was entirely translatable, but I'm too much of a gentleman to translate it. ". . . air vent."

It was closed when we found it. So very little air was being vented.

Without hesitation or doubt, the dwarf replied, "Then it was meant to be."

I wonder if we haven't got off on the wrong foot. I apologize for the damage to your mine; it was undertaken to prevent that mine from being invaded by monsters, not out of any malice.

The dwarf tutted. "Easier to cut through wolves than collapsed limestone."

Perhaps, but at least the limestone isn't actively trying to kill you back.

For a moment there was silence, then this strange sound began to echo up from beneath me, like someone gargling with gravel in their mouth. It took some time for me to realize it was a laugh. "Never been in a mine, have you?"

Well, if you intend to rid yourself of me, likely sending me off to my doom, might I at least know the name of my executioner?

As if reciting it by rote, the dwarf announced, "Geotech Surveyor Second Class Cygni Khnuteson."

A pleasure to meet you, Cygni. I am Absalom . . .

Cygni cut me off. "Said already."

Yes, well, I wasn't entirely certain that you caught it, given how swiftly I was taken from your head.

"Not used to voices in my . . ." The word he said here was probably sufficient to start a barfight with anyone in earshot and made reference to an unlikely culmination of carnal events involving several of my blood relatives and a squid. ". . . head."

Perfectly understandable, my friend.

"Ain't friends." Cygni cut me off. "Don't need any friends."

Ah, but that is where you are wrong. Imagine, if you will, a world in which you are possessed of the art of magic. Capable of reshaping reality to your will. The highest art, at your beck and call. This could be yours if we were friends.

"We don't do magic." There was a finality to that statement that should have put an end to all conversation on this topic, but beneath the words, in the tidal shift of emotions within Cygni Khnuteson, Second-Class Surveyor, there was something unexpected. Something that I had not expected to find in so stolid a creature. A dull, low pang of longing.

Before you placed me upon your head, that may have been true. But if you knew my name before this day, you would know that I am the greatest wizard in all the world, capable of teaching anyone. For instance, I took Ig, a kobold of little intellect and capability, and taught him the High Art to such a degree that he was capable of defeating an army of ogres without even needing to cast a single spell.

A little guffaw emerged from beneath me, accompanied by a cloud of stone dust. "Unlikely."

Just as I can sense your feelings, I am certain that mine are readily available to you, and if I were attempting to deceive you in any way, such a thing would be instantly obvious.

There was something like a sneer underneath the dwarf's beard. "Everything you say feels like a lie dressed up in fancy words."

Then let me speak plainly with you. If I taught an imbecilic kobold magic, I can certainly teach you.

"Go on then." The dwarf stopped in his progress through the myriad twists and turns of the tunnels that had already rendered me thoroughly lost.

Had I eyes of my own, I would have blinked at this sudden turnabout. *I beg your pardon?*

"Teach me," Cygni said. "Now."

I mean, it isn't an instantaneous project, it will take time to convey the required knowledge to you . . .

"You've got until we reach the king." Cygni started off walking again. "If I don't know magic by then, you're his."

Oh . . . I . . . uh . . .

The dwarf made a noise like he was regurgitating something, which I eventually parsed as a scoff. "So you can't."

Had I eyes of my own, they would have narrowed at this challenge. *The heck I can't.*

What followed, as we trundled along through the dark, was the most comprehensive introduction to magic that has ever been committed to memory. The ancient language of the arcane archons, building blocks of all magic, I conveyed to the dwarf, then explained how it had to be combined with an understanding of the elements to produce the intended results. To my surprise and delight, dwarven education, or at least education for those fulfilling the role of a second-class geotech surveyor, included a more than basic understanding of many of the various elements that compose the world already. The exotic elements that had only ever been successfully manifested in laboratory conditions within the various universities of magic around the world were not on the dwarven curriculum, but such was Cygni's grasp of the existent elements that they had encountered in their day-to-day life that these new elements could be incorporated into his belief system without much in the way of argument.

This degree of condensed knowledge delivered into Ig's head would likely have resulted in instantaneous combustion, but teaching a dwarf was like a dream come true. Cygni remembered every single word that I said perfectly, and could recite my descriptions and understandings of the various elements back to me perfectly within a few hours.

Over a hundred elements, we rattled through as we went, neither one of us tiring, and soon I switched over to the basic grammar and structure of Archaic, which the dwarf absorbed with equal diligence.

Earlier in my life, my contact with the minds of others had been limited to conversation, which in itself is an inherently clunky system of conveying ideas. There had been a few occasions when it had become necessary to use magic to infiltrate the minds of others and bend them to my will, such as when there was only one apricot croissant left in the university canteen, but generally my mind and those of others had been entirely separate. And now, I had the experience of two completely different and completely alien minds.

Ig's mind had been chaotic, a mess devoid of all the structures that I would have considered necessary for the formation of thoughts, but this dwarf was at the opposite end of the spectrum. His mind was rigid in the way that a vast and ancient building was rigid, the weight of the higher thoughts pressing down to hold the foundational ideas in place. It was a place of hard right angles and careful filing according to a system that had been passed down either through careful education or some sort of genetic memory. Regardless, the net result was an eidetic memory, and a train of thought that it would have taken some extremely heavy impacts to derail.

I could not understand how it was possible that a dwarf had never been a wizard. They had these incredible minds, capable of filing away every detail for instant recall at a moment's notice, that put even my incredible faculties to shame. Not to mention that every one of them came pre-equipped with a luxuriant beard, which many consider to be a vital component of a wizard's garb.

You are a natural, I finally declared after exhausting every readily available word of Archaic that I could call to mind. *For more complex workings, we must construct a balance of different elements and different words of Archaic, but for the most part, they can simply be assembled sequentially, with only the rare spell requiring simultaneously holding knowledge of multiple elements at the same time. This leaves only two matters to address and you can call yourself a wizard. The first matter is that of focus.*

"Made it through listening to you warble all day without falling asleep, how's that for focus," Cygni grunted.

Well I never . . . you . . . For not the first time since meeting this dwarf, I had to force myself to ignore his insults and shut up, for the greater good. The greater good in this case being avoiding being tossed into some dwarf-king's treasure room for the next few centuries. I reminded myself of this, ignored the insult, and moved on. *It is a matter we can turn to during practical training, now that you have the fundamentals down.*

I am not a dwarf, as I am sure you know by now, and as such, my familiarity with mining, caves, and so forth is relatively limited. Yet despite my inexperience, my perception was colored by the eyes that I saw the world through, and Cygni most definitely recognized the various minerals and types of stone that we were passing through, and more importantly, that the areas we were moving into now had stone that had been freshly worked, rather than carved out decades or more before our arrival. This was the living and breathing part of the mine, where at any moment we might encounter another dwarf. Something that I cannot say I was relishing. It had taken me all day working on Cygni just to get to the point where he was reluctantly considering not handing me over to his king and nigh-inevitable banishment back into the senseless void. To start over fresh with another dwarf, just because they happened to snatch me off this dwarf's head, would have been less than ideal.

But we did not come upon any miners in our progress, though here and there, tools lay about and there was a certain freshly mined smell in the air. Stone dust, predominantly, with an undercurrent of heat from the friction of tools on rock.

Might I suggest that we pause in our journey for just a moment so that we might attempt some practical applications of what you have been taught?

"No."

It will take but a moment and be an excellent example of all that you have already learned.

Once more Cygni answered with a grumble. "Not now."

I was not entirely certain how I was meant to prove to the dwarf that they would be capable of performing magic if they wouldn't actually try to do any. But his refusal to even attempt it suggested to me some sort of philosophical issue with the idea. As though perhaps dwarves had always known how to use magic but chose not to on moral grounds.

I'm sure a druid would have said not to use magic unless you had to because it disrupts the natural balance of life and nature, but to all druids out there, I have a few choice words that I refuse to translate from the original Dwarvish. Quintessence is bountiful, it is flowing throughout the world, and any small amount that an individual wizard can take in is rapidly replaced in the natural drift, not to mention the bountiful amounts of Quintessence we pour out into the world with our spells.

Why, some places where magic has struck are so overwhelmingly saturated with Quintessence that entirely new forms of life develop. Admittedly they tend to have the mangled features of two disparate creatures melted into one and get called monsters, but you cannot deny that chimera is alive! Not unless you want to argue that its component lion, snake, bird, and dragon parts are not alive independently. So up yours, druids.

Might I ask why you do not wish to . . .

"People around. Hush."

I would have said that Cygni must have had far superior hearing to me, for him to be able to detect the presence of others in the coming tunnels without me noticing them at all, but I was using that same set of ears for the same purpose. Anything he heard, I should have been able to hear. Anything he saw, I should have been able to see.

Yet despite this incongruity, we rounded the next bend and, lo and behold, there were indeed dwarves there. A great many dwarves. Some might argue, too many dwarves.

This section of the mine had once been a natural cavern, and it now served as a natural junction point between the veritable warren of tunnels stretching out from it in every direction. The cavern itself had long ago been pillaged of all mineral value, but it had not been prettified in any way, there was no carving or shaping of the stone—what had been cut remained cut, no matter how blunt and bizarre such a thing might look. This was not a living space; it was firmly a part of the mine. A distinction that most dwarves probably wouldn't ever make, but that I as a once-human was intent on establishing. Living where you work is never a good idea, even if where you work isn't sporadically filled with poisonous gases released from beneath the earth.

Anyway, back to the matter at hand. There were a great many dwarves blocking our way, and as we emerged fully into the vast hall, it became apparent that was a deliberate move on their part. Many of them were linked, arm in arm, to prevent any access to the tunnels of the mine still being worked, and those that were not linked stood nearby to reinforce the resolve of the linked-armed dwarves, holding up placards and chanting in their guttural tongue.

I was not accustomed to hearing Dwarvish sung, so it took some time to decipher the chants. Typically if a dwarf was singing, it would be about gold, but in this instance it seemed to be about working hours.

"King Khnute is awful bold. He takes more than just our gold. Every hour we work and slave. Digging out another cave."

They were fairly coherent in terms of rhythm, even if they couldn't all seem to agree on which note they were trying to hit. There was one soprano somewhere in the mix who kept on trying to hold the last note of each line, even though they were clearly meant to be moving on to the next. It was the auditory equivalent of a minor industrial disaster. Which I supposed was appropriate. The singing picked up again.

"Overworked and underpaid! King Khnute has got it made. We're down choking on cave gas. He sits on his big fat throne!"

"What do we want?" bellowed one red-in-the-face dwarf.

"A comprehensive overhaul of our working hours and conditions, appropriate pensions for those injured in the line of duty, and on-site healthcare to minimize the loss of limbs."

"When do we want it?" Red Face yelled back.

"Rolled out within a reasonable timescale that won't be overly disruptive to our collective goals of maximizing profit and tapping that promising new iron vein in section thirty-four."

"Damn right!" Red Face roared. "Power to the people!"

"Power to the miners!" the gathered crowd echoed back.

I suppose that it was something of a problem for dwarves to go on strike, given that their entire lives from waking to passing out again were entirely devoted to work, and that in their little hive society they were all fervently devoted toward their communal goal of digging up everything that the earth beneath our feet had to offer. It would be rather like asking fish to stop swimming until all the sharks had been ordered out of the ocean, I supposed.

Does any of this actually work?

"Watch," was the only reply I got from Cygni.

From out of one of the unguarded tunnels emerged a group of dwarves clad in the heaviest armor that I could have conceived of. Thick slabs of iron so heavy I was surprised they could even move, let alone see through the narrow slit on the helm.

A cry went up from the miners just before the king's strikebreakers hit the line. It was not the grand melee that I had been anticipating. The miners didn't fight back, they had no intention of doing their fellow dwarves harm, but they did hold their ground, pressing back against the rush of bodies, though with enemies in that heavy armor it must have been like trying to hold back a landslide. They wrestled and jostled back and forth, cudgels swinging down on the miners as they held their line.

"Wouldn't be trying to beat them down if it wasn't going to work, would he?" Cygni seemed oddly satisfied. Where his loyalties lay in this conflict I couldn't really say. On the one hand his heart seemed to sing along with the miners, on the other his loyalty to his king was absolute. It was an awkward position that I suspected every dwarf in the chamber was currently occupying. They were a people so accustomed to order, so built for it, that even disobedience for the preservation of their own lives became hard for them.

So I assume that we have a little extra time for your education since ingress into the inner parts of your mine are currently blocked by this little scuffle?

It was the wrong thing to say. Every moment that we were out here, away from the oppressive structures of dwarvish society, I had more time to work on Cygni, to derail that train of thought and shift it in a new direction. The direction of taking me where I wanted to go instead of handing me over to some accursed authority figure. But now that I had pointed out the problem, Cygni's mind immediately switched to solving it.

"We'll go around."

Through Cygni's eyes I took in all of the blocked tunnels, the fighting, the picket line that had already formed an insurmountable barricade inadvertently reinforced by the very people trying to break it up.

I'm not certain that there is an "around" to go.

Cygni just grunted and set off along one of the unguarded tunnels.

CHAPTER TWO

CONCERNING SCABS

These tunnels looked less well-kept than the ones we had already traversed, and given that we'd started out in an ancient and disused part of the mine, that was a little concerning. The supports were bowed under the weight of the stone above, hastily assembled instead of carefully crafted, and there was a sourness to the air that felt both familiar and wrong.

Where exactly are you taking us?

Cygni did not reply.

While every part of the tunnel complex up until this point had been pristine to the point of near cleanliness despite it being a working mine, there were signs of habitation here. A pile of rags in a corner. A broken oil lantern that had been pushed aside instead of being collected for painstaking repairs. A smudge on the wall, possibly coal dust, that had not been buffed out. If this were a human city rather than a dwarf mine, I'd say that Cygni was taking us into a rough neighborhood. This was the equivalent of graffiti and broken windows to a dwarf.

Let me guess, there is some secret tunnel that only you know about.

"Not yet."

That was the sort of comment that made me immediately more concerned.

I realize that we have been covering the destructive properties of magic, and that you are an exceptionally quick study, but that does not mean that you will be capable of producing a safe and traversable . . .

"Hadn't even thought of that." Cygni seemed rather taken with the idea. Of course a dwarf would be excited about using magic for mining. "Could magic make a tunnel?"

I mean, typically a wizard would sidestep the issue by using some sort of stonepass spell and walking right through the solid earth rather than risk bringing a mountain down on our heads through excavation . . .

His beetled brow drew down. "Isn't that how I found you to start with?"

I may have taught the kobold all he knows, but that doesn't mean I've taught him all that I know.

Another grunt, another turn, another tunnel, even dingier than the last.

Might I inquire as to where we're going?

"Yes."

Where are we going?

"Left."

We made the next turn and I began to suspect that the dwarf was being taciturn out of spite.

And why, pray tell, are we going left?

"Because that leads to the third tunnel on the right."

Which leads us to . . .

"Want me to draw you a . . ." He said a word in Dwarvish which should not strictly have been spoken outside of a whorehouse, and even then, not one of the classier ones. ". . . map?"

I fell into silence—sulky silence, if I were being entirely honest. I had become entirely too accustomed to Ig obediently following my commands. If Ig had the attitude of this dwarf, we'd still be in his muddy hole under a rotten tree instead of on the doorstep of civilization.

We did take the third tunnel on the right, then a dozen more turns through the increasingly desolate tunnels. They hadn't been finished properly in places. You could still see the raw shapes of the natural rock instead of the smoothness of walls. At first, I'd assumed that we were headed into older tunnels that had become disused, but rather, these seemed to have been relatively new when they were abandoned.

I would have liked to have asked why these tunnels were abandoned, given that Cygni's gaze could pick out hints at valuable minerals hidden in the stone around us with every glance, but as my answer would at best have been a grunt, I elected not to.

The journey in its totality probably didn't take all that long, but without conversation to pass the time, or the intense attempts at education that we'd been undertaking thus far, it felt like considerably longer. In an attempt to break up the silence, I did offer to begin teaching some further words of Archaic to my solemn bearer, but Cygni grunt-refused that too. There was a tension in the dwarf that had not been immediately apparent to me, not the wild terror that had possessed Ig through every waking moment, but a kind of fear nonetheless, manifesting itself in the desire for silence so that he might focus upon what his senses told him.

This tension somewhat invariably began trickling its way up through the dwarf's roughly shorn scalp and into me. I found myself paying too much attention to every little detail of each chamber and tunnel we passed through. When I caught sight of actual graffiti on one of the walls, I very nearly jumped clean off Cygni's head in surprise.

In a human settlement, this would have been the equivalent of an overturned cart in the middle of the road that someone had set on fire.

As we passed the little scribble by, I could see that it was not of dwarvish make, but rather a dull brown smear that might have been blood once upon a time. Something resembling a face, or possibly genitalia. The artist was not particularly talented.

Goblins.

Another grunt from Cygni. This tunnel complex must have intruded upon a goblin nest, and that was why it had been abandoned, which begged the question of why Cygni was taking us there now, given that goblins are not typically the friendliest lot. One might actually argue that they were the least friendly lot, in fact. Limited in their cruelty and ambition only by the fact that in the place of the bulging musculature of their distant cousins the orcs, nature had imbued them with something resembling rubber bands beneath their skin. Still, they might have been a real danger to civilized people in sufficient numbers thanks to their considerable cunning, which had proven more than a match for many an adventurer, but that too had been thankfully tempered by impulse control usually only found in hyperactive children after a day of eating nothing but sugar.

Despite all of these shortcomings, the bottom line was that it was not a particularly sensible course of action for a dwarf to go wandering into one of their nests alone. Even if Cygni was wearing no small amount of padded armor and carrying that rather nasty-looking mining pick, enough goblins could be a problem.

So you can imagine my relief when I heard a dwarf voice echoing along the tunnels toward us. The gruffness with undercurrents of gargling gravel was unmistakable, even if the language that the dwarf was speaking was not Dwarvish.

A couple more corners and we came upon the source of the chatter. More of the strikebreakers in their heavy armor were lounging around, trying to look vaguely threatening with the minimum amount of effort, while the one I assumed was their leader from his lack of helmet continued his negotiations with the gathered goblin tribe.

It was not a particularly large chamber, as goblins tend to just hole up in whatever has naturally formed and spill out a little if there are too many of them, so they were pressed in close in front of the dwarf, yet there was still a barrier of air between them that the goblin horde did not seem inclined to break through.

In halting Goblinese, the dwarf continued, ". . .you can swaptrade shinygold for eatthings."

The goblins' mouths fell open at this startling concept. "Or swaptrade other shinies we dig?"

"No . . ." The dwarf had the harried and exhausted look of someone who was having the same conversation for the fourteenth time. ". . . No. You no keep shinies you dig. You dig shinies and give us. Then we give shinygold to swaptrade."

"Not swaptrade shinies?" another goblin asked.

"No. That is not how . . ." He struggled for a word, as goblins had no concept of employment or jobs in their language, lucky bastards. ". . . timetrade works."

A wise leader among the goblins held up her hand. "Me brain this. We digs. Digs up shinies. You swaptrade us shinygold for shinies?"

"For the love of the stone." The dwarf groaned in his own language. "No. No swaptrade. You give us all shinies you dig. That how timetrade work. Then we give you shinygold for time you spend digging shinies."

One of the little goblins guffawed. "But time not cost anything."

"You give time to us, we give shinygold to you," the dwarf tried to explain yet again.

One of the smallest goblins, a little blue around his batlike ears, yelped in terror. "You steal time?!"

"No . . . No . . . Damn it all." He cast a baleful look over his armored cohort, who appeared to be trying not to giggle within their blank-faced armor. His gaze finally settled on Cygni. "Oh thank the stone, you there, are you the translator?"

"Could be," Cygni replied. Lying through his teeth and mustache.

I could translate the goblin's speech for you.

A soft grunt this time. Acceptance perhaps.

"Well, go on then, I'm getting nowhere with these . . ." The word in Dwarvish does not translate to the common tongue of humans, which is for the best, as if you were to understand how he was describing the goblins in that one harsh syllable, you most likely would have vomited. Even I felt a tad queasy, and I had no stomach.

Cygni ambled up to the goblins and held up his hands for silence. A few moments later the goblins noticed him doing so in the midst of their own myriad arguments, and they all held their hands up too. It looked like the beginning of the world's worst religion. "We pay you shinygold. You dig for us."

"Yes!" The goblins all bobbed their heads. "We dig. Then we find shinygolds."

"No." Cygni had not yet had his temper tested by these creatures, so there was no ire as he repeated, "You no need find shinygold, we give."

This seemed to present some confusion to the goblins. Many literally began scratching their heads. The wise leader of the goblins posed a philosophical question. "Then why dig?"

"So we give shinygold."

One of the guffawing goblins from earlier now looked deathly serious as they all tried to work through the problem. "But what find is . . ."

Cygni thumped a fist against his chest. "Mine."

"Mine!" chirped one goblin, then another. The whole lot of them were peeping it back and forth to one another. "Mine! Mine!"

Cygni's raised voice drowned them out. "That why called a mine."

This profound wisdom, a blatant lie, was enough to entirely silence them all. It seemed that now they understood. With that clarity, the true negotiations could begin. The wise one rose to her feet. "How much shinygold give?"

Cygni held up a finger to silence the goblins for a moment while conferring with the strikebreaker's boss about the rate they were going to offer them, but there was already a round of cheering going up from the goblins. The wise one had tears shining in her eyes when she asked, "One each?"

The strikebreaker leader nodded vigorously at Cygni and the cheers rose to almost deafening levels.

From there it was simply a matter of standing back and waiting as picks as big as the goblins themselves were handed out, and we guided them back through some of the tunnels we'd traveled until we reached a dead end.

By this point I hadn't a clue where under the earth we were, but Cygni's incredible memory was accompanied by a mental map that seemed to overlay everything. He could see where this tunnel would lead when expanded forward, how it might intersect with other tunnels on the far side of the picket line and from there, how this alternate route could be used to access the city proper.

Whatever doubts I may have had about the potential competence of these goblin miners were certainly confirmed when they began to work. These creatures lacked even the most basic of common sense, hitting each other with their tools as often as the stone itself, and they undertook their task with a kind of deranged enthusiasm that I suspected would have been present regardless of whether they were being paid or not.

The strikebreakers had been assigned to stand watch over these goblins and direct them, but now they were mostly just scrambling to stay out of the way as chips of stone began to fly. Cygni had already foreseen this turn of events and was quite a distance back along the tunnel.

I hope that you are proud of yourself, exploiting the ignorance of these goblins.

Cygni shrugged. "They agreed to one gold."

You don't think that you should have mentioned how much a miner usually gets paid?

"They aren't . . ." A word of Dwarvish describing a very specific carnal act. ". . . miners."

There was a genuine undercurrent of disgust and anger toward the goblins that we were relying on to clear our path that reminded me entirely too much of how I used to look on the monstrous peoples of the world before being forced to spend time in their company for a time.

No, of course. How could you possibly treat people of another species with respect.

"Don't care that they're goblins." Cygni scoffed. "I care that they're scabs."

Scabs?

"Working through a strike. Helping the bosses. Disgusting."

That undercurrent of anger was once more present, but it was tinged with self-loathing. It was a weakness that I could work on. *Aren't you also working through a strike?*

His voice dropped to a rumble at that line of questioning. "Surveyors ain't striking."

And aren't we reliant upon these "scabs" to progress toward your goal?

He huffed and a cloud of dust drifted off his beard. "Doesn't mean I have to like it."

You know, we don't actually have to go and see your king . . .

"Yes. We do." He cut me off dead. "He'll know what to do with you."

I also know what the best course of action is in that regard. You can take me to find my friends, or failing that, you could take me to Arpanpholigon, where I'll be sure to meet up with them again.

"No." Cygni's blunt answer gave me very little wiggle room to negotiate.

I could teach you the ways of magic. Make you the first of your kind to . . .

"Already did."

You haven't even cast a spell yet. And the practical applications of magic are considerably more difficult to . . .

His tone brooked no argument. "We're going to the king."

Would you not at least like to attempt a little magic before then, so that you can observe firsthand the incredible gift that I'm offering you?

"No."

It took an abominably long time for the goblins to work their way through the stone, despite their numbers and the expert direction of the dwarfs.

I'm not entirely clear on why the gentlemen in armor couldn't simply dig for themselves.

"Ain't miners. Not their job."

Surely this strike constitutes the sort of unusual circumstances that might lead them to . . .

"Guards ain't miners." Again that totalitarian worldview pressed in on us.

And I suppose that you never do anything other than surveying.

"Right."

You've never swung that pick of yours?

"Course I have. For samples."

But that is not mining?

Cygni rolled his eyes as if I were a simpleton. "That's surveying."

Had I been back in the Invisible College of Arpanpholigon, surrounded by my peers and all of my resources, to get this quality of conversation I would have had to move aside a decorative tapestry to reveal one of the building's many stone walls and struck up a chat with it.

When the goblins did finally break through it was something of a relief, in truth. Certainly it meant that I was going to be moving forward toward an uncertain but likely miserable fate, but at least I wouldn't be left standing around here with Cygni and his many firm opinions any longer.

While the goblin miners sifted through the rocks produced by their latest burst of hyperactivity for anything of value, Cygni picked his way over the rubble to the small opening into the adjoining shaft. A human could not have squeezed through such a gap, and I had my doubts about a dwarf managing it either, but I had not accounted for the many years of underground experience that the dwarf had accumulated. Drawing out his pick, he placed it across the hole, using it to measure. Satisfied, he then crammed himself into the hole, headfirst.

I supposed that I should have been thankful for this bullet-like approach, really. At least this way I wasn't getting scraped across the ceiling.

There was just barely enough room for the dwarf's shoulders in the gap, and were it not for the impressive way that he undulated his stout body through the hole, I doubt that any progress could have been made at all. I supposed that this was the advantage of the average dwarf's rather square build. If any one part of their body could make it through a gap, the rest would too. Pushing and squeezing and twisting and pulling, he dragged his way out the far side to land in the same kind of pristine tunnels we'd seen before heading toward the goblins. Much better. A sense of relief flooded through Cygni too as tension I hadn't even noticed left him. Home. He was home.

It was difficult not to let a pang of my own pain spread through him then. It had been so long since I had been home. It could have been years for all that I knew. Nobody thus far had been kind enough to furnish me with a calendar.

That first passage soon became another and another, the distant rumble of the picket line echoed back to us from the direction that we'd first tried to approach, and now the center of the dwarves' civilization began to unfold before us.

It was, to put it in the simplest possible terms, a chasm. Up both sides of the vast hole in the world, buildings had been hammered into the solid stone, some of them more ramshackle wooden constructs that had been thrown up hastily and held in place with guy-lines, but the majority of them carved into the face of the chasm wall itself.

For all that I may have been contemptuous about the idea of living in a hole in the ground, there could be no denying that this was a city, one splayed out vertically instead of horizontally perhaps, but a city all the same. Everywhere that I looked, torches burned, making the pitch-black of this underground chamber look like the stars at night, or perhaps more accurately like a swarm of fireflies flitting around, because though many of the torches illuminating this place were affixed to walls, the majority were being carried by dwarves going about their business.

We entered somewhere about three-quarters of the way up the wall and I was relieved to find Cygni holding on to me by the brim as we stepped out into the sweeping winds that flowed through. The two vast walls of the crevasse leaned back in to kiss one another up above us, but even that high, I could still make out more homes chipped into the rock.

Beneath the beard, I was pretty certain Cygni was grinning as he announced, "Welcome to Khnute's Crack."

CHAPTER THREE

A PAIN IN THE CRACK

Transportation around the city seemed to be mainly by hooking a boot and a hand onto constantly moving chains rotated by some sort of great wheel mechanism up and down all over the place. What made it rotate was beyond me; anywhere else I would have assumed magic, but perhaps there was some dwarf down in the dark at the bottom of the city who had the thankless job of keeping it in motion.

I fully expected for Cygni to head up to the very top of the chasm if we were off to meet the king, a kingly place from which he might survey his whole kingdom, but it seemed my judgment in this matter, as in so many others, was flawed. Dwarf kingdoms are not built like wizards' towers, but in quite the opposite manner. We headed down as deep as the spinning-chain elevator could take us.

It was perhaps the best possible tour that I could have had of this city, akin to soaring over a human city from above and taking in all the sights in one swoop. Here were the great forges where tools were made and jewels set, the stone around them carved into workings of titanic dwarves using their hammers to beat the stone into shape.

We dismounted there and headed across to the next of the rotating chains, slowly migrating our way along the cavern wall, crossing the length of the horizontal stretch of the city too. All about us there was industry. Armor and weapons were forged, because to be without them in the underworld came with an implicit death sentence—I tried not to think about Ig, helpless without me—but for the most part all of the iron, gold, and various other metals were actually being made into more practical things. Pick heads and jewelry for trade. Cutlery seemed to be one smith's entire livelihood. Dwarves were nothing if not focused, picking one particular niche in their society and hammering at it until they got as close to perfection as could be. Well, I say they picked a niche, but more likely it was assigned to them based on the needs of the hive. I knew that Cygni had hopes and dreams, I could feel them, crushed down flat under the weight of his duty. But the dwarf hive was not a place for individuality.

Visibility was incredibly limited as we proceeded, even to eyes adapted to such a place. There was smoke as thick as soup surrounding us everywhere we went, with the dwarves roaming around, hauling products and ingots looming out of the dark for only a moment at a time before vanishing again. The heat in this part of the chasm was almost unbearable—beneath the many layers that he wore, Cygni was beginning to sweat from just our brief journey across this stretch of thoroughfare, so I dreaded to think how roasted the resident workforce had to be. A dwarf suddenly loomed out of the smog and Cygni had to jump aside or be run down by the handcart that the beardy little bastard was charging along behind.

You know, I have always wondered, why do all dwarves have beards?

"What?"

In human society, some of them have beards, or mustaches, or some mismatched combination of the two, but dwarves, you all have that thick hair on your faces. I mean, I'm a wizard, I know a little something about the importance of a long flowing beard, but surely it is impractical for people working with tools and fire all day long.

Grumbling, Cygni carried on past another wagonload of ingots. "Ain't for looks. It's for breathing."

Breathing? You breathe through your beards?

"There's some thought like you. Rebels. Show-offs. Chin-displayers." He sneered as he said the term, as if it was worse than some of the truly horrific words he'd already belched out today. "They died."

Your people die without beards?!

"Black lungs." Cygni nodded, hooking a boot into the passing chain now that we'd finally reached it. "Metal dust shredding your insides."

The beards are a filtration system! Oh, I tell you, once I get a body again, I'm going to have so many treatises and texts to correct. The accepted texts say that the beards are to signal social standing! I knew it made no sense for so practical a people to have such a frivolous affectation.

Unsure how to respond to being treated as a subject of academic interest, but pleased at being called practical, Cygni remained silent.

Down below the level of the forges, vast furnaces blazed day and night, heating all the residential quarters above them through convection and ensuring that the steady flow of ore coming into the city was processed swiftly enough that it had no opportunity to pile up. At first I wondered at the choice to position it halfway down the chasm when gravity would surely have made it easier to deliver ores directly to the bottom, but I supposed that it made a degree of sense to have it here if there were tunnels wending off through the rock at all heights. It was central.

Another reason for the positioning of the furnaces became clear when we made it through the furnace layer. Cygni's ears popped as we went farther and farther into the depths. Deeper than the practical areas of the city came another round of housing, not drowned in the rising smog of the furnaces but heated from within by their own stoves. A far higher class of home than any of the miners could have ever hoped to dwell in, so low in the city that the unstoppable industry didn't even coat them with soot.

Lovely place, quite charming, thank you so much for the tour, but the longer we dally, the more likely it is that we shall not catch up to my companions. Do you think that we might just skip the audience with the king and hurry on toward that instead?

"Going to the king. Shut up or I'm taking you off."

You know, I could knock you from this chain with a thought.

Cygni sneered. "Go on then."

We continued down for another few floors of housing before I mumbled back. *I didn't say that I would, just that I could.*

Down below what I would have to term the upmarket region of the city, things began to change once more. The stonework that had been so pristine just a little farther up the crevasse in the wealthy neighborhood now began to crumble, not from lack of care or disrepair, but due to the sheer age of the structures on display. What the dwarves had built up above was beautiful, in that very clean and precise manner of all their architecture, but down here it became art more suited to frame a temple than the public halls that were so venerated by being granted this space.

As we passed by the entryways, I realized that there was lichen spread out inside these edifices. Mushroom farms and insect ranches, the breadbox of the city.

The carvings on the walls flowed like water into the structures themselves, a coil of what had once been a faux vine now spread out in a lattice, connecting the overhanging entryway to the stone beyond. The pillars were similarly graven, not only with surface decorations but with a startling degree of depth. In some places it was quite possible to see all the way through to the other side, the torchlight passing through the gaps warping and wavering before our eyes. The wind that blew through those punctures whistled faintly as it passed in a haunting melody.

Well, that isn't natural.

Cygni scoffed. "Of course they ain't, we made everything here."

I mean that they are a magical construct, my obstinate friend.

"We ain't friends," Cygni grumbled. But they were looking at the pillars with renewed interest. Eventually asking, "What kind of magic?"

So there was some curiosity in his soul after all.

I cannot say for certain what purpose it once served without examining the structure more closely, but I'd imagine that it was human in origin, given the relationship between your people and the elves.

"Never been humans in Khnute's Crack."

Well, someone capable of magic was here, and unless your people have some wizards hidden away that neither of us knows about, I have to assume that they invited in a human to do the necessary enchanting work.

"How do you know it's magic?" Cygni's brows drew down as he tried to outthink me. Which was rather like bringing a rock to a swordfight, setting it on the ground, and expecting it to defend you.

Quintessence lingers. Those trained in the use of magic become sensitive to it. I have immense levels of arcane awareness. Also, the whole structure on this side of the chasm would fall down if they weren't magic. Holey pillars don't hold up weight. Plus there is the whole whistling thing.

"Whistling?"

The sound that the wind makes as it passes through is musical. That smacks of enchantment to me.

Cygni's frown was in danger of consuming both his eyes and cheekbones by this point as he tried to reason this all through. "What's this 'musical' thing?"

You are unfamiliar with the concept of music?

"Did I say a thing to you when you couldn't tell shale from slate? Or an inselberg from a monadnock? No. I knew you weren't an underworlder, and I ain't rude."

I'm sorry, did you just claim that you aren't rude after repeatedly telling me to shut up for the past hour?

"Not shutting up when you're asked is ruder."

I assure you that it is not.

"What's music?" Cygni grumbled. "And none of your cheek."

It was actually a rather philosophical question to pose to someone who was already dealing with their new reality of not only being a hat but being a hat from an entirely different world from their current location.

Sounds that are played for entertainment or the pleasure of hearing them?

"Sounds for fun?" The dwarf snorted. "Sounds like something an elf would do."

There were abundant theories that humanity learned the art of music from the elvish, so I couldn't exactly deny that, but I did mislike his tone as he scoffed at all human achievement.

Actually, while the elvish musical scene is rather stagnant, humanity has been pushing the art form forward for several centuries now.

"Like whistling pillars."

I could not help but feel that I was being mocked somehow, so I returned my gaze to the city we were passing down through.

Ornate didn't even begin to describe the structures set into the walls now; there was a density to the carving work that bordered on pathological, as if the maximum amount of detail and beauty had to be inscribed in each square foot of the stone. There were histories of the dwarven sagas writ here, myths and legends intermingled with reports of particularly valuable minerals that had been discovered. Here a dragon, there a deposit of calcite, long mined out. To my knowledge the dwarves had no religion as such, so what these vast halls of worship might be, I could not have said.

What purpose do those beautiful buildings serve?

Cygni smiled beneath his beard. "That's the pub."

The templelike area had given way to what must have been the royal palace, judging by the abundant blank-faceplated guards hanging around.

As we approached that lowest level of the crevasse, a dull glow permeated the air, not from the torches slung about, but from the stone itself. Another enchantment that combined with the dwarf's natural low-light vision to make this place as visible as midday on the surface.

So the floating obelisks, it never occurred to anyone that they might in fact be some sort of magic.

Cygni mumbled something that sounded like, "Magnets?"

Really . . .

"Can do amazing things with magnets."

The perfectly octagonal constructs hung above the chasm floor, surrounded by the ambient glow of magic. Each one of them slowly rotating on the spot and marking the path to the huge entryway to the palace. The columns holding up the façade of the ornate building were similarly eight-sided, suggesting to me that both things had been constructed about the same time, to the same design. Magnets. Pfft.

It would only occur to me after we had passed them by that they were rotating at exactly the same rate as the chains had been rotating up and down along the chasm walls. The lifts had been magic, just as I'd first thought. Probably one or more of these obelisks turned to a practical purpose by the residents. There was magic all over the place, but the dwarf population had been here for so long that they thought these things were mundane.

There seemed to be more and more of the blank-faced guards as we proceeded, but nobody made any attempt to stop Cygni. I supposed that political assassinations weren't really a concern when there could only ever be one king at a time and the whole civilization was built around them. That or they believed that the loyalty of dwarves was absolute.

As we passed through the gaping doorway, a rhythmic thumping began to resonate from up ahead, like the heartbeat of the kingdom. I had not a clue what it might have been, assuming it was either some vast beast that the dwarves had enslaved, some working of machinery that I could not understand, or some other work of magic that they all ignored. Cygni made no comment on it and spared it no thought.

So on we plodded toward my doom. I wondered for a moment if I'd be dumped in some storeroom within the palace itself to wait out eternity, or if they had a separate building for all of the artifacts that they never had any intention of looking at again.

Somewhere in this palace would dwell the only things that humans would have defined as males in the hive, hairless and helpless in comparison to their kinfolk, unrecognizable to outsiders as dwarves at all. Or so I'd read. So far as I could tell, the males were as closely guarded a secret as the king himself. Not for the eyes of outsiders.

On we plodded and on the rhythmic thumping went.

I had expected there to be courtiers and the like lingering around, trying to convince the king to follow the course that they had planned, but I supposed that self-aggrandizement wasn't really in the nature of dwarves either. The only people here seemed to be servants, all scurrying around industriously, carrying odd lumpy packages out of what must have been some sort of storeroom up ahead. They entered with cloth, emerged with a hunk of something that was probably stone, judging by how they strained under the weight of it. They were oddly garbed for dwarves, chainmail veils hiding their features from sight, except where their beards emerged underneath, and those same veils were lined with little bells that made sorrowful jingles as they walked.

Perhaps they were the undertakers of the dwarf kingdom.

Unchallenged, Cygni strolled right into the storeroom, only for his eyes to rapidly adjust and the reality become apparent to me. This was not in fact a storeroom, unless that which you were storing was a king.

A vast stone throne occupied the rear wall, raised up so that the king's trailing skirts of robes and mail did not pool on the ground. King Khnute was garbed as any dwarf was, in layers of armor and cloth, but unlike the other dwarves, he was positively titanic in proportions. Not in height, of course, but in girth, the king was unmatched. I found myself thinking that it was lucky that the chair they'd plopped him on was made of stone or it likely would have collapsed under the creature's weight.

The king's face was flushed, his eyes heavily lidded, and his beard was an extraordinary mixture of braids and trinkets of gold. Even the armor that he bore was golden, and on reflection I thought that the chainmail may have been gold once too, though it was tarnished beyond recognition from the waist down. Khnute's lazy stare turned slowly toward Cygni as he approached the throne. "GS2 C76111, what do you want?"

"Hi, Dad." Cygni's voice squeaked a little before he could clear his throat. "Reporting on tunnel collapse in Sector Eight."

Khnute's expression had not changed since we arrived, but now there was a slight narrowing of the eyes, and a noise somewhat akin to a grunt. A moment later, the source of the rhythmic thumping was revealed.

Down the length of the king's skirts from between his legs, an object tumbled before hitting the solid stone floor of the chamber. One of the long parade of servants stepped forward and scooped up the object from the wet patch on the floor below. It was only as they were walking by, swaddling it, that I realized it was a baby.

When humans are born, they have big heads. This has been the source of much discomfort on the part of those humans who have to push that head out of them. But dwarf babies are essentially cubes of meat. One end is the head, the other the backside, and there are limbs tucked in toward a torso as thick as either end. This one appeared to have landed on the solid stone beneath it headfirst, but thanks to the wonders of genetics, had suffered no harm from this drop apart from a slight increase in the squareness of their head. It was carried away, and Khnute carried on as if nothing had happened. "The old pit quarry overflow adit. Well, what of it?"

"Medium-sized explosion. Cause: wizard."

"Disgusting." Khnute's eyes briefly crossed as they grunted in their labors. "Is it still inside the mine?"

Cygni shifted uncomfortably as he tried to formulate an answer. "Yes and no."

Another baby dropped to the rock, letting out a squeak of surprise on impact. "Yes or no?"

Cygni tried again to get his words together. "It's complicated."

"Wrong." Khnute cut off the explanation. I was starting to see where Cygni got his exceptional manners from. "Yes or no?"

Cygni opened and shut his mouth. "No. The wizard was . . . cut in two."

Technically true, I supposed.

Khnute nodded in satisfaction. "Good."

"I have his hat."

For the first time, Khnute actually seemed to look at his son. The lazy stare slowly rose to take in the hat that was me atop the dwarf. Eventually the king grunted. "Why?"

I was amazed that Cygni was willing to endure this intensely uncomfortable conversation, even out of a sense of duty. Particularly when every answer he made to his king-father made him sound stupider than the last. He cleared his throat and answered, "It talks."

Another baby hit the floor with a wet splat.

"It talks?"

I do talk, that is true. It is perhaps the least remarkable thing about me, but I do talk.

Khnute's eyes narrowed once more, this time not with labor pains. "Is it talking to you right now, C76111?"

"I've not gone softheaded!" Cygni was quick to reassure his father. "It is magic. Says it wants to go to the human city."

"The hat." Khnute spoke carefully. "Wants to go to the city?"

I'm not a hat! I'm a wizard. I'm a wizard and on return to Arpanpholigon I shall resume my manly form and those who have assisted me will be greatly rewarded. The king likes gold? I can conjure more gold than he's ever seen. He wants help with his mine, I can craft enchantments that will make your efforts laughably easy. Whatever you desire, I can make so.

In a rush, Cygni tried to finish his tale. "It says that it is a wizard, that it has been turned into a hat, and wants to go home and be turned back."

"Take off the hat, C76." Khnute's eyes narrowed once more, but this time I did not think it was due to birthing pains.

Don't take off the hat. Do not take me off! I don't want to go back to the darkness.

"Father?" Cygni asked, but I could already feel his blunt fingers seizing me.

Don't take me off! Let me speak to him! I'll convince him, just let me . . .

Darkness consumed me. The senseless nothingness that I'd been so desperate to avoid overtook me once more. It was the loathsome oblivion that I'd feared all along, and for all I knew it would be eternal.

Shit.

CHAPTER FOUR

A VERY DWARVISH REBELLION

I assume that time passed. Without a brain to think with, eyes to see, or any other sensory information, this was entirely hypothetical.

Death would have been better, I suspect. Because at least with death, there is the absence of awareness. But throughout all of the nothingness, I was. Even with nothing to think with, or about, I still existed. Someday, I am certain that those philosophers who make their money through thought experiments about whether reality is real or not will come upon this account and be startled to learn that existence is not actually dependent on thinking, but until then, only I knew this unique form of terrible existence.

Then, abruptly, I could see again.

There was not much to see; it was near enough to pitch-black in whatever place I had been sequestered. Some dismal and forgotten corner of the dwarf king's hoard, no doubt. While there was a touch of gold in my embroidery, what I'd seen of Khnute definitely suggested a preference for treasures with a little more bling.

"Hat?"

To my immense surprise, I was atop the bullet-head of one Cygni Khnuteson once more. I wasn't sure that I particularly wanted to speak to Cygni, after he'd entirely ignored me and doomed me to the void, but beggars could not be choosers.

Dwarf.

There was another bout of extended silence. Presumably Cygni had assumed that I'd have a lot to say to him. I did not.

"You . . . I . . . I'm taking you up on your offer."

Which offer is that, precisely?

He grumbled a Dwarvish curse word involving a correlation between a mineshaft and one's rear end. "The magic one. I'll take you to your mates. You teach me about magic."

Hmm, I'm not sure if that offer still stands. It was rather time sensitive . . .

"You've been here a day, no more. Whatever your mates might be, they ain't dwarves, ain't no way they made their way through these mines faster than I can get you through 'em."

Hmmmmm. I droned directly into his brain. *Hmmmmm. I'm still not sure . . . What if they've already made it out the other side . . .*

"Then I'll take you all the way to your . . ." I'm hesitant to even give the vaguest translation for the swear word that he used next, lest anyone attempt to recreate the physically impossible sexual act being described. ". . . city."

Do you swear an oath to that effect?

Oaths are a very important thing to dwarves, almost as important as grudges. In fact, violating an oath is a very good way to create a grudge against you. They're considered sacrosanct in a society that is already obsessed with order. Of course, this particular dwarf was already breaking the rules a bit by stealing me from his king, but hopefully the seriousness of the oath would keep him honest in regards to our dealings at least. Besides, I wasn't exactly going to remind him of the fact that he was going against everything he believed in to help me. He might change his mind.

"I will," Cygni said with a little hesitation, then, "I do."

Then away we go!

I settled a little more comfortably on his head as he began sneaking off through the darkened chamber. I dimly made out rows upon rows of shelving, but not what was upon those shelves. I could only hope that the whole place wasn't stuffed full of priceless arcane relics that the dwarves had set aside for further study and then forgotten about.

As we stepped out into a torchlit hallway, still somewhere in the palace judging by the rhythmic splat of baby on rock in the distance, he paused. "Where are we going exactly?"

Ah yes. My stalwart companions would have been heading for Arpanpholigon, so whichever direction that is, please. Also, they would have been heading from the collapsed tunnel where you found me. So if that influences the course at all, now you know.

"Right, yes." He slipped back into stoic silence as he passed a little too close by some of the faceless guards. Luckily, I was riding a surveyor, second class, accustomed to sneaking around tunnels in silence just in case there was anything nasty lurking out there, and the guards' ears were conveniently blocked by big slabs of metal on their heads.

Has the strike ended? Will we be able to get free passage?

Cygni seemed confused for just a moment. "The strike? It's been over since they saw the goblin scabs. No dwarf could abide watching their mine being defiled by such shoddy workmanship. Everyone's back to it." Wistfully, he added, "I hear there's a really promising new andesite deposit in Sector Nineteen."

Would you rather be learning magic, or looking at andesite?

To my immense lack of surprise, I could feel him beginning to have an internal debate over this particular question.

With magic you can make all the andesite you want, now can we please get moving, I hissed into the metaphorical ear of his mind.

"Shut up," he snapped as we rounded a corner.

I would appreciate it if you stopped talking to me in such a manner. I will have you know that . . .

Wherever that thought was going, it stopped dead as I was torn from the dwarf's scalp.

Blissful nothingness again, then I was back on Cygni. Blinking metaphorically in the sudden return of light.

"Patrols about," he said without a hint of apology in his tone. "Couldn't let them see you."

We were now outside of the palace proper, as I could tell from the lack of percussive midwifery.

Well, now that you are well and truly committed to this minor act of larceny, might I ask what prompted the sudden change of heart? One moment you haven't the faintest inkling of interest in magic and now you are willing to defy your king for a lesson?

He huffed. "I had an inkling."

Not even the faintest inkling.

"Half an inkling, at least." This dwarf would argue that the sky wasn't blue.

Can you stop dodging the question?

"Wouldn't call it dodging, just following the rational train of thought," he said, attempting to dodge the question yet again with more haphazard sophistry.

You are deliberately avoiding answering my question, using other subjects as obfuscation. The very definition of dodging a question. Now please be kind enough to speak plainly.

"Well . . . I . . . my reasons are my own." He puffed out his little chest, proud of himself for standing up to me.

You are aware that I'm attached to your brain and can go raking through your memories to find the real answer if need be. I'm just being polite by asking.

There was a brief spike of genuine fear. "You stay out of my head, hat."

I am literally talking to you, in your own head, right now. I don't really have the facilities to talk elsewhere at present.

"Fine!" he said too loudly, catching the attention of a passing dwarf in the tunnel we were currently traversing. He ducked his behatted head down and mumbled the rest into his chest. "There's holes."

Well, we are in a mine.

"Holes in our history," he grumbled. "Things that don't make sense."

Well, that's history for you. People forget things. The tomes get lost. All the world is an amnesiac when it comes time to recall the ways that they've wronged others. It is quite remarkable that we even manage to recall our own personal histories without drowning in shame at the behavior of our younger selves. And when our younger

*selves were in their fur-clad enslavement and conquering phases, very embarrassing to
recall in polite company.*

"It isn't like that," Cygni lied. "Not for dwarves."

*I'm aware that your kind are blessed with nigh-perfect recall, but that does not
necessarily translate into an intergenerational history without gaps. For instance . . .*

"There are holes in stories that are there. How a battle was won. How a
treasure was found. How the dwarves of old did the things that they did. Know
what they did, but don't know how."

Yes, again, this is the nature of history, I'm afraid.

"It's deliberate, is what it is. Somebody has been . . ." Now, the word that
Cygni used next was definitely used with the kind of malice attributed to his
usual cussing, but in this case it does have a direct translation that I do not believe
fully conveys the weight of disgust. So, imagine the following word spoken with
the utmost disgust and disdain, as though any person who would do such a thing
were the very worst kind of pervert or criminal. "Editing."

And you think it is magic.

"No, I reckon someone's just been fiddling with the books."

For a brief moment there I had forgotten that Ig and kobold-kind did not
in fact hold a monopoly on stupidity. They held a concentration, certainly, and
Ig himself was a veritable nexus of all the flows of dumbassery throughout the
universe, but even that tangled knot of dumb was but a single thread in the
grand tapestry of life, a tapestry woven entirely from the stupidity of all history
and the present.

You think that the part that has been edited out is magic?

Cygni nodded to himself. "I think it might explain some . . . discrepancies."

I could not help but be a little intrigued by this turn of events, even if they
were in my favor. Here was a most devoted dwarf, entirely subservient to the
social order in which he was born, trained from birth to fulfill only a single
purpose, but instead of being trapped within that role for all time, he had broken
out. Not because of the injustice and oppression inherent in that system fueling
his rage, but by the raw force of curiosity alone.

*So, rather than a surveyor, you are in fact some sort of historian? An archae-
ologist, perhaps?*

It was perhaps the wrong thing to prod, but prodding it did let me hear the
hasty justification that Cygni had made up to justify his actions to himself. "I'm
a surveyor. Going looking for things is my job. I point them out to them that
need to dig them up. This seems like my wheelhouse."

*Plus there was the rather obvious evidence that your ancestors made use of magic
that we spotted back in town.*

Another firm nod that one of the passing dwarves took as greeting. "Another
discrepancy."

One might even say that it is a mystery that there is no record of dwarves ever having worked with magic, yet such ample evidence of magic having been worked.

Cygni's was a mind of planning and order, and so he had formulated a carefully structured plan, even for his little act of rebellion. "I'm coming with you, I'm learning magic, then I'm coming back, and I'm solving the mystery."

Very reasonable. I had to approve, since it was essentially my plan, framed through his own viewpoint.

We dawdled along until the crowds of dwarves around us in the passages began to thin and we were quite clearly away from the city itself, before Cygni felt safe enough to begin a proper conversation. "If your friends from Sector Eight are heading toward the human trade-post adit, they'd have quite a distance to go."

I have no doubt in their navigational capabilities. Ildrit would keep Ig heading in vaguely the right direction, surely. Or Ig would accidentally wander the right way eventually with Ildrit trailing along after him. Or they'd both have made straight for the surface. Regardless, the only place either of them knew to go to find me was Arpanpholigon, so I was quite sure that was the best direction to find them. Unless they assumed I was dead and destroyed. Who could say, really?

"Best chance to intercept is to take the steam line out to Sector Twenty-One and cut across from there."

I ignored the mining jargon and focused upon the important information. *What would be our most direct route? Without adjusting to, uh, intercept.*

He didn't point out that we might have been abandoning my friends to starvation, roaming lost through the mine tunnels for the rest of their natural lives. "Straight out from Twenty-One along the chalk channels to Deadman's Deep, skirt it, then out the mine."

Oh, that isn't so bad. I had no notion that we were so close.

Cygni snorted. "Out the mine and into natural caves. The trade adit ain't been used in decades. Direct passages are all gone."

Ah. But these natural caves will guide us to our destination?

"No," Cygni said flatly. "I'll guide us to our destination, I'll guide us through the caves."

Oh, so you've been there before?

"No," Cygni said again, but didn't expand with any self-congratulatory commentary this time around. Right, unknown territory. Grand.

"Are we looking for your friends, or pressing on?" Cygni asked.

The image of poor little Ig lost and wandering through the dark tunnels until he weakened and died was truly a tragic one, but I considered it to be fundamentally unlikely. Whatever else Ildrit was, the man was a survivor. He'd find a way out for them. I had faith in his abilities. Besides, without me there to torment, I doubted that Ig would get into much mischief. What would be the point if I weren't there to be incredibly disappointed in every decision the kobold made?

Let us reach this Twenty-One place and make our decision from the information available to us there.

Cygni clearly didn't like not knowing the next step of the plan, but he plodded on all the same like the good little workhorse he was. Ildrit and Ig may have cut across toward the direction in which I had been flung in the hopes of retrieving me from another angle, and thus we may have hope of encountering them en route. Failing that, we could always linger for a time at these chalk channels and await their arrival. Assuming that they hadn't been set upon by the various monsters and rather unfriendly dwarves down here.

Out of curiosity, are there any other exits to the surface nearby that they might have taken?

"Quarry adit ain't used anymore, but we've got other shale dumps where we need them. Could be your friends found one." He was trying to offer me comfort, I knew, but it is difficult to lie, even by omission, while sharing a brain.

I shall hope that is so. Although . . . they may not do so well in civilized lands without me to guide them.

"Thought you said one was human." Cygni scowled. "He'll vouch for the . . ." The exact word that he used to describe Ig is essentially untranslatable, but it is a term that I believe the dwarves use to refer to parasites that infest the undergarments.

There may have been some minor misunderstanding with the Arpanpholigon ruling council that might prevent them from recognizing him as such.

Cygni's beetled brows must have appeared as though they were attempting to mate with one another with the way that he was scowling. "What will they think he is?"

There was little point in hesitating further. *A criminal.*

Disgust washed through the dwarf. "You associate with lawbreakers and monsters, and you expect me to trust you?"

Well, to be fair, I didn't exactly have a full dance card out in the Badlands, I had to travel with whosoever was available to me.

"But you're still looking for them?" There was a definite accusatory tone to his voice now that I didn't much care for.

Well yes, they helped me, it would be rather caddish of me to abandon them now, don't you think?

Cygni spat. "I'd think you'd be glad to be rid of them."

They weren't all bad. Ildrit hasn't done anything particularly evil in quite a long time, and Ig . . . I'm not sure he's even capable of doing anything bad, really. Stupid, certainly, but he lacks the capacity for malice.

"A monster is a monster, and a lawbreaker is worse. You should leave them to rot."

A criminal is worse than a monster?

"Monsters are what they are, but a lawbreaker chose to be that way."

By doing something like stealing a hat from their king?

That brought our progress to an abrupt halt. "That's different. He's . . . he's busy is all. He doesn't have time to investigate you, being king and all. I'm doing it for him."

Oh, so your breaking of the law is an entirely different matter. I understand now. Forgive my confusion.

"Listen here, you . . ." Something that one inserts into a very private place, presumably with the assistance of some lubrication or a running start. ". . . hat . . ."

We are all faced with complex situations in the real world, where the right choice and the one that is dictated to us by law diverge. I would suggest that as a newly made criminal, you become accustomed to this idea.

"I am not a . . ." His mouth worked silently on its own as his brain caught up to the reality that he'd put himself in. ". . . I am. I'm a lawbreaker."

Welcome to the club, I break the laws of physics all day every day. It is part and parcel of being a wizard. To make something where there was nothing is unnatural, yet we do it, because we have the power to do so, and the wisdom to decide when doing so is right. If you are to be a wizard, I'd suggest that you become accustomed to that idea also. That you need to trust in your own judgment over what you have been told.

"They're going to cut off my head." Cygni apparently missed that rather insightful speech in the midst of his mental breakdown. "I stole . . . from the king. Oh stone above . . ."

He sank to his knees in a little cubby off the main tunnel, hyperventilating so hard that his beard and mustache were flapping in toward the mouth that I assumed was under there somewhere. I wasn't sure exactly what would happen if the dwarf I was riding had a full-blown panic attack while wearing me, but I had to assume it would not be good.

It was necessary to solve the mystery. And I'm sure that solving said mystery will invariably result in you being welcomed back with open arms.

"I'm a lawbreaker, I should go turn myself in right now." He recited it as if by rote. "I'm just making it worse for myself. Maybe they'll only lock me up forever if I give up."

Cygni, I assure you that nobody is going to execute you for taking your own hat back from someone who wasn't using it.

"It was the king's hat . . ." He choked on the words. Of course robbing a fellow dwarf would have been a terrible, unforgivable crime to him, but robbing the king, his father, father of all the hive . . . That was probably right up there with poking a god in the eye.

I needed to change his thinking rapidly, or we were both going to end up back imprisoned.

Did the king find it? Wear it? No. You were the one who discovered me, abandoned. You have the right to claim me. I belong to you. At least for now. All that you did was . . . assert your right to your own property. That's a very dwarvish thing to do, isn't it? Don't you people have territory wars over practically nothing?

"I . . . I . . ." A short, sharp curse that technically described the water used to sluice dust from a freshly cut piece of stone but was more often attributed to mean a bowel movement. ". . . you're my hat. I just took you back."

The lie clicked into place, the perfect justification for his actions. I really should have known better than to aggravate his mental state when he was already doing what I wanted. It would have been like yelling "boo" at Ig.

That's right.

Whether he heard me or not, I couldn't say, but he went on rambling all the same. "And you'll teach me magic, and I'll show everyone dwarves can do magic, and that the lore is wrong."

Exactly.

He started quivering like an angry chihuahua in a blizzard. "And then they'll execute me for that instead."

So close.

I'm sure that once you have returned your people's natural birthright to them, the king will forgive any transgressions.

"I'm questioning! I'm questioning the sacred texts! The lore!" The hyperventilating was back, the whole beard now rising to whap him rhythmically in the face. "I'm a lore-breaker! That's even worse!"

Cygni Khnuteson, Second-Class Surveyor of the kingdom of Khnute's Crack, you are nothing of the sort! Whoever edited the lore, they are the ones who broke it. They are the liars, you are restoring truth . . . you are restoring order.

It was exactly the right thing to say, which is somewhat inevitable given that I am one of the most intelligent people on the planet, even if I have been temporarily reduced to headgear. Cygni's frantic panting stopped, the shaking ceased, his beard flopped back down to its natural position atop his chest and stomach.

"I'm restoring order . . . I'm restoring our birthright . . . I'm getting us back what was stolen from us!"

Precisely! Isn't that much more important than a hat?

"It is!" He finally reached the point of epiphany, considerably later than I would have preferred, but at least he hadn't lost his mind in the midst of a crisis. Just in the midst of an escape attempt.

He got back to his feet and coughed. "Let's, uh . . . not talk about this. Ever."

Please.

It wouldn't exactly do wonders for my reputation if people found out I was offering psychiatric counseling to distraught dwarves any more than it would help his for people to know that he was a distraught dwarf.

A shrill shriek cut through the air, high-pitched enough that for a moment I felt it on Cygni's skin before it descended deep enough to be heard. Some massive, monstrous beast was clearly making its presence known. The very air around us was buffeted by its breath washing over us, stale and moist.

Cygni grinned. "Right on time."

CHAPTER FIVE

A SONG OF STEAM AND STEEL

Whatever monstrosity Cygni was walking us toward filled me with considerably more fear than it did him. Apparently vast monsters were just a normal part of living underground. Something I probably should have taken into account before heading down here. I had thought it oh-so-clever to conduct the remainder of our journey to the city out of sight of those who might misunderstand Ig's nature but hadn't considered the unique dangers of the underworld.

Is there perhaps some course that we could take that avoids the territory of this creature? Not that I doubt your ability to fend for yourself, of course, I'm sure you are a stalwart warrior, but . . .

"Are you scared, hat?" Cygni chuckled.

I do not believe that having a healthy sense of self-preservation is indicative of some moral fault.

The precise word that he laughed at me then is once again untranslatable if one wishes to maintain one's sensibilities, but it implied cowardice, childishness, a fear of the dark, a diminished stature, and an undersized pickaxe that may have been metaphorical. Needless to say, this hardened my resolve somewhat.

The tunnel we had been traversing opened out into a wider one, and then joined a half dozen others all converging on a single point. It seemed that this was some sort of main thoroughfare, though why they had constructed it with that odd ditch running up the middle between the smooth stone platforms was beyond me.

From farther down that tunnel, the screeching sound emerged once more, and the fog began to seep along the ceiling. It had to be some sort of dragon, that was the only explanation. Some subterranean dragon living in these tunnels with the dwarves. I could not imagine how they might co-exist.

A great many dwarves were just standing around on the platform on the far side of the trench, as though they were simply waiting to be eaten. Was this some sort of sacrifice? Was that how peace was achieved with the dragon, a steady supply of free meat? With a fresh twinge of horror, I realized that Cygni had assumed the same position on this side of the ditch. I had thought that his mental turmoil had been broken through, but clearly he had decided to end himself, and me with him.

We can talk about this, dwarf. There is no need to make any hasty decisions.

"This is the quickest way." Cygni shrugged.

I couldn't imagine that being devoured by a dragon was all that swift and painless, but presumably he had some firsthand experience to the contrary. Perhaps he meant to be devoured by the most merciful of dragons?

It may be the quickest, but does that make it the best? Is this really the course that you want to take?

"It's either this or hike tunnels for days."

Would a little walk really be so terrible? We could continue your education, and discuss any other matters that are troubling you, and . . .

Before I could get another word out, the beast arrived.

Heralded by a fresh gout of steam, it came bursting from the tunnel, scuttling along the ditch between the platforms. Not a dragon but some vast worm from the glimpse of it I got. Huge and black with the steam pluming up from some blowhole atop its face. The awful shriek came again, and from beneath its hidden underside, sparks chattered across the dirt.

Just as I felt certain that it would lunge up and snatch Cygni in its as-yet-unseen jaws, it breezed right by. Slowing in this cavern but overlooking him entirely. I was awash with relief from my tip to my rim. But just as I thought that we were safe, and in its hurry to be away the great worm had left us in peace, it came to a complete halt and a booming voice echoed out from it. An echoing, cacophonic version of Dwarvish speech filled the room. "Mind the gap."

Had I the musculature, I feel certain that I would have been shaking. And then that awful voice came again. "Mind the gap."

I had convinced myself, in my foolishness, that we were safe now that the head of the beast was past, but this was no normal creature. The aberrations of the deep dark take many forms, and I had overlooked that this abomination would not necessarily keep its mouth on its face. All along the length of the monster's body, its jaws snapped open, dozens of them springing wide, and the worm's last meal came vomiting out. A veritable tide of dwarves who had all been crammed inside of it. Densely packed within its gut until it must have been fit to burst. No wonder it was regurgitating so many now.

Once more the awful voice boomed out. "Mind the gap."

What is the gap?!

Cygni snorted again, pointing down at the space betwixt the gaping maw of the metallic worm and the platform of solid stone. And then, once the disgorged dwarves had all fled, he stepped forward and strolled right inside the monster, pausing to carefully step over the gap, as though that were the thing to be concerned with.

What in the nine hecks are you doing?! I didn't yelp. It would not be becoming for a wizard to yelp; I merely expressed my opinion in a somewhat heightened tone of voice, conveying my surprise with his choice to jump directly into the mouth of the monster.

Cygni rolled his eyes. "Taking the steam line out to Twenty-One."

I paused for just a moment, taking in the straps hanging from the roof of the creature's innards, the various dwarves holding on to said straps for stability and the seating arrayed along the sides of the guts, already occupied with those dwarves of seniority, possessed of grayer beards than the rest. My first assumption was that this steam line idiom was a convoluted means of describing self-destruction, like the many familiars through the years of my study that had mysteriously moved to a nice farm out in the countryside following bouts of sickness, but it was obvious that I had actually fundamentally misunderstood the situation.

The steam line . . . is what we are inside?

"Never seen a train before?" He snorked. Snorking, in this context, was attempting to muffle laughter through his nose while simultaneously attempting not to draw attention from the other passengers, who were already looking curiously at his hat.

Not underground, no, I responded as wryly as I was able while still coming down from the adrenaline high of being flung into the guts of a giant metal monster by a suicidal dwarf.

"Coal engine, steam power." Cygni was entirely too pleased with himself. "Goes the length of the mines in minutes instead of days."

Yes, I'm sure it is very impressive. Of course, with magic, one could simply teleport the distance in an instant, but your contraption is very exciting.

That pushed the dwarf back into sullen silence as the steam engine lurched back to life and he had to grab for a roof strap or risk spilling into the other passengers. At last I had the opportunity to properly observe dwarvish life. Most of the seated dwarves were reading little stone tablets and doing their best to ignore everyone. Most of the standing dwarves were hanging from their straps like rhesus monkeys, dangling beards swaying as we rounded curves in the track, but otherwise as motionless as the stone that entombed us all. Not the most exciting subjects for anthropological study, really.

That is not to say that dwarves are boring—I perish the thought; their entire social structure is fascinating, their biology a mystery shrouded in multiple layers of chainmail and the structure of their incredible brains sufficiently dense that it would take me a lifetime to fully explore and understand how they came to be this way. None of which I could achieve by watching them on a train. Nobody was even humming. Though I supposed that if the concept of music was entirely alien to them, that was hardly a surprise.

Are there any other mechanical marvels that you're going to inflict upon me before our journey is through? Some sort of mechanical bird that will carry us through the sky, perhaps?

I wouldn't say that Cygni was pouting, as such, but there was a certain protrusion of the lips as he grumbled, "Don't be ridiculous."

There was a lot more trundling in silence. A strange chattering noise sounded from beneath our feet as we went along that I had to tap into Cygni's memories to translate into our passage over wooden slats laid under the solid metal bars of the tracks. He fidgeted as I raked through his memories. Ig had never been a fidget. Though I suppose that exploring through his thoughts had been more akin to diving into a vast expanse of empty ocean hoping to encounter a single idea than sifting through carefully organized files.

"Stop it."

I did. Both because pushing the dwarf too far was liable to end with me plucked off his head, and because ultimately, I was being rather rude. Inviting myself in, eating the hors d'oeuvres, putting my feet up on the table. It was pretty obnoxious, if truth be told, and I felt compelled to apologize to Cygni for the imposition. Perhaps I owed Ig something of an apology too, given how readily I'd commandeered all of his faculties. Though, to my credit, he hadn't been using any of them. As I tried to formulate the correct string of words to make the dwarf forgive me, we were both distracted by a sudden lurch. The train was slowing once more, that awful screeching sound vibrating up through the dwarf's feet, up through his bones, all the way up to me atop his skull.

I am not fond of that noise.

"Me neither," Cygni grumbled.

The train stopped, new passengers boarded, old passengers departed. And among the new passengers, there were armored guards like we had seen at the palace and the picket line. The king's enforcers.

Immediately a spike of fear shot through Cygni, and that perfectly organized mind of his began diligently plodding through all the steps that would follow his arrest. I missed Ig. At least his panic was explosive and rapid, and he lacked the imagination to detail every torturous step of our impending miseries. Cygni had his own anxiety refined to a plod.

Do not be afraid, my friend. All will be well. There is no way that they have even discovered my absence yet, let alone begun pursuit.

It was well that I could hear his thoughts, as he was so breathless scarcely a sound came out. "The king is the king, he knows everything."

Speaking as someone who has made a pretty solid effort at actually knowing everything that there is to be known, I can assure you that someone stuck scooting baby dwarves out their nether regions all day is unlikely to have the full breadth of all available information at any given time. I doubt he even reads.

"We should get off the train." He started to move and I was forced to seize control of his legs before he could actually get us in trouble.

Yes, lurching away at the sight of guardsmen and running isn't at all suspicious.

He was so concerned with the arrival of the guards that he entirely overlooked the fact that I could, at least briefly, seize control of his body. That was good. "What do we do?"

We ride the steam line out to Twenty-One, as planned. You stare vacantly into space like everyone else on the train, and you say nothing unless questioned.

His voice had taken on a higher pitch, which made it south of most bass, but was still amusing. "What do I say if they . . ."

I cut him off before he could get any more worked up. *Let us burn that bridge when we come to it.*

"Cross."

Hmm?

"Cross that bridge."

Really? I've always assumed that setting them alight was the better way to avoid pursuers.

The dwarf opened and closed his mouth several times after that without making comment, and I, in an attempt at politeness, avoided listening to his surface thoughts.

Gradually, after eyeballing everyone as much as it was possible to eyeball people without exposed eyeballs, the guards muscled their way off down the train to find someone new to hassle. We had avoided detection for now, presumably because nobody was looking for us and Cygni was simply being a paranoid wreck.

There were a great many stops as we progressed our way through the mines, which was the only reason that the trip was taking any time at all given the pace at which this technological wonder traversed the dark tunnels. Cygni was no longer in the mood to play tour guide, so we maintained the same dumbfounded silence as everyone else on the train. If I did not know better, I would have sworn that there was some silencing spell upon the vehicle, or perhaps some mental compulsion that prevented those aboard from continuing their conversations. Yet gradually I came to the conclusion that we were in fact bearing witness to dwarven politeness at its finest. A dwarf mine was essentially a closed system for the vast majority of the time: nobody in, nobody out. So if you annoyed someone today by taking up too much space, then three years down the line you might end up crossing paths again and getting your foot trod upon. It was no wonder the dwarves held grudges for so long, trapped in such proximity at all times. Their highest form of politeness was attempting not to intrude on one another's lives despite being shoved up against each other so tightly that their beards had to be manually detangled.

Cygni was rammed right up into the armpit of a miner who clearly hadn't had a post-work wash yet, judging by the shifting of all of the bodies on the train, yet both he and the miner were pretending that the other did not exist. The whole thing was mildly confounding.

It was with great relief that we finally decanted ourselves onto a fresh platform that looked remarkably similar to the one we had just departed from. Cygni breathed a sigh of relief to no longer be smelling the aromas of hard work, as interpreted by an armpit.

"Right, this is Twenty-One. Now what?" He asked it casually, as if he weren't asking me to consign my dearest friends in the world to potential death.

I . . . don't know.

"You don't know." Cygni let out a humph. "When will you know?"

Can we find somewhere a little more private to have this conversation?

Cygni glanced around at the staring miners, these ones powdered with white rather than black dust, just to liven things up a little. They stared back with the same suspicious expressions. "Right."

At the same rolling pace as he did everything, Cygni made his way off into a tunnel running parallel to the train line. The stone about us changed as he went, with the gray rock giving way to pale chalk. *Do dwarves have a great many blackboards that need written upon?*

Cygni began counting off the various uses of chalk on his fingers. "Filtration, filler, pigment, quicklime, lowering acidity . . ."

Forget that I asked.

I missed Ig. I don't know how that happened. The kobold had been a pain in my backside since the moment I met him, but somehow, he was better company than this grumpy little know-it-all.

Yet having someone along who knew the local terrain was definitely providing some degree of utility. It was not long at all before we'd found our way to some little cul-de-sac off the side of the main corridor in total isolation.

He cleared his throat. "Well?"

Given the inevitability of my companions passing this way if they are headed for Arpanpholigon, I would suggest that we wait here for a time, to see if they catch up to us.

"The king is going to notice you're missing eventually, then stone help us." Cygni shook himself as though he could get the thought out of his head with sufficiently violent movement. "We need to be out of the mines by then, or at least have something to show for the time."

Then might I turn your attentions back to your studies for a while? You have a spectacularly good grasp of the nature of elements, and your ability to pick out associations has also been excellent, as has your grasp on the fundamentals of Archaic. It is my heartfelt belief that you will be quite a competent wizard once you begin practicing.

He started trying to sidetrack me once again. "How do you 'heartfeel' something with no heart?"

It was simply a turn of phrase.

"Like burning bridges?" He snorted his amusement. Ig would never treat me like this.

Can we focus upon the magic, perhaps? Just think, if the worst were to happen and you were to encounter some sort of trouble with your father, being able to show off a grasp of magic might be beneficial. Wouldn't you say? Something to show for your little adventure.

He conceded the point. "You ain't wrong, hat."

I rarely am.

Clapping his hands together, he turned to face the chalk wall. "Right then, teach me."

If I were to be entirely honest, I had expected the argument to occupy more of our time than it had. I was somewhat let down; I had so many arguments and counter arguments prepared. The whole train trip here I'd been practicing. Now I felt a little like I'd been invited to dance and then someone struck me across the backs of the knees with a broom handle. *Teach you. Yes. Right. Okay. Let me think of the best way to approach this . . .*

One of his fuzzy little eyebrows rose enough that a stray hair tickled the underside of my rim. "Thought you knew all about this?"

Well, with Ig it was rather simple, he surrendered control of his body and allowed me to draw in Quintessence for the first time, then he merely had to continue the process.

Without hesitation, he responded, "So do that."

I suspected that you might object to surrendering your bodily autonomy to me.

"Like when you grabbed me on the train?" he grumbled.

You noticed that, did you?

When he answered, it was so flat you could have set a spirit level using it. "Full-body paralysis."

I do apologize, it is not my intention to impinge upon you in any way, I greatly appreciate that you are putting in the effort to help me, and I would also like to apologize for those moments when I have intruded upon the autonomy of your mind, it had become . . . habitual to sift through Ig's mind without warning, but I can understand why a higher lifeform may not appreciate it.

Despite my typically excellent diction, I rushed it all out before I could be interrupted. I was not accustomed to apologizing to my intellectual lessers, and since my intellectual lessers encompassed every sentient creature that I'd ever encountered, you can imagine how alien this whole experience was for me. Yet despite the monumental effort that I'd put in, Cygni did not seem to be impressed. Quite the opposite in fact; the background buzz of his thoughts had a distinctly contemptuous flavor.

"Are we doing this or ain't we?"

With such a clean-cut invitation, I could hardly refuse to possess his body and flood him with Quintessence.

In the interest of fairness, this may be rather uncomfortable. The first time that I do it, it's rather like opening a mouth that has sealed shut from lack of use.

Cygni snorted. "Pain's my every day."

I had not seen much evidence of that so far, but I decided to plunge ahead before second thoughts could get the best of him. Seizing control of his body, opening up his arcane senses to the world, and drawing the Quintessence that surrounded us into his . . . nowhere. He had nowhere to contain the Quintessence; he had the channels through which it could flood but no reserves in which it could be stored. He was simply built differently. *Ah.*

"Ah?" he asked, reasserting control over his body to bitch at me.

It seems that there is nowhere for me to hold the power that I am drawing into your body.

"So what?"

Well, unless you can conceive of some other way of retaining Quintessence for long enough to shape it into magical effects, I'm afraid this rather stymies our progress. You will be able to draw in magic so long as you use it in the same moment that it is drawn, and you will be able to replenish such power as you inadvertently draw from your body, but the places where reserves within you would be held are . . . absent.

"So dwarves can't do magic?" Cygni's tone was not impressed, I can tell you that much.

Yes and no. There is no reason that you cannot make use of the rather small amount of Quintessence that you'll be able to draw in an instant to produce minor effects, but anything too elaborate is likely to overtax you and result in your body's natural Quintessence being consumed. Which will in turn result in . . . death.

"So what is . . . too elaborate?"

Well . . . the spells that we've been discussing up until now are right out. We will have to look to low magic in the immediate future, and I'll contemplate some . . . simplifications of some archaic words for further down the line.

"So all my knowledge of Archaic . . ."

Will kill you.

"And my knowledge of the elements?"

Will kill you.

"You know, I'm starting to think that maybe your lessons weren't worth much."

But you can feel the flows of Quintessence through you now?

"Like a static buildup."

So our theory is sound, we'll just have to work around the limitations.

"The limitations being I'm going to . . ." This particular word of Dwarvish is actually a reference to a beautiful folk tale about . . . no, of course it wasn't. It was a vile and anatomically impossible sexual act. ". . . die."

The obstacles that we face in our journey become the path itself.

"What's that mean?"

I don't know, but didn't it sound wise? Regardless, we shall work on some low magic for now, while you resist the urge to perform any higher acts of magic, and I shall consider any possible uses for the rather limited Quintessence that shall be at your disposal as you make your attempts.

"So I draw it in like . . ."

He succeeded on his very first attempt. Even I hadn't succeeded in my first attempt at drawing Quintessence from the environment. Ig . . . was a whole other story, obviously, but the vast majority of students took weeks to achieve the necessary concentration and force of will. Again, he was a natural. It was just unfortunate that all of the Quintessence he drew in immediately forced the Quintessence that already resided within him out the other end.

Most impressive.

"And I use it by . . ."

Expelling it with your breath as you concentrate on your understanding of an element. But don't . . .

He whispered, "***Lux.***"

All of the Quintessence in his body was stripped out of him and he would have dropped dead then and there if I hadn't immediately seized control of his still-standing corpse and hauled in a fresh flood of Quintessence to replace what he'd used.

Cygni dropped to his knees, gasping for air as though it had been all the breath ripped out of his body with the word instead of all his vital essence.

As I was saying, do not make use of it in that manner, because it will be entirely too taxing for your limited supply.

To his credit, there had been the briefest glimmer of golden light before he keeled over. The spell had been a success, but it had been a purric victory: so named for the time that the Archmage of Arpanpholigon's cat had succeeded in capturing a mouse within his laboratory at the cost of shattering every piece of glassware within. Ending in his immediate termination from the position of familiar and reassignment to being an outside cat.

Last time I kept a bloody familiar, I can tell you that.

Still panting for breath, Cygni let out a half sob, half gasp, entirely pathetic little moan. "That nearly . . . killed me."

Yes, I was trying to tell you that was what was going to happen.

"All . . . these words . . . Archaic . . . they'll all . . . do the same?"

If you try to cast with them, most assuredly, the majority will draw considerably more Quintessence from you. It was just luck that you chose one of the most basic options from your considerable vocabulary.

"Poisoned . . . chalice . . ." He was getting his breath back properly now after that brief moment of his lungs and heart stopping. "You . . . hat . . ."

Shall we skip past the recriminations and blame to focus on what we have learned?

"Why . . . dwarves . . . don't do magic."

Perhaps, or it may just be that you have some unfortunate deformity of arcane anatomy. Without another dwarf to test on, I'm afraid that we shall not know. Perhaps if we partnered you with someone capable of drawing significant amounts of . . . Ig. Ig would be ideal. More Quintessence than he knows what to do with most of the time. Literally. Although that isn't saying much; you could hand that kobold two orbs and he'd immediately drop them both.

"You got a point in there somewhere?"

An external source of Quintessence will allow you to perform magic, but for now, we shall focus your training upon the direct application of small amounts of Quintessence in what is known as low magic.

"Low magic? Sounds like the best kind."

To a dwarf, I supposed that it would.

And so it was that we wasted the remainder of our day, slowly acclimating Cygni to the direct applications of Quintessence. He moved some rocks around. Then he moved them around in a slightly different way. Then he tried to stack them, overdid it, and had to have a nice lie down for an hour or so. Riveting stuff.

Congratulations on your fruitful day.

"You decided if we're leaving your mates behind yet?"

It had in fact been the sole topic to which I had turned my considerable intellect for the duration of his practice session. When I wasn't gently intervening to stop him from destroying himself utterly by overextending his limited reach.

The following conclusions were what I had reached in all of that remediation:

Ildrit was competent. Whatever other troubles may have afflicted him, he was a survivor most capable of ensuring his own continuing survival. To wit, he would have recognized that the mines were a fundamentally hostile environment and departed from them with all haste.

Ig was fundamentally incompetent, and without my presence upon his brow, his intellectual capacity would have immediately begun to degenerate. As such, he would have presented no argument to Ildrit, following the typical kobold policy of following after whoever seemed strongest.

Ergo, the likelihood that they would still be in the mines was practically nil. And in the miniscule percentage of outcomes in which they did remain underground and attempt to travel in this direction, they would have had a sufficient head start, without the detour to goblin-town and Khnute's Crack, to arrive around about now. Since they had failed to do so, I was forced to work off the assumption that for once, they had done the smart thing without me intervening.

We shall depart once you have taken what rest and succor you require.

Cygni hopped back up to his feet with surprising spryness for a creature that was essentially a cuboid. "We can go now."

Perhaps sleep and food might be . . .

The dwarf shouldered his pack. "Don't need it, don't want it. Let's go."

My dear friend . . .

"Not friends," he interjected, but I carried on regardless.

Even the most valiant and stalwart of warriors are still enslaved by their biology. We all must consume energy and sleep, lest our bodies break down.

"Maybe you pansy humans do." A furtive grin appeared beneath his beard. "We're dwarves."

While I'm sure that you are the marathon runners of the remaining conscious races, the truth remains . . .

He interrupted me once more. I was not accustomed to being interrupted. The one and only time it had occurred during a lecture at the university, the student in question had lived out the remainder of the year as a newt. Yet I was not currently in a position to newt anyone. So I swallowed my irritation as Cygni said, "How long's my shift?"

You don't appear to be wearing an under-dress.

"Harr harr." He laughed utterly humorlessly. "How many hours?"

I suppose it is something ridiculously long if it has made even dwarves rise up in protest against it. Ten hours? Twelve?

"Seventy-two."

My mind boggled at that number, trying to interpret what he had said in some other way that made any degree of sense.

I beg your pardon. Seventy-two hours? That's three days!

"Aye, used to be longer, but some slackers started falling asleep on the machines." He sneered. "Too cozy by the forges."

How is it possible that you could work for three days without rest?

"Dwarves are built different." He seemed genuinely proud of his ability to work endless hours, as if it were not symptomatic of a social structure that was entirely broken.

Might I inquire how long you have been awake thus far?

"I've got another day or two in me."

That wasn't strictly an answer.

He cocked his head to the side like a confused spaniel. "Wasn't it?"

I was not going to engage in this nonsense again; it was disrespectful. The pointless redirection, the mockery of it all, I wasn't going to do it.

"Are you sure it wasn't?"

Had I teeth, I would have gritted them. As it was, I simply made myself as uncomfortable to wear as possible. Every inch that I could pinch or itch, I did. Every time that a flop of my brim could block his direct line of sight, I flopped it. It was a small and petty revenge unbecoming of my station, but at this present moment in time, I had unbecome my station entirely and become a hat, so I had to work with what I had.

If there was even the slightest twinge of irritation in Cygni, it was buried so deep that it would take some sort of psychiatric archaeologist to uncover it. I will admit that I was accustomed to Ig, and his emotions. He didn't so much wear them on his sleeve as vomit them out at everyone in the blast radius. Cygni was at the opposite end of that same spectrum, in that you could probably spend a lifetime with him and never for a single moment know what was going on behind his black-beetle eyes.

Even I, with a direct line to his meticulous little brain, was rebuffed each time I sought the emotions behind his choices. As though he were insulted at the idea that he was anything but a being of pure logic. I would not dig deeper, as I could scarcely afford to make an enemy of my only ally, but I will admit that I felt somewhat adrift, not knowing his thoughts, his drives, any part of him beyond what he told me.

The chalk channels lived up to their name, long and white with little else to recommend them. Cygni's boots gradually became clotted with white dust. There were lanterns strung up along the length of the roof, but since nobody seemed to come down here, they remained unlit, a little reminder of how dark it actually was down here.

I had Cygni's wonderful dwarven eyes to light the way, but without them, the darkness would have been absolute. I don't mean *blow out the candle it is time for bed*, or *the moon has slipped behind a cloud*, I mean absolute darkness. Total oblivion. Like I get to experience every time someone isn't wearing me.

I'm not a big fan.

Yet with Cygni's natural gifts, it would have felt quite churlish to request a torch be lit. Here he was bestowing upon me the treasures of his genetics, and I'd throw them all away for a candle. It would be difficult not to offend in making such a request. So I endured the deep shadows cast across the pale nothingness of this channel through the earth in poor humor.

"Scared of the dark?" It seemed that the good manners that I was extending by not prying into my dwarven companion's thoughts had not been reciprocated.

I have delved into the eternal darkness between worlds, I have gazed into the void and made it blink when it tried to look back, I am a wizard, master of all creation, and I fear nothing.

"You know we ain't able to lie to each other, right?" Cygni chuckled.

You want the truth? The darkness is a gruesome reminder of the oblivion that you damned me to when you took me from your head and gave me to your father. Without eyes to see, ears to hear, or even a mind to think. All I knew was nothingness. I cannot conceive of a worse heck, and you banished me to it gladly.

"I . . ." Cygni at least had the good grace to lose the gruff laughter now. "I didn't know that."

You didn't ask. You didn't care.

"I came back for you," he interjected.

When you thought that you were missing out on a prize. When you thought magic was just out of reach. Not because you give half a damn about me.

His mustache twitched in a manner that might have suggested a smirk. "Maybe . . . a quarter."

Very droll.

He grumped and stomped his feet to loosen some of the chalk. "Well, you aren't teaching me magic now, and I'm still helping you."

Well, yes, of course, because you are intelligent enough to recognize that my immense genius, turned to the problem of providing you with a means of channeling a greater amount of Quintessence without doing yourself harm, will result in the goal that you seek. Even if there is a temporary roadblock. You are many things, but impatient is not one of them.

"I didn't know that, actually," Cygni mumbled in surprise. Voice echoing only faintly along the length of the chalk channels.

Oh please, I'm the greatest wizard that the world has ever known, you don't think I've already come up with a half dozen potential solutions to allow you to become the second greatest? With that memory of yours, all we need to do is construct some sort of artificial reserve in my workshop back in Arpanpholigon and you'll put every under-ling and apprentice I've ever had the displeasure of dealing with to shame. You'll likely be able to give me a run for my money, given enough time and study. So, you're being patient and sensible and assisting me in returning to the one place in the world where I'll have access to all the resources required to pay you back for your services tenfold.

When he spoke now, he seemed awkward. In front of his father, I'd seen him on the back foot, but with me he'd always been supremely confident. "I was taking you because I promised to."

But you don't even like me?!

He shrugged. "Promise is a promise, no matter who it is to."

The vast gulf in our understanding of the world loomed betwixt us once more. To me, a promise had never been anything so binding. It had been an expression of my intent at a given moment, that I was willing to adjust as circumstances changed. For a dwarf, and in particular for Cygni, it seemed that a promise carried an entirely different spiritual weight. I had to pry further to truly grasp this. *So you are telling me that even though you thought that you were no longer going to receive any sort of recompense, you still intended to march all the way to the human kingdoms?*

With no small amount of bitterness, he let out a sigh, blowing a cloud of chalk dust from his mustaches. "Not like there's anything left for me down here. I'm a traitor now."

Most likely I was obliged at this point to offer some sort of comfort, but the truth of the matter was that he was likely correct. Dwarves saw the world in black and white. Any degree of disobedience was tantamount to a capital crime. Still, I had to try.

You moved a hat nobody was wearing. It seems like a very mild sort of treachery.

He scoffed. "As soon as you're discovered missing, they'll look for me. And when they can't find me . . . my name will be in the book of grudges."

And how swiftly do you suppose that the theft might be uncovered? Are the troves of sequestered treasures toured regularly?

"They're the king's private property. Folks can't just go wandering 'round in there." There was a drift in cadence as enlightenment began to dawn on Cygni. A lilt of realization.

So it won't be noticed for months, if not years, is what you're saying?

"Probably not in my lifetime . . ."

A human king would of course have had some lackey in their treasury every day of the week, counting every penny to ensure that nothing had been pilfered. That lackey would begin pocketing gold immediately, resulting in another lackey being brought in to prove lackey one was lacking in the morals department, then they would discover that there was hot and cold running gold on tap provided that they kept their mouth shut about a little bit of embezzlement, and so on and so forth. Meanwhile, a dwarf king's treasures were left alone, untouched, and the absolute trust placed in the hive was repaid in kind.

Or perhaps it wasn't. Cygni could not be the only dwarf to have ever pilfered a little something from the master's coffers. All of the hidden treasures shoved up into the hidden recesses of Khnute's Crack could have been plundered without anyone the wiser, because the dwarves were all so certain of their own virtue, each one of them with a little guardsman in his head, commanding utter obedience. The actual guards felt like they were almost superfluous. An affectation borrowed from other cultures to convince the dwarves that their king was as important as any other.

Throughout this brief consideration, Cygni had still been absorbing the realization that his life was not actually over. ". . . I could still be back. With magic. Before anyone knows."

You most certainly could. And even if you aren't back before anyone notices, when you come back with magic, I have a sneaking suspicion that will overpower any concerns about a little hat borrowing, wouldn't you think?

"I . . . I told them you were a magic hat, maybe I'll tell them . . . you vanished on your own!" The concept of lying was so novel to Cygni that the bounce in his step almost tripped him up.

Seems plausible enough.

"Thanks, hat."

Thank you, Cygni, for upholding your side of our arrangement even when you thought that it may not bear fruit.

"Don't know that one." Cygni stroked his beard. "Like . . . apples with fur and claws?"

I'm not doing this again.

CHAPTER SIX

APERTURES AND AQUATICS

There are a great many things that dwarves learn to fear in their early lives, hidden in the granite womb of their civilization. They are a species that will, if all goes well, remain subterranean for the duration of their existence. The Dwarvish word for an exit to the surface is basically a direct translation for our words "waste" and "dump" merged together.

As such, while a human parent might be teaching their children not to wander into traffic or into the deep dark woods or whatnot, a dwarf is taught an entirely different set of terrors to keep them on the straight and narrow. They are taught that the tapping sound in the walls of the mines might be goblins trying to undermine you, or it might be the structure giving out under the weight from above, and that in either case you should probably run until you can't hear it anymore, no matter how promising that quartz deposit looks.

But among the many lessons that a dwarf is taught, the one that seems to take the deepest root in their psyche is a fear of water. This may seem like I'm making a jibe about their cleanliness, but honestly, they don't smell at all bad, especially if you've spent some time as a kobold. Rather, it is that water found underground is almost exclusively going to be bad news for a dwarf.

There are obvious reasons for this from a miner's perspective—you don't want to be breaking through into a flooded chamber and drown your whole tunnel—but the particulars of why dwarves fear deep water seem to be less about that practical aspect and more about another.

One of the big restraints on life developing in the deep dark beneath the world is the absence of anything that might sustain it. There is little in the way of warmth or light, littler still in the way of consumable resources that might sustain such creatures as require fodder. But in the water, this is not so.

Life was born in black waters like this, far back in the dim recesses of prehistory. From soup cometh us all, and to soup we shall return. In fact, I returned to soup not so long ago when I was placed upon a tureen, though that isn't the particular soup to which I was referring. It was a rather under-seasoned chicken broth.

Regardless, while there may have been an anxiety well hidden beneath the carefully layered structures of Cygni's mind up until this point, he now was tapping into a far more primal terror, the kind inserted alongside all of the other insecurities that parents bestow upon their children. As such, his gaze flicked incessantly toward the vast pond of Deadman's Deep as we approached.

From beneath the myriad layers of padded cloth that composed his uniform, a lantern had at some point emerged and been lit by some mechanical contraption that I'd been unable to identify in the brief moment it had flickered into sight. As such, we now had a golden glow hovering about crotch height, shimmering across the surface of what should really have been still water.

The water was not still. Ripples far larger than Cygni's little boot-stomps should have been producing were swishing back and forth across the surface. Unfamiliar as he was with bodies of water, Cygni's anxiety was not heightened by this, but being a surface dweller with a passing knowledge of the kind of creatures that lived in deep dark water elsewhere, it is fair to say that I myself was experiencing some degree of trepidation.

Might I suggest that we accelerate our progress somewhat?

"Want me to slip on the wet rocks?" Cygni grumbled.

It took all that I had not to point out that the only way the rocks could be wet was if something large was in the water, displacing things with its motion. *I do not want to alarm you . . .*

He cut me off. "Then don't."

Which was about the moment that the sound emanated across the surface of the water, so low and deep that it made Cygni's voice sound like a mosquito playing a mosquito-sized piccolo. He didn't hear it, he felt it on his skin. In his bones. So low that his conscious mind could not make sense of it, but that tiny little stem at the root of his tiny little brain immediately started screaming to itself.

Luckily for us, I was not so ignorant. For while it had simply sounded like some sort of tectonic shift to dear Cygni, I was versed in the more esoteric languages of our world, and I understood it to be Abyssal.

Heck is where you go if you are very bad in life or inclined toward enjoying being barbecued and prodded in the scrotum with pitchforks. I don't judge, to each their own.

It bore no relation whatsoever to the Abyss. Which was an altogether different kind of place, with much less heavy metal music, and a lot more crushing pressure. It was said that it was a place so hostile to existence itself that nothing could live there, yet as you have likely surmised from the fact that there is a language named for the place, something dwelled within that eternal night. And whatever those eldritch beings may have been, it seemed that their spawn were now in the lake of Deadman's Deep, having a rather spirited conversation amongst themselves.

Deep in the darkness, a being of unfathomable form and horror rippled some organ evolved long before bone, pushing water and air through it to reverberate out through the cavern, setting every hair on the back of Cygni's neck standing to attention. And that droning reverberation, once translated into a tongue that would not drive mere mortals mad to comprehend, was saying, "That's a dwarf."

From far beneath the waves came an answering rumble. It could have been from the very heart of the earth, so deep and resounding were the waves that it sent rippling up through stone and water. "Dwarves aren't pointy."

There were some distant sloshing sounds that set Cygni's heart hammering and his feet finally moving a little bit faster. Some of those sloshing sounds were presumably the extrusion of some sort of sensory apparatus from the pool's surface. "It isn't very pointy."

The first voice came again. To describe Abyssal in human terms is extremely difficult. It is a language comprised of layered, repetitive rippling sounds. Like whale song, if all of the whales were singing in harmony and had multiple throats to work with. Not to mention, much deeper voices. "Look at the top."

More ripples and consideration. "Could be a stalactite."

The language of the Abyss is one of a cold place, where things move so slowly that they cannot be perceived to be in motion at all. As such, when there was a pause in the conversation, it actually stretched out a fair period of time. "Don't sit still that long, do they?"

If one did not have shoulders, if one did not have a skeleton at all, was it possible for one to shrug? What visible contortion of protoplasm and tentacular extrusions would accompany such a motion? We shall never know, as it all took place deep beneath the surface of the water, before the voice returned. "This one might have."

Another long period of silent contemplation occurred, during which Cygni continued to scramble on forward at maximum speed while also making no noise whatsoever. A tricky feat that would require some tricky feet. "If it isn't a dwarf, what is it?"

Something in the distant dark broke the surface, setting forth more ripples across the great pond. Judging by the commentary, this particular organ was not an eyeball. Though I had little clue whether such creatures had eyes as we knew them at all. "Hairy. Scent tastes like land-meat and dirt."

The first voice was raised in some mild excitement, lifting the surface level of the lake into a fine mist. "That's a dwarf."

It is difficult to say which of these two monstrous disembodied voices could be considered the voice of reason. I suspect both of them thought that they were. "Could be a goblin."

As if they were a philosopher decrying a misspoken logical loop, the other amorphous glob replied, "Goblins aren't pointy."

The point was conceded to the good spokesman from the darkest recesses of human nightmares. "And they smell worse. Oily."

With the tone of a geriatric cephalopod proclaiming something of vital importance to the future of its pod: "I can't have goblin on my new diet, you know that."

Sotto voce is not actually possible when you're speaking in infrasound that vibrates through the bones of the earth. "We all know that. You haven't shut up about it in eons."

Huffing is also not something that is strictly possible when you don't breathe air, but the word certainly described the manner in which the eldritch abomination spoke. "Excuse me for watching my figure."

"You're the only one watching it." The phrase "under their breath" wasn't really appropriate either given that there was no actual breathing involved. I could certainly say that it was said out of the side of the thing's mouth. But given how many orifices the thing was capable of opening, that turn of phrase probably wasn't apt either. This is why nobody likes eldritch abominations, they're bloody impossible to describe, which makes conversations about them a linguistic nightmare.

"Excuse you?" The affronted sound was higher than the others. Such that it made Cygni's teeth ache and his eyes boggle in his head.

"What was that?" The dwarf gasped in terror.

Just keep moving. I'm monitoring the situation.

Meanwhile the aquatic argument raged on.

"What? Everyone knows that . . ."—eldritch gender seventeens—". . . like a . . ."—eldritch gender four—". . . with some lumps to them."

"Well, maybe after millennia not dead but dreaming they'll have developed some slightly more refined tastes than back in your day, when you had to store fat in lumps just to make it through the pre-atomic winter."

How does one define sass? Is it in the particular phrasing? In the tone of voice? Regardless, this eldritch beast did manage to personify that abstract concept for the duration of its rebuttal.

They weren't shouting exactly. They were certainly louder than they should have been if they meant to remain incognito and snatch people up from the shore without being noticed.

"Yes, yes, we all know you were spawned when the stars themselves were lit. You're young and hip and us boring old lumps with our lumps aren't worth listening to. Couldn't be we'd acquired any wisdom in a lifespan that eclipses that of the universe . . ."

The argument descended below the limits of dwarvish hearing as the two beasts beneath the waves descended into grumbling and bitching.

Finally, the sound returned. "It's stalagmites anyway."

"What?" The other argumentative monster was completely knocked off-kilter by this unexpected attack.

There are things that man was not meant to know of. The language of the Abyss is probably one of them, but more specifically, the sound of an eldritch abomination singsonging the phrase, "Tights come down, might go up again," must have qualified.

"It is down."

Bubbles rose with an exasperated sigh. "No, you're upside down. The water is up. The pointy bit was on top. Like a stalagmite."

"Diets. Pah!" The first of the abominations sprayed a stream of chill water into the air. "Well, even if you aren't going to have anything to eat, doesn't mean I've got to starve myself another century until something else comes this way. I'm grabbing it, stalagmite or not."

The dieting abomination sounded intensely smug as it informed the other, "You can't."

Pseudopods writhed beneath the surface in barely contained wrath. "And why's that, smarty-tentacles?"

"It's buggered off."

Cygni and I cleared the cavern chamber quite some time before the argument concluded. It was a vast chamber, but Abyssal is a terribly slow language. I considered, briefly, filling him in on what all of the eerie sounds had been as we passed by the water, but ultimately decided that it probably wouldn't have been to his advantage to know that he'd been mistaken for a goblin. That was the sort of thing that could really plague a man's ego.

The passages were still good dwarven work as we proceeded beyond the cavern, but eventually we reached a point where natural tunnels stretched out before us and Cygni came to a dead halt.

He looked down at the floor of the tunnel, to the clear delineation between carefully smoothed stone and the heaped gravel lining the tunnel ahead. Taking a deep breath, he lifted his foot, then it just hovered there. Not quite coming down.

Is there some sort of problem?

Cygni gave a gruff chuckle. "No. No problem. Just . . ."

Oh, spit it out, we haven't got all day.

"Farthest I've ever been from home," he said. "Next step I take."

Well, I suppose some degree of sentiment is in order then, by all means. Take a moment.

I did my even best not to listen in to his internal thought processes, even though that basically meant that I had nothing to occupy me other than staring off down a dark tunnel. Finally, with a little sigh, Cygni brought his foot down.

There we are, that wasn't so bad, was it.

He chuckled, then lifted his other foot and paused once more.

What is it now?

Solemn once more, he declared, "Next step I take will be the farthest from home I've ever been."

I waited for him to put his foot down, to continue our journey, but he was lost in thought once more.

This is a joke, right?

There was a twinge of annoyance in his voice. "Dwarves don't go wandering like you people."

Yes, but you've already done the dramatic pause, can we just . . .

"That was then," he cut me off sternly. "Now this is the farthest I've ever been."

He did this, step by step, for another fifteen minutes as I slowly but surely tried to work out how I could kill him and still somehow escape from this mine. Killing him would be easy enough. All I really needed to do was suck all the Quintessence up out of him to restore my own reserves and he'd drop like a fly.

At some point the emotional pangs that the dwarf had been experiencing finally seemed to fade enough that we could get back up to a walking pace, but my irritation with the creature remained. Just because dwarves were more like humans in appearance than kobolds did not mean that they were in any way more like us. Their minds were different, their bodies built for a different purpose, and the manner in which they approached things was sufficiently alien to be aggravating while still being just familiar enough for me to understand it.

So what is it exactly about being away from the hive that is causing you such anxiety?

"Not scared," Cygni was quick to say. "Just . . . not . . . comfy."

I could see very little that might bring comfort in your solid stone hometown. I was not aware that comfort was one of the things that drive dwarves. Indeed, I would argue that you throw yourselves directly into discomfort as much as possible, what with the devotion to mining—one of the professions that surface dwellers consider the harshest of work.

"Hard is comfy," Cygni tried to explain. "Soft is . . . hard?"

I believe we may be slipping from philosophical debate into gibberish.

"You know where you are with hard. It's obvious." He seemed to be trying to work this through for himself as much as for me. "But when things are soft . . . when there's no order to what you're meant to be doing . . ."

I should really have foreseen this possibility. Without the carefully structured life that he was accustomed to, Cygni was already beginning to lose cohesion. The external structure of society shaped him into what he was, and without it there was the possibility for boundless outward growth. He could become anyone without a king telling him who to be all the time. Which would have been fine if either one of us had any clue what kind of person he might turn into without peer pressure keeping him focused.

Allow me to suggest that you treat me as your king until such time as you have returned home, unerringly obeying all of my commands so as to alleviate this feeling of confusion.

He snorted at that, contempt overpowering whatever existential crisis he was facing. "Trust you?"

Have I shown myself to be untrustworthy in any way?

There was a long moment of silence, as though he expected me to confess to something when there had been no wrongdoing at all on my part. Then he sighed. "You just spent fifteen minutes thinking about killing me."

Ah, I forget that when I'm thinking using your brain, you sometimes overhear it. If it is any consolation, it wasn't a serious contemplation of killing you.

"He'd drop like a fly." He quoted my thoughts back to me.

I'll admit that particular one did sound a little damning without context.

Oh, that was just casual malice as a result of irritation at our slow progress. Everyone has the odd murderous thought, it doesn't mean that I'd act upon it.

"I ain't trusting you farther than I can throw you," he stated flatly.

To be fair, I am rather light in my current form, with the right directional wind that could account for a good distance. Add in a push of that low magic that you're on your way to mastering and I may in fact make quite a journey.

We had been making better progress since his initial hopscotch performance, and had now traversed no small number of naturally formed tunnels through the earth. I supposed that it made a degree of sense that the dwarves' mines might intersect with existing subterranean regions at some point; they would just continue expanding outwards until they did so. Likely how they ended up with goblins and other unpleasant critters in their mines all the time.

There was a growl to his voice now. Like two slabs scraping against one another. "You aren't helping."

I am trying to.

"Yeah." He scoffed. "Helping yourself."

When our goals are aligned, helping me is helping you . . .

He cut that off with another scoff—pretty soon he was going to choke on one of them. "If you could leave without me, you would! You just thought it."

It was an idle fancy! You cannot hold every passing thought against me as though it were a serious intention.

This was all Ig's fault. I had become so accustomed to a brain that was never in use, where the owner never paid the faintest bit of attention to what was going on inside of it, that now I was confronted with a normal, functioning mind, I was forgetting myself.

Meanwhile, Cygni's latest mental collapse was well underway. "I need . . . I need somebody to tell me what to do."

And I'm more than willing to fulfill that role for you.

"No. I need . . ." He cast about himself as though the answer might be written on the cavern walls. "I need me to tell me what to do."

Back when I'd first been placed upon the head of Ig, I had brought about a transformation within him. All of the atrophied parts of his mind had been forced to life, and he had become—perhaps uniquely among kobold-kind—sentient. He had not used that sentience for much after that point, other than to be a persistent pain in my . . . rim . . . but the fact remained that before, he had no will of his own, no awareness of himself, and after my intervention: he did.

By contrast, Cygni had been sentient from the very beginning but deliberately suppressed all sense of self so as to fit neatly into the mold into which he had been cast. It was the same of all dwarves, I supposed. The hive, the mine, it was their whole being, and each of them was meant to play the role of but a single cell in the greater organism.

And now, this cell had been excised. It had been given the opportunity to grow, beyond the constriction of the body in which it had been trapped. Admittedly this metaphor was getting away from me somewhat, as I didn't actually want to compare Cygni to a skin-flake or cancerous growth. Regardless, the most important thing was that for the first time in his life, Cygni was in command of their own actions, their own destiny!

So you're promoting yourself to king?

For a moment the enormity of that statement overwhelmed him. He fumbled his words. "I . . . yes. Hive of two." He took a deep breath. "I'm king."

You don't suppose that the greatest thinker in living memory might be a better choice of leader?

His eyes narrowed. "Are you a dwarf?"

Not so far as I can recall.

He cleared his throat, pushing away all doubts, as kings are prone to. "Then I'm the only one qualified."

And what is your first command as king of our little hive?

"Stop thinking about home." He barked the order to himself. "Get moving. Sooner you're done, sooner you're home."

I think that still qualifies as thinking about home.

"And you can shut up too."

CHAPTER SEVEN

BURROWS AND BODY-BORROWING

The natural stone of the tunnels continued throughout most of the day as we strayed farther and farther from the dwarven sections of the underworld. Yet there was still some degree of uniformity to these tunnels that did not speak of entirely natural formations. Cygni did not recognize them as lava tubes or anything of the like. It seemed that the pooled water we had left long behind us had not hollowed these passages through the stone either.

Rather it seemed that some other hand was at work, making chambers where there had been stone, tunnels where there had been stone, and . . . look, it was all stone down here before someone or something came along and did a number on it.

Cygni had no complaints, as these mysterious tunnels were all leading us in more or less the correct direction, but I was still a little dubious about how convenient all of this was.

"If there weren't already tunnels here, we'd have dug them" was the only response that my prying received.

Yet for all that this was an unfamiliar world to me, and for all that I lacked Cygni's fundamental grasp of the meaning of subterranean structures, as we progressed through various-sized chambers and passages there was a pattern to them that I was beginning to discern. A sort of rhythm that I was beginning to suspect.

Adventurers are, by and large, a profoundly stupid lot. They develop a complex set of skills that are almost entirely non-transferable to more lucrative trades, then engage in a gig economy with pretty reasonable odds of every single gig ending in their own deaths. Even if there were better odds, it still wasn't a valuable use of anyone's time. In particular because as the more literate among us have noted, it doesn't matter how many dark lords are defeated or dragons slain when there are always more of them ready to pop up again the moment that your back is turned.

Yet despite the obvious deficiencies in their reasoning, there is one thing that adventurers and I do agree on. We have not always seen eye to eye on the subject, but I have finally come around to their way of thinking in this one particular matter. Dungeons are excellent.

Initially I could think of nothing more pointless than to explore a hole in the ground on the off chance that whatever treasure had originally been buried there might not have been made off with in the intervening decades, but having experienced a little taste of the dungeon life firsthand, I can now say without a doubt that I understand their appeal.

Within a dungeon you have a self-contained ecosystem of monsters, all of which are guaranteed to be evil enough that you need feel no moral qualms about killing them with the most spectacular magical innovations that you can pull together on the fly. The real treasure is not the gold or prizes stowed away in the dungeon's lowest levels; it is the freedom to murder that you cannot get anywhere else in the world.

Now I realize that I may be coming across as a little bloodthirsty, when adding this little opinion on to the idle thoughts of dwarf-slaughter that I'd casually entertained earlier, but you need to understand something: I am an academic. I have spent my entire life in one institution of learning or another, smothered by a million layers of bureaucracy, peer review, and the eternal constraints of propriety that accompany such a life. Despite being capable of wielding awesome cosmic powers that would make the gods themselves weep, I was frequently forbidden from using a single scrap of that power for myself. Indeed, despite the many allegedly educated people who passed through the university during my tenure there who sought to disrupt my work, dispute my findings, and spark my ire, almost every single one of them emerged alive, well, and in their original form, give or take a little discoloration. There was no sudden abundance of newts, no cataclysmic explosions that inexplicably only killed people who talked to me before I had eaten my breakfast, not even a single student turned inside out after using a slice of bacon as a bookmark in one of my tomes. I was the very pinnacle of restraint and reason.

So it should come as absolutely no surprise to any of you that now that I was confronted with an opportunity to actually let loose all of my incredible power without guilt or restraint, I was delighted by the possibility.

Let us all be honest with ourselves: there are few people who live lives entirely devoid of frustration, and fewer still who have the moral fortitude to say that if given the opportunity to beat small, ugly, and evil creatures to relieve some of that frustration, they would not take it.

Cygni had produced his pick from where it had been nestled across his back and was giving it a few practice swings already. There was no question of the moral high ground between the two of us, not in this. He'd lived in a system as oppressive as academia since birth. He must have been practically brimming over with restrained fury.

It was small wonder that when you did find stray dwarves out roaming the world, they were always drinking heavily and charging into battle with berserk roars, despite their natural state of being containing as much excitement as the average flower-arranging class.

Confirmation of all our suspicions arrived when we approached the next chamber and realized that there was an unadorned wooden door separating it from the various tunnels beyond. There was nothing of note about the door, in fact its complete absence of any decoration or interesting material made me instantly suspicious of it. Why would you build a dungeon and then furnish it with so bland a door?

Search it for traps.

Cygni looked up at my brim or rolled his eyes. Possibly both. "Do you know how to search for traps?"

Why would I know how to search for traps? Spells, I could sniff out in an instant. Enchantments and curses? Of course. But mechanical traps definitely seem to be more your sort of thing.

He grumbled. "Because I'm a dwarf?"

Because you're a . . . surveyor. Survey for traps.

"Don't know how." He peered at the door with his own mounting suspicion. "It just looks like a plain wooden door."

And can you even conceive of anything more suspicious than a plain wooden door in a dungeon? Whence came the wood to such a place? Who summoned a carpenter of moderate but not exceptional skill? Why place a door here, and not in any of the other various passages? Its very presence confounds all reason!

"Maybe they bought them premade." He shrugged. "In bulk."

And carved the very stone tunnels of a dungeon to accommodate their mediocrity?!

He stared at the door for a long moment, as though pondering some deeper secret that he chose not to share, then finally said, "Makes sense to me."

Then you may open the door, but be ready to cast me aside in case there are devious traps awaiting you. Pits full of acid, poisoned darts, harpoons that are filled with lightning . . .

He had already been reaching for the handle when I said all that, but it gave him pause. "Will you shut up. You're making me nervous."

He reached out once more with a quaking hand, then thought better of it, and instead stepped back and stretched as far as possible to extend his pick, using its full length to push against the door.

The door did not budge. "It's locked."

Perhaps there is another way around.

He snapped back, the tension of the situation clearly getting to him. "Maybe you should do some magic to unlock it."

There was magic that could unlock a door, high-level conceptual stuff involving a blending of elemental properties to produce something akin to the ontological equivalent of "freedom," but ultimately it was typically much faster to rely upon a good old-fashioned fireball. Of course, with the limited Quintessence available to us, neither of these were viable options.

If you were to approach it and reach out with your low magic, it would be possible to manipulate the mechanism of the lock within. Pushing the individual pins of the lock into place and rotating the drum without ever needing to touch them. You would likely hover on the verge of death throughout the complex procedure, but I could guide you.

"Or I can kick it down."

Oh yes, I'm certain that won't attract any attention from the devious denizens of the dungeon at all. Why didn't I think of that?

"I'm kicking it down."

Will you just wait a moment and let me think!

Fireball. Fireball. Fireball.

They say that if you are provided with only a hammer, then every problem you encounter looks like a nail, and I have to say that the plain wooden door before us was screaming out for a fireball. Begging for one, really. Calling out in all of its fragile, flammable glory.

Let's try the low magic thing. Extend your hand toward the handle and let's have a feel.

Obedient as a mule, Cygni grumbled the whole way, slowly extending his pick-free hand, and edging slowly toward the door.

Close your eyes and extend your arcane senses.

"Don't have any of those."

You do, because all living things do, you can feel the Quintessence within you, it is connected to the Quintessence in all things, it is one thing, it resonates in harmony with all of creation. Feel for the resonation, like a bat listening to the returning echoes of its own cries, feel the returning pressure of the structures you seek . . .

"I feel . . . wood."

Without lungs I did not have the physical capacity to sigh, but mentally, I would like you all to know that I was definitely sighing.

Try just a little harder. Extend your will out toward the door, as if you mean to use low magic to manipulate it. Feel where your will and the solid object coincide.

"Just wood."

You don't make a lock out of bloody wood, do you?

"Suppose you could do . . ." I could feel the moment that Cygni's mind tried to drift into contriving wood-lock contraptions, and I was having none of it. I seized control of his body, thrust out with his senses, and discovered . . .

Wood.

He pushed my will back up into the hat with a heave of mental effort and beetled his brows once more. "Told you."

This was unexpected. Perhaps there was some complex system of interlocking wooden pieces within the door that would instantly trigger some lethal trap.

Perhaps there was some ancient enchantment placed upon this door so potent and well cloaked that even I, the greatest living wizard, could not perceive it.

"Well?"

There are many possibilities that we need to consider. These are ancient halls, after all; it is quite possible that the chamber beyond has simply collapsed. Or that there is some barrier assembled beyond the door to keep us from entering. Or . . .

The door swung open, pushed out toward us. We were confronted by a goblin holding a crooked stick with a rock tied to the end and wearing an expression of the utmost surprise. It said, "Wah?"

Cygni yelled, "It's pull, not push!" and swung.

The pick did its job magnificently, plowing straight through the goblin's skull and into what it probably considered a brain. Cygni shook it off with a satisfied grunt.

You . . . just murdered it.

"It's a monster; this is a dungeon."

We were just talking to them earlier, the other goblins.

"And now we're killing these ones. That's goblins."

And you feel no twinge of morality?

"They're goblins?" He seemed to be genuinely perplexed.

I was also perplexed, in truth. If you had told me before all of this began that I would be feeling bad over the death of a goblin, I would have laughed in your face. Actually, I would probably have wondered how the hell you got into my study and why you were talking to me, but the point remains, I had stopped seeing monsters as monsters and began seeing them as slightly different-looking people. I had seen our negotiations with the goblins earlier as the normal state of affairs rather than some sort of outlier. I was some sort of bleeding-heart monster sympathizer like the news criers back home were always mocking.

Ig. It was all his fault. He was a monster, but he was so pathetic that you forgot about it until it was too late and you already cared about him. The bastard.

Well, perhaps our progress through what is clearly going to be monstrous territory might go easier if we were to befriend rather than massacre them?

"Don't know." He shook some gray matter off his pick. "That was pretty quick."

Well, perhaps it would simply make me happier if we didn't indiscriminately massacre everyone and everything that we met.

"Is this your first time in a dungeon?"

I . . . no. Technically it was my second, although the last one was out of order at the time.

Cygni chuckled. "If they didn't want murdering, they wouldn't be in a dungeon to start with. Everybody knows how dungeons work. Even gobs."

With that, he stepped over the dead goblin and strolled into the next room of the dungeon. It was a five-foot cube, previously containing only that single goblin, and a treasure chest that the goblin was presumably meant to be defending.

Compelled by some force that neither of us could name, Cygni wandered over and flicked the lid of the chest open with his pick, only to discover three gold coins inside. What could possibly have compelled a goblin with no concept of economics to hoard these three gold coins in a chest was entirely beyond me. It was three coins. They would have fit quite comfortably into a pocket or—more likely, given that this was a goblin we were talking about—an orifice. Dungeons were strange places that shaped the behavior of their inhabitants in strange ways.

There was one door leading out of the room, so it was to that we proceeded. Much like the previous one, it was constructed so plainly as to be entirely nondescript.

Perhaps . . .

Cygni reached out and pulled on the handle. The door swung open.

Ah.

"Smartest hat in the world forgot you have to pull some doors." He grumbled to himself.

Listen, I'm not exactly in my element here.

The next room was somewhat larger than the first. There were some signs of goblin habitation, which is to say, droppings and some broken furniture, but no goblins seemed to currently be present, for which I was grateful.

Cygni looked around the room in all of its decrepitude, and then moved on to the next door.

You aren't looking for gold?

"Did you forget why we're here?"

I'm just trying to be accommodating, I know that you people love looking for gold.

"You people?" Cygni asked, with steel hidden behind his soft words.

Yes, you people; surveyors.

He opened and shut his mouth a couple of times then conceded the point with a bob of his head. "I do like looking for gold."

Well, feel free. I imagine that we'll need it once we're out of here.

In the next chamber we encountered one of the first hallmarks of a true dungeon. There was a statue with various bowls held in its multitudinous arms and an inscription that Cygni didn't focus on long enough for me to read.

Oh, a puzzle. Excellent. Finally I will have something to test my mind. Logic is a skill, a blade that must be whetted if you mean for it to remain sharp, and I . . .

Cygni laid into the statue with his pick.

What are you . . .

He went on hacking at it until all the stone began to fall away from around the metal frame that was, in effect, the mechanism of the puzzle. He went on chipping until the central post of the device was revealed, then adjusted each of the various arms by hand until a click could be heard and the section of wall beside the statue swung open right where there had been a suspiciously door-shaped outline on the stone.

You were meant to put things in the bowls.

"And they'd have weighed different and moved the levers to unlock the lock," Cygni agreed. "This was quicker."

I don't feel like you're really getting into the spirit of things.

"Shortest route." Cygni slipped through the secret door and into a passageway, leading us on to the next room.

I just do not feel as though my strengths are being fully utilized.

"Course you are." Cygni grimaced in what might have been a smile. "My head's warm."

Seething was not the appropriate response to so casual a comment. I refrained from speaking at all as we entered the next room, and Cygni set to work once more. There were no goblins here, thankfully, but there was some system set up to shoot flames out from the walls that immediately stopped functioning after the dwarf knocked on the walls a couple of times and then, judging the appropriate spot, hammered the spike of his pick into what must have been a gas supply pipe.

This one was meant to be resolved through learning the pattern of the ignitions and proceeding while they were inactive, I believe.

"Probably." Cygni swaggered across the chamber without a backwards glance at the soot stains.

For all of my complaints, there could be no denying that we were making swift progress through the dungeon so far. But at the same time, I supposed that we were on the periphery of it. If I remembered my ecology lessons correctly, and I did, then the more fearsome foes and substantive defenses would be found farther into the edifice. Adventurers referred to this as a difficulty curve, but it was actually a result of the more serious traps typically only having a single use before they were depleted, and more people reaching the serious traps closest to dungeon entrances. Similarly, the larger and more fearsome monsters claimed the prime territory that was still defended well near to the deepest part of the dungeon, forcing the lesser creatures out to face the invasive adventurers—or in this case, Cygni's pick.

I was beginning to hope that the goblin had been an outlier and that the dungeon had been abandoned, despite all evidence to the contrary. But the next chamber that we entered soon put paid to that hope. Within the next chamber towered a creature that resembled a bipedal crocodile. To the learned, these beasts were known as Ophidians, though in the common parlance they were more often referred to as lizardmen. When encountered in the wild, they typically murdered and ate anyone that they came across, but some fringe scholars also believed that they controlled the media and lived in disguise among us.

Sadly I had never uncovered any sources that could confirm such ideas, with the majority of the citations in these Ophidian commentaries being somewhat circular in nature, occasionally diversifying into insistence that real evidence was being suppressed or destroyed by the Ophidians themselves.

Given that every Ophidian that had ever been observed was illiterate and barely capable of speech in their own tongue, it seemed moderately unlikely to me that the fringe scholars were onto something, but what did I know. I was only the smartest man in the world, after all.

Regardless, this particular lizardman seemed to have no intention of controlling the value of gold on the stock exchange and seemed markedly more interested in beating Cygni to death with a club.

"We come in peace." I seized control of Cygni's mouth and called out to the Ophidian in what I hoped was a vaguely accurate composite of his native tongue.

The lizardman cocked his head to the side. "One peace?"

Cygni halted in his charge, pick still at the ready, but willing to let me talk matters out with the massive muscular hulk of rippling scales. *"Yes, yes!"* I was delighted that he understood me. *"Peace."*

He hefted his club. "Make many peaces."

Ah.

Cygni barreled forward between the thing's legs before the club could come crashing down on his head, and by proxy, me. Turning as he passed to hammer the spiky end of his pick through the back of the unfortunate lizardman's knee. This one certainly wouldn't be impersonating any members of a royal family anytime soon. At least not any of them capable of walking upright.

"We do not need to fight, my friend."

"No fight." The lizardman used his tail to maintain some sort of equilibrium without his left kneecap, leaning heavily on his club as a makeshift crutch to turn and face us once more. "Stand still. No fight back."

He flung himself at us once more, showing none of the eloquence and savvy that would have been required to control global banking, but showing a great many teeth in his gigantic alligator mouth.

Cygni swung his pick up only for it to deflect off the hard scales of the creature's hide. The only thing that I could say in favor of the swing was that it knocked the champing jaws off target so they closed next to us rather than directly on us.

"Please stop trying to bite me," I shouted over the roaring. *"I am not your enemy!"*

"I don't think he's listening," Cygni bellowed, ducking under another sweep of the lizardman's club.

After the swipe failed to connect, the lizardman paused to look offended. "Me listen."

Cygni did not. Instead he swung his pick down and buried it through the unfortunate creature's foot.

There was a considerably more strained-sounding roar this time around. But when Cygni tried to draw the weapon back out again, it stuck. Whether in bone, meat, or stone, I could not say, only that it slipped from his grip as he staggered back and the Ophidian chomped on the empty air where he had once stood.

"Just stay there a moment, we'll talk this out," I told the lizard before turning my attention inwards. *I believe that this creature can be reasoned with.*

"He's chewing off his own foot to get at me."

That's just overenthusiasm, I'm sure that he'll stop before he hits bone.

There was a wet crunching sound and the Ophidian was after us again. Albeit with more of a crawling motion now that it had lost the use of both legs.

"Do some magic!"

I'm a hat, remember? I'm only good for keeping your head warm.

There was a squeak to Cygni's voice now that in other circumstances I might have found rather amusing. "It's going to eat us!"

Actually, it is going to eat you; I'm quite unpalatable. More likely it will wear me, and I'll have a nice mindless minion to boss around.

The lizardman pursued Cygni across the room at a pace that was frankly impressive given its lack of lower limbs. Cygni reached the far wall of the chamber just a moment before the arrival of the bestial creature, just long enough to make a noise somewhere between a yell and the sound of a steam whistle and fling me violently at the oncoming monster.

For an instant there was darkness, and then, *"Agh! MY LEGS!"*

There had been some moments as Ig when there was discomfort, but actual agony had been in short supply, and now I was a legless lizard. Not a snake, a legless lizard. They are different. But now is not the time for a taxonomy lesson, because my legs were buggered.

My voice came garbled from the crocodilian mouth. *"Oh! OH! This really hurts. Why would he keep crawling when it hurts this much?! Why would he bite off his own foot?! How was he still moving?!"*

In the moment, I was so overwhelmed with sensation that I did not realize I was a lizardman, but that realization hit not long after. And with that awareness came the mind of the Ophidian, bucking up and growling from beneath what had seemed like the entirely placid surface of his mind.

Hi there, friend. It's me again. Uh . . . your conscience. I think killing this dwarf would be bad and wrong and you should not do that.

"Hungry!" came the calm and reasoned response from the gentleman with scales.

We can find food that isn't sentient.

"HUNGRY!" he roared, overpowering my tenuous grasp over his body and surging forward once more. With all of my will, I clamped down on his arms once more, and I got all the joy of experiencing his chin clattering against the stone floor.

Using this opportunity, I called out to Cygni, *"It is the sign of intelligence that one can adapt one's views to the latest information and . . ."*

"Get to the point!" Cygni bellowed as he leapt on top of the lizardman's head and ran along the length of him.

"Kill it!"

The crocodilian head whipped around so fast that I almost slid right off. The downside of it having a flat skull rather than something with better topography. "Hungry!"

"How?!" Cygni yelped as he tumbled end over end to land beside the bloody hunk of lizard foot, and his pick.

"Stabbing? Bludgeoning? I'm not picky!" Controlling Ig had been so easy; he'd been essentially mindless, yes, but also completely devoid of any will of his own, completely and utterly subservient to anyone with a commanding tone. But this thing was mindless in an entirely different way, driven by instincts and impulses so ancient and powerful that it was less like a wrestling match for control, and more like attempting to ride out an earthquake.

Cygni tugged at the handle of his pick to no avail, and the slithering monstrosity I had become was closing on him fast, despite my more focused and selective attempts at limiting his progress by freezing one limb at a time. If I could just use magic, this would all be so much simpler.

Yanking hard on the thing's leg as it tried to bite down on Cygni, who I had to admit did look particularly delicious at that moment, I brought the lizardman down on the pick's upturned spike. Yet despite all the momentum and weight at work, it was more of a painful poke than a lethal impalement. The creature's scales were simply too thick.

"You're going to have to use magic, it's the only way to get through."

"It'll kill me!" Cygni yelped, ducking under the Ophidian's flailing arms to try and pry his pick free.

I barely managed to stop one of the hooked claws catching him around the back of the head. *"So will the bloody lizard!"*

He grabbed for the creature's discarded club, but it was too heavy for him to lift, let alone swing. While I was no longer party to his thoughts—instead drowning in the steady internal monologue of meat meat meat—I could recognize the moment when he made his decision. To go out swinging, figuratively, with magic.

Taking one last deep breath, as though that might help, he raised a hand toward the Ophidian, prepared his knowledge of an element in his mind, and then . . .

"Wait!"

Cygni's eyes snapped open in surprise.

For the most intelligent creature in the world, you would think that ideas might come to me a little faster sometimes. I pulled on the Ophidian's Quintessence just as I'd been threatening to do to Cygni earlier. All of the energy that made this heaving, furious creature alive instead of merely a pile of angry meat flooded up through its head, out at a jaunty angle into me. Refilling my depleted reserves and slowly robbing it of all vitality.

Thankfully the beast was too stupid to understand what was happening, or to recognize that I was the parasite latched on to its vital strength. Before Cygni's eyes, the creature's scales lost their luster, its beady eyes went dry and dark, and the hunger, the terrible hunger that dominated the monster's mind was replaced with an awful, gut-gnawing terror as it recognized its own end.

These were all experiences I would have been much happier never experiencing, if I were to be entirely honest. The sort of thing that will be burned into my memory until I myself shuffle off this mortal coil in a more permanent way than simply becoming a hat. So if you ever want to know the awful betrayal as you realize that your life has been stripped away from you in an instant by something you thought was an inanimate object, I am your man.

The Ophidian dropped dead. I returned to the empty darkness.

Although in truth, it was not entirely empty this time. I still had some awareness of the body that I rested atop. There were still some chemical processes at work there, even if the life had departed. Hypothetically, I supposed that I might be able to do a little minor necromancy and puppeteer the corpse around, but given that it had no legs, that didn't seem like the best idea at this moment in time. Not to mention that I had absolutely no idea how to prevent decomposition. So instead I remained still and calm, taking care not to animate the corpse, until I felt Cygni's stubby little fingers lifting me up once more.

His hands were shaking. His pick, still embedded in the floor. He had taken a moment to calm himself after the fight, yet there was still adrenaline rushing through him. Not because of the monster or how close he'd come to death, but because he'd had to work himself up enough to put me back on now that he'd seen how easily I could drain the life out of someone. "Alright, hat?"

Perfectly well, apart from having experienced death. And you, any injuries?

"Pick's seen better days . . ." He jiggled the loose handle of it and chuckled nervously. "Ego's a bit sore, too."

To be fair to you, I don't think anyone could have expected a feral bipedal crocodilian to be waiting for us.

"Probably should have, it's a dungeon."

One that I intend to take a little more seriously, moving forward. I apologize for my earlier complaints. The sooner we are gone from this dangerous demesne, the happier that I shall be. For all that the idea of such a place may intoxicate me, the truth remains that it places you in mortal peril, and I should not have made light of that.

He shrugged, looking as bashful as a dwarf can. "I've been breaking it just to spite you. So I think we're even."

Quite.

CHAPTER EIGHT

CAVERNS AND CRYPTOCURRENCY

With that charming little diversion finally completed, Cygni and I departed the room posthaste. There was another door, leading to another passage, with another nondescript wooden door at its end. There was also a rather cunning little pitfall trap that we likely would have fallen victim to were it not for the fact that nobody had dusted in here for centuries and our reptilian friend from earlier had left a trail of footprints, including a blank patch that he always jumped.

Even in death, he was still helping us. Just as he had helped us put aside our differences.

There was no longer a debate each time that we tried to open a door, or a fraction as much trepidation. On reflection, we probably should have maintained a healthier respect for whoever designed this deathtrap of a dungeon. Cygni reached out to open the next door without a second thought, and immediately upon yanking on the handle realized that something was wrong.

He leapt back as the mechanical apparatus hidden in the doorframe and walls sprang into action, very slowly.

As it turns out, if you build a complex mechanical trap out of iron and then leave it for decades, it rusts, which makes the ever-so-threatening spikes shooting out of the walls to penetrate anyone standing in front of them a little on the slow side to actually catch anyone out. At least the screeching as they emerged was giving Cygni a headache; that was some sort of damage at least, albeit very brief.

Finally, once they were fully extended, the rusty spikes spun their barbs ever so slightly out of position, to twist the knife in the wound presumably, though on closer examination it turned out that they were actually moved aside to allow the contents of the hollow pipe to emerge.

Once upon a time, the fire ants would have come streaming out, biting everything in sight and making life extremely miserable for anyone who had survived their impalement, but now they emerged as a fine gray trickle of insectile corpses, heaping up on the floor before the door.

Oh, now that's just sad.

"But why . . ."

So it would hurt more.

"But surely . . ."

Yes, I would have thought impaling someone to death would have been sufficient too, but the people who design dungeons have other things in mind. It isn't enough to efficiently murder everyone who attempts to gain ingress, you must also do it with some degree of flamboyance so as to impress whosoever is purchasing your traps.

"But . . ." He stared at the heap of dead ants, more perplexed by this than he had been a sentient talking hat. "Why?"

It isn't much, but it is honest work.

Sidestepping the trap, which was making some whining noises as though it wanted to retract back into the stone but didn't quite have the strength, Cygni pushed open the door fully.

Inside of the chamber ahead of us, there was magic.

It wasn't particularly potent magic, but it was a complex and long-lasting sort of enchantment. The room was not very big, with two doors leading out of it, other than the one by which we had entered. The enchantment was upon the statuary between us and them. Two rather simple-looking, faceless dwarvish guardsmen in armor, each about half the height of Cygni, one cast in white stone, the other in black.

Oh, I know this one.

"Behind one of these doors is certain death!" proclaimed the statues in harmony. "Behind the other is the way forward. We know which door leads to which, but one of us always tells the truth, and one of us always lies. You may ask of us only a single question."

"If one always lies, did they lie explaining the rules? And if they lied explaining the rules, does that mean . . ."

I'm not certain if the deception kicks in until after the questioning.

"And we can't ask, because that would be our question." Cygni seemed to be getting the hang of this quicker than anticipated. "So are they . . . people?"

The statues? Well, form tends to define intellect, so they'll more likely think like people than not. Regardless, this is a classic dungeon puzzle with a very simple solution. A classic, if you will. What you need to do is ask . . .

"Wait, wait." The dwarf cut me off. "Let me see if I can work it out."

Genuinely delighted that he was now taking part in the fun, I settled in silence.

If Cygni were to ask either of the statues, "What door would the other guard say doesn't lead to death?" then the puzzle would be solved, as the liar would tell us the door that led to death, and the truth teller would also tell us the door that led to death, and we'd simply pick the other one.

Simple if you know the answer, impossible if you don't like every logical puzzle. Yet Cygni still stood, stroking his beard.

Finally, he released the chin fluff and straightened up. "I've got it."

Then, without consulting me, he hefted his pickaxe and smashed right through the podium that the closest guardian statue was standing on. It could not speak, as such, within the bounds of its enchantment, but it did make a little "erk" noise as it hit the ground.

"Alright, statue," Cygni said as he hauled the carved stone upright. "I don't have any questions for you, but I'm telling you now, I'm going through the right door, and I'm carrying you in front of me. If you've got any objections, say something."

For a moment, it was trapped by the confines of its original enchantment, but this thing had been sitting for centuries with plenty of time to think about its own limitations. It could definitely talk outside the confines of the enchantment, and it definitely seemed to care about its own continued existence. It wasn't an elegant solution, by any stretch of the imagination, but . . .

The statue vibrated for a moment in Cygni's arms, then burst out with, "Take the other one!"

From its podium the other statue let out a gasp, then cried out, "He's lying, you should definitely go through the right one."

"Screw you, Clarence!" wailed the statue in Cygni's arms. "You've had it in for me since day one. I am not dying for this stupid job. Go left!"

"This stupid job is the only reason you exist!" the still-upright statue insisted. "Go right!"

While all of this was going on, I was carefully parsing all of their statements, trying to work out if the telling of truth and lies was limited to the answering of questions, or whether we were still being deceived by their nonsense.

Cygni continued walking toward the right door, markedly slower than he really needed to despite the burden of the statue's weight. Had these contrivances of magic and stone pores, then I would say that the dwarf was trying to make them sweat.

"The right door is the death door! Don't go right. Whatever you do, don't go right!"

Clarence tried to drown the other statue out. "Ignore him! He's the liar; the death door is the left one. You want to go right."

"Do you really want to be stuck here for the rest of time with nobody to talk to?" The doomed statue made a sound like a sob.

"I'll be quite satisfied in silence actually," Clarence sneered. "Anything is better than your endless inane whistling."

There was a wounded gasp from in Cygni's arms. "You said you like my tunes!"

"I lied!" There was some real venom when that got spat back.

"You can't lie!"

Clarence hissed, "Can't I?"

"Wait, can you?"

The other statue was at a loss for words for a moment, making flabbergasted sounds before finally yelling, "Have you forgotten which one of us is meant to be telling the truth?!"

"It's been a long time since anyone came through!"

Clarence was practically screaming by this point. "You had one job! One!"

"Like you are any better!"

"What's that supposed to mean?"

"Oh, you know what that's supposed to mean!"

It wasn't possible for a faceless statue's eyes to narrow, but that was still the impression that was given. "Do I? Or am I lying about not knowing what it is supposed to mean?"

Cygni carefully placed the statue he'd been carrying down in front of the right door, then walked over to open the other.

You are so certain of your solution?

"Not like we'll get any sense out of them one way or the other now." The dwarf shrugged, then pulled the door open. Beyond was a passageway that seemed to be entirely devoid of instant death, so either his cunning solution to the problem worked, or whatever had been meant to kill us had broken down in the intervening years. I was tempted to ask Cygni to go check behind the other door, but suspected that second-guessing their solution would have been taken as an insult, even if my interest was purely academic at this point.

As we departed, the argument in the chamber behind continued unabated.

"Well, I've never heard you say a single word against my whistling before now."

"Because I didn't want to have an argument about it."

"So you just put up with something that made you miserable for centuries because you didn't want to have an argument?"

"I know how you get if we disagree."

"And what is that supposed to mean?"

Thankfully the bickering faded by the time that we reached the end of the passage, and the next room opened up before us from behind yet another deliberately nondescript door.

Within the next chamber, there was a large chest, sitting partially open due to the vast amounts of gold heaped up inside it. There was also a door leading out, and nothing much else of interest.

Cygni had a degree more sense than most of the people I had met on my journey thus far, so he approached the chest slowly and in a circuitous manner, observing it from all angles before moving a little closer and repeating the process.

I sense no magic from it.

"I don't see any traps."

Yet . . . I do not trust it. Why would there be a box full of treasure just sitting here?

Cygni crept a little closer, searching the uneven floor for any hint of a pressure plate or trip wire. "Suppose they've got to keep the money somewhere?"

It must be a mimic.

"A what?" He readied his pick.

As I'm sure all of you remember, a mimic is an ambush predator that takes on the appearance of an inanimate object so as to lure prey closer to it. During my time with Ig, we fed one so many bananas it felt sick. But now we had a hungry one before us, ready to spring forward with pointy teeth and slathering tongue and devour poor Cygni before he had a chance to blink.

I conveyed the gist of this to Cygni, who laughed. "Those aren't real."

I can assure you, they are.

"They're just a baby story to stop little dwarves touching treasures that aren't theirs."

They are real creatures, my friend. I have encountered them before.

"What?!" Cygni had entirely forgotten about the mimic, just outside of pouncing distance. "What else is real?"

Most things?

"What about birds? They're made-up, right?"

It took me a moment to grasp what he was saying, and then I too lost my focus on the ambush predator in the room. *Birds?*

"They're made-up," Cygni said. "I knew it."

I spoke very carefully in the tone usually reserved for addressing very small children or very large men with sharp objects. *Birds are one of the most common species of animal on the planet. How can you possibly not believe in birds?!*

"Things that can fly without magic? Rubbish." Cygni brayed with laughter. "You're pulling my leg, ain't you."

Birds are very much real. The skies are filled with them. They nest in trees. Some of them have even been trained to carry messages. Wait, you've really never seen a bird?

The idea that someone could go their whole life without ever encountering one of the most numerous creatures on the planet struck me as ludicrous, but Cygni did have his reasons. "I live underground. How would I see something that lives in the sky?"

You've never . . . hang on. You have birds in mines. I remember reading about this. You definitely have birds. You carry them in little cages so that you know when there is poisonous gas in the air.

Cygni cocked his head to the side in confusion. "Pixies aren't birds."

You use pixies?!

I generally try not to raise my voice when I'm speaking inside someone's brain, just in case I rupture anything, but that was certainly worthy of a little intercranial bleeding.

Throughout this entire conversation, the chest had begun quietly shuffling sideways in the hope that it would not be on the receiving end of the pickaxe still being brandished in the air. While it was hungry after so long alone down here in the dungeon, the metabolism of a creature that plays inanimate for years at a time is exceptionally low, so it could afford to pass up this ironclad meal. A couple of coins fell out of it with a jingle as it went, but neither of us noticed in the moment.

Pixies are sentient creatures! They're protected under our accords with the elves! They have their own civilization and art and . . . well, I'm sure they do useful things too.

With a gruff humph, Cygni crossed his arms. "We didn't sign any accords."

Well, of course not, you and the elves have been fighting since you first crawled out of a hole in the ground. That's neither here nor there, you can't use sentient creatures as poison monitors!

He tried to shut me up. "They don't mind."

What do you mean they don't mind, you are poisoning them?!

"Isn't really my place to say, but most of them seem to be into it."

Would that I had saliva to choke on to express my disbelief. Into it?!

"They enjoy it. They like huffing fumes . . ." He said this softly, as though he were sharing some shameful secret that he had no right to share. "They get high."

In many ways, despite my age, a lifetime in academia had left me with a rather childlike outlook on some matters. And left my vocabulary deprived of a great deal of useful slang. *How high can they get when they're trapped in cages?!*

"They agreed to the cages after the biting. We only use the cages in case they get fighty after huffing lamp-damp."

I cannot believe that I'm hearing this. You have enslaved a sentient species to use them as . . .

He cut me off again. "They signed up."

They what?!

"I told you, they like it."

But that . . . I . . . they . . . what?

It takes a lot to flabbergast me, but in this one instance, Cygni had been entirely successful. I could not conceive of the degree of heroism and bravery that these pixies committed to when they agreed to go forth into the mines and breathe poison to protect the dwarves. It was truly awe-inspiring. The stuff of legends.

Finally, Cygni spotted the chest trying to nudge the door to the chamber open.

"Oi!"

The mimic dropped back down onto the floor and pretended to be an immobile and inanimate object once more, but the jig was up.

"I know you're a mimic. You moved," Cygni told it. "Just drop all your gold and you can go back to sitting."

I must admit, I would not have thought of robbing the monster in exchange for its life, so Cygni was definitely better equipped for dungeoneering than I.

As for the mimic, it shifted uncomfortably from side to side, as though it were weighing its options. As I saw those options, there was: a) get murdered and lose all your money or, b) live and lose all your money. Neither was a good option, but one of them definitely had more long-term planning involved. Option c), murder the person threatening you, was probably what the mimic was contemplating, but without the element of surprise on its side, it seemed unlikely that it would be able to pull it off.

"I haven't got all day."

The tilting of the mimic from side to side became more pronounced as its internal struggle mounted. Finally, with a slam, it came to a halt on the floor, its lid flipped open, and it disgorged a wave of coins.

Cygni took half a step forward at the promising glint of gold, and then caution prevailed. "Alright, back to your spot."

The mimic made some little grumbling noises that might just have been the creak of its hinges but began edging its way back across the room again, away from what it had probably considered to be a pretty cunning trap that might have made Cygni bend over and put his head into chomping distance.

So at last Cygni began to plunder the gold: shining, perfect coins that looked as though they had been freshly minted.

Wait.

"Oh, what now?"

This is not right. Put them down, quickly.

"It's gold!" he insisted, just as the first baby mimic chomped off his finger.

For the second time in an hour, I experienced loss of limb. I cannot recommend it; there is something about not just the pain but the absence of feeling afterwards that is haunting. Both the coin and finger flipped end over end as they fell to the ground, but we did not pause to check whether it landed heads or tails up.

On the plus side, the sudden loss of a finger made Cygni extremely compliant with my suggestion. Roaring with pain, he tossed the handful of coins into the air, stumbling away from them as their edges opened up into tiny golden razor-mawed mouths.

Once they'd scattered to the floor, they began pursuing him, chattering their way across the floor toward him blindly, like the tiny sets of disembodied teeth that they were. He made a hasty exit toward the door as I heard the mother mimic chuckling.

In other circumstances, I'd have tossed a fireball at it for having the temerity, but in that moment my attention was elsewhere. Cygni was bleeding. He burst through the door to the next chamber, slamming it behind him before the chattering money monsters could pursue.

The ring finger on Cygni's left hand was now entirely absent and blood was squirting rhythmically from the stump. More blood than he really had to spare, if truth be told.

The next chamber was another puzzle, thankfully, so we didn't have to navigate combat in addition to massive blood loss. The dwarf dropped his pick and delved into one of the many pouches secreted about his person to retrieve a little oily rag, which he pressed to the wound as if it might be sufficient, but he bled through it in mere moments.

"What . . . what do I do?"

You aren't going to like it, but I have a spell . . .

"I'm not killing myself to . . ."

It's a small working, barely enough to drain half your . . . well, I don't think calling them reserves is appropriate. It should not injure you to cast. Except for the injury it is intended to cause you.

"What?"

Focus on your knowledge of hydrogen and speak the word **Igniculus***.*

"What's hydrogen got to do with . . ."

Do as I tell you or bleed to death!

With a whimper of pain, he cast. I did not need to tell him where to turn his attentions; the pain was enough to center him on one spot specifically.

The scent of barbecue filled the room. Sizzling, delicious meat. If he had not already been so queasy from blood loss, Cygni's appetite would almost certainly have been whetted as he cauterized the wound. Luckily for us, hydrogen burned so swiftly that the spell was complete before he could be distracted by the searing pain and mispronounce anything.

"AGH!" he exclaimed.

AGH! I replied, having experienced the exact same pain as him in the exact same moment.

"Why didn't you warn me that . . ."

Because you might have hesitated.

"I wouldn't have!" He was shouting at me as if I couldn't hear every word before it even reached the surface of his mind.

Well, I for one, wasn't willing to bet your life on that.

"I . . ." He stopped shouting, then took a shaky breath to steady himself. "Thanks."

You are most welcome. Don't forget to restore your Quintessence to its usual levels or you will begin to decay.

"I'm starting to think this whole magic thing might be more trouble than it's worth." He sank down to sit on the floor, still eyeballing the bottom of the door in case any gold came scurrying under.

You and me both.

CHAPTER NINE

DUNGEONS AND DEPRECIATION

The puzzle in the next room was a relatively complex matter of adjusting the positions of mirrors to reflect light into the gem above the door, but Cygni's hand was sore enough that he let me walk him through the solution rather than picking it apart.

From there our progress was intermittent. The puzzle rooms we moved through as swiftly as I was able to perceive them, but the traps and monsters required a little more of his input.

The traps, for the most part, were relatively easy to navigate thanks to their advanced age having crippled their motion, but some of them were more based in physics than cunning engineering, and as such remained moderately dangerous. A tonnage of solid stone remained a tonnage of stone regardless of how long it had remained in place, and dislodging it was just as likely to render a dwarf into a pancake now as on the day that it was first installed. Many of these traps had been triggered by the resident monsters having clumsy moments, but the few that remained had been thankfully marked out with chalk by the residents. The better for them to avoid them.

Cygni had been gruff thus far, a little unpleasant to deal with, but typically manageable. Much as I would have expected from any dwarf. But with the addition of the throbbing pain of his missing finger, he had now graduated to downright irritable.

"Three gold coins in the whole dungeon . . ." He grumbled as we left another dead goblin in our wake.

It is my understanding that the majority of the hoard will be located nearer to the center.

"Knowing my luck it will be in a pit of acid."

Don't be ridiculous. Acid would dissolve the gold.

"You know, for such a smart hat, you'd think you'd be smart enough to know when to shut your mouth."

I don't have a mouth.

"It isn't too late for me to put you back on that shelf," he growled.

The next puzzle was simple enough, a children's puzzle game involving various liquids in different-sized containers and their measurement that resulted in the next door opening. I wasn't entirely sure what the purpose of all the puzzles in dungeons actually was—I mean, I enjoyed them, certainly, but was it some sort of child-proofing? No toddlers allowed beyond this point if you cannot solve our basic mathematical problems? If it was meant to stop monsters wandering in, it was most assuredly not working.

While it had been a rather trying journey thus far, we did at last seem to be making some sort of progress. The rather bland entry-level dungeon rooms that we had begun with had given way to ornately carved murals of dragons and their various reptilian minions, which hilariously included kobolds in some depictions. It was nice to know that even ancient dungeon masters weren't sure what species to classify those useless little sacks of flesh alongside. Are they lizards? Are they rats?

They are a bloody nuisance is what they are. As I'd be sure to make extremely clear to Ig as soon as I tracked him down and ensured that he was hale and healthy.

From the gradual adjustments to the decor, to the gradual heightening of the ceilings in each room we passed, I was filled with a certainty that we were definitely making progress. A certainty that was somewhat undercut by Cygni's mounting dread.

Yes, I would admit that the higher roof might allow for slightly larger creatures to dwell in the upcoming chambers, and that yes, that sooty outline on the wall we just passed did look rather like the outline of a man. But that, along with the dragon-themed embellishments to the walls, floors, and doors did not necessarily mean that we were about to stroll directly into the den of a dragon. The smoke-stained cavern-tops may have simply been a result of adventurers' campfires. Or perhaps an infestation of those lava lizard things . . . salamanders. There were many non-dragon reasons for all of these little signs that seemed to point to a dragon.

Cygni pushed open the elaborate stone doorway into the next chamber and revealed the dragon lying in wait.

The chamber itself was markedly less impressive than one would have thought. Vast, yes, but only so vast as to contain the colossal beast within, not to dwarf it. There was no swooping cavern containing a primordial reptilian nightmare, just a neatly constructed box that prevented the dragon from wandering off anywhere. More concerningly to Cygni—even though you'd have thought his attention would have been firmly affixed to the giant fire-breathing monster—was the fact that the dragon lay sleeping atop a pile of bones rather than a mound of treasure. Had they been golden bones, I doubt he would have been so concerned, so it was not a matter of mortal dread, but one of an investment that was not paying off. If he had to face down a dragon, he at least expected a giant mound of gold as payment.

Honestly, that was fair. Even at the height of my powers, in my own body, with every resource available to me, I would have resisted the pseudo-suicidal urge to go toe to toe with an adult dragon. Those things are powerful, both physically and magically. Not to mention that they grow like goldfish through-out their entire lives, which would make the one in front of us right now somewhere in the region of two thousand. That was a very long time to learn a lot of tricks. Not that Cygni had a great many tricks up his own sleeves at this moment in time.

We had some incredibly minor magic and a bloody mining pick with a wobbly head. These were not tools one chose when heading out to face a dragon. I'd probably have thought twice about facing down an oversized newt with that list of assets at my disposal. A regular newt, I'm confident that we could have whittled down given enough time and energy, but if it came up to Cygni's knee, in his current exhausted state, I'd have placed the odds at about 50/50.

For a shin height beast, I'd put it at 75 percent in Cygni's favor despite the blood loss. It was not about the size of the dwarf in the fight, but the size of the fight in the dwarf, and what Cygni lacked in energy, he made up for in decades of repression. That had to find an outlet somewhere, and judging by the widespread destruction thus far, I was guessing it was going to come out through violence.

At present, the only reason that we had not been reduced to embers in the breeze was that the dragon was sleeping. Its vast neck, like some colossal serpent, lay coiled around the central mass of its body so that its nose lay just above the root of the equally massive, serpentine tail. Lizards, on the whole, are not known for eyelids, but this one seemed to have a set, as the eyes bigger than dinner plates were currently closed. This was a great relief, as eye contact may have been enough to push Cygni over the edge into actually relieving himself in his trousers.

Now is the time to be extremely calm and collected. To make no sudden dashes or movements at all. To be as gentle in each step as a petal falling from a flower.

Cygni nodded carefully, as though worried their neck might loudly squeak.

Now, we are going to navigate slowly and carefully around the dragon, taking a great deal of care not to step on any of the bones. Our natural instinct is going to be to stare at the massive predator, but we are going to ignore that instinct unless we hear it move, and we are going to concentrate on where we are putting our feet.

Another very careful nod that stopped once Cygni was looking down at the ground, then away we went, plodding along with a degree of daintiness that I had not foreseen him being capable of. Picking his way through the scattered bones with delicacy and care, on tiptoes, there were ballerinas who would have shown less grace than terror brought out in Cygni.

Slowly, oh so painstakingly slowly, we navigated around the room, staying as close to the outer wall as we could muster without disrupting the bones and whatnots that were propped up there. There were some bits of armor long gone to rust, and the walls themselves bore an interesting patina of soot stains, forming a kind of historical catalogue of this chamber's prior visitors. Great kings may have had tapestries of their victories adorning the walls, but these murals told them in real time. Here, the arms of a knight thrown up in outline. Over here, some barbarian warrior reduced to ash and splattered on the stone. Dozens upon dozens of them over the years, decades, centuries. There were recognizable styles to armor connected to different periods of time and cultures. From historical accounts, I could recognize more than a few, and some of these silhouettes and remains had been outdated since the invention of steel.

There was a sound, so soft that in any other circumstance I doubt we would have heard it—a gentle tapping. Cygni twisted around, looking for its source, and discovered it only after craning his neck around all over the place.

There was a rib bone dangling from a mostly intact rib cage, and with the soft vibrations of Cygni's steps it had begun to jiggle. Slowly at first but gradually increasing in its swings, the bone had begun to wiggle back and forth, back and forth, swinging like a pendulum, slowly working its way loose of the bone it hung upon.

Don't panic.

I could hear a low whine, just at the edge of Cygni's hearing, and realized after a moment of it building up that it was actually coming from Cygni. I grabbed hold of his vocal cords before his terror could wake the beast. This resulted in a rather unpleasant glucking sound, but at least it was over quickly.

And still the bone continued to wiggle its way along the curvature of the rib cage, getting closer and closer to the end.

Alright, here is what we are going to do . . .

Before I'd even managed to lay out the most basic of plans, Cygni flung out his hand and grabbed for the bone. Now, the bone was at the other side of the room, beyond the dragon, and as such, he obviously wasn't reaching out his hand with the intent to physically grab the thing. Rather, he cast out with the Quintessence within him to seize it using the low magic that he had essentially mastered.

The distance was the trouble. He had so little Quintessence to stretch out, and while he could have manipulated the dense clouds of ambient magic that surrounded the dragon with my guidance, the amount of disruption such an act would cause was liable to wake the beast all on its own. So I had to just watch as he struggled and strained and sweated, all to arrest the wibbling motion of the bone. Yet in his panic, he did the job all too well. The force of his will slammed into the wibbly bone and it was knocked right off the cage on which it had hung.

If I could have looked away or even winced, then I imagine that I would have, but instead all I could do was watch as the rib flipped end over end through the air, slowly coming down on another heap of calcified remains, which might as well have been the dragon's dinner gong announcing that dwarf a la mode was being served.

With one last desperate push, bringing his heartbeat—which had until now been hammering—to a stuttering halt, Cygni caught the flipping bone with his magic and held it still.

All was silent, unless you happened to be in skin-to-skin contact with this dwarf, in which case you might have heard the veritable floodgates of sweat opening as he tried to lower his burden softly to the ground.

Gently. Gently!

I could hear all of the bitter, backbiting comments simmering on the surface level of his consciousness, just barely restrained by his survival instincts.

Oh so carefully, he lowered the dangling bone down to the ground and let it settle before releasing his grip. The bone budged just a tiny fraction, then went entirely still. Silence once more, except for the frantic thumping heartbeat of the dwarf.

Phew.

Taking a steadying breath to try and calm himself, Cygni turned back in the direction of the door and took a step. This was a mistake.

While he had glanced at the floor, his full attention was not directed toward it, and as such he did not recognize that the cobbled patch that he was stepping onto was not in fact a cobbled patch, but rather a discarded bit of molted dragon skin.

As such, when Cygni's foot came down, it also skidded forward.

He teetered briefly upon the verge of doing the front splits, but lacked the necessary flexibility, and so after making it about halfway down, then toppled. Landing bodily in a massed pile of bones with a sound somewhat akin to sledge-hammering a xylophone.

"Ow."

It has been a pleasure knowing you, Cygni, even if your idiocy has resulted in our untimely death.

The dragon's eyes opened.

That should have been the moment of our death, if the universe were a sane place. Either Cygni's heart should have stopped beating out of pure unadulterated terror, or the dragon should have snapped around and eaten us whole. There was no logical world in which we survived that coming moment.

At least, it made no sense until Cygni, already half curled up on himself, focused enough on the dragon to realize that the huge eyeball pointed our way was entirely milky. A cataract bigger than many people I know was directed our way. The dragon was blind. "Who goes there?"

The voice should have been booming and volcanic, but instead sounded dry and wispy. As though coming to us from a great distance away through many shuffled sheets of paper.

Cygni opened and shut his mouth a couple of times.

Answer her! She's extending us the opportunity for conversation instead of anni-hilating us in a fireball after we strolled into her home uninvited, the least you can do is feign politeness.

"Uh, hello," Cygni mumbled out.

The dragon was unimpressed. "What awful times we live in when even knights have no manners. Introduce yourself, sir, that I might know the name of my supper."

"Sorry, I'm Cygni Khnuteson," the dwarf managed to blurt out despite the tremor of terror in his voice. "And I'm not a knight. I'm a surveyor, second class."

"A what?" the dragon snarled, cocking her head to the side. "Speak up, boy!"

"I'm not a knight!" Cygni raised his voice as loud as he dared, which was still markedly lower than when he was chastising me for absolutely nothing. "I'm a dwarf."

"A what?" The dragon's roar had a gristly moaning quality to it that I did not appreciate. "They send dwarves to slay dragons now? Why, in my day you had to be at least a knight, preferably a prince."

A little light of recognition went on in Cygni's eyes. "I mean, I'm the son of a king, does that count?"

"Then why didn't you say that? Young people these days don't do anything right. You come in, you announce yourself, you tell me what princess you're here to save, then I roast you. Have you all forgotten how things are done?" She began to ramble. "In the good old days, they'd never send a dwarf to kill a dragon. There would have been questing knights in shiny armor queued up around the block waiting for the opportunity to come and be killed by me. They'd walk uphill in a blizzard in full plate armor to fight a dragon without complaining once."

All of this was a little too much for poor Cygni, who was just barely man-aging to keep up with the fact he wasn't on fire yet. "Is there a princess here that needs saving?"

The dragon coughed out a plume of smoke, but it sounded like there was more still caught in her throat. "That isn't the point! There's a way you're meant to do things."

Cygni winced as the cloud of soot washed over him. "Sorry, it's my first time meeting a dragon."

"No excuse! And did you track blood in here? I can smell blood."

Cygni looked down at his feet, then back across the stone. There was no sign of a single bloody footprint. "I don't think . . ."

"None of you do, you youths . . ." The dragon stretched out her wings, and we could see for the first time that the leather stretched between the pinions was tattered as old lace. "You invite yourself in without anyone's by-your-leave. Trample over my carefully arranged lair. And don't even offer me a princess to stop me from destroying your home. It is damnably rude is what it is! Here I am taking a well-earned nap for a couple of years, and you come stomping in . . ."

My god, this is worse than I ever could have realized. This dragon isn't just mature and powerful, it is geriatric.

"Why is that worse?" Cygni whispered.

Because the elderly are annoying.

"What are you muttering over there? Speak up! That's the trouble with young people today, nobody speaks up properly, you're all always muttering away and expecting us to hear you. If you've got something to say then spit it out, boy!"

Caught unawares, Cygni spat it out. "I don't think old people are annoying."

"OLD?!" thundered the dragon.

Oh, now you've done it. There is nothing that old people are more angry about than being old.

The dragon's head shot out toward where she thought Cygni stood and roared in what she thought was his face. She was about three feet to the left, but we were not about to correct her. "I am in the prime of my life! I have millennia of fuel left burning in my belly. You dare to call me old?!"

"I . . . I didn't call you old . . ."

Her head snapped around once more. The eye, so thick with cataracts that you could not have guessed the original color, was turned to face Cygni now, and in the face of that eye as big as his head, his courage wavered.

There was a dangerous edge to her dusty voice when she said, "So now you're calling me a liar too?!"

At last, panic overtook Cygni and he turned to the only person in all of creation who could save him. The only one who was so much smarter than the dwarf himself. "Hat! Do something!"

Sadly, he had come to me in search of solutions when, as far as I could see, there were none. He'd barely made it back to his feet after his little pratfall, and there wasn't enough magic in him to kill a gnat, let alone a millennia-old dragon.

Try to throw me out of scorching range when she flames you.

He reached up and grabbed me by the rim with a grunt of terror, and I genuinely thought he was actually going to take my advice and try to preserve me. I was mistaken. "Then I'll do something!"

Wait, no! No! That will not . . .

For a brief, almost blissful moment, I was in the dark land of no senses, then I landed atop the dragon's head, nestled neatly upon a horn that had seen better days. If she'd thought that we were rude wandering into her house uninvited, wandering into her head was almost certainly going to be much less polite. So I did the right thing, even though it was probably not as smart an idea as lying low and subtly influencing her into wanting to fly toward Arpanpholigon in search of treasure, maidens, and all the other things dragons like.

Good evening, madam. I am Absalom Scryne, typically the greatest living wizard, currently reduced to being a hat.

"What?!" The dragon's voice boomed inside the echo chamber of her own head. "Who's there? Who is that? Where are you?!"

As grim a sight as the exterior of the dragon had been, a glimpse into the mind of this once incredible beast was all the more terrible. While Ig's mind was a wind-swept plain, devoid of all structure, and Cygni's was a meticulously constructed library of orderly thoughts, I now found myself in the ruins of some great castle or cathedral, long gone to ruin and disrepair. Looking around it, I could see the majesty of the place that had once been, the incredible ambition that had gone into such a creation, and the cracks and holes where now only darkness showed through. Ig's mind had been disordered because he left thoughts to drop where they formed, but here there had once been as perfect order as could be found in Cygni, now turned to chaos as the foundations had crumbled, setting everything toppling over on top of itself. Here was a memory from centuries before, bleeding out and blending with one from yesterday. There was soaring through the sky as a freshly molted hatchling, flowing into the first clutch of eggs she'd ever laid, and her own little babies taking flight and leaving her behind. Such a life she had lived, stretched out over so long that continents had risen and fallen and empires crumbled, but now all of it was forgotten. All became dust and blended into the desert winds blowing through the ruins of her mind.

But as sad as all of that was, it was not frightening in the same way that the power still burning within the dragon was. All of the magic that let a seven-ton lizard fly and breathe fire was still there inside her, a vaster reserve than I could ever have hoped to muster if I lived a dozen lifetimes. She had lost her mind, but not her power, and that made her as dangerous as a crossbow-wielding baby.

Meanwhile, Cygni was bellowing, "Drain her! Suck her dry! Do it!"

The dragon turned her murky vision that way. Cygni was little more than a blurred shadow to her sight. Flickering out of being when he wasn't in motion. She opened her mouth to chastise him for existing in such an ethereal state when I snuck in to hijack her mouth. *"I can't! She's too powerful. If I tried to drain her Quintessence, I'd explode. That trick will only work on the powerless. Unless you want me dead."*

"Better you than me!" Cygni snapped back, though from the expression of shame that washed over his face I knew that sentiment was not his true feelings. Probably. It was strange not being able to hear his thoughts . . .

"YOU!" the dragon roared, all of that unbalanced power and will slamming into me and rocking me on my metaphorical feet. "What are you doing in my head, little man?"

I managed to deflect the worst of the wild blow, and avoided my own utter annihilation as a result, but it still hurt. And it was rude.

Madam, how dare you treat a guest in this manner? What is wrong with the dragons of today? In my day, we would have had some polite back-and-forth, maybe some sort of shapeshifting duel or riddles. I am a wizard of the highest order, and I deserve to be treated with the respect due to my position and seniority.

That's right. I was going to out-old the ancient dragon.

"You come into my lair, and you demand . . ."

I cut her off with all the pomposity that a lifetime of being better than everyone else had granted me. *Demand? I demand nothing, madam, I simply have the expectation that a dragon of your stature would know how to entertain.*

She let loose a great cloud of sooty smoke, enveloping Cygni in a cloud that I sincerely hoped he would use as cover to run away. He did not. He was still staring up at the squabble with wide eyes. "Entertain?!"

When a guest comes to visit, there is an implicit social contract, whether they were invited or not. That was insufficient, I needed to add in a jibe too . . . *In my day, dragons knew that.*

The decrepit dragon gasped in dismay. "You dare to lecture me on etiquette after invading my mind."

Madam, it is hardly an invasion when the door is left wide open. You may as well have been sending out gilded invitation cards to any who cared to come wandering by.

The noise she made this time was less a roar, more a squawk. "My mind is a fortress!"

I scoffed, not because I was feeling particularly contemptuous toward this unfortunate beast, but because it was necessary to provoke her further, and further provocation seemed our only way through this morass.

You are aware that I'm inside that particular fortress right now, looking out through the myriad holes that have formed?

"Get out!" she roared, covering both the ceiling and herself in a phlegmy coating of soot. "Get out right now! I've never been so insulted in my whole life. Just leave!"

Fine! I shall, and needless to say, you can forget any invitation to Arpanpholigon in your near future!

She flicked her head to be rid of me and I landed comfortably back in Cygni's grip. "Get out! Both of you! Don't ever darken my lair again!"

With the first indication that he had any good sense at all, Cygni took off running for the exit, diving into the narrow cave, skidding across the smaller bones that had been scattered this way and then slipping on down the slope into the treasury.

Emotions were not Cygni's typical domain of preference. He had repression up the wazoo. Logic, reason, these were the things in his head that he was comfortable with. Yet when he slip-and-slid down into a giant pile of treasure, something was awoken within him. Some primal urge of all dwarf-kind to hoard shiny things and sing songs about it. Impulses took over him.

His first instinct was to grab all the treasure in reach. His second instinct, newly formed, was to get as far away as possible from every single coin in sight in case it nibbled on him. The third instinct was to count all the coins, which may actually have been a manifestation of some deep-rooted need for order slowly turning into a compulsive disorder.

Trapped between these initial instincts, he simply sat and stared for a while. The chamber was bigger than my tower back home, at least in terms of circumference, and every surface of it was heaped with coins, crowns, jewels, and miscellaneous other items of value. More gold than he'd ever seen in his life, despite having spent that life mining up gold, among other minerals.

Slowly, as though worried that this was all a dream that might fall apart, Cygni rose. "Did I die?"

Not that I'm aware of.

"I lived a good life, I think. I did right." He still didn't touch any of the treasure, just in case it all turned out to be a dream. "If I died, I'd end up here."

First and foremost, I must inform you that you are still alive, your heart is still beating, and thanks to my persistent genius, we survived the encounter with the dragon of this dungeon. Secondly, I'm pretty sure that you are aiming too low in terms of an afterlife if a dusty old pile of coins is all you get.

He looked at it with unabashed adoration and sighed, "What could be better?"

I cannot say that I'd given much thought to an afterlife prior to this point. I was honestly so exhausted with my current life that I genuinely wasn't sure if I'd want to keep things going beyond that. Not to mention that my own personal afterlife appeared to be happening concurrently with this conversation, and in the place of any imagined delights, I got to be a hat. Still, I had vague impressions from some of my more religious peers. *Nubile virgins feeding you peeled grapes?*

Cygni snorted. "Gold will buy you that."

Divinely inspired bliss? I'll admit that this one was a stretch, but I'd definitely heard someone talking about it as if it were a real thing one could hope for.

"Gold will buy you that."

An eternity in some paradise plane? I already knew this one was available for a very reasonable price considering the cost of interdimensional travel, but maybe he didn't know it.

"Gold will buy you that."

Either he had connections on the surface that I didn't know about, or a degree of faith in gold that others usually reserved for their deities.

He carefully picked up one coin, keeping a close eye on it, and turned it around slowly before his eyes. The light from his lantern glinted off its yellowed surface.

That is most certainly a coin.

"Not a monster?"

Nope, a coin. The monsters look freshly minted, and this one is . . . wait . . . look at it again.

On one side of the coin there was a depiction of a palace; on the other, where one would usually find a king or queen, there was some sort of bird.

Oh dear.

Cygni had slowly sunk down and sunk their hands into the heaps of gold, lifting them up and letting them trickle through his fingers with abundant glee. In a moment I imagined he was going to knock himself unconscious by trying to slam his face into them as though he could swim through solid metal. But my little comment brought him to an abrupt halt.

"Oh dear, what?"

The coins, they're, uh, very old.

He rubbed his greedy little hands together. "That's good, old stuff is worth more, right?"

Typically yes, but in this instance . . . I wasn't sure how to break the news to him when he was having what amounted to a religious moment for dwarves. It felt petty and mean, but at the same time, it was going to be necessary to avoid certain . . . complications.

Cygni got tired of waiting. "Oh, just spit it out, will you."

These are third-century republican spingars. The coin with the lowest gold-to-filler ratio in history. At the time of their minting during a massive economic crisis, each of them would have been considered to be worth one gold piece apiece, but their value has depreciated somewhat.

Cygni was still cradling the handful of coins to his chest as though they were an abandoned baby that he'd rescued. "So how much is one of them worth?"

One of them? Oh, practically nothing.

His brows drew down so far that the fuzz was blocking the upper part of our shared vision. "But all of this, all added together, that must make . . ."

I did some quick mental mathematics.

Enough to buy a nice lunch in Arpanpholigon if you don't mind skipping dessert. And a small drink.

"No . . . no . . ." He scooped up another double handful of coins, and I could actually feel his heartbeat speed up at the sight of them. It was like Ig and Rhinolyta all over again, unrequited love. "Look at all this gold, surely it's worth . . ." Despair overran him and he trailed off.

Time gets us all eventually. Present company excluded, of course.

"Not gold! Gold is forever! Gold is . . . gold is . . ." He sounded like he was about to break down crying.

I apologize for being the bearer of bad news. If it is any consolation, I imagine that some of the gemstones here may have some worth. Perhaps there are even artifacts worthy of our attention.

His lower lip was wobbling. "But the gold . . ."

Try not to think of it as gold; consider it to be, uh, chaff to be sorted from the wheat.

"But all that gold . . ."

Cygni, my dear fellow, all that glitters is not gold.

The metal dug painfully into his palms as he grasped it tighter. "But they're gold coins!"

I would like to propose that we take a moment for you to get your head around the idea that these particular coins are worthless so that we can move on.

"Gold?!" He sobbed.

For the next hour or so, I remained quiet as Cygni passed through the many stages of grief. At times stuffing his pockets with worthless coins, at others sobbing inconsolably as he threw them around the room. Typically I would have had more to say about the time being wasted, but in truth the whole experience was quite helpful. As Cygni abandoned his senses in the depths of despair, I picked them up and used them.

The sense for magic was barely developed in this dwarf, having only been activated by me some scant hours before we reached this point, but I was accustomed to working with far less to far greater result, and by the time that his pacing, sobbing, vomiting into a helmet, sobbing, pacing, and sobbing were complete, so too was my complete inventory of all the magical items now available to us. Minus one Helm of Arrow Protection, which would remain unavailable until after it had received a good dry-cleaning.

To summarize the various dweomers and enchantments that had been bestowed upon items of great value, handed off to adventurers who were off to slay a dragon and then abandoned here following their death by burning, we had:

Four separate but unrelated shields of fire protection. None of them had a single scorch mark on them, yet all of them had been separated from their owners following their dissolution into ash. Ergo, the shields were protected against fire, but they should have gotten armor with the same enchantment.

Three cursed swords, each less useful than the last. One made you murder the person you loved the most in the world and fed on their soul. One drank the blood of your enemies, but also yours if it wasn't used often enough. The third took a little longer to untangle, as it was a rather nasty and complex piece of work that meant that everyone killed with the sword would retain enmity toward the user if and when they were reincarnated, to the net effect that the user's enemies would be endless throughout their life. Alternately, it would mean that they got attacked by a lot of babies.

Two rings of jumping, something I'd always considered to be of questionable usefulness when exploring underground, but I'm sure adventurers could present some very sensible reasoning for their need for them, other than their love of concussions.

Two wands, one that still retained its charge but had been so badly scorched that the spell bound in it would no longer function, and the other holding on to its charge only barely. Unfortunately the spell that the latter could cast was one of water-walking, which I cannot imagine was going to be immediately helpful to us anytime soon.

Two mirrors of communication that had presumably been used by different members of the same adventuring party to coordinate their plans. One still had part of a glove melted onto the handle, so the plans can't have been very good.

Two bags of holding, which would have been immensely helpful if we were making off with the whole hoard of money, but at present would only be helpful for holding the handful of miscellanea that we were going to be taking.

Well, that was one of them. The other was entirely waterlogged to the point that it was dripping. I had a sneaking suspicion that at some point it may have been dropped in a lake while open and retrieved once said body of water was depleted. There was a possibility that some fish might be retrieved from it later, to be used as sustenance for Cygni when he finally tired of the dry tack he'd been nibbling every so often, but given his aversion to water in general, I suspected that his feelings toward fish might not have been entirely friendly.

One gauntlet of giant's strength. If it were a pair, then it would have been useful. As it was, we were going to end up throwing out Cygni's back the first time he tried to use it.

By no means an entirely useless assortment of trinkets, but neither was it all that helpful in our current circumstances.

Still, it did give Cygni something to pick up and stuff into his pockets that might actually have some value, and that helped to tease him back from the precipice of the chasm of depression that he had found himself teetering on.

"What's the point of . . ."

Resale value. Just put it all in the bag and let's go. Don't forget the diamonds.

"Diamonds?!"

That seemed to perk him up a bit. He was like a puppy really, you just had to give him little treats to keep his attention pointed in the right direction.

"Ain't sure what a puppy is, but that didn't sound flattering."

Sorry, sometimes my thoughts get away from me.

After a degree of excavation to get through all the heaped worthless metal, we uncovered an exit from the treasure hoard that was not going to require us to pass by the geriatric dragon again, which was a huge relief as there is an upper limit to how snooty even I can get.

"Comes with being old."

I am in the prime of my life!

"Aren't you dead?"

Well, apart from that.

The way out had been blocked with one of the fire-resistant shields, one that still had a sticky paste on the rear side that had presumably been its owner learning about the convection of heat a little too late in life to be helpful. But now Cygni was able to squeeze down into it and proceed through a tight tunnel heading in what he believed to be the right direction with only a small amount of hunching over.

Cygni grumbled, "This is the right way."

I have no doubt about your underground navigational skills, dear dwarf. I, myself, am simply a little turned around by all the twists and turns.

CHAPTER TEN

ARSENIC AND OLD STONE

There was no short period of time spent traversing through the dim and entirely too tight tunnel, with Cygni constantly ducking to avoid having me knocked off by a lower ridge in the roof. I have never been terribly prone to claustrophobia thanks to the fact that, from about the age of nine, I've been quite capable of exploding anything constraining me with an ending blast radius that would leave agoraphobes quite troubled. Yet now, here, deep underground with my ability to level everything in sight currently restrained, I began to feel it. A tightness along the lines of my stitched seam.

"Nearly there," Cygni assured me.

You have never been here before in your life, nor is the region mapped anywhere in your recollection, so that is a gross supposition on your part. Presumably meant to calm me. I do not require calming; I am not some animal to be tamed.

"Just saying, we must be nearly through."

And I am "just saying" that you have no possible way of knowing that.

"The stone speaks to me."

Listen, there is already one voice too many in this head . . .

Yet despite this obviously just being an attempt to placate me, I did find myself placated. The tension began to ease, and when Cygni felt a breeze upon his face, it was I and not he that felt compelled to let loose a sigh of relief.

The tunnel gradually gained height, even as it lost width, until Cygni was standing up straight and edging along sideways to make it through the crack we had just found ourselves in. Stone brushed against my rim to the front and the back, and while I'm rather a wide-rimmed hat, I was not so much bigger than the girth of Cygni that I didn't fear what would happen should he grow stuck. I suppose that after a few days of starvation, he might slim down enough to continue on our route, but I did not really want to experience that particular discomfort.

"Just don't think about it," he whispered to me. Whispered, because the stone was compressing him too much for him to get a full breath to speak normally.

What else should I think of when stony death encroaches on every side?

"What . . . is the first thing you'll do, when you get a body back?"

Wreak horrible vengeance upon whoever deprived me of one to begin with.

He chuckled. "You hold grudges like a dwarf."

I wish that I knew who I should be holding my grudge against. It would make it so much easier to come up with an appropriate method of punishment.

"You mean planning for the battle?"

Battle? I am the greatest living wizard in all of the world; there will be no battle. Whoever stands against me shall be promptly annihilated. No, I mean that the sooner I know which of my upstart ingrate colleagues at the university managed to assassinate me and steal my position, the sooner I can begin devising a particularly torturous spell to slowly destroy them, playing to their most terrible fears.

"You're a real charmer."

I can assure you that once you have been killed and subjected to such posthumous degradations as I have, you too might develop something of a mean streak when it comes to repaying the one who put you in such a position.

With one final grunt of effort, Cygni squeezed out of the crack and into a cavern. The air here was stale, but cool compared to the cramped quarters we had just passed through, and Cygni and I both profoundly enjoyed the first few deep breaths that he drew.

Congratulations on successfully distracting me from our predicament. I . . . appreciate your efforts.

"You'd do the same for me."

Perhaps I would have, if given the proper motivation, like getting him to continue on through a dangerous scenario to my benefit, but he had done that just to be kind, and that struck me as unusual. He was a practical sort of dwarf usually; sentiment seemed out of character.

The cavern had not narrowed to our entryway, rather we had passed through one of a great many crevasses leading into this massive chamber. When I say massive, I do not mean it was simply large, I mean that it was like an inverse mountain, a cavernous gap in the world so vast that it was awe-inspiring. Khnute's Crack was a huge hole in the ground, but it had been filled with people and industry and construction and life. This was simply an emptiness on a tectonic scale.

"Big cave," Cygni succinctly described it.

Very large.

"Yup." He craned his neck to look straight up, but it was to no avail—we were so deep under the earth that even though this cavern stretched up so large that he couldn't see the top, it still didn't break the surface. Pitch-blackness hung above us like a vulture, just waiting to drop down on us when we least expected it.

Charming place, really. Perhaps we should traverse it as swiftly as possible.

"Just thinking that myself." He took off at a brisk pace in what he seemed sure was the right direction. Since the cavern seemed to stretch off in more or less every direction, we were soon just a little circle of lit-up floor in the middle of a big nothingness. Sometimes there was rubble to break up the monotony, but more often than not, just rough stone underfoot and distant shadows that might have been walls.

If that had been all that there was, I do not think that there would have been any problems really. Darkness, caves, all these things were very much inside of Cygni's wheelhouse, and I was in his wheelhouse also, the head-shaped part of his wheelhouse. This metaphor is a mess. I shouldn't have been unsettled by the darkness and the tons of stone weighing down above us because currently I was a dwarf, at least in the physical sense, and that was normally enough to keep my concerns about the current situation at bay, but there was something else at play.

Cygni's magical senses were pitiful in comparison to my natural capabilities of course, but they were not entirely blunted by a lifetime of disuse. He could feel something, even if he didn't know what it was. And I, with my more enlightened understanding of the nature of magic, felt the thrumming in the Quintessence around us as a master harpist would recognize a note distantly played. A discordant note.

There was something wrong with the magic in this cavern. Everywhere else in the world Quintessence flows freely and smoothly through all space, but here it was not moving as it should. Even when I, at the height of my strength, drew upon Quintessence to refill my reserves, I could never pull on so much as to disrupt the natural flow—as I'm sure druids would be swift to brag about—but here something was. It was twisting magic out of shape.

If magic was a grand tapestry incorporating all of existence, and in a way it is, then somewhere in this cavern there was a snag. A tangle. Something wrong. Small wonder then that it made Cygni edgy and me . . . well.

Might I offer a proposal?

"Hmm?" Cygni replied, even more monosyllabically than usual.

What if, rather than continuing this way, we sought out a different route.

He raised an eyebrow and the bushiness of it tickled my rim. "You see one?"

Well, hear me out. What if we head back in the direction that we came, go back through the crack in the wall, go past the dragon, and then find a different path from back in the dungeon?

He kept plodding on, even though it was clearly in the opposite direction to the one in which we should be going. "Back in the crack you thought we were going to get stuck in?"

Yes, well, we know that you can fit through now.

"To the dragon that will roast us?" His eyebrow had gone down now, but there was a pulling in the muscles on his cheeks that I could have sworn was the beginning of a smile. You couldn't see it under the beard, but I could feel it.

She actually seemed quite reasonable. I'm sure that if we talk to her a little, we will be able to negotiate our safe passage.

Alright, even I'll admit I was stretching the truth a little too far with that one, but there was probably some way we could sneak past a blind dragon.

The tugging at his cheeks was getting worse. If I had hands, I'd have squished his face back into its usual surly expression. "Back into the dungeon full of monsters and traps that is leading the wrong way?"

Perhaps it would be the preferable option?

For some reason, the more concerned that I became for his safety, the more amused the dwarf became. He chuckled, actually chuckled. "Really spooked, ain't you?"

Apprehension about a potentially dangerous situation is not "being spooked."

"Thought wizards were meant to be brave. All that power . . ."

A common misapprehension. A healthy dose of caution can mean all the difference in the field of magic. In fact, I would posit that the world would have considerably more wizards in it if they had all been blessed with my instincts for self-preservation. Do you even know how many students of magic end up annihilating themselves entirely because of overconfidence in their abilities? They concoct some new spell, feel entirely certain of all their calculations and casting language, empower it with Quintessence, and poof.

Cygni's smile slipped a little as he shuddered. "They drain themselves?"

No, their spells work perfectly. Too perfectly. Do you know what happens when you cast a spell that encases you in an impenetrable sphere so that no enemy can harm you? Air can't get in. Do you know what happens when you conjure a flame that can never be extinguished? You can't put it out when you brush against it and catch on fire. Do you know what happens when you create a curse of such incalculable cruelty that . . .

"I get the idea." Cygni cut me off, mid-thought.

Then you grasp that there is a reason I am redirecting our course. Just because something seems like the fastest route does not mean that it will be. Sometimes it is better to take a more circuitous path to avoid destruction.

"Wizards are amazing." I felt myself swell with pride involuntarily as he spoke. "You find a thousand words to say what I can say in two. You're scared."

I think that's technically three.

"You're." Cygni enunciated each word carefully. As though savoring them. "Scared."

"You're" would be a compound of you and are, in this instance.

"Still counts as one," he grumbled.

I cannot say I'm familiar enough with dwarven grammar to correct you. However, I will be happy to correct you upon your initial point. Which is to say that good sense is not cowardice. Sometimes it takes true courage to divert from conventional wisdom and seek the circuitous route that leads to victory rather than plowing ahead into certain doom.

With an unpleasant lurch, I could feel his stomach drop at the thought. Or possibly because we were drawing ever closer to whatever was causing the warp in the weft of magic. "I'm not going back to the dragon."

Then I suppose this is my opportunity to accuse you of cowardice, simply because you will not face a danger that you consider to be overwhelming. A danger which, I will add, is a known quantity at this point, unlike whatever it is we are soon to encounter. A danger which exists within the usual realms of knowledge and natural laws and has been known to be defeated by means both arcane and mundane that are within our grasp.

"Dragons: certain death. Whatever is in here: uncertain."

Cygni didn't seem too fazed by my implication of his cowardice. Perhaps he was correct, and I was too needlessly verbose to get my point across. I needed a change of tack, a less garrulous approach to make him understand. The sort of thing that would work on children or the mentally infirm.

Be a man! Take the risk! Fight the dragon!

The perfect call to action if I do say so myself. The kind of thing that would have had peasants arming themselves with pitchforks, knights puffing out their chests, and PE teachers shedding a tear at the perfection of the phrasing.

"I'm not a man," Cygni replied with a smirk under his . . . her beard.

I mean, cosmetically . . . to humans you appear . . . and socially . . .

"I'm a dwarf." She cut my meandering off with a snort. "It ain't going to work. We're going this way."

It brooked no argument.

The scent of almonds filled the air as we progressed. Along with the odd whiff of rotten eggs. Cygni began to breath only through her mouth, and the filter of her mustache, without even seeming to realize she was doing it. Poisons were not uncommon down here in the depths of the world, and even the king of poisons had to be mined from somewhere, but it was rather unusual for it to exist in a place in such concentration that the air itself tasted of arsenic. The stone beneath our feet, sheets of uneven rock that had served just fine up until now, shone in places where the torchlight touched them. Grays and yellows and reds reflecting back, not quite metallic but not quite not. Here and there a yellow stain spattered upon the stone from within, reeking of heck.

Noxious chemicals in the air, doesn't seem like an ideal place to be strolling around.

"Ain't going back." Cygni didn't even bother to engage with my nonsense this time. Perhaps I was becoming tiresome. Perhaps if she grew tired enough, she'd turn back just to make me stop.

Isn't the king of poisons one of those terrible ones that slowly builds up in your body the longer that you're exposed to it?

"You know the answer to that, same as I do," she hissed, trying not to breathe too much.

So really, the longer that we are here the closer you come to certain death?

The shallow breaths and long steps were beginning to take their toll on Cygni. "Wish . . . you were a lantern fairy."

Because then you might believe me when I warn you of all the toxicity in the air?

"Because . . . you'd have passed out . . . and shut up by now."

You are exceptionally rude.

"Not . . . exceptional . . ." Cygni spluttered as some beard-filter tickled the back of her throat. "Pretty . . . normal amount."

Ironically, if Ig were here, he could have solved our current predicament. Using low magic, he could have held all of the poison in the air away from us. Unfortunately for both Cygni and I, we were capable of focusing our attention on a single thing, which meant that any attempt by either of us would result in but a single mote being cast off.

Of course that useless little runt was never around when you needed him.

With all seriousness now, would it be better for us to turn back than to proceed?

"Only way . . . out . . ." Cygni was holding her breath now as the reek of the place grew ever stronger. "Is . . . through."

There were cracks and fissures in the stone now, no great pressure was working from beneath them, so the gases that eked out came with no force. It was almost like a spill of noxious cloud rather than an eruption. It swirled away from Cygni's stubby legs as she stomped on through, but one could not help but wonder what the more dilute version hanging in the air at breathing level might have been doing to her as we proceeded.

Yet despite this obvious impediment, she did make it through. We reached what must have been the far side of this great ravine, and after a moment to reorient herself, Cygni set off along the distant wall, now no longer so distant. It was streaked all the way up with yellow from the delightful egg-fart gas escaping all around us, but on the plus side, we could no longer smell the telltale hints of almonds, so perhaps we would only die of sulfur poisoning instead. Perhaps not preferable, but less insidious, certainly.

Sulfur at least had the great benefit of you dying then and there, rather than sneaking up on you years down the line when you crossed some arbitrary threshold of sulfur inhalation and clubbing you over the back of the head. With the head in this metaphor being your mortality.

Regardless, we trailed along the stained wall until it ceased to be stained and began to look abnormally smooth.

Is it my imagination, or does it rather look like the wall here has been . . . melted.

"Water does that, over time." Cygni was as dismissive as always despite her senses jangling just as badly as my own.

And there is an abundance of water in this cavern, isn't there? I can tell from the way your lips are chapping and your eyeballs are becoming raisins.

"Time changes things," Cygni grumbled. "Water moves deeper."

Yes, but it doesn't move sideways, and that is the direction in which the wall has been smoothed. As if exposed to some intense . . .

If she had rolled her eyes any harder, they might have escaped their sockets. "Teach the dwarf more about how stone behaves, oh wise wizard."

If the dragon had eaten you, at least I wouldn't have had to endure any of this sass.

"Sass?"

Indeed.

And so, for a time, I was silent. Taking in the changes in the stone. The smooth, molten expanse where some immense blast had cut out this side of the cavern, the places where crystals had begun to grow back from their blighted roots, the places where, even here, the magic felt subtly wrong. As Cygni followed the wall along, I half wondered if it was because of that tugging in the Quintessence that we were going in this direction. If the warp in the magic was drawing her in. I wanted to ask, but truth be told, I doubted that she would even know the answer. Even a mage of my caliber might struggle to discern the invisible hand of magic itself upon me.

So onward we waddled with nary a backwards glance and the poisons that had filled the air began to give way to two new scents. Ozone and staleness.

The former would doubtless be related to whatever magical mishap had occurred up ahead and created the tangle, while the latter spoke to the age of this place, and how long it had been since fresh air had swept through. One would have thought that so gigantic a chamber as the cavern we had traversed, with all of it leaking gases, would have had some sort of air current cycling through, but I supposed that given enough time, even that would be insufficient to scrub the incredible age of the place from our olfactory senses.

You might wonder as to why I speak so much of the scents in this dark and dank expanse, whether there is some uniquely sharp faculty of the somewhat beaky dwarven nose that allowed me to drink in information through it. Alas, this was not the case. Rather, it was simply a matter of input. There was nothing to see or hear, which left us only with touch and scent to perceive the world around us. Thankfully Cygni had not yet begun licking rocks.

As we came to the distant end of the chasm, there was a glow. Not a glow as would be perceptible to the eye of any nascent traveler, but the sort that a wizard could not overlook if they tried. Quintessence of such density was gathered in front of us that even Cygni, so deprived of her magical senses through her life, could perceive it. The hair on the back of her neck prickled and her beard puffed out like a startled housecat.

"Is that . . ."

Whatever I have been trying to convince you to stay away from since we emerged into this tomb, yes.

"Isn't a tomb. Nothing's dead here."

She meant it to be a comment on the thankful absence of corpses—and don't get me wrong, I was always thankful that there were no decaying bodies lying around—but she was of course quite correct in a less literal sense.

Quintessence, magic, it is life. Formless life, but life all the same. When gathered in quantities such as this, it should have spontaneously formed living creatures. We should not have been able to move ahead for a veritable carpet of bunny rabbits that had just sprung into existence for no particular reason, yet there was no fur rug underfoot.

The magic should not be gathering like this.

"I figured from all your bitching." Cygni's lip quirked up into a sneer.

Allow me to clarify: It should not be possible for magic to gather like this. It should not remain Quintessence in this . . . density. It should form other things. The rocks should be transforming into little trolls. The gases should be forming elemental creatures. This much magic should not . . . cannot remain inert in these quantities.

Cygni's eye rolling was getting to the point where I was starting to feel a little seasick staring out through her eyes. "So we've finally found a mystery you don't already have the answer to, and you want to run away?"

Discretion is key. This phenomenon requires study, of course, but that does not mean that we should be the ones to make that study. Perhaps some more disposable undergraduates would be a better initial team, just in case the ambient Quintessence decides to ground itself through a magician and reduces them to ash.

That finally brought the relentless trudge toward our doom to a halt. "Wait, it can do that?"

Well, that is rather the nature of the unknown, is it not? We cannot know *what this amalgamation is capable of.*

Her eyes narrowed. "You're just making stuff up now, aren't you?"

I am being forced to make suppositions due to the complete absence of any data about this phenomenon.

"So . . . making it up?" she finished for me.

Based on prior knowledge of arcane accidents and Quintessence buildups.

There was a momentary pause until she recognized the contradiction and called me on it. "You said it can't build up like this?"

The point is, we should not blithely stroll into the midst of whatever is occurring.

"It's in the way." She wasn't willing to let me just bluster past the facts, which was very annoying. If Ig were here, he would have gladly agreed to just about anything I said.

In desperation I said, *We can find another way.*

But by then it was too late. Her eyes had locked on to the subtle patterning in the stone that she had until now overlooked, mistaking it for a natural grain.

She dropped into a squat by the wall and ran her fingers along the lines. "This is carved."

Probably just that sideways water you were talking about digging channels.

"It's dwarf made. Look at the joins in the lines, the precision."

As you're so quick to point out, I know little of stonework, so can neither confirm nor deny your suggestion.

She opened and closed her mouth, realization sinking in. "You knew?"

I had my suspicions.

Having my rim grasped and twisted betwixt her sausage-like fingers was an unpleasant experience, but not a painful one. Pain would have required nerves, rather than a vague awareness of my own form. "Why didn't you say something?"

Because it would have encouraged you to carry on in this direction when I'm quite sure that . . .

"Of course I want to carry on!" Cygni yelled so loud that, had I musculature, I would have flinched. "This is dwarf-wrought stone, and we're heading in the direction of something magical. This could be the answer to what happened to us! Where our magic went."

Again, precisely why I did not point out the signs.

"Listen here, hat." I got the impression that if she could have pulled me off her head to look me in the nonexistent eyes while yelling at me, she would have. "You and me are in this together. Right?"

This seemed to be a leading question, but I had no inkling of where she was trying to lead me.

I suppose . . .

"And that means that we work to the same goals. You want to get back to the city and grow yourself a new longshanks body. I want to find out why dwarves don't have magic. Both of us can get what we want, but only if both of us help each other."

Indisputable. With my mind turned to any problem, it could be resolved, and she had thus far proved a capable "leg man" for the operation. Even if the legs were stumpy and the man part seemed subject to change.

I . . . yes. Fine. I noticed some degree of striation in the stone back there that looked graven, and as we passed the smoothed section, I could perceive areas that had not been scorched so thoroughly that carried carved friezes of great dwarvish deeds, and there was a certain . . . angular quality to the way that the cavern was constructed that did not speak to a natural formation. The walls and floors met at a right angle, for instance. A corroded angle thanks to the various eruptions, but a right one all the same.

In the beautiful library of her mind, Cygni shuffled things around until she too could see what I had seen, at which point such details as I had just indicated became abundantly obvious even to her. She let out a heavy breath. "How did you see all that and I didn't?"

I believe you were preoccupied with the poison situation. Not to mention that just because you have the same sensory apparatus as I'm currently using, it does not mean that it is being processed by so well-developed a mind.

It took her less developed mind a moment to process what had just been said. "Did you just call me stupid?"

This was one of those rhetorical questions that druids and philosophers liked to trot out when they had no facts to support them. I could recognize that, and knew that the correct way to sidestep the sidestep was to reach for something equally abstract and leave them to puzzle it out after.

A being with a mind that had been somewhat more honed might have been able to discern that for themselves.

Clearly, Cygni's mind was sufficiently honed to decipher that without too much pondering. "I'm shoving you down the next sulfur geyser we find."

Ah yes, that will prove your superior intellect.

Her confusion washed over me. She understood that I was being petty, vindictive, and cruel, but assumed that I was doing so because of some higher purpose. She was ascribing me a degree of maturity and intellect beyond what I was portraying, even now. She growled out, "I'm not stupid."

Among your own kind, I'd argue that you are likely one of the brightest. Compared to all of elf, human, and monster-kind, you exceed their capabilities in every metric.

I could feel her heart softening as I spoke. This interpersonal relationship stuff is far easier than all the books made out.

But alas, we are not making a comparison to the average, we are making our comparison to an outlier, and when compared to me, I am sorry to say that the world's smartest dwarf is little different from the world's smartest cuttlefish. Both incredibly impressive specimens, but operating on a somewhat different level.

She had been feeling appreciated and comforted; now she was feeling angry, but not so angry that it interfered with her being pedantic. "The hell is a cuttlefish?"

I projected an image into her mind, of the humble cuttlefish at sea. Doing its cuttling in peace. *A kind of mollusk. They are remarkably intelligent, for being a mollusk.*

Her jaw almost cramped from the force with which she grit her teeth together before barking out, "Forget the sulfur, first hole I find, you're going in."

I do not mean to offend you, I lied, *merely to point out that it is no great loss to be outsmarted by a being who is defined entirely by his superior intelligence. It would be akin to becoming enraged at your ability to fly when confronted with a bird.*

She stomped on without acknowledging that, though under her breath, she grumbled. "Going to make you fly in the next ravine I see."

Which I shall do in a very ineffectual manner, because I was not built for flight in the manner that a bird was. And it would be foolish for me to envy the bird, would it not?

"I still don't know what a bird is!" she yelled into the dark.

You do take my meaning though? That you should not be jealous of my jaw-dropping intellect.

"Amazing all that ego could fit in one hat." Her words dripped with contempt, but I got the sense that equilibrium between us had returned. I had broken whatever bond was twisting her out of shape before it could do either of us harm.

It would do her no good to go along thinking she was doing me favors, or that my suggestions were rooted in cowardice; some degree of adversarial prejudice in our interactions would serve her well. It wouldn't do for her to think we were equal partners in all this, as her demands seemed to imply. She was getting too . . . chummy. *The difference between arrogance and confidence is ability.*

Pinching the bridge of her nose, she sighed. "Can we get back to the rocks, please?"

It was a subject I was considerably more comfortable discussing. Painting myself as such a caricature was unpleasant, if necessary.

Age has not badly affected the carvings, but the buildup of crystalline growth and other residues has shallowed the cuts. As such, it is difficult to discern any details.

The tension that had been so abated by her paternal . . . maternal . . . whatever instincts she'd been having toward me returned. "Nothing useful?"

Beyond placing the date of dwarvish habitation in this area at several millennia back, nothing pertinent that I can see.

She plodded along a little farther, then paused. "Why is my skin crawling?"

Magic.

"Isn't that your area of expertise?"

Rather like asking a smith his opinion on an impossibly large lump of ore floating in the middle of the room, I'm afraid.

Perhaps that metaphor got away from me slightly, but my hope was that it correctly conveyed my confusion at how the primal material from which my art is formed came to be in such an unnatural state.

And then, finally, after what felt like hours of slowly creeping up on it, the source of the warping effect was right before us.

Sitting at a slight angle where it jutted up from betwixt the stones of the floor was a crystalline material, probably closer in construction to stone than any real gem. It was glowing, but not in the way that the eyes could sense. It radiated magic. Quintessence had been gathered here, compressed until it made a solid form. It was . . . impossible.

There was nothing dense enough to compress Quintessence, and the only tools one had to manipulate Quintessence were made of Quintessence. Which was, inherently, no denser than Quintessence, for obvious reasons. There was no way in which anyone could have condensed or congealed it into this form either. Such things were beyond the ken of modern sorcery. Which is to say, even I didn't know how to do it. And if I didn't know how to do something, it couldn't be done. Ergo, impossible.

Cygni stared at it with awestruck eyes. "Is that . . ."

Quintessence given solid form, yes.

The knowledge I had bequeathed to her through our connection and her own prodigious knowledge of the elements both presented her with the same obvious fact as I myself had run up against. "But it . . ."

Entirely impossible, I can assure you.

She stroked her beard while peering into the lightless glow. "So how . . ."

Whatever process was used is entirely beyond me, but it must have involved some exotic matter that we have not had access to in living memory.

She had squatted down before the crystal, barely larger than her thumb, but dominating our thoughts. "It couldn't . . ."

No, I assure you that this is not a naturally occurring phenomenon. If it were, someone would have encountered it at some point throughout the history of the world, and written it down, and I would know about it.

She rolled her eyes. "You haven't read everything that . . ."

No, I have not read everything ever written, only everything pertaining to the art of magic. Some things I have not troubled myself to read. Halfling romance novels, for instance. Instruction manuals for goat carts. Orcish philosophy. But anything even tangentially related to magic, I have at least skimmed, and I assure you that if Quintessence made solid had ever come up, I would have bloody well remembered it.

It seemed that my tone had become somewhat overwrought as the conversation proceeded. "Alright, calm down."

I cannot be calm, because the situation calls for alarm. If one impossible thing has occurred, what is to say that another will not? Our entire understanding of reality is inductive rather than deductive, with our ongoing assumption that everything will continue as it always has predicated upon our observation of that which has gone before. Now we are in the presence of the impossible and so all our reality may splinter without a moment's notice. Gravity may cease to hold us. Cats and dogs will start living together in sin. A kobold will be elected Archmage of Arpanpholigon.

I lapsed into silence for a moment as I tried to compose my thoughts. It was an opportunity that it seemed Cygni could not pass up. "You done?"

I believe I have several more hours of histrionics within me, but in the interest of brevity, please just assume that I am finished and move closer so that we can examine this little impossibility, shall we?

She chuckled as she shuffled forward. "Thought you wanted to stay away from . . ."

That was before I saw it.

To form a solid mass, the floaty little particles of Quintessence had to be tightly packed together before they were enclosed in this particular crystalline form. As such, the tiny fragment in front of us was so radiant with power that it actually made me a little nervous. More magic than most lesser witches and wizards would get through in a lifetime contained in something the size of pebble.

It seems we have the answer to how dwarves, congenitally incapable of retaining Quintessence, were historically capable of casting.

"You think . . ."

Yes, I do, famously. But the question remains of how this . . . lost element could have been contrived.

"If it's lost . . . does that mean we get to name it?"

Scrynium, I suggested as Cygni blundered out, "Cygnite."

We can discuss it later. For now it is less important what we name it, and more important how it came into being.

"Probably end up called Quintium or something."

It doesn't matter for now.

Which was to say that it would be named Scrynium, of course. History was written by the victors, or in this case, by the people who knew how to write. I could have my discovery in a dozen arcane journals before you could say "peer review."

Whatever is producing the unnatural warping of the flows of Quintessence is doubtless responsible for this accumulation, so I suggest that we move farther into the cavern toward that font of discomfort.

"What about the Cygnite?" she asked, trying not to smirk as she said it.

I cannot tell how stable it is at a glance, and touching it may very well result in an unexpected discharge of Quintessence.

"So . . . just leave it there?"

I believe that would be the course of wisdom, yes.

Cygni reached out and grabbed it while I was mid-sentence.

As predicted, the Quintessence was stable within the crystal, but the moment that it had an out—into Cygni's magical channels—it began dumping out its contents. Her beard bushed out, her hair stood on end, sparks began bursting from her fingertips and her eyes. I could vaguely make out her skeleton, glowing under her skin, when the Quintessence peaked.

Dump it out, you fool! Dump it out!

To me, that logically would have meant to cast a spell of vast power rather than risk the accumulation of magic incinerating me, but to Cygni, clearly the command meant something different. She did precisely what nobody in the history of magic has ever been stupid enough to do, and instead of redirecting the overwhelming power of raw Quintessence, she pushed back.

The magic stopped flowing. The crystal in her hand vibrated. All of the energy dammed up inside of it once more, and then, inch by inch, she shoved the magic back. All of that overwhelming power, enough to cast a dozen spells, inched its way back along the channels in her body, all the way back out through her fingertips and into the Scrynium.

Cygni then spoke a word of Dwarvish so coarse that I cannot even attempt to translate it into the common tongue lest it do you permanent psychological damage. I, for one, was quite queasy after hearing it. For those of you who are familiar with the dwarf tongue, I shall provide only the hint that it related to four elephants, silk ropes, your mother, candles being turned upside down, and a mushroom of unusual size.

After that initial cussing, she gathered herself enough to say, "That hurt."

Yes, I'd imagine it would have. Loath as I am to point out the obvious, perhaps you should not draw on the power of the . . . I had no lungs, yet I needed to sigh. *Cygnite, unless it becomes necessary?*

Her voice lowered to a growl. "It wasn't on purpose."

I assumed it was, since completely ignoring me and grabbing it was deliberate.

"It's done now." Cygni lifted the Scrynium off the floor. It snapped cleanly from the stone where it had been nestled and growing through all these years. "No point moaning."

That sample should be ample to prove our claims regarding the new material we have discovered. We should proceed toward Arpanpholigon with all haste. At the university, we should be able to contain it without any further danger.

"You don't want to know where it came from?" She seemed genuinely surprised at my reluctance.

I desperately want to know where it came from, and fully intend to accompany you back here once I am restored to the flesh so that we can more properly explore this cave complex. As it stands, I am incapable of protecting either one of us from the chaotic effects of so much magic, and thus, wish to depart with all haste.

"You love your own voice, don't you?" Cygni snorted in amusement.

When one is forced to be the voice of reason, one finds oneself speaking at length. Particularly when your good advice about not touching things is ignored and people almost explode themselves with an overabundance of Quintessence, I snapped back.

"I ain't exploding."

My natural urge in such circumstances would of course have normally been to threaten my erstwhile student with some minor explosion of some part of their person, but I was attempting to maintain civility with this particular apprentice and was currently lacking in any explosive capability myself. Ergo, I remained silent.

We proceeded along the remaining distance of the vast scarred chamber in relative silence, the distant, high-pitched hum of magic just beyond the limits of Cygni's hearing, but close enough to set all the other stones and crystals of the chamber jangling and chiming, exacerbated by the dwarf's heavy footsteps.

More crystals of Scrynium protruded here and there in the rougher areas of the stone where intense forces had not entirely smoothed the surface. Cygni saw them, felt the draw of them, but resisted. I doubt I would have had her self-control if confronted with such riches. The value of the little crystal in her pocket was probably about sufficient to buy a kingdom. Give or take a few ramparts.

Yet those riches paled in comparison to what we saw up ahead, looming into the lantern light. What had been crystals in the farther parts of this vast cavern were now greater, angularly jutting spikes of Scrynium rising up from the floor and descending from the ceiling as though they were simple stalagmites and stalactites. By mass, each of them had to be triple the size of Cygni, bigger than a full-grown man, yet with some delicacy to them all the same, some sense of fragility, as though the crystals knew that they were not meant to exist in this world and were clinging to their existence tentatively.

Cygni felt me looking from the corner of her eye. "Shall I pick up one of them?"

Could you carry one of them?

She chuckled. "Probably not."

Well then.

Her inability to lift many times her own body weight in crystal would soon become a problem as they became more prevalent, with the ones descending from the roof intersecting with the ones rising from the floor to create solid pillars. At first this was no issue, we could simply walk around, but gradually these pillars became more clustered, solid walls of raw Scrynium blocking our path.

"Looks like there is a lot more Cygnite than we expected, eh?" she needled me.

A small sample was sufficient to convince me that there was something most seriously wrong. How do you suppose I feel at this sight?

She took her time, weighing what she knew of me from our conversations, and what she knew of my levelheadedness in the face of such an amazing discovery. Then finally she replied, "Horny."

It was an answer so unexpected that even I, master of the arcane arts and in particular the languages used to craft it, was temporarily deprived of my ability to speak. In fact, had I the required jaw, I would have been gawking. I hadn't even the capacity to get flustered as I hissed out, *What?*

"Spent your life trying to get power, now there is more than you know what to do with. Reckon you'd probably be humping those crystals if I wasn't in charge."

First of all, to claim that you are "in charge" simply because you are in possession of flesh and I am deprived of it is rude. Secondly, I do not get . . . horny . . . over magic.

Cygni was vibrating with barely contained amusement. I knew that she was winding me up. I knew that this was not all being spoken in seriousness, but I still couldn't allow her to say such things without challenge. "Aye, you've never sat up all night, working yourself into a frenzy about some spell or another."

That was not . . . just because I devoted my time to the study of magic did not mean that I had some prurient obsession!

Academic interest is not . . .

She cut me off with a smirk. "And I'm sure you've had loads of girlfriends."

My dating life had never been particularly active. There had been some teenage fumbling in the libraries and laboratories of various schools of magic, but none of them had come to a relationship because I was devoted to my work. And, I will admit, a tad awkward.

I've been very busy! I am the most . . .

She was in, sharp as a knife before I could get another word out. "And you haven't poured all the energy people normally put into having healthy relation-ships into magic instead."

Just because I have my priorities in order does not mean . . .

"Magic is your girlfriend. You're horny for power." Her grin was broad enough now that her cheery apple cheeks were starting to feel the strain. "Accept it and move on."

I do not appreciate this disparagement of my character.

"I've never met anyone as in love with anyone as you are with magic," she said, somewhat more softly now. Less of a jibe, and more of an observation. "The way you talk about it. The way you think about it. It's like there's nothing else in the world that matters."

There was no way that I could refute that, because ultimately, she was entirely correct. Not about my being sexual with magic, but about my love for it superseding all else in my life.

Of course she had chosen to unleash this revelation at this moment to keep me distracted so that she could continue pushing on into the forest of crystalline pillars without my intervention, but that did nothing to deplete it of its significance.

Throughout my journey thus far, I could quite easily have settled myself upon the head of someone already competent and capable and already have made it home, but instead I kept on trying to teach magic to the most unlikely of stu-dents, even when it was obviously to my detriment. Had I ridden an ogre all the way to Arpanpholigon, I would not even have needed magic to proceed. Brute force would have gotten me home, but each time that I'd even contemplated such a course, I'd found some excuse to do otherwise. I might have moralized it, but I knew as well as anyone else that I was entirely amoral. It was the siren call of magic and learning that had kept me atop Ig, and now Cygni.

I shall not try to stop you from proceeding any further. I know that your heart is set on it, and my curiosity is . . . piqued.

"That's what I thought." She chuckled to herself. "Wizard-horn."

Where the stone could still be seen through the crystalline growths, it was almost entirely blighted by whatever ungodly force had melted the stone of the rest of the chasm, but here and there were still glimpses of the carvings beneath. Dwarvish work all the way. Cygni saw it too, but just as I was trying to temper my feelings about magic, so too was she trying to temper her excitement about archaeology. Her own mounting excitement over the potential discovery ahead of us drove her on at a pace that might have been called feverish if dwarves moved any faster than a steady plod in any situation.

The density of the crystals would eventually have created a solid barrier to advancement if all had remained constant, but from the moment that the Quintessence had taken on a physical form, it had begun to experience the same exacting pressures as any other stone, and that meant that time had worn at it. And given the sheer volume of time that had passed since the Quintessence began to crystallize, that meant that gravity had cracked and snapped some of these great pillars. Not to mention whatever force was being exerted to create them to begin with.

As we proceeded deeper into the nested layers of crystal, we reached older stratum, and they had suffered all the more for their longevity. What had been a solid wall earlier was now mostly a proliferation of shards scattered across the floor where they had fallen. Pure magic crunched under Cygni's boots, but still she did not falter. Even as she felt it crackle and hum beneath each steady step.

Clambering over some stumps of what had once been vast crystal pillars, we finally came to the center of it all. The source of the warping, an act of magic so profound that it had changed the very nature of the world.

It was a very large rock.

CHAPTER ELEVEN

ETERNAL LIE

Cygni gazed upon this incredible creation and sighed. "Bit of an anticlimax, eh?"

Open your other senses and recognize the incredible sight before you.

"It's a big rock, we don't have to pretend that it's . . ." Her mouth hung open for a moment as she did what I'd recommended to her and the intensity of the arcane working before her became apparent. A spell of stasis so complex that it called upon every known element to some degree. A kind of magic beyond what even I was capable of with all of my study and mastery. ". . . Oh."

"Oh" is correct.

Carefully now, and ever so slowly, she came closer to the menhir at the center of all this chaos. The power within it outmatched even the raw Quintessence made solid all around it. It would have taken a dozen wizards, no, a hundred—all with as much power at their disposal as I wielded at the height of my powers— to invest so much Quintessence. And judging from the carvings still set upon the lower parts of the menhir of plain-looking stone, it had been done by dwarves.

There were a set of three runes set higher on the stone, the metal that had been so carefully gilded into them now sloughed away to droplets at its base by the forces being exerted. Cygni looked upon them and could not read a single one.

"What . . ."

An older dialect, predating your own. Likely, a native magical tongue used in parallel to Archaic. I believe that I shall be able to piece their meaning together if given some time to study them and plumb the depths of my memories.

She was still too overwhelmed by it all to compose a proper thought yet. One of the few advantages of a lifetime studying ancient relics of impossible power was that I was at least a little more capable of rolling with the proverbial punches. "Aye . . . you, uh . . . you do that."

She was reaching out a hand to touch the stone before I had even begun my translation, and I was forced to abandon such important work to seize control of the body of this idiot. She froze in place as I exerted control.

Perhaps we do not touch the artifact of ancient and immeasurable power with our bare hands just yet?

"We did this . . . We made this . . . Dwarves had magic . . ."

I think that we've already established that your people once had magic at their disposal; that doesn't mean that whatever this working is will not immediately result in your death on contact.

"The writing here . . ."

That is probably markedly less important than the runes I was translating.

"It isn't . . . it isn't magic words . . . it's almost . . . religious?"

I was under the impression that your kind were rather agnostic.

I did my best not to say "logical" there, but I fear that the meaning may have bled through the carefully picked words.

"We are . . . now." She regained control of her hand and drew it back from the scripture in the stone carefully. "Maybe we weren't then?"

Please don't become one of those weird religious zealots that believe magic is a gift from the gods. I'm not sure that I could stomach dealing with that.

She ignored me entirely, as most women always have, and warbled on. "Maybe . . . maybe we had priests . . . And they were the ones who could do magic?"

Or perhaps your people insisted that only shoemakers were capable of the arcane arts; we do not yet have enough information to make such suppositions.

That little jibe was enough to tug her back out of her reverie. "What do the runes say?"

They say stand still and shut up long enough for me to translate them.

Disgruntled but silent, Cygni and I wrestled for control of her eyes, ending with one pointing up at the untranslated runes and the other down at the texts and images inscribed at eye level. From an outside perspective, I'm sure it was an amusing sight, but from the inside it mostly felt like consistent eye strain.

The shapes of the runes bore some resemblance to the Archaic that I knew, but broken up and reshaped into more angular forms. They were still recognizable, vaguely, but I found that not a one of them formed an actual word in Archaic even when I deciphered them back into their original shapes. They were sounds. Syllables, really. Noises. Nothing to do with the magic that had been done. Ergo, my translation had to be wrong, and simply rearranging these words into Archaic was not the correct course.

"They bound it here, all the magic they had, they poured it in." Her hand hovered over the shapes carved into the stone, the little dwarves with their little beards, all their little hands raised and pointed at the rock we stood before, and wibbly lines leading from them. "But the spell . . . it was too big."

She craned her neck up, reading from the bottom to the top, as dwarves do. Eyes straining in the dim light until she unclipped her lantern from her belt and held it aloft.

No matter which dialect of Ancient Dwarvish I compared these runes to, none of them seemed to match, not even partially. I couldn't get a single fragment of a word right. So I went back to the first idea that had at least produced sounds, even if they weren't terribly useful sounds. I started to run through them, reading this time from the bottom to the top, as a dwarf would.

Nun.

The other eye, under Cygni's control, snapped up to the runes. "What?"

The first rune.

Her brow furrowed, hiding the uppermost rune from sight in a bristle. "Like . . . the human ladies with the funny robes who're all married to the same guy?"

I'll admit that one took me a moment to parse.

I do not believe that actual nuns are involved, no. These may be phonetics. Or potentially an entirely different language translated into runes via Archaic.

Her bristly eyebrows must have appeared like a pair of caterpillars attempting to mate above her nose. "It could mean nothing?"

Once more, I will have to invest the time to properly translate the . . .

"Get on with it then," she growled. Quite rudely, I'd say, given that she was the one who kept interrupting me.

She went back to eyeballing the lower inscriptions, hand hovering perilously close to the surface of the stone despite my earlier interventions. "It took too much power, but the dwarves, the priests, they wouldn't stop. They . . . took more Quintessence in. They took it from everyone else. They drained us all dry, and then they died anyway."

And that neatly explains why dwarves no longer have magic. It is all in this big rock.

There was a tremor in her voice as her hand continued to drift perilously close to the surface of the stone. "Wouldn't everyone they drained have died too?"

Mhor.

That snapped her out of it, albeit briefly. "What?"

Rune two says "Mhor."

"The dwarves?" She was sounding increasingly exasperated with me, as if I were the one constantly interrupting her hard work. "Drained of their magic."

A shudder ran through her body as she remembered what it felt like. The bone-deep chill of having all the Quintessence in your body drained away. The absence of agony that you knew should have been there, but you couldn't even feel because without magic, you had nothing.

Oh yes, almost certainly, every dwarf that was capable of performing magic was likely drained to death to fuel whatever this working was meant to be. All that would have been leftover were your ancestors, the mutants born incapable of storing Quintessence.

Her mouth fell open. "Mutants?!"

That is the technical term, dear, there is no point getting grumpy with me about it. When there is a genetic deviation from the norm, that is mutation, but do not be so taken aback. Your ancestor's mutation allowed them to survive while the vast majority of your species was made extinct by a single deranged act of magic. I would thank my lucky stars for that mutation, were I you.

She stepped away from the menhir, backing off toward the shattered crystals all around us. "So . . . that's it. I can't learn magic. All the dwarves that could learn magic died . . ."

Oh, nonsense.

I cut her off before she could sink into another pit of emotional despair. They were becoming entirely too regular.

I am a wizard, you know. Give me a little time in a library and I'll have a spell puffing your atrophied little Quintessence stores back to full size and you'll be casting like a champion in a week or so.

This seemed to curb the worst of her pain, but she was still sullen and facing away from the big rock that I needed her to look at.

You've solved one of the greatest mysteries of dwarf-kind today. You'd think that you could draw some degree of satisfaction from that knowledge? We now know why dwarves don't have magic. We know the specific extinction event that removed magic from the gene pool. Not to mention discovering a physical substance that should allow every single dwarf in the world to cast again if they so pleased. From any perspective, this has been a tremendous victory.

A single tear trailed down her cheek into her beard. "My people . . . my ancestors . . . they all killed themselves for some spell, and you think this is good?"

I mean, historically speaking, there have been stupider reasons for self-destruction. I'd also argue that it is somewhat foolish to mourn their deaths when they all would have been long dead by now anyway, regardless of their actions that day.

She reached up and seized my brim, implicitly threatening to tear me off, again. She spun on the spot and through her watering eyes I could see the menhir once more. "How can you . . . all those people . . . all the dwarves in the world . . ."

As I said, they're history. We are not. And as such, I believe that our attention should be turned to the present, and future. Which is to say . . . oh. Goth.

"Goth?!" She let out an exasperated huff as I interrupted her and myself.

Nun. Mhor. Goth. The runes on the stone. Something to do with the spell, most certainly. But what does it mean?

"Nun Mhor Goth," Cygni repeated back to me, and the chamber all about us shook.

Until now there had been no sign of seismic disturbance, no hint of any instability, but the distant walls cracked and crumbled, the circle of crystals at the periphery of our vision shattered and fell, and most importantly, the stone that we stood before became heavier.

I do not mean heavier in the sense of weight, but rather in the sense that it had become more real than a moment before. Anything that magic works upon is divorced from reality to some degree so that the minor rewrites to the script of existence that we wizards craft can take hold. Yet as Cygni spoke the words of the runes aloud, they had reverberated with the stone. Name and stone were one and the same, and speaking the name was all that it took to draw both back closer to the real world they had been banished from, to some degree.

Let's not say that again for a little bit, shall we?

Her head snapped around as she searched for some source for the chaos that had just swept over us. "What in the nine hecks was that?"

Let's not find out, hmm?

"The whole cave . . . the whole world just shook." Her voice definitely did sound more feminine now. I wondered if the gruffness was an affectation for other dwarves, or if she'd been using it on me because I'd initially gone with conventional wisdom and called her *him*. "And all you've got to say for yourself is . . ."

Don't do it again. At least not until we know why it all shook?

She turned back to the rock. "The carvings don't tell us anything else. Just that all the magic went into this stone. And all the dwarves died."

What of the areas farther up?

Hoisting her lantern once more, she peered at the upper scritchings. "Looks like . . . the magic coming back out of the rock?"

So perhaps the situation was intentional? They planned to reserve their Quintessence here to be retrieved at a later date? I have heard tales of sickness that afflict users of magic through the ages. Restless Wand Syndrome. Dragonpox. Hodgkin's Lymphoma. Although that one mostly affects necromancers. Perhaps there was some plague that they were attempting to circumvent?

She shook her head. "Whatever happened, it must have been bad if this seemed better."

Or perhaps some enemy that could sense them with their magic? I imagine that the date of this menhir's creation was close to the outbreak of war with the elves. And elves are an inherently magical people.

Frustration bubbled up in her chest. "You'd think that if they were sealing it all away for later, they'd at least explain why."

There is nothing in the carving to shed any light on the . . .

"Nothing." She cut me off before I could even finish the thought. "There is no reason. Nothing but what they did and . . . those runes."

And so it fell to me once again to make sense of a senseless situation. The self-genocide of the magical dwarves, the menhir of power, the mysterious tongue spoken by nobody alive but probably very familiar to all those magical dwarves who decided it was better to die than leave this spell incomplete.

The runes are the reason. They are the explanation. They just didn't expect every-one who could read them to die.

"They bloody should have," Cygni snarled. "They killed them!"

To be fair to the ancient dwarvish shoemakers or whatever they were, I don't think they were expecting to not only die but to also wipe out everyone else in their casting caste. These were probably very simple and sensible precautions at the time. It is just the passing of eons that has robbed them of their utility.

"We need to get the magic back out."

I would not suggest it. The stasis spell is unlikely to come apart gently; we might experience some . . . turbulence if it were undone. The kind of turbulence that might, say, collapse this whole cavern?

"I don't care," she cried out in anguish.

Well, I do. I have no intention of spending the rest of eternity atop a broken thick-skull underneath a rockslide.

"You are a hat." I couldn't tell if she was mustering her courage or trying to control her anger; everything was so repressed in this dwarf that it was hard to keep track. "You'll do as you're told."

I can assure you that I will not. I will not assist you in undoing this spell until we have more thoroughly analyzed precisely what . . .

She slapped her hand against the side of the stone, smearing it with blood from her coin-severed finger, and before I even had a chance to react to that, she bellowed out, "NUN MHOR GOTH!"

I really wish she hadn't done that.

The whole chamber shook and rattled. The crystalline towers of pure con-densed magic that had served as pillars shattered apart and toppled like dominos, the few that had survived and remained upright after the initial concussive wave swept over the room soon floored by their toppling brethren. Distantly Cygni caught a glimpse of a way out, a tunnel at the far side of the chamber, but it was only a glimpse before a toppling pillar blocked it off from sight. Which was truly unfortunate, because had there been a way out, I might very well have seized control of her body and attempted to bolt.

Now the reason that I wish that she hadn't touched the menhir, smeared it with dwarvish blood, and bellowed whatever the runes meant out loud was that it provided three potential reasons for the spell to begin unraveling. If it had just been one, I might have understood the chain of cause and effects. Even two, I might have managed to parse through, but all three? There was no possible way of knowing which option had switched the deafening low tone of magic within the menhir to ascend to a shrill, nails-on-the-chalkboard kind of pitch that had her snatching her bloody mitt back and pressing her hands over her ears.

She had to yell to be heard over it, and honestly, if I'd been standing beside her rather than in her head, I still probably wouldn't have heard her cry, "What is that?!"

If only someone had analyzed the spell more, then I'd be able to tell you. Might I suggest running away very quickly?

She had at least enough self-preservation that she had begun to back away as the trilling screech of the menhir mounted louder and louder, setting all the Scrynium in the chamber vibrating in awful harmony. "Run?"

Run!

As fast as her little legs could carry her, Cygni did attempt to run away to the relative safety of literally anywhere else in the world, but her progress was somewhat hindered. The spell, which had until now been silently drawing in Quintessence to continue fueling itself—so much Quintessence that it had begun coalescing and crystalizing around it—had now kicked up into overdrive. All of the Quintessence in the room was being dragged toward the stone as it rose slowly off the little podium it had been set upon and floated up into the air, slowly turning just like the rocks back in Khnute's Crack.

Something that probably wouldn't have been so much of a problem if it weren't for the fact that: a) the Scrynium in her pocket was made of pure Quintessence, b) I was full of Quintessence, and c) she was full of Quintessence. Not to mention, d) all of the crystallized Quintessence all around us was being dragged in too, pulling the proverbial carpet of shards out from underfoot and dragging us back toward the rock.

To her credit, Cygni did not abandon the idea of running for her life; her feet still pistoned up and down with the same mechanical efficiency that she did everything and she was able to maintain her position in the room instead of being hauled back into whatever was happening in the rock right now. Of course, that meant we were still considerably closer than I would like to what I couldn't help but feel was going to be a massive implosion at any moment, but she was trying. Credit where it was due.

When the vast pillars of fallen Scrynium began lifting off the floor and floating toward us though, all bets were off. A massive lump of it that would have put masonry to shame came tumbling end over end toward us, Cygni threw up her hands as though she had strength enough to stop it, and the moment that it touched her bare skin, we abruptly had new options. I grabbed control of her vocal cords as the Quintessence surged into her uncontrollably and directed it.

"Saltus!"

Cygni might not have had helium in her mind as I spoke the word, but I was in her mind, and I was concentrating on it quite firmly. The Quintessence surged through her, through her mind, out through her throat, and the spell took hold.

She vanished. Not invisible, but transformed into something lighter than air, launched across the room before re-forming into her more solid state beyond the encroaching ring of shattering crystals all colliding with one another around the levitating menhir.

Cygni gasped for air as her lungs came back into being and staggered. With a little distance, the pull of the Quintessence well that was drawing everything in loosened, and with all the Scrynium dust already whipped away by the drawing, her feet found solid ground to press forward from. Step by agonizing step, she pulled us away from the maelstrom's maw.

"Don't do that again," she asked, very politely for someone who had been briefly atomized.

I don't plan to.

The massive pillar of Scrynium that had toppled to block our exit was still in place despite the menhir's sucking. As were many of the broken pillars that had toppled in the initial reality-quake. Less than ideal, since I'd flung us in that direction hoping that we might have continued our escape, or at least put some solid stone between us and the active implosion.

At this point, anything between us and that thing would be good news.

The awful, shrill grating noise stopped, which was nice, but the lingering silence that followed was almost worse. It was what I believe the bards would describe as a pregnant pause. An uncomfortable silence. A momentary void in sensory input.

The dragging force trying to pull us into the rock came to a halt too, so Cygni's attempts at running became much easier and much more successful. We fairly zipped across the cavern floor.

A loud *crack!* broke the silence.

CHAPTER TWELVE

CONCERNING THE MAKING OF AN OMELET

If wizards had rules, and we fundamentally do not, then the first of them would have been this. *Do not look back.* If you have been given the opportunity to run away from something cataclysmic that you may or may not have caused, keep on running.

Alas, I had not yet imparted that vital lesson to dear Cygni, so when she heard the crack, she stopped running and turned back to look.

This was an error in judgment.

The menhir had split lengthwise like a very professionally but incorrectly cracked egg. The stone was in the process of falling neatly apart in two opposite directions, and the contents, the ridiculous amounts of Quintessence that had been flung into the spell of stasis that should have been coming out in the kind of explosion usually only observed through telescopes in the younger regions of the night sky, should have been consuming us.

Yet, as the spell unraveled before our eyes, there was no catastrophic explosion, not even the traditional flash of blinding light. Quite the opposite, in fact. All of the Scrynium and Quintessence had been putting out a fairly healthy glow up until this point in proceedings, but now . . . now there was only darkness.

I do not speak of the kind of darkness that most people are accustomed to. The absence of light, the drawing of blinds and the snuffing of candles. This was an older darkness, the primeval, primordial darkness that may have retreated when creation came into being, but which has always lingered there just beyond our perception. We catch glimpses of it sometimes in places like this, deep beneath the surface of the world where the sun's warmth has never touched, but this true, deepest darkness that now unfolded before us is usually reserved only for the eyes of the dead. Or me, when I'm taken off somebody's head.

Cygni's guts churned at the sight of it, and I was thankful that she had not stopped to rest and eat as I'd often chided her to, as in all likelihood anything that she had consumed would now have been fleeing out of her body through every orifice at high speeds. It was only through the impressive discipline that ruled every part of her that we were able to sidestep the issue of running away in urine-soaked trousers.

Had I the physical capability to void my contents, I likely would have too. Perhaps there were some unforeseen benefits to being a hat after all.

I feel quite certain that Cygni was trying to speak in that moment, just as I was trying to corral my thoughts into something rational, but all that escaped her was a gentle grunt. An exhalation born not of terror, as you might have expected, but instead from a complete abandonment of all control over her bodily functions. Were I not here to keep things turning over, I suspect her heart would have stopped at the sight of the Thing before us.

At the center of all that spilling liquid darkness, there stood a figure. A silhouette, really. Darkness given form. It was as tall as a man at least, but you got the distinct impression that was only because of the angle that you were viewing it from, as though this were some optical illusion and the Thing itself was infinitely vaster than you could perceive, stretching off into dimensions unknown.

This Thing, this entity of unbridled darkness, moved like the flickering of shadows at the heart of darkness. The part at its top, which reason told me I should call its head, rotated, not toward us, but in a slow circle. With a crackling sound. The extensions at its sides that reason would have called its arms rose up and the farthest extremities of those arms, that in any other creature I would have called hands, flexed against the base of what I wanted to call its neck, but could not, because it would be applying human terms to something so very, very inhuman.

The Thing squeezed and undulated at the back of its own neck, then turned to face us. It had no face. Just darkness. A slice cut out of reality in the shape of a man. And from within that darkness came the voice.

"Man, I've got such a crick in my neck. Can't recommend sleeping inside a big rock for thousands of years." The Thing wrenched its head from side to side once more, releasing yet more of the same awful crackling noises. **"You know how it is, you think to yourself, I'll take a quick nap, and then when you wake up, it's eons later!"**

Cygni and I remained at a loss for words as the shadow Thing dusted what had to be imaginary fragments of stone off itself and descended from the podium. All the shadows in the room trailed after it like a bridal train. Every flicker of Cygni's torch set the shadows around it dancing, but never, not once, did any light penetrate to the dark heart of the Thing.

"Whew, tough crowd." The thing mimed wiping sweat from its brow, then pointed at Cygni with a snap of its fingers and sudden recognition. **"Hey! You're one of those dwarves, ain't you? I thought I smoked you all the last time around."**

That, finally, was enough to get Cygni's mouth moving again, even if she was just noiselessly mouthing obscenities.

"Yeah, I seem to remember you all trying to trap me in a rock forever or something. How'd that work out for you guys? Good? Did it turn out good? You still the biggest empire out there? Still rocking that world domination?"

It was as though the thing were trying to goad her into anger with the deaths of her kin. As if it had known that it was destroying them all, even as it was bound.

"Yeah, it doesn't take a genius to work out that you don't screw around with a god and live, you know? I mean, if I went easy on you, you'd all get ideas. Things would get totally out of control." The thing continued stretching, rolling nonexistent shoulders, and generally behaving as though it were rising from a long nap. Yet all of this must have been affectation. A creature of pure darkness would possess no muscles to warm up. In this, the thing was like a wizard.

While I am not entirely certain of what this creature is, I would not assume that its claims of godhood are genuine. There have been many . . .

The Thing cocked its head to the side and paused in its manipulation of its physical form. **"Hold on now, is there somebody else in here?"**

I remained silent and still as Ig had done when confronted by a wolf, just hoping that this predator might overlook me if I drew no attention to myself. He had also tried that with a large fish, a crow, and a particularly aggressive-looking shrub. There weren't many things that didn't prey on kobolds in this world. For the first time, I was confronted by something that felt like it preyed on wizards.

The Thing raised its head and sniffed at the air, despite having no nose or other facial features to speak of. **"Is that a little wizard in there! Hey, little wizard! What are you doing riding that dwarf around? Don't you know that's a good way to catch coal-crotch?"**

Cygni let out a disgusted noise but was still too overwrought to snap back at the Thing, leaving me to handle all of the conversational heavy lifting.

You can hear me? That makes things much more pleasant and easy. Greetings to you, I am Absalom Scryne, the greatest living wizard in the world. By my talents were you freed from your imprisonment. You are most welcome.

"Haha! The cojones on this guy! I mean, I get that you're a hat right now, so the big brass ones you should have dangling would probably look like jingle bells, but you should definitely still have them." It was making some sort of cradling gestures with its clawed hands for emphasis.

I'm afraid that I'm not familiar with the term . . .

"Balls. Buddy. You've got a pair like wrinkly boulders." Despite the lack of eyes, I felt distinctly as though it were winking at me. **"You tell a god to its face that it isn't a god, then you try to make it feel like it owes you a favor?"**

I apologize if I offended you, but it has been my experience that most people claiming to be deities are simply megalomaniacs getting carried away flexing their own limited power.

The Thing threw back its head and laughed. A callback to that lovely nails-on-chalkboard sound that we'd been so enjoying but moments ago. **"Well, I ain't most people. I'm darkness incarnate, baby."**

Much like my companion, I found myself at something of a loss for words in the face of this creature. As such, my repartee was perhaps a touch sharper than I had intended when I blurted out, *Yes, you do certainly seem quite . . . shady.*

"Haha!" Its laughter came in an awful roar, hitting Cygni like a cave-in and sending her staggering back as the Thing stalked closer. A liquid, languid gait that belied the bulk that it was gradually putting on. **"Again with the sass! Oh man, I should keep you around. Every king needs a jester, right? And what's a jester but a silly little man in a silly little hat. You can fill both jobs!"**

Rarely in my life have I been on the receiving end of such mockery, presumably because, up until this point, the immediate result of speaking to me in such a manner was a rain of comets directly upon said speaker's head. As that was not currently an option, I composed myself as best I could.

There is no need to be rude.

"Rude? You think this is rude? Last people that talked to me like you're talking? They don't even have words for what I did to them. There isn't even dust left that used to be them. There is nothing. They're nothing." As the rambling tale went on, its voice had become harsher and harsher, booming back and forth within the cave, until with that final "nothing" a tiny trickle of blood escaped from poor Cygni's ears. **"So maybe that's something to bear in mind the next time you're thinking of telling a god they ain't a god. Hmm?"**

Divinity seemed to be in short supply in our new acquaintance, but power was overabundant. Quintessence was the element of life, and no matter what else this thing was, it was not lacking in that vital component. Were magic light, it would have been blinding.

Forgive my impertinence, but I have yet to see any evidence of a deity here. For all that I know, you're simply some sort of . . . elemental.

"Darkness elemental! Nice guess. Swing and a miss though." The Thing sprang forward until it was almost within striking distance of Cygni, whose heels had caught on a toppled pillar as she tried to back away. **"Plus, I've got to tell you, trying to prove to a god that it isn't a god, not your smartest play."**

I suppose that if one were to prove to an actual god that they weren't real, then they'd cease to exist.

"Can't prove a negative," Cygni mumbled under her breath.

"Don't know how to break it to you, kid, but you couldn't prove an actual god isn't a god anyway. Because they are." The face of the Thing tilted down toward the face beneath my form, and I got the awful sense that it was smiling at her. Probably in what it considered a friendly way. As friendly as a shark smiling at a delicious baby seal. **"Anyway, who's the broad?"**

Once more I was flustered by the sudden change of direction, and after all that we'd been through together, I was feeling rather protective of my dwarven companion.

She is hardly wide enough for that to be her sole descriptor!

The thing, it had no eyes, no mouth, nothing of the sort, just like me. Yet even so, I could not help but feel that it just blinked.

"I'm Cygni Khnutesdottir," she announced before there could be any more nonsense. I hadn't realized the surname would change too. "Surveyor Second Class."

The Thing leaned in close enough that if it had breath, she would have felt it on her face. Her beard began to bristle with discomfort. **"Bet you wish you'd taken a few more classes before surveying me, hmm?"**

In a display of defiance, courage, or madness, Cygni looked away from the Thing and pointed to the shattered egg of stone from which it had hatched. "Don't know who you are, don't rightly care, but I know my ancestors put all their magic in that rock with you. I want it back."

Luckily for us, it seemed that the Thing appreciated her gall considerably more than I would have. It brayed with painful laughter once more. **"You really think I'm going to repay that favor? You think I wanted to nap for longer than it takes stars to die? Your folks, they really screwed me over, kid. And now, well, I ain't the vindictive type; I'm not going to go all vengeance and doom on the ones of you that are left, the past is the past, but I wouldn't go demanding any blessings from me either. You know?"**

It was a rare treat, being able to converse with someone without having to take over the vocal cords of someone else, and in any other circumstances I imagine that I would have been quite delighted about the situation. Unfortunately, these were the circumstances, and there was nothing that I would have liked more than to talk to Cygni in the privacy of her own head without anyone listening in. If only so I could scream at her to run repeatedly.

The magic was fueling the spell of stasis that kept this creature contained. With the spell broken, the Quintessence has returned to its usual inert state. There is no magic potion to be drunk or spell to be cast that will return the gift to dwarf-kind.

"Who's this creature you're talking about?" The thing was back in her face again, all its features concealed by the darkness it was composed of, yet still I got the sense of bared and sharpened teeth snapping shut mere inches from Cygni's face. **"I've got a name. Use it."**

"We introduced ourselves," Cygni sneered into that awful sense of sharpness. "You didn't."

The man-shaped shadow flung its arms out to the sides with theatrical flare. **"You know me, dwarf. I'm the deepest dark, the blackest night, and you know my name. You spoke it to call me forth. I'm Nun-Mhorgoth."**

The whole room shook and shuddered once more as the Thing spoke its name. There was some distant tinkling as the few crystals still standing upright toppled over. I imagine if we had been up on the surface, this quaking would have been replaced by a toll of thunder and a flash of lightning, but that was just supposition on my part.

I don't suppose that this is one of those "dark is not evil" situations, where you're literally just the god of darkness, as in the absence of light, and not some awful monster of evil and destruction too?

"What do you think?" I had the distinct sense of a smirk. **"Has anybody ever been that lucky?"**

Cygni's shoulders slumped. "We never have."

"Got it in one."

So to clarify, we have just unleashed some antediluvian horror from the dawn of time on the world?

I was sincerely hoping that this wasn't the case. I had more than enough to be getting on with, without the rise of some new dark lord that needed a solid spanking.

The unseen smirk became another jagged-toothed grin. **"Nailed it."**

For an instant it seemed that all our lives hung in the balance. Whatever was said next, whatever was done next, it would change the course of history. I tried to gather my thoughts, to compose a statement so powerful that it could turn the literal god of darkness and evil into an ally instead of an enemy. But while I was thinking, Cygni was already talking. "If it is so powerful and scary, how has it been stuck down here so long?"

She pissed it off. Of course she did. What else could she possibly have done other than make it angry. It only had enough power contained in one little finger to completely obliterate us, why wouldn't she say the most pointedly passive-aggressive thing possible.

For a brief instant I truly thought that it was going to just kill us then and there; the hate and rage radiating off it were enough to curl Cygni's eyebrows. But showing remarkable restraint in the face of her backchat, the dark god said, **"Funny story actually—not ha ha funny, more eh, weird funny. Anyways, I've been reaching into your dreams and calling you here your whole life, but all you dwarves, it's like you're tuned out or something. Only managed to get into your head just the other day, and I'm pretty sure that's thanks to bozo the clown hat."**

I was not fool enough to rise to the challenge either; it seemed that this game of provocation would go back and forth until someone succumbed. *There is really no need for childish name-calling.*

It didn't have eyes to roll, but Nun-Mhorgoth gave a distinct sense of eyes being rolled all the same. **"Anyways, I sometimes hooked a human or an elf up top, but getting them down here? Forget about it. Impossible. Can't dig to save their lives. And the dungeon monsters? Useless, the lot of them."**

It leaned in closer to Cygni, trying to make her uncomfortable with its lack of awareness of personal space. It was pretty effective, but despite her guts clenching up, she didn't take a step back. She stood her ground. I found myself obscenely proud of her. **"I needed one of you, one of the ones that trapped me here. And along you came strolling, just when I needed you. Ain't that lucky?"**

"This . . . this was the quickest way." Her brows had furrowed so completely this time that I could already feel a tension headache beginning to build. She was in denial, but I could not afford that luxury. I began tracking back through my own thoughts, looking for the malign influence of the Thing.

"Was it, though? Was it really? Some completely blank part of your map was the right way to go to get to the biggest human city in miles, where your little hive does all its trading?"

For the first time, Cygni showed a hint of weakness. A shiver ran through her as she questioned everything. "No . . . you didn't . . . I . . ."

The dark god giggled. **"Don't feel too bad about it, babe. I made wizard boy my brain-bitch too. Didn't I? Otherwise he'd have noticed that something wasn't right. What with him being so super smart and all."**

My mind is a fortress, protected against any and all intrusions. There has never been anyone who could get through my psychic shielding.

Rather than the giggle reserved for Cygni, I received what could only be called a guffaw. If there were a donkey comprised of pure evil, that was the sound it would make. Though anyone who has spent any time with donkeys will tell you that they aren't far off that 100 percent mark at the best of times. **"Buddy, your mind is a fortress made of felt and embroidery. You've got no spells to protect you, and if you even want to talk to the poor puppet under you, you've got to fling your gates wide open. I've met larvae with better defenses. And I'm not talking preternatural superbugs or anything, I mean the regular dirt kind."**

"I'm nobody's plaything." Cygni squared her shoulders, hands in fists at her sides. Something sharp bit into her palm, helping her maintain her focus, her rage, even as Nun-Mhorgoth's psychic intrusion washed over her. "Not the hat's. Not yours."

"Oh, that's cute. She still hasn't worked out how insignificant she is compared to us. Maybe you should just let the grown-ups do the talking for now, hmm?"

"Only got one more thing to say anyway." I realized that the shard of Scrynium she had retrieved earlier was what was in her hand, but it was far too late to stop her now. Not with her understanding of osmium already boiling to the surface of her mind.

The thing cocked its head to one side. **"Hmm?"**

She thrust out her empty hand and bellowed *"ALAPAM!"*

A perfect casting of Anaxian's Platinum Palm leapt from her own to blast Nun-Mhorgoth away from us, launching it back across the room with a sound somewhat similar to a whistling.

It was the kind of magical blow that would have killed most wizards on the spot, a direct, physical attack instead of the more elemental damage that we typically preferred. Yet there was no questioning that it was the right choice in this moment.

The Thing slid to a halt just a few feet away from the shattered menhir and clapped its hands with glee. **"Oh, I just knew you were going to be fun!"**

The shadows that had been trailing after it coiled in now, like the tendrils of some vast black anemone that had finally snared some prey. It seemed that gods didn't need to speak words of magic to use the Quintessence inside of them, but that was just fine by me. The less I had to hear of that Thing's insufferable voice, the happier I'd be. Besides it wasn't hard to work out what was being cast from the shimmers of dulled light within the shadows.

Fermium. You need to dodge the blast or you'll melt.

"Melt?!" Cygni yelped. She concentrated as best she could on oxygen with a mental image of her melting competing for headspace, and yelped out, "***Saltus!***"

It was not quite the same as when I'd effortlessly transported us across the room, but it was more or less effective. She exploded apart into thin air then re-formed behind Nun-Mhorgoth as it unleashed a wave of destructive power that tore the side of the cavern where we'd been standing a moment before apart.

Once more the crystals shattered and dust and fragments filled the air, glowing faintly with the radioactive aftermath of the fermium blast.

Unfortunately, this had played right into the dark not-yet-proven-to-be-a-god's hands. It was already twisting around, unleashing those coils of shadow toward us. Cygni fended one off with the gradually depleting crystal in her hand, letting the pure Quintessence surge out and startling that particular whip of shadow back, but the other struck home. Plunging not into her, as I would have assumed that the murderous monster intended, but rather, into me.

For an instant the world vanished into the endless oblivion of senselessness, then I saw it all through the Thing's eyes.

The Thing saw the world the way that I did in my dreams, in the palace of my mind. Every flow of Quintessence visible, every physical structure just a mixture of the various elements and forces at work. All of the invisible world that I had thought only I could truly understand was known to this creature, known instinctually, where I had spent a lifetime learning to superimpose it over my flawed human vision.

I could see my own physical form, the hat, wrapped in decades of enchantments and absorbed Quintessence, with just the tiniest spark of sentience within it like the Thing could sense in Cygni. I was dangling from the tentacular extrusion and being wheeled back closer to the possibly-a-god and out of Cygni's reach. Though to be fair, if I'd been placed on a high shelf, I would have been out of a dwarf's reach too. So it didn't take much to outstretch her grasping hand.

And just like that, we're done. The greatest living wizard? I thought you'd have put up a fight at least. That was just sad.

It was in my mind. Probing tentacles of darkness pushing into my memories, my thoughts, taking everything that I had ever been and siphoning it away.

Thanks for getting me up to speed on current events; it would have taken ages to find someone as well-informed as you to drain up on the surface, and until then I'd have been blundering around killing all the little pointless people willy-nilly instead of the little important people that I really need gone if I'm going to take over again.

It hurt. I have suffered in my life. I have experienced death, thanks to my brief sojourn atop the lizardman earlier in the dungeon, but nothing could have prepared me for these agonies.

You cannot . . . do this . . . to me . . .

Sorry, does it hurt when I suck right there? What was that, your childhood? Yeesh, no wonder you're such a stuck-up prig. Don't worry about it. All gone now.

Everything that I am. Everything that I was. Nun-Mhorgoth was taking from me. I couldn't let it. I had to remember.

I am . . . Absalom Scryne, the greatest wizard . . .

You're a snack. Not even a filling one. I'm probably going to have to eat your mule just so I don't get hungry again before I break the surface. Not that there will be anything worth eating in that pinhead of hers that you didn't put there.

There was a spark of anger in me when I heard those words, but it wasn't attached to anything real. I didn't know why I was angry. All I knew was pain. I had to resist, but that hurt even more.

I . . . am . . .

The awful laughter returned. The scraping on the chalkboard on the inside of my skull. Except I had no skull. I had no body. All I had was a mind, and that . . . that was fading.

You're the little fish in the big pond now, baby. Welcome to the big leagues.

Then even the pain was ripped away from me and all I knew was darkness.

CHAPTER THIRTEEN

NEXT TO GODLINESS

And so ends my tale. I was once a wizard, then a hat, and now nothing at all. Entirely destroyed by the unexpected assault of a creature that I could not possibly have predicted that I might encounter in a place that I was never supposed to be. As far as endings go, I realize that it feels like something of an anticlimax, but that's life for you. I'd never see Ig again. Never learn who killed me when I was a mortal being. Never see the shining towers of Arpanpholigon again. It was all over.

Except . . . I was still aware of the nothingness. I was still sentient enough to recognize that there was darkness all around me. I could still remember . . . most of my life, if I went prodding a little. Not all of it. Not by a long shot. But then again, when I wasn't on someone's head, using their brain to process my thoughts, I had little access to my memories either.

I wasn't dead. I should have been dead. I most assuredly should have been dead after what was done to me, but still I lingered. That meant something. Surely that meant something. How could I be thinking if I was dead? How could I be having the very thoughts that you are currently reading, if I had nothing left to think with? Was this some awful lingering aftereffect of whatever had transferred my consciousness into my hat when I died? Was I incapable of passing on, even now?!

Then Cygni put me back on her head.

Memories came rushing back in, the last few moments played out from her perspective rather than my own rather limited one. She had watched as the tentacle punched me off her head and grabbed me. She had seen me suffering and writhing as much as a hat can as I was reeled back in toward the Thing of shadows.

Reaching into the pouch on her belt, she had deposited the Scrynium crystal, scooped out the pair of jumping rings, and shoved them onto her fingers despite them clearly having been made for considerably more delicate hands. I could feel the sting and pinch of them as they went on, then the sudden rush of weightlessness as first one then the other took effect.

She had leapt from where she stood, both hands now empty, lunging through the open air of the cavern to intercept me as I was dragged off, smoking from the seams, to my doom. And then she'd caught me.

The following moments were a confusing blur of motion, as she bounded and rebounded off the toppled crystal pillars, always staying just ahead of Nun-Mhorgoth's slapping tendrils and spells. Outpacing the incredible speed and power of a creature that I was now willing to concede may have actually been a dark god of some sort, to finally come to a halt here by the distant blocked exit of the chamber just long enough to tuck me back on top of her head.

Thank you.

"You'd do the same for me." She managed a smile, despite it all, and had I a body of my own, I feel quite certain I could have kissed her then and there, beard or not.

We have to escape. There is no way to face this beast head-on.

"Agreed," she replied, back to her usual curt self. Then she turned from the approaching dark tide to look at the crystal pillar laid across our path. She snatched the bag of holding from her belt and a painful rictus of a grin spread across her face. "Hope this works."

"Give me back that hat without any more hopping and I'll let you keep your torso and head." Nun-Mhorgoth's voice washed over Cygni, bringing fresh trickles of blood from her ears, but she paid it no mind. Bending her knees and then leaping into the air.

I had not the faintest idea of what she was hoping to achieve with this. She jumped so high that she soared right up and over the pillar blocking our way, but it would be to no avail. There was no route of ingress from above, just a different angle to look at the pillar from.

She yanked the bag of holding wide open as she began to fall, and I realized only in the final moment of our descent what it was precisely that she was playing at.

The opening of the bag was wide, but not wider than the pillar. When it came down on top of the crystallized Quintessence, we hung there for a long and ungainly moment, swinging back and forth, before a little tear in the seam of the bag opened it out a fraction of an inch more and it began to slide down the smooth crystal's surface, swallowing it whole.

Had the pillar been upright, this likely would have been a near-instant journey back to the ground, but thanks to the angle it had settled at, we instead slid slowly down the length of it, drifting to the side as we went until the entire massive lump of Scrynium had been consumed.

In any other circumstance, this would have been absolutely fine and perfect, providing us with a soft landing. Cygni gave the bag a little twist when we got to the bottom and the pillar that had once been a massive impediment no longer even had any weight as she tucked the bag back onto her belt. But in the current circumstances, the slow slide down to the bottom of the pillar had bought Nun-Mhorgoth all the time it needed to cross the room. **"Clever trick with the baggage, but it won't save you."**

The cloak of shadows all around the maybe-god swirled and then lunged out toward her, sharp-clawed tendrils ready to hook into her flesh and wear her the same way that they'd worn me. Except bloodier, obviously.

Cygni brought the other bag of holding up as I internally screamed and then she ripped off the drawstring holding it closed.

Inside of that bag, there was an ocean. I'd thought lake before, but no, that was definitely saltwater exploding out of the mouth of the bag with all the force of a high-pressure hose.

If Nun-Mhorgoth had been an actual shadow, then the water would have passed right through the center of its mass, but luckily for us, it was solid.

The shadow Thing was taken in the guts by the stream, blasted back across the room to smash back into its broken menhir with what would have been an awful crack if you could hear anything over the sound of roaring water.

Physics took hold and launched Cygni backwards with almost as much force as the expulsion of water that had struck the Thing. She was lifted off her feet, shot across the chamber and right out through the doorway she'd just opened. She hit the far wall hard enough to black out, even though her skull was thick enough to make short work of most walnuts with a headbutt. And then I was in control of her body, puppeteering it awfully, like a marionette with half its strings cut.

The bag continued its violent expulsion, vomiting out so much seawater that when a dolphin went flying by, I didn't give it a second thought. The force of the spray was such that the bag had pinned itself to the wall, and while it might have been handy to retrieve it and use this trick again someday, I didn't have enough control over Cygni's unconscious body to make her hands do what I wanted.

Water lapped up around her ankles as the flood got worse and worse. We needed to move, or we'd be drowned as surely as the Thing from the stone.

I dragged one of her legs along, then the other. I remembered that I had to make her breathe halfway through the next step and huffed in some air quick so that she didn't keel over dead from that. Her arms dangled limp at her sides, her upper body flopping back and forth, as I forgot that you had to tighten the muscles there to stay upright. It was amazing just how much bodies took care of themselves without our conscious effort. When I finally got a body of my own again, I would not take it for granted. I might even do some exercise or something. Well, probably not, but I'd certainly eat better. Well, probably not that either, but I'd definitely complain less about my various aches and pains. Well, probably not that either, but for the first day or so, that new body would be treated like a temple.

We'd made it a few feet along the tunnel under my firm but fair guidance before I banged Cygni's head off the wall and almost dislodged myself. The sharp pain of it was enough to stir her from her slumber. "What?"

Oh, thank goodness. I have no idea how to steer this thing. We need to keep moving, this place is flooding fast.

"The bag worked?" She was still dazed but at least her legs were still moving, and I hadn't broken anything important while she was gone.

It was a truly inspired idea. You are a most capable mage, well on the way to the title of wizard, in my humble opinion.

That managed to shake a laugh out of her. "Humble?"

An opinion can be humble while the originator of said opinion holds himself in high esteem.

That was unpleasant. I came dangerously close to self-deprecation for a moment there. It was time to correct course. *Using oxygen as the catalyst for your teleportation was inefficient; I showed you the correct element to invoke only a moment before.*

"Bite me." She chuckled. "It worked, didn't it?"

I will not deny that it was effective, just inefficient by comparison.

"You're welcome."

The water around her ankles was continuing to rise, as was her anxiety. I would have thought that the vast cathedral of a cavern that we had just departed would have had plenty of space for the water to spread out before heading our way, but I suppose that given the potentially infinite amount of water inside the bag of holding, I should have realized it was going to present problems sooner rather than later.

We may need to pick up the pace somewhat, what with the rising tide and all.

"Going fast as I can," she grumbled.

We seemed to be moving markedly faster when you were leaping around earlier.

It was nice to get back into our usual eye-rolling routine. "I'll jump right into the tunnel roof, will I?"

It was admittedly somewhat lower than the high ceilings of the chamber before, but she couldn't touch it without standing on her tiptoes, so it wasn't exactly scraping my tip. Still, she was taking my suggestion and trying to make little bounding jumps as we went. It wasn't terribly effective thanks to her sodden boots and the water working against us, but at least we were moving somewhat quicker.

The water was up to her knees and there was still no end of the tunnel in sight. Even if there had been, we would have had to resort to swimming before much longer, and the moment that this newly created underwater sea came into contact with any of the other bodies of water down here, all bets were off regarding our survival. The land-based predators of the dungeon ecosystem, we could contend with, but the bizarre and monstrous things that dwelled below the glassy surface of the subterranean seas were an entirely different kettle of giant, blind, murderous fish.

The wand of water-walking might assist us.

She scoffed. "How?"

We could traverse over the top of the water rather than wading through it.

"And crawl?"

Perhaps when the roof rises somewhat.

Cygni's mounting fear of the rising waters had eroded her goodwill over her successes faster than even I had expected. She was afraid, and rather than feeling afraid, she was channeling that fear into anger. Frustration, really. After everything that she'd been through, drowning in a hole in the ground didn't feel fair.

There was also a lot of subsurface internal argument going on. She was trying to work out if she had abandoned her principles and her post in the dwarven mine of her own volition or if it had been the work of Nun-Mhorgoth probing at her mind. She was trying to work out how much of what she knew of herself was true, and how much of it was planted there by this . . . Thing.

The water was now lapping around her waist, and she had to pluck the other bag of holding from her belt or risk it being filled with water in turn. The pick that she had proudly borne since we first departed the dwarven tunnels had been lost somewhere in the turmoil of fighting and magic and her empty hand flexed now, wishing for it. Wishing she could be doing violence as a way to ignore what I was saying and she was thinking.

You may not be able to trust the contents of your mind, but you can trust in the structure.

There was a proper snarl on her face when she snapped back. "What's that meant to mean?"

Your memories may have been tampered with, your impulses adjusted—it is possible that both of our minds have been toyed with—but that does not change who you are.

"It changes everything." I think I preferred it when she sounded furious to when she sounded so utterly defeated. She moved faster when she was mad.

You cannot trust the things that are in your mind, but your mind itself remains intact, the structures it has formed in. You are a methodical and logical person with an incredible memory and an incredible ambition. These things could not be changed, and they are things that would have driven you to take the actions you took, even without interference.

"What are you saying?" she snapped, a little anger creeping back in. Energizing her plodding. "It doesn't matter somebody was poking around my brain?"

However powerful your oppressor may have been, you could not have been compelled to act against your fundamental nature, and as I see it, you have done nothing wrong.

A bitter laugh escaped her lips. "We freed a monster my people committed mass suicide to stop. We might have flooded out the whole of Khnute's Crack. I . . . I left home. Ignored my orders. Betrayed my king. You're telling me I did nothing wrong? When that thing finds a way around the sea we dropped on it, how many people are going to die? How much damage is it going to do?"

This was why I had been quite insistent on veering toward a more conservative approach to the unknown. My suggestion had been to navigate around the problem area. My suggestion had been to leave the menhir untouched and to speak no more the dark name inscribed upon it. My suggestions had been thoroughly ignored, and now something truly evil was loose in the world through no fault of mine. If there had ever been a better time for somebody to say "I told you so" then I could not conceive of it. Yet . . . Cygni had saved me. Over and over again, she had put herself in harm's way so that I might be spared, and time and again, I had repaid her very poorly in my treatment of her. Had I the lungs to take a deep breath before I spoke, I would have, but that luxury was denied to me.

If it had not been you, it would have been someone else. Nun-Mhorgoth had been waiting for an opportunity and would have continued to wait for all eternity. It is . . . unfortunate that you were compelled to free it, but I do not hold you responsible.

"I hold me responsible." It came out in a rather snotty sob. "I did it. I . . . chose to do it. I freed that . . . thing."

You believed that it would return your people to their former glory. It was an understandable choice.

"And now the world is going to pay for it." Anguish was back in her voice, and I wondered how much of the water on her face had splashed up, and how much was originating from her eyes.

Of course not, some hero will come along and kill that thing before it does more than conquer a few villages. That's what heroes are for. They're like the antibodies of the world, protecting against infection.

I spoke of the matter lightly, as though Nun-Mhorgoth's raw power had not also left me petrified. I'd hoped that my blasé tone might have helped, but it only encouraged her to question more. "You know any heroes that can beat that thing?"

Throughout my life, I had known no heroes. I had read about their great feats in books of legends, I had heard tales through the grapevine about the incredible victories that they had won and the awful costs that they had paid, and I had decided very young that I was never going to number among them because I had entirely too much sense. There had only been two people to cross my path since my unfortunate hat-ification that might have qualified for the title of hero, and unfortunately both of them had done the same thing that heroes always do in the real world. They had died. Wyn and Rhinolyta were dead and gone, their memories an ache in my mind that I kept probing at like a cavity in a tooth that I just couldn't resist shoving my tongue into.

As such, it was difficult to come back to Cygni with something appropriately lighthearted.

None immediately spring to mind.

"And now we're going to drown." The water had made its way up to her chest by this point and a sea turtle was bumping into the back of her thighs insistently as if it was in a hurry to get past her.

We are not going to drown.

She scoffed. Or possibly just coughed when a wave rebounded off the wall to hit her in the face. "You know how to breathe underwater?"

I do, as a matter of fact, but I was thinking of a rather more complete solution to our current situation.

It took her a moment to realize that I was not making a joke. That was the problem with people who were not wizards, they kept on thinking in terms of what was possible instead of recognizing that through magic there was no limit to the possibilities. "What?"

While you have been wallowing in self-pity and, uh, water, I have been composing a spell. All that you need do is extract that shard of Scrynium and follow my instructions perfectly. You have been thinking like a dwarf instead of a wizard, I have not.

"You can make us . . ."

Oh no, I have no intention of transforming you into a fish so you can learn a valuable lesson or any nonsense like that. I was thinking of something rather more . . . direct.

She continued sloshing on forward, finally sidestepping enough for the turtle to swim by, as I laid out my plan, culminating in her finally asking, "Is that . . . can we do that?"

When I had a physical body, I often treated it as an impediment. A disability that my mind, which was the real "me," had to deal with. I slept because my body demanded it. I ate because my body demanded it. I washed because my body smelled without doing so, but otherwise I wanted as little as possible to do with my body. But in that moment, deprived of my body, I felt for the first time a serious stirring of desire for flesh once more. I wished that I had a body, just for that moment, so that she could see my smile. It would have unnerved her.

Oh yes.

I recited the words of Archaic in her mind, worked her through the order in which the elements needed to be drawn up as catalyst. Her memory was not eidetic, but it was so close that I was somewhat amazed at how easily she managed to recite the full list of both things back to me. Of course, remembering a list was considerably easier than trying to remember the full string of words, and elements, and maintain focus on each of them at the appropriate times. At least I didn't have to concern myself with her overdrawing on her Quintessence thanks to the lump of Scrynium serving as a battery. Maintaining a steady flow of Quintessence as a longer spell unfolded was the downfall of many an unprepared apprentice, so I was pleased to have that particular problem eliminated.

Cygni's whole beard was underwater, and the salt spray was slapping against her face by the time that I was convinced of her ability to successfully cast the spell, by which point her anxiety had mounted to such a level as would have made Ig envious.

Are you ready?

She reached her hand into the bag held overhead and nodded, splashing her face with water all over again before gasping in a desperate lungful of salty air.

Then begin.

"Perfodi usque ad superficiem et deduces me ex hoc pulmentum humidum."

Every word was perfect, the cycle of elements in her forebrain was perfect— the power flowed through her from the solid Quintessence pressed against her palm and took form.

I didn't tell her what the spell would do. Perhaps I should have, but in the moment it seemed like a waste of the precious moments she had to learn the magic, and, of course, if she had known what I intended, then she might very well have argued. We did not have the time for arguments; we did not have the time for anything at all.

All of which was to say that when the Archaic ripped the Quintessence out of her mouth, she had no idea that it was about to burst into flames, nor that those flames would instantly gulp down all the air in the area, turning from orange to blue and through to invisible as their heat increased and they rose. That was a helpful fundamental of the natural world. Heat did rise. That was particularly lucky for us, as if the flames she had conjured fell then we would have been reduced to a pile of ash and barbecue in record time. Actually, perhaps the closeness of all the water would have poached the dwarf instead, who is to say. Regardless, the fire went up.

First as a widespread spilling along the narrow tunnel roof, then swirling into the proscribed spiral, turning inwards and upwards into a point, a wedge, driving up into the stone above us and superheating it to melting point. This was why the conical structure of the blaze was necessary: if it had been but a pillar of flame, all of the superheated rock losing its grip on the stones around it as its bonds were broken by the impossible heat would have come right down on top of us. Instead, using the spinning top, the lava sloughed down and out, the centrifuge of force at work in the rising fire cone flicking it away from the central point where we stood and all around us instead.

As the heat rose, so too did the roof. It shot straight up through strata of stone that had been there since time immemorial, likely completely obliterating the archaeological value of everything between here and the sky. In that moment, as Cygni gasped for air in the temporary vacuum, I could not bring myself to care.

The panic within her was rising once more, but it was with good reason that I had not warned her what was about to transpire. If she had tried to hold back enough breath to carry her through this phase of the plan then the spell would not have cast.

It hurt to feel her lungs burning so, but it was necessary, and I have never been one to shy away from taking the painful option if it is also the best one. That is practically the definition of wisdom. Of course, it is definitely easier to choose the path of pain when someone else is going to have to walk it for you.

With the flaming drill rising above us, one might have thought that it was just a matter of watching and waiting for freedom, but alas, the world around a spell did not cease the instant it was cast, and now the water about us began to boil with the backwash of warmth, and the encircling lava fall trapped us in here with it. At first it was only a cloud, but as the lava touched down, the gentle hiss of rising vapors became a roar, and her vision was stolen from her by the stinging fog.

Endure, my friend. This too shall pass.

She couldn't answer without air, and breathing in steam was not a better option than trying to inhale the vacuum earlier, so I enjoyed blissful quiet as the gathered steam was seized by the next part of the spell and gathered beneath Cygni in one dense cloud. When she could, abruptly, breathe again, it took her only one ragged gasp before she roared at me.

"Why didn't you warn me?!"

Which probably would have been quite dramatic were it not for all the hydrogen being sapped out of the water in the freshly made air causing her voice to rise a fair few octaves. She was less bellowing like an angry dwarf, and more tinkling like one of those fairies her companion miners kept in lanterns.

No time, I lied.

And then the hydrogen was also consumed by the rising flames, ripping the air away from us again abruptly.

The sudden destruction of the hydrogen created a small explosion, forcing us and all the remaining gases downwards, but then there was that wonderful vacuum being created again. The lava had formed a solid shell around us and this hollowed pillar, so there was no way for the consuming flames to draw in any more gases from outside, which left only the option of devouring everything in here with us. That in turn drew the little cloud that Cygni was standing on upwards with the kind of velocity one usually associated with a crossbow bolt being fired.

She yelped as best she could without air, apparently unaware that the cloud around her ankles had solidified to hold on to her, despite how biting the cold must have been even through her substantial hobnail boots. And then we were off, flying straight up to the swirling maelstrom of fire overhead.

The initial yelp I could have forgiven, but her ongoing squeal was downright annoying. Even if she wasn't able to vocalize it, I could hear it echoing in her head. By now she surely had worked out what we were doing. Yet still she flailed and struggled, kicking at the cloud that was carrying her up and out of this cesspit of a cave complex as though a good nudge might make it let her go.

The flailing about shouldn't technically have caused that much of a problem. It wasn't as though anyone, even a stoutly built dwarf, had the strength to break through one of my spells with muscle power. Except, unfortunately for us, I had forgotten in my haste that Cygni still had not one, but two rings of jumping rammed onto her fingers.

When she tried to leap free of the cloud carrying her up the shaft, she kicked off with all the power of a kangaroo that had recently been introduced to a branding iron to its nether regions. If the cloud had been carrying her up to the flames with all the haste of a crossbow bolt, now she moved like a lightning bolt instead. So fast that even her own eyes could not perceive the motion, which I suppose means that she was moving faster than nerve impulses, which is pretty fast, I must say.

Which presented a problem. I had carefully constructed the spell so that the fire would rise, clearing out all of the stone above us, and then the cloud would carry us up in the wake, allowing immediate departure from the dungeon, and piggybacking the spell of flight on the initial spell that was going to be quite potent, and likely shed a lot of excess Quintessence. As the hydrogen produced by the dissolution of the water we had been drowning in rose to be consumed by our conjured flames, so too would the steam. I had constructed the spell so that we would be carried up just below the level of the fires, just in case there were any catastrophic collapses or the like later on, blocking our exit route before we had the opportunity to use it.

By leaping like this, with her magically enhanced hopping abilities, Cygni had now accelerated herself, and more importantly me, to a rate that meant we would overtake the fire. With the correct protections in place, this would have resulted in us cracking our heads off the as-yet-unmelted stone above, but of course, we had none of the correct protections in place, as I had not a moment to spare in the construction of our escape plan for the careful laying out of a safety net. There would be no flattening for me and concussion for Cygni; instead we would rise into the white-hot flames still soaring up to the surface and we would die most horribly. Sizzled to a crisp by our own arcane working.

A little embarrassing as deaths go, but not an unexpected end to my career. And of course, there was no possibility of avoiding it. Not at the speed she was moving. Her velocity would have her in the flames before a rational thought could pass through her mind, and she certainly didn't have the time to cast.

I have never believed in instinct. When some part of me tried to make me act in an irrational manner, I had quashed it. Yet here and now, moving faster than even my own thoughts, came the flow of Quintessence through me. My paltry reserves, the only thing that kept me alive and whole, were flung down. I did it, but I never thought of doing it. I never thought of unleashing the full weight of my massively diminished strength into low magic, to push against Cygni enough that her ascent was slowed.

The loss of all my magic was the end of me. Magic was all that I really was at this point. It would, kill me, but she might live, and for some reason that treacherous bastard of an instinct had wanted it that way.

In the same moment that I was experiencing my own instinctual impulse, so too was Cygni, reaching up against the wind whipping by to seize me by the rim, and then flinging me down so that I might survive at the expense of her life. Noble and heroic, while my actions had been brash and foolish.

I fell away from her grasp and down into the darkness in the same second that my magic caught hold of Cygni and pushed her down toward the cloud that would catch her. Together but separate, falling while still being carried up, we parted ways.

Without senses, I would never know if she survived or not, but at least I had the comfort of eternal oblivion to dwell on it in.

CHAPTER FOURTEEN

THE ROAD GOES EVER ON

Oblivion and death are two different things, I suppose. Death has a finality to it while oblivion stretches out for eternity. To my knowledge, no time really passed when I was not atop someone's head, but it could have been months, decades, or millennia between Cygni throwing me off to try and save me, and the next living hand to touch me.

I felt it, the tingle of sensory feedback filtering through that brush of skin. My fabric did not feel how it should. There were holes, here and there, tiny little ember burns, and the smooth silk inside me was twisted and puckered in places where fire had licked at it.

Life and awareness returned to me, ever so slowly. The sensation of smooth, warm skin beneath my headband. The gentle cool breeze blowing over me, through the little holes that had been punched in my surface by the sparks that had rained back down on me. At last, my new carrier opened her eyes and I knew where we were.

The stars shone down on us from above.

We got out.

Cygni had never seen stars before, but she had felt my memories of them. In the abstract, she had understood precisely what she was going to see when the clouds parted, but that was not the same as actually experiencing it. She let out a gentle sigh that soon turned into a soot-riddled cough. "We got out."

Turning around slowly and carefully, Cygni showed me the pit that I had made, the circle of blackened trees and shrubs that our spell had surged up and scorched to charcoal.

Looking for some landmark to guide her, Cygni stared out into the night, but there was nothing immediately apparent, at least to her. After all, she'd spent her whole life underground. Everything up here was unfamiliar, and she kept on going weak at the knees if she looked up for too long, as though afraid gravity might lose its grip and she'd go floating off into the nothingness above.

As for me, I cannot tell you what a relief it was to be free of the underworld. The endless total darkness felt like an all-too-familiar companion by now; the crushing weight of the stone above us had begun to be a comfort instead of a font of dread. I had spent enough time atop a dwarf that their dwarvish ways of thinking had begun to infect me.

Beyond the destruction that we had wrought upon this otherwise quiet place, I could distantly make out the glow and smoke of a little hamlet, some assorted forestry, and the telltale ridge of one of the kingsroads that crisscrossed the region.

Following along that would have us in Arpanpholigon in no time at all. They weren't enchanted, and they didn't have carriage services running along them day and night, but they did have one distinct advantage over the Badlands. They were flat. A smooth expanse of brickwork leading all the way back to home sweet home. Even Cygni and her stumpy legs would make short work of the miles we still had to travel if there were no interruptions. Finally, I was going to be back where I belong.

I can't believe we made it . . . and in mostly one piece.

Cygni made a noncommittal sound as I thought that, which I did not trust in the least. I'll admit that after being propelled out of the earth like a cannonball from its usual receptacle, most people would show some degree of reticence, but this was something different. Something . . . sinister.

We did make it out in one piece, didn't we? I know I'm a little singed, but surely that's as far as the damage goes.

Another sound, like a grunt, grumble, or huff. Neither confirming nor denying. It would have set my teeth on edge, had I teeth, but as it stood, it instead merely made me tremble with the sense of impending doom that can only precede extremely bad news.

Find a mirror, a pool, something reflective. I need to see how bad it is.

"It's bad," she whispered, her voice cracking. I could not tell if it was smoke inhalation or good old-fashioned trauma making her speak so, but neither was particularly good news.

Let me see for myself and judge.

I felt a shudder run through her, a sudden chill. The weather underground was consistent, if not pleasant—the temperature rarely changed unless you did something like melt a huge shaft up to the surface with magic. As such, poor Cygni was not accustomed to such things as breezes. "Not . . . survivable."

Nonsense, I feel fine.

With a heavy sigh, she began digging through her pocket pouches, flinching every time the wind brushed by, until eventually she retrieved what she was looking for: a mirror on an extendable stick, presumably used to look around corners in the mine. She took hold of it by the handle, took a deep breath, and then hoisted it up so she could see herself.

There I was in all of my glory, perched atop her head. There were several distinct scorch marks interrupting my exquisite embroidery and more than a few holes punched through where an ember had settled, but despite the damage, it seemed to me that my structural integrity had not been compromised, and nor had my mind. Though I suppose that if I had lost a bit of my mind, I might not have been immediately aware of its absence, due to lacking the bit of mind that remembered what bits of mind I had. Regardless, I suspected that Cygni was grossly overstating my state of disrepair, presumably that perfectionist streak coming through.

Then, as the mirror panned down, I realized my mistake.

She was not talking about me. I was in more or less shipshape. She was not.

As she had been flung upwards, I had managed to slow her ascent, but not completely. Instead of there being a healthy buffer of vacuum between her rising cloud platform and the inferno overhead, she had been thrown not into the flames, but into reach of the heat that the fire left behind. Here and there on her face, I could see the resultant burns. Little patches on her forehead and chin that were red and raw. The overall tone was somewhat more similar to a tomato than not. Mostly akin to a long day out in the sunshine rather than the brush with death that she had experienced.

In the first moment I did not recognize her, then I looked into her eyes and knew it was the same Cygni as had been carrying me forward all along. There was no mistaking her eyes.

The more observant among you may have noticed that I commented extensively upon her face and chin right then, and that was a subtle hint as to the major transformation that her brush with flaming death had catalyzed. The luscious beard that had defined her features, along with the bushy eyebrows that had looked so like caterpillars, were gone.

She had rosy apple cheeks and a little cleft in her chin, and dimples. She was, to put it in no uncertain terms, adorable. If a little lightly roasted.

It is certainly . . . a dramatic change.

"I'm dead," she whispered in her harsh and broken voice.

Let me be the first to assure you that you are in fact very much alive. Is this some sort of cultural thing? Do dwarves only get a shave when they have expired? Or is it like an excommunication thing, where you're no longer considered a dwarf without the beard?

"First patch of bad air we hit, I'm done for. You need to find somebody else to ride; I'm finished."

She had the expression of one expecting her immediate death, and it took me longer than it should have to realize that this was not an elaborate joke.

We don't have that here.

She blinked. "You what?"

Bad air is pretty much exclusively an underground sort of problem. All the air up here, it is good. Or at least there is sufficient ventilation that the bad air is diluted before it can do much in the way of harm. You never wondered why so many humans, elves, and miscellaneous other creatures managed to survive without beards?

"Thought they couldn't grow them." She shifted uncomfortably. "Felt bad for them."

I mean, women can't grow them, generally. Or elves. But as to humans, on the surface, beards are typically an aesthetic affectation rather than a survival necessity.

"So you all just grow them for . . . fun?"

Some of us grow them to convey our majesty, others because they are simply too lazy to shave. I have always been firmly in the former camp, of course.

"Why would you have one if you don't need it? They're itchy and food gets stuck in them and . . ."

Perhaps we can focus on more pressing matters now that your impending death is no longer our primary concern.

She snapped the extending rod of the mirror shut again and set about returning it to her pocket. "Can you fix this?"

The actual regrowth will occur with time and I'm loath to interfere lest you end up with double the correct amount or worse. Bodily manipulation can be tricky, even with your talents and my knowledge at our disposal. There is a chance that you might be permanently altered in a manner we do not desire.

She let out a huffing sound.

I could apply an illusion of a beard and eyebrows if you wish, but it seems a squanderous use of our limited Scrynium supplies.

"I've got half a ton of Cygnite in my bag." She put extra emphasis on her nonsense made-up name for Scrynium.

Which I've no doubt will come in very handy.

"Right, fine," she grumbled. "Whatever."

Would you be so kind as to look up.

Before she could think of a reason to say no, her eyes darted to the heavens of their own accord. Her knees buckled at the sight of the open skies above her and her first impulse was to throw herself down and grab on to the ground, but in the moment that I had before she dragged her eyes back to the earth beneath her feet I saw the stars.

"Why did I have to do that?" she hissed between chattering teeth.

So that I could see where we were.

"We're here."

If you'd be so kind as to head toward that ridge over there?

Between her traumatic encounter with open air and the traumatic exposure of her lower face, Cygni would have been quite within her rights to sit down and have a good tantrum about now, but as was always the case with her, practicality seemed to win out. We began the trudge across to the road, even as she went on grumbling wordlessly.

The position of the stars allowed me to ascertain our location and the direction in which we must travel.

More grumbling and mumbling ensued. Though by the time she had lumbered up onto the road, enough of her irritation had deflated that she could appreciate the workmanship of it. She stared down at it constantly, if only to avoid seeing the horizon and the terrors above it. I almost didn't notice when she finally spoke, my mind so full of plans for the future that the present didn't seem to matter a whit; the way that it always had back when I was still studying and learning and growing. "What does the pattern mean?"

Pattern? What pattern?

She nodded at the road as though it should mean something to me, and then, after an embarrassingly long couple of seconds, I understood.

You think it is a single piece of stone that has been carved, as in your cities, but in fact it is constructed out of many pieces of what we call brick. Baked clay formed into uniform pieces and slotted together. The pattern you perceive is the places where the bricks intersect.

I could almost hear her brain rumbling to life. "Staggered to give it better stability. Smart."

Humanity isn't entirely devoid of innovation.

"Don't have stone, so they make their own." Cygni almost managed a smile.

Just as you had no magic, and now you can cast with the best of them.

She snorted. "Prefer to know what what I'm doing does."

It was the closest that she came to an admonishment after our escapade had almost incinerated her, so I was going to go ahead and take it without complaint or excuse. We trudged on along the road, sadly heading away from the little hamlet where we might have found somewhere comfortable to hunker down for the night. I could feel the exhaustion aching in Cygni's bones, but once she had a mission in mind, I felt that there was little that could be done to waylay her from it. With a little luck we would come across another village or traveler's inn along the road before she passed out.

That inevitable unconsciousness grew more and more likely the farther we progressed, and I began trying to calculate from my memory of the sky just how long it would be until the sun rose. I had a sneaking suspicion that sunrise might provoke a reaction from a young lady who had never seen celestial bodies before tonight. Perhaps something in the way of screaming and blind panic. Broaching the subject with her when she was in her current zombified state seemed to be rather foolish, however.

No sign of a handy inn showed up, and with the temperature dropping with the fall of night, Cygni began to shiver.

Might I propose a campfire?

"What's that?"

A stack of sticks that you ignite and use to stay warm.

I could feel her revulsion at the idea—not because she was scared of trees the way that elves often snidely implied about her people, though she did seem to be glancing at them with some degree of wariness, but because an open flame down in a mine is asking for the kind of trouble that leaves you missing limbs.

I can assure you that it is perfectly safe.

"Said that about your last trick too," she grumbled. "Now look at me."

Madam, your beard will grow back. The rest of you would not have, if I'd left you to drown.

Her grumbles were definitely more muted after that as she gathered up bits of wood and carefully formed them into an orderly stack. This was not, typically, the method used for the creation of campfires, but as I was more of an indoors sort of person, I can't really claim that I had any better ideas as to how it should be put together. Luckily we had something that would allow us to overcome any shortcomings of airflow and construction. She reached into her bag of holding and, after some substantial rummaging, came up with the little shard of Scrynium.

Despite everything that it had been used for, it had barely shed more than a few inches in size. That was some extremely condensed Quintessence.

I didn't even have to guide her from there, she was more than capable of casting a little sulfur-infused Igniculus without input. The oddly cuboid campfire caught alight without any more effort, and she huddled close to it.

There are some preparations that we should make for tomorrow.

Her eyes were already drifting shut but she dutifully mumbled, "Uh-huh."

In a few hours the sun will rise, and you may want to find some sort of protection for your eyes as this whole place is going to become rather bright. My first idea would be to . . . you're already asleep, aren't you?

If you have never heard the snores of a dwarf, then you will just have to trust in me when I say that there was no danger of any predator or stranger approaching us despite our proximity to the road. I did my best to keep Cygni's ears open for any signs of approaching danger, of course, but it was difficult when there was an intermittent blast of something between heavy logging equipment on the exhale and a squeaking not unlike a foghorn on the inhale. It was a wonder that there had not been more tunnel collapses in the mines given the volume and intensity of the harmonics at work.

Anything that was brave enough to approach such a sound would likely have been blasted back a fair distance if they got into too close proximity. When Cygni awoke, I would have to check to see if the grass around her had been laid out flat by the concussive force of the unholy snorkeling sounds.

But I remained diligent and steadfast in between the trombone blasts of her sinuses. I listened for the faintest sound of danger, the jingle of chainmail, the soft footfalls of a cutpurse, anything that might bring my new friend harm. It was sort of heroic of me, I suppose, to be sitting there all night doing that. The sort of thing a really good person would do for someone else. Even though there was no benefit to them. Because now that we were beyond the wall and close enough to Arpanpholigon to spit, I didn't really need Cygni anymore, not really. Anyone that came across a wizard's hat out here would know precisely where to take it if they wanted some sort of reward, and whichever wizard in the Invisible College slapped me onto their head would become the puppet of my vengeance or risk having me suck all their Quintessence out. Cygni was now surplus to requirements, yet, like the living saint that I am, I stood guard over her all night long. Inasmuch as an inanimate object can stand guard.

Needless to say, after spending all night listening intently for the approach of anyone who might do her harm, for the slightest of sounds suggesting banditry afoot, it came as something of a surprise to me to hear music drifting to us from somewhere beyond the horizon. Not the lilting lullabies of the elves, used to lure unwary travelers astray, nor the grunting, rhythmic marching songs I had come to associate with the ogres of the Badlands, but something else, something . . . queasy. An awful undulating racket that I gradually came to realize was not the death rattle of some tremendous beast, but rather a rather incompetent attempt at playing the calliope.

It wheezed its way toward us, sounding increasingly nervous as it went, each toot slightly discordant, as though it were not taking steps toward us but rather going up and down flights of stairs between notes.

Cygni, wake up.

As it turned out, the reason that my dwarven companion had been so reluctant to take some rest was that as soon as the lights went out, there was no getting them back on. In many ways, dwarves are like the stone that surrounds them in their natural habitat. Unrelenting, solid, reliable, and entirely incapable of waking up.

Cygni! Something approaches! Wake up!

She snorted and made a little mumbling noise, but her awareness of the world around her did not increase in any way. If anything, disturbing her seemed to have instead encouraged her to roll over and sink deeper into sleep now that the sharp rock that had been digging into her buttock was no longer stuck in.

Cygni! Monsters! Mayhem! Death and doom! All approach!

Not an inch did the dwarf budge. Not one solitary inch.

Balls.

As it turned out, the thing that was required to wake a sleeping dwarf was in fact a sharp prod with a stick.

"Is it dead?" asked the poker.

"No I'm bloody not," Cygni grumbled as she jerked back upright to a sitting position.

The poker, as it turned out, was a young gentleman in a fool's regalia, who made a rather amusing jingle as he leapt back with his stick held up like a fencer's foil.

"Ah!" he exclaimed loudly enough for his companions on the road to hear. "It's alive!"

Cygni's hand had been fumbling around for her pick, but given that she'd left it somewhere down in the guts of the earth, she was understandably unsuccessful in arming herself. What she found instead was the bag of holding, which she readied like a cosh. "What do you want?"

Her grasp of the common tongue would have been surprising if it hadn't been taken almost verbatim from my own mind due to the connection between us. It certainly seemed to surprise the fool. "Sorry to bother you, sir." He was tripping over both his words and his own feet as he backpedaled away from her. "Didn't mean you no offense."

The sunlight shining down on Cygni, warming her face for the very first time, was definitely causing some troubles for her eyes. It took her a great deal of blinking and squinting before she could make out that there was an entire caravan on the road, including the accursed calliope, which seemed to take up an entire caravan on its own.

She had come from a world of practical brutalism. Clothes were made to serve only their functional purpose; some minor engraving was the extent of the gaiety that dwarves allowed—and even that mostly as an expression of their talents for stonework rather than any desire for beauty. As such, these mule-drawn caravans painted in all the gaudy colors of the rainbow and more were something of a shock to her system. Even the fool's garb, so obviously useless for absolutely everything that clothes were meant to do, was a font of confusion.

It is a circus. A party of mummers and showmen. Have no fear of them, they are . . . entertainers.

Cygni blinked a few more times before she finally grumbled once more, "What do you want?"

The fool looked askance to the caravan once more, as though someone there might save him from the horrors of polite conversation. With no clear script to follow, he defaulted. "Knock knock."

Cygni's eyes narrowed even further, until they were tiny slits in her rosy-cheeked face. "If you want me to knock you, don't have to ask twice."

"Oh, no. You're meant to say, 'Who's there?'"

"It's you."

"No, I know it's me . . . I'm . . ." He truly looked to be entirely out of his depth. "An interrupting ape."

"You are," she agreed, as he yelled, "Ook!" at the top of his lungs.

The two stared at one another for a time, entirely immobile, the immovable object and the unstoppable urge to make stupid jokes.

The calliope made a rather unpleasant crunching sound as whoever was playing it abruptly ceased, and just a moment later the door to that pipe-sprouting caravan swung open. "What are we stopped for?"

Many words sprang to mind when it came time to describe this gentleman. Rakish. Rugged. Roguish. He had a little goatee beard and a scar on his face that only seemed to accentuate his handsomeness rather than detract. Pale blue eyes shone out from his tanned face, so pale as to be almost white. His long hair looked like a mess, but a very deliberate mess, falling down to frame his face in so artful a manner that it might have passed for accidental. As though there were ever a moment when he didn't look so good and it was coincidence that he happened to look so at this moment. Muscles shifted beneath a shirt that was unbuttoned half the way down, and there was chest hair poking out.

By contrast to the bandy-legged and pasty-skinned fool who we had first encountered, this man was a demigod, an Adonis who combined handsomeness with a smirk that hinted at just a little danger.

Cygni swallowed down a mouthful of unexpected drool.

Oh no.

He met her gaze and smiled. "Well hello there, stranger."

To her credit, Cygni did realize who was being spoken to just a moment after the words were said. The delay was mostly as words tried to fight their way past the newly awakened part of her brain, a part which exists in most sentient beings and which I was lucky enough to have encountered only very briefly while riding atop the head of Ig. A part of the brain which I regret to label "horny."

"Hi," she managed to squeak out.

Try to control your raging hormones for just a moment and actually think . . .

I may as well have been talking to myself. Her ears were only for the startlingly handsome man who strolled down the embankment of the road to shoulder aside the fool and hold out a hand. "It's always a joy to meet a fellow traveler on the road, always new stories to share, new delights to be found in each other. Won't you come along with us?"

Once more, she managed to squeeze words out past the part of her brain that was screaming "hubba hubba" repeatedly. "Yes."

She held out her hand, expecting it to be shaken, and was startled when he seized hold and kissed her right on the calloused knuckles. "We're headed to Arpanpholigon, is that the right direction for you?"

It was entirely possible that steam was actually rising off Cygni in that moment. "Uh-huh."

Still holding her hand in a surprisingly gentle grip, this smoldering meatloaf of a man led Cygni back to the caravan and helped her up onto the bench in front of his oversized instrument. But a moment later, the whole procession began again in earnest.

"It is truly a pleasure to meet you, madame dwarf. Might I know your name?"

Cygni fought to keep her eyes from crossing. "Cygni."

"Such a beautiful name for so beautiful a woman." His smile was not affecting me in the same manner as her, I can assure you. If I was quiet for a time, it was simply because I did not want her to look a fool trying to carry out a conversation with an item of clothing simultaneously to meeting new people. I was not swayed by his grin. Nor was I sinking into his eyes the longer that he looked at Cygni. "Cygni, it sounds like music to my ears."

He leaned in closer and sniffed. Typically when a gentleman does something like that, it is about time to call the human resources department of wherever you happen to work, but to Cygni, entirely deprived of male companionship her entire life, the gesture carried a heady eroticism that made me extremely uncomfortable.

"You smell so sweetly of the sea, Cygni. How did you come to smell of the sea when we're miles inland?"

Tell him nothing. The less strangers know of our purpose and our journey, the safer we both shall be.

"There's seas beneath the surface too." She spoke in an almost falsetto voice, as though trying to pass for a human girl. It would have been comedic were it not so sad.

Every word that spills past your pouting lips is going to get us into more trouble.

"What a wonder, to think that such things could be?" He hadn't leaned back since sniffing her, and the proximity of his chest to her face was making her heart thump. "You must take me someday, to see these oceans beneath the earth. An adventure for just the two of us."

"Okay," she squeaked out.

Pull yourself together, woman. You can't go simpering after every mildly attractive carny that comes strolling along. You don't even know his name and you're ready to give him your firstborn child.

He put his arm around her with a casual stretch and all thoughts, including mine, immediately left her head. If, in that moment, she had melted and slopped down off the bench, I would have remained entirely unsurprised.

"What brings you up here to the world, dear Cygni?" He wasn't prying so much as making polite conversation, but Cygni clearly had no grasp of our precarious situation.

While I remained Absalom Scryne, greatest living wizard of our time, internally, from the outside I would simply appear to be an incredibly potent magical item that granted the bearer all the knowledge of an archmage. The sort of thing worth even more than the giant slab of Scrynium that she was hauling around in her bag. The sort of thing wars were waged over.

Tell him nothing!

Cygni cleared her throat in her typical guttural manner, strangling it off into a more coquettish cough toward the end. Then replied, "Nothing."

Idiot.

"So you've abandoned your people to go wandering in the sun just for the fun of it?" He chuckled wryly. "You sound like my kind of woman."

Cygni had managed to pull her thoughts together enough to blurt out, "Meeting friends. In the city."

"Friends, eh?" He chuckled, deep and low. "Anyone I should be jealous of?"

Internally, Cygni was screaming, but it showed only in a blush upon her exterior.

Once more, you do not need to divulge anything.

"Don't think so," she mumbled. "Not even sure they'll be there."

The rake chuckled once more and the vibration of it passed through his chest and directly into Cygni's shoulder. "Then I'd say you've got a little extra time to dawdle with me in that case."

Within the palace of my mind, the endless beautifully crafted rooms, the endless index card racks containing something that amounts to something akin to the sum of human knowledge, a ransacking was taking place. The meanings of words were stowed in this wing of my mind, and it was here that Cygni focused her furious assault. Digging frantically through drawer after drawer, desperately trying to find out what dawdling was, and if she needed a special outfit for it.

It means wasting time together, you hopeless romantic.

She managed a smile then, and still feeling self-conscious, let the rocking of the caravan as we passed over the rutted road tip her over to nestle against the man's side. He closed a hand over her far shoulder, ensuring that she could not be wobbled off the side. His grip was not tight, but it was solid. Safe. As though he might protect her from anything in this world that might do her harm.

"You must forgive my ill manners," the rake said in a tone that implied he was about to be even ruder, or perhaps lewder, in a moment. "Here I am with my arm around you, and I haven't even told you my name."

"What is it?" She really didn't care what he was called so long as he went on looking at her like that. Preferably from so close that she could feel the warmth of his breath on her face, on her lips.

"Why, haven't you heard of the traveling troupe of Stjepan the bard?" He chuckled, pointing to his name painted on the back of the wagon in front of us in peeling gold foil.

That name is ringing a bell.

"They say that I'm one of the greatest singers to ever grace the land, but I would entirely disagree. My talents lie almost exclusively in the lute, you see." He extended his empty hand and flexed it slowly. "I might be able to carry a sweet enough tune with my voice alone, but my finger-work is what really drives everyone wild."

Cygni's eyes were on his fingers and her mind was in the gutter.

Stjepan . . . where have I heard of a bard named Stjepan?

He leaned in so close to her now that his whiskers were brushing against her ear as he spoke. "Perhaps you and I might make some beautiful music together, if you travel with us for a time? My troupe always needs more beautiful women."

Flattery was not something that Cygni was accustomed to. In fact, this may have been the very first time that she encountered it in her lifetime. She also wasn't terribly familiar with the concept of beauty, on the whole. She knew when she looked upon certain formations of crystal and ore it made her a little weepy. She knew that gold made her chest tight. But as for other people, before encountering this moderately handsome man, she had never really registered any of them as something to be admired.

Yet whatever it was that made a person beautiful, she felt that as a dwarf, she fundamentally lacked it. Her most cherished feature, her soft and luscious beard, had been torn away from her in the firestorm, leaving a chin that was nothing to write home about, despite the rather adorable dimple at its middle. Her lips were dry and chapped after the aforementioned inferno, her skin had the kind of gritty quality that only a lifetime without washing can give you, and the hair on her head had been shorn down to the bone so as to prevent the spread of lice. None of these things added up to beauty in her mind.

So the disconnection between his words and how she perceived reality finally made her recognize that she was being flattered, or, as she would have called it . . . lied to. In an instant, she started to see clearly once more. The rose-tinted lenses of lust fell away from her eyes.

It didn't hurt exactly, to realize that she wasn't the beautiful woman he was treating her as. It wasn't even uncomfortable, as such. But there was a sadness in her after that. A little sorrow that she couldn't have been all that he'd implied she was.

"What exactly would I do, in your circus." Her voice wasn't quite back to its usual timbre, but there was a hint of gravel in there that I found supremely reassuring.

That same sharp grin returned, but it didn't send the same thrill through her now that she thought it was an affectation. "A girl like you could do whatever she set her mind to, I'm sure."

"Shoeing your mules?" she asked with just a hint of bitterness.

He laughed. "Don't be silly. It isn't like one of these wagons has a smithy in it. No, I was thinking that you might be up on the stage with me. Letting the whole world see your beauty for themselves."

Once more the incongruity of Cygni and beauty in the same thought jarred her back to reality. If I had been asked, I likely would have described her as handsome or perhaps as the prettiest dwarf that I'd ever seen, if I were being clever about it. Meanwhile he kept pressing on, despite losing her a little more each time he tried the same tactic.

"I don't sing. I don't dance."

"Just seeing you would be enough to make most people's day. I know the sight of you brightened my life right up." That rakish smile seemed to be missing more than it was hitting now. "It isn't often that there are dwarves up here on the surface, and it is ever rarer to see a . . . lady dwarf."

They're all lady dwarves, you simpering buffoon. Just because this one has no beard doesn't mean that she's any different from the rest.

Cygni's hands jumped up to her face to cover her bared chin in a reflex reaction at the mention of her hair loss. She was not happy, but I couldn't tell the depths of her unhappiness until she turned to Stjepan and placed a gentle kiss upon his lips.

This seemed to startle him, as though a seduction hadn't been precisely what he'd planned. Perhaps because his target had taken the initiative to do something for herself. For her part, Cygni drew back and smiled. "Sweet of you, but I'm as much a man as every other dwarf you've ever met."

To his credit, Stjepan did not immediately leap out of the seat as Cygni clearly expected him to. Instead he sat for a moment, processing this new information. Then, calculating the next best move, he threw back his head and laughed. "You dwarves, how is anyone supposed to know?"

One might try asking before putting the moves on them, I suppose.

Regardless, he did not remove his arm from around Cygni's shoulders, and I began to suspect that despite him oozing toxic masculinity from every pore, he might have been a little more flexible than anticipated with regards to his lovers. Cygni cleared her throat. "Suppose there's some stuff I could do to earn my keep. Knock on wheels. Carry boxes. That sort of thing."

Stjepan looked askance at Cygni with the eyebrow that was neatly intersected by his roguish scar raised. "Have you ever put up a tent?"

She shrugged. He shrugged? Either way, the dwarf's shoulders moved under the rake's hand. "Ain't sure."

"How could that be so?"

Cygni shrugged once more. Definitely not just to feel his hand tighten its grip on her shoulder ever so slightly. "Ain't sure what a tent is."

Another laugh, low in his throat, with a little rumble that still made all the surviving hair on Cygni's body stand on end.

There was a brief moment without any more flirting as they rolled along in something like companionable silence, then Stjepan turned to her once more with the same slightly sinister smile that seemed to delight her so much. "Now what shall we do to fill the time until we arrive at the next village and I teach you how to put up a tent . . ."

He leaned in closer still, and like the heroine in every romance I'd ever had the displeasure of reading, her chin tilted up so that their lips could meet.

Oh, I remember now. Stjepan was the werewolf.

At some point since our ascension to the world of men, you might have thought that Cygni might have removed the rings of jumping that she had so hastily jammed onto her fingers during the fight with the monster below the earth. But between everything else that had been going on, she had entirely forgotten.

As such, upon hearing the word "werewolf" and jumping with surprise, she did not merely headbutt and startle the lothario with his arm around her, but instead launched straight up about twelve feet into the open air.

CHAPTER FIFTEEN

THE SHOW MUST GO ON

It took a considerable amount of time for Cygni to rejoin the caravan after that. The fool and a bearded woman came to retrieve her from the tree that she was trapped dangling upside-down in. She would have thought that a ladder might have been required, but there was a helpful acrobat with a helpful trampoline that made the whole thing considerably less serious of a rescue operation.

"Must have been quite a fright you got, jumping like that," the bearded woman said. It had taken a fair bit of explanation to get Cygni to understand that female humans did not typically have facial hair to quite this degree, but now she was staring admiringly at the soft curls upon her chin. Her name was Angelina, she had been with this circus since she married one of the members of the troupe, and her unique features had earned her a permanent home in the freakshow side-tent where I assume Stjepan had intended upon placing Cygni, had he convinced her to join this little mess of his.

"Just a dog." Cygni attempted to laugh it off, but that isn't easy when you're dangling upside down from a tree and the bough is making some concerning groans.

The fool's eyes narrowed at that. Cogs were spinning behind his eyes despite the fact that his mouth was mumbling out, "How is a dog like a tree?"

Both Cygni and Angelina ignored him entirely.

"I suppose you'll be joining the acrobats with legs like those." Angelina's smile could not be described as infectious, but it was certainly close enough that you should consider consulting a doctor.

Cygni opened and shut her mouth a few times just before she was untangled and dropped headfirst onto the trampoline below.

As she rebounded up to brush the leaves time and again, the fool spoke once more, clearly still stuck on his theme but trying to move along with the conversation. "What do you call a vicious dog with no legs?"

A few bounces and considerably more nausea had her back in an upright position surprisingly quickly, and from there it was just a matter of straightening me out on her head before she could manage to untangle her thoughts enough to answer.

"It wasn't me." She was struggling not to give too much away, but there were certain things that were too obvious to entirely steamroll over. "It was magic."

"Oh!" The bearded woman looked positively delighted. "You'll do so well in the magic tent then. Folks have been awful bored of the magician we've got just now. I haven't a clue how he does his tricks, but they've got no patter."

"Patter?" Cygni had finally stopped bouncing entirely and now dismounted the trampoline with as much dignity as she had left.

"I met a very short baker by the name of Peter the other day, he told me all about how he makes flat breads." The fool opened up his mouth to unleash the punch line but the bearded woman talked right over him.

"It's all very well being the best at whatever you're doing, but if you can't sell it to the crowd, nobody cares. The magician, I'd swear his act would make him a hill of gold if he had the patter, but as is, folks don't even bother with his tent half the time. My husband though, his patter is the best. Could sell bicycles to fish."

"Where does a fish keep his money?"

The fool was not the wisest of men, but he had consistency, the kind of relentless energy that one usually associates with the desperate and the mad. I supposed that if one were to dress in a body-sock, attach bells to their head, and repeat the same awful puns for all one's life, then this might have been the kind of psychological damage that would be dealt.

"Why would a fish need a bicycle?" Cygni's brows drew down, and I was relieved that there was a fine ashy layer of hair leftover there, since it seemed that about 90 percent of her self-expression was through wiggling them.

"They don't." She chuckled. "That's the point?"

Cygni blinked at her, and the conversation moved on.

Despite Cygni's best efforts to remain as stoic as she ever had been, Angelina was as relentless as the fool in her own way. Asking question after question about Cygni—not any of the big questions that might have gotten us in trouble, but all the little ones that make a friendship.

Or so I'd assume. The closest I ever came to friendship in my long life was having a smattering of lesser enemies that I hadn't gotten around to turning into amphibians yet. Once I had a body again, I would really have to be sure to newt them once and for all. Just to be on the safe side.

Despite herself, Cygni soon found herself being toured up and down the procession with Angelina, learning about the incredibly large family that the woman had grown up in. All of the children that she herself hoped to someday have and her retirement plans that all seemed to revolve around a seaside cottage. Not to mention her current family of jugglers, percussionists, sword swallowers, mace swallowers, and clowns.

It was the latter category that made me uncomfortable. The freak show crew were all pretty pleasant people with some mild abnormalities that made them of interest to the common moron, but the clowns—the people who spent their lives desperately scrabbling to get a laugh out of people who actively wanted them dead for being what they were—they were abnormal in an entirely different way. There was some aching hole in their souls that made them don the face paint and squeaky noses that no amount of applause could ever fill, and the harder that they japed and punned, the more obvious that became.

As for the fool who had ostensibly been sent along to rescue us from the tree originally, I believe that he may have been the most twisted soul of the lot of them.

Long before we made it to the end of the line and the alleged "magician," the front of the train reached the next village. Cygni went bounding off gleefully to find Stjepan, apparently having set aside any concerns about him being a werewolf, and I was forced to endure a lesson on the correct assembly of a tent.

As you know, new knowledge is my succor; there is nothing in this world that I enjoy more than the discovery and gradual journey to understanding some unknown facet of the world. Yet despite this, if you were to ask me any question involving guy-ropes, pegs, poles, or canvas, more likely than not I would be able to provide you with no supplemental material. Some portion of this was of course my own utter disinterest in the whole matter, but more relevant was my ongoing attempt to absolutely ignore everything that was going on as Stjepan wrapped his arms around Cygni and showed her how to swing a hammer.

"Don't worry about being strong enough. All you've got to do is lift it up, and the weight of the hammer will bring it down," he growled into her ear. "Up and down."

Yes, that's right, he decided he needed to teach a dwarf how to swing a hammer. And she pretended that she needed instruction so that they could rub up against one another.

Sex may have eluded me as a mortal, but if all this grotesquery was what I had been missing out on, then I was extremely glad to have sidestepped it.

Cygni, who had marched and fought for almost a full day without so much as a heavy breath, was flushed and sweating by the time that they were done with their rutting. Both still fully clothed, thankfully, and both ostensibly just having put up a tent. In twice the time it had taken everyone else in the caravan trail to perform the same task.

Perhaps it is the fact that I am now made of a dry-clean-only material coloring my judgment, but sex definitely seemed to involve far too much sweating and . . . fluids in general.

While they had been bumping and grinding, the rest of the circus had set itself up around them, and now the calliope began to wheeze and Stjepan, like the dutiful master of a terrible beast, had gone off to pet it in the hopes of making it sing rather than roar.

Once more, Cygni and I were alone.

You can do better than that horndog.

"Jealous?" she jeered softly.

That you've acquired friction burns on your rump? Shockingly no.

She reached up to pat me. "I ain't leaving you behind just because there's somebody else in my life now."

The idea that man intends to be in your anything for longer than about three minutes is laughable.

"Definitely jealous." She snorted.

Madam, I am a hat. The things you intend to do with this cretin are entirely outside my wheelhouse.

"I've got a lot of intentions."

It was an active effort to distance myself from her mind before she sank into her fantasies. As grotesque as witnessing their flirting and frotting had been, the full act might have actually induced nausea. Something that, as an item of clothing, I would not have had any means of dispensing with.

Well, do bear in mind that lycanthropy is a magical disease passed through saliva and blood. Unless you wish to grow hair in places other than your beard, I would attempt to keep things chaste.

She casually shrugged. "Some things are worth getting a bit hairy for."

As we spoke, or rather, as I spoke and she completely ignored everything I was telling her, we made our way through the early crowds that had gathered for what was liable to be the greatest evening of entertainment in their pitiful little peasant lives.

For a time, we lived as they did. Strolling around the various amusements. Cygni seemed oddly delighted with the whole place and grew annoyed with me when I pointed out the manner in which the games the peasants were playing were rigged. As though I were the one spoiling the fun rather than whoever had nailed those coconuts to the shy or weighted those ducks so they couldn't be flipped over.

Going into the tents for the main amusements cost money, and while Cygni had been introduced to a fair number of the members of this circus during the journey, the hawkers who stood watch selling their tickets to each little event had not been among their number. Presumably getting some sleep in the caravans themselves in preparation for an evening of yelling.

So Cygni decided to preserve the scant copper coins in her pouches and instead took in the ambience. There were children screaming, adults laughing, and beneath it all, the hellish hurdy-gurdy of the calliope was never-ending. Stjepan may not have been physically out and about among the fairgoers, but his presence was being felt, nonetheless. His presence was being felt so thoroughly, in fact, that I suspected a great many people would be leaving with a migraine.

Here were the tumblers, the jugglers, and those people impressed by movement. Over there were the fire eaters and the fireworks, for people more impressed with flashing lights. I imagine that there was something exciting for people who liked pretty colors around here somewhere too. Needless to say, none of it was particularly intellectually stimulating.

Well, not for me anyway.

Cygni wandered around taking in the sights as though witnessing the wonders of the universe for the first time. I suppose that coming from a world without any entertainment beyond the recitation of histories and grudges to this was probably something of a shock to the system, but nonetheless it was embarrassing to see her behaving like such a tourist when she had an entirely adequate tour guide atop her skull.

She had made it almost the full length of the place before stopping in front of one striped tent not dissimilar to all the others, with the exception of the slightly more depleted crowds crammed inside it. This was clearly the magician's tent, given the rather faded and oft repainted posters. The current act was enti-tled "The Incredible Ignoramus," which I must confess did nothing to assuage my firm belief that every stage magician in the world should be rounded up, placed in a confined space, and then liquidated.

Yet there was something that had made Cygni halt in her meanderings here, and it was not her abiding desire to irritate me as much as possible. Rather, there was something just barely touching on the periphery of her arcane senses. A tingle. An itch. A brush of cool air across the back of her neck.

"What?"

Magic, of course.

It was not any wizard; none of them would have lowered themselves to per-forming in a place like this, using their incredible power for the entertainment of the common folk. That was not what magic was for, in my opinion, and that of the establishment at large.

So some hedge witch in a backwoods somewhere had lucked into a little bit of natural ability and combined it with a hand-me-down grimoire and now they were probably pulling eggs out of their ears or some such nonsense.

The hawker on the door interpreted Cygni's interest in the flows of Quintessence as a desire to buy a ticket, but instead of protesting or declining, she just handed over her last few coppers and ducked inside the tent. If this was where she was going to end up working on the way to Arpanpholigon, I suppose it made sense to scope the place out.

There were rows upon rows of benches set up but only half of them filled. The commoners with their rears planted upon those benches looked halfway to bored despite the display going on down on the grass.

In the middle of the room, blades danced. A dozen knives swirled around, sweeping and weaving and flashing in the torchlight. It left me stunned into silence. There was no spell at work here. Only low magic.

By all rights, I should have expected to look around and find a whole team of lesser witches waving their arms around and showing off, as according to all conventional logic it is impossible for a single practitioner to divide their attention in so many directions at once. Yet that was not what I hoped for.

In my heart of hearts, which was currently a fold in some silk lining within a tattered hat, I hoped that when Cygni's eyes turned to the middle of the tent, there would be but a single figure standing at the center of it all. A short and wiry creature, that looked something like a bipedal rat with a horrid skin condition. The only living creature I had ever encountered capable of dividing its attention across so many different items at once when exercising low magic. The one, the only, Ig the kobold.

He saw me and his mouth fell open. His concentration faltered and the knives that had until now been politely orbiting fell to earth. He flung his little arms open wide, his eyes even wider, and at that moment, at that precise moment when he was at his most distracted by my presence, somebody threw a sword at him.

The audience let out a cry of dismay. Cygni let out a cry of dismay. Ig let out a noise like a herniated weasel. But all our horror meant nothing to the inevitability of physics. The blade soared through the air toward the side of Ig's head, just as all the other daggers had when his lovely assistant had launched them.

How Cygni reacted faster than the rest of us entirely escapes me. Our reflexes should have been more or less simultaneous, what with us sharing the same nervous system in that moment, yet while I was trying to think of what to do and Ig was trying not to piss himself again, she was leaping across the room, not to rescue the kobold in danger, but to intercept the sword in flight.

She caught it by the handle. It jerked at her grasp from the force of the throw, spinning her through the air, but she managed to maintain her hold on it all the same. Neither audience members nor kobold were slain, and Cygni's new hopping and jumping act was debuted to great applause.

From the shadows, casting aside his bedazzled cowl, came Ildrit. The lovely assistant who had just thrown his sword. He seized Cygni up in his arms and crushed her to his chest. "Thank you! That could have been really bad if you weren't here."

Then he noticed that I was poking him in the nostril. "Wait one minute. Is that . . ."

Cygni had until this moment been lost in a sort of hormonal bliss, with her face crushed against Ildrit's pectoral muscles. But abruptly she pulled herself back from his grip. "What?"

But by then it was too late for any sort of diffusion of the situation, because Ig had come bounding over and rammed his snout directly into Cygni's liver as he tried to hug her too.

"Hat-friend save me!" he bellowed, to a smattering of chuckles from the crowd, who clearly thought this was still part of the act.

Those chuckles seemed to bring Ildrit back to reality faster than the rest of them, and he quickly spun to address the crowd. "Give us just a minute, folks! We need to catch our breath."

Cygni had managed to pry Ig free from her hip, but now his grasping little paws were upheld, toward me. "Gives! Gives!"

"What is that thing?!" she yelped in dismay as Ig essentially humped his way up her leg, trying to climb.

That is Ig.

"That's . . ." Her head didn't literally spin, nor did she experience any sense of vertigo, yet the realignment of her preconceptions and the evidence of her senses certainly put her off balance. "I thought you said he was a kobold."

That is a kobold.

It seemed that in her life, she had never encountered this particular species before, and was confusing kobold and cobalt. I suppose that if I were expecting a bluish metal and was instead confronted with Ig, it would have thrown me somewhat also.

"That's a kobold?! It looks like . . ."

I cut her off before this could get too offensive. *Yes, we're all aware of his appearance, and aroma, let's not belabor it.*

Ildrit had to step up and be the voice of reason, easing Widowtaker out of Cygni's hand and sheathing it on his back once more. "While I'm glad to have us all back together again, these people are still expecting a show."

Be so kind as to place me atop Ig, dear girl.

I was surprised at her reluctance to take me off. For all her fears and complaints about me, I would have thought that getting shot of me would be a delight, but no. She actually didn't want to give me up. How bizarre.

I will return, have no fear. Ig is simply the one who needs my assistance in this moment.

She still wavered, but in the face of what Ig probably thought were puppy-dog eyes, it was difficult. Mostly because you had an immense desire to do whatever he wanted just so he'd stop staring at you like that. His beady little eyes began to water, and Cygni plopped the hat onto his head without further ceremony.

Reality flickered in and out of existence for but a moment, then I was back with Ig again. And curse my soul if it didn't feel like home.

Hello, old friend.

Ig let out a noise like a kettle left too long on a stove and his entire memory dumped out into mine. The escape from the tunnels beneath the earth, just inside the Great Wall. The long trek without any company but Ildrit, and the slow decline of his faculties without me there to keep them fine-tuned. The passing circus, the job offer, the long hard road to Arpanpholigon. The nightly shows. His inability to focus well enough to cast, his inability to even use low magic until his life was endangered by a snapping guy-rope flinging a metal peg at his head. Ildrit's plan to keep them both with the caravan. Showing off as a knife-thrower outside of show times to get his hand back in.

"Hi" was about all that he managed to say. The atrophied tissue of his brain was still inflating back to a degree of usefulness now that I was there to fill it. I drew upon the Quintessence within him, refilling my depleted reserves, and just as swiftly, he refilled his own. If I could have combined him with Cygni, we would have had the ideal host. Competent with magic, and with a boundless font of power to draw upon. Alas, he remained an idiot and Cygni remained a dwarf. And never should the two meet.

While he was still nice and stupid, there was nobody really running things in terms of his higher functions. His brain stem was up to its usual tricks, flooding him with constant anxiety and keeping his heart hammering away, but the rest of the slop he called a brain was essentially inert. It made it so easy to take control of him.

I flexed my little paws and smiled, stepping back out into the ring. *"Greetings once more to you, oh prurient peasants. I am returned with a degree more intellect at my disposal. The world's first kobold wizard."*

There was some confused murmuring from the crowd, but as with my lectures back at the college, questions would have to be saved for the end. *"Until now, you have witnessed only the lowest of magics, the application of raw power to physical objects, but I believe it is time to reveal some of the deeper mysteries of the cosmos to you this eve."*

Quintessence flowed through me, through us, empowering Ig and I as it always had. This need not be anything fancy, not even a word of Archaic needed to be spoken; I simply reached down into the mystical core of Ig, seized control of the Quintessence hidden there, and released it.

From beneath every bench in the room, bunnies began to lope out. Bouncing and bounding in every direction, to the amazement and delight of the crowds. It was the simplest thing that I could think of, as I certainly wasn't going to be wasting any real magic on these buffoons.

"My missed you, hat," the kobold said as the tide of rabbits swept past him, scampering for the freedom of the night air.

And I have missed you, Ig, you scrabbling moron. More than you can ever know.

Quite satisfied with the show's grand finale, the various guests of the circus applauded a little and then began shuffling out. Ig basked in their approval, even as that same approval filled me with contempt for everyone involved, and then turned back to our friends.

Cygni had a shard of Scrynium in one hand, a glowing ball of fire growing in the other. Ildrit was on all fours, with a dead rabbit dangling from his mouth and an expression of extreme embarrassment on the rest of his face.

Oh for the love of . . . he fell for the bloody bard too?

Ig nodded sadly, even as Cygni readied to blast our twice-cursed friend into ash.

Perhaps I should do the talking?

Outside of our little tarpaulin-covered haven, the screaming began in earnest. All the people of the crowd who were briefly amused by the flood of rabbits escaping the magic tent, thinking that something had gone amusingly wrong, were now confronted with all the other werewolves in the circus succumbing to the instinct to hunt and bite the ultimate prey animals as they scampered for safety.

"Cygni, please refrain from blasting any werewolves with fire for the moment. It seems that your beau has been rather . . . modern when it came to sharing his bed. And teeth." Then Ig added, "Magic no work good on wolfses neither."

The tonal shift between the two voices coming out of Ig seemed to startle Cygni for a moment, a particularly vital moment in which she should never have allowed herself to be distracted. The fireball that she had conjured so casually was now simmering at the required temperature and beginning to pulse a rhythmic countdown to its detonation.

I cleared Ig's throat. *"You may want to get rid of that before we all die."*

"Not wolfses," the charming little creature piped up.

I sighed. *"You may want to get rid of that before all of us who have not been seduced and bitten by a werewolf die."*

Cygni glanced around, her lovely logical brain ticking over each option. She couldn't throw the fireball outside into the already terrified crowd lest it slaughter them wholesale. She couldn't throw it at the ground lest it destroy all of us. Her eyes turned to the heavens as though pleading with some deity for rescue, but she remained the non-religious sort, despite her encounter with a creature who may possibly actually have been a god earlier. She was looking up at the peaked point of the canvas tent and working out whether it was far enough from the epicenter of the blast to keep us all alive.

"Throw it!" Ig and I yelled together.

She did.

Now, typically at this point, I would simply have had her weave a simple protective shield overhead, invoking both air and some heavy metal to produce a solid blockade that would vanish after the heat had washed over it. Sadly, I was currently situated on the head of Ig, rather than the far more competent caster I had now become accustomed to, and as such, when he flung up his hands and tried to invoke elements that he couldn't even spell let alone understand, it was less than effective.

Rather than the word of Archaic that I had in mind, Ig unleashed a terrified sound somewhat akin to a large hog suffering testicular torsion. Unsurprisingly, this was not effective in constructing any arcane protections.

The fireball detonated at the top of the tent. Every one of us was knocked from our feet by the sudden outburst of heat and concussive force. The top of the tent opened out like a hastily peeled banana, blackened and burst by the sudden pop of fire. The stars shone down on us for but a moment before the smoke rising from the smoldering remains of the rest of the tent obscured them.

"Well, that could have gone worse," Ildrit said, spitting out the bundle of fur still stuck in his mouth.

"You're a werewolf too?!" Cygni bellowed in dismay once she was quite certain no fire was going to come raining back down on her.

The werewolf looked sheepish. "Listen . . ."

"Clearly this is how Stjepan secures the obedience and compliance of those he wishes to recruit to his circus. A new iteration of his old ransom-were plan." Ig was fighting me for control of his throat. Curious.

"Wolf man says we all needs stick together. Like wolf pack."

And let me guess, he is the alpha of this particular pack?

"He was saying alpha!" Ig exclaimed in surprise.

An outmoded understanding of animal pack structures; hardly surprising that lout subscribes to it.

"I made a mistake. I trusted someone I shouldn't have. You'd think I'd have learned my lesson after . . ." Ildrit trailed off before mentioning Bonetaker.

To my surprise, it was actually Cygni that came to his rescue. "That bard's fooled smarter than you."

Her, for instance.

Ig cocked his head to the side in confusion, and gods help me, I found it endearing instead of annoying. What dire transformation had been wrought upon my soul that this creature, once so loathsome to me, was now a source of delight? How low had I sunk that I truly thought of a kobold as a friend rather than simply a tool to serve my purposes? Was I like every other fool doomed for a dullard's death mired in sentiment? What was I thinking?

He gave her a grateful smile, then held out a hand to shake. She just stared at it. Not a dwarf tradition. "The name's Ildrit. Though I'm sure the hat's told you all about me already."

"Hat only had eyes for the rat." She sneered in Ig's general direction.

Ildrit chuckled at that, slowly lowering his hand. "Well, the two of them were basically made for each other, the way I figure it."

Cygni looked up at him with the same expression she would have used when confronted with a particularly unusual vein of mineral. And I stepped up to make the introductions. *"This gentleman is . . ."*

She cut me off before I could repeat her lies to Stjepan for her. "Cygni Khnutesdottir, Surveyor Second Class."

"Dottir . . ." Ildrit's brow furrowed. "You're a girl?"

In most places, a question of that sort would end abruptly in a heavy blow to the crotch. But it seemed that Cygni was feeling magnanimous after almost blowing everyone up. Instead, the dwarf squinted up at him in what I fear she thought was a smoldering fashion and announced, "I'm a woman."

That briefly stunned everyone into silence for just long enough for the screams outside to reach a crescendo. *"Am I to take it that every employee of this circus is in fact a werewolf?"*

Ildrit stared at Ig for a moment. "Weird hearing real words coming out that mouth in the right order."

"It does of course beg the question why you did not immediately remove the problem in the manner for which you are famed to remove problems." I sighed through Ig's mouth; it was nice to be able to sigh again. *"Lycanthropy may be both curse and disease, but whosoever infected you is ontologically load-bearing regardless. With Stjepan slain, all that he has wrought would be undone."*

Ildrit blinked. "Can anyone translate that for me?"

"Why no stabby wolf-boss?"

"Thanks, Ig."

It was strange how casual the two of them had become in my absence. I would never have called this cursed swordsman a friend, I simply did not feel that either of us had earned that closeness, but Ig and Ildrit seemed to be getting along like old pals after my absence, something that felt all the stranger because the looks of affection from the human were directed at the same face I was looking out of. "Because he's married to the bearded lady. And she's . . ."

"Nices." Ig finished his sentence for him as he trailed off.

Cygni looked from Ig to Ildrit and back again. "So what? Be a slave instead of hurting her feelings?"

"Our dear companion bears a magical sword that slays the spouse of whoever it strikes down. The black blade Widowtaker."

Cygni looked at the sword in question on Ildrit's back, then looked at Ig once more. "And?"

How could she be so dense? Even Ig could see the problem here. "We is not wanting to kills her too."

She rolled her eyes and walked out. I must admit, I didn't fully expect both of my wearers to get along perfectly, but the contempt she was showing toward

Ig just because he was a kobold was an uncomfortable reminder of how I had thought of him when we first met.

There was an awkward silence where all we could hear was the screaming outside, then for some reason I felt compelled to fill that silence. *"So that was Cygni, and despite her . . . gruffness, she has been absolutely invaluable in reuniting us."*

"She's certainly got character," Ildrit said in as neutral a tone as he could muster.

Ig was perhaps a little less flattering in his description. "She grumpy."

As well she should be, having been stolen from her home and forced to assist me in my quest.

"Me also was too."

Yes, but her home wasn't a hole in the ground . . . okay, well, technically it was . . . but . . .

"What in the nine hecks have you idiots done?!" bellowed the newly arrived Stjepan, saving me from having to articulate any more of that train of thought.

The werewolf looked somewhat the worse for wear. His hair was still artfully draped, and his stubble still made even Ig want to caress his jawline, but there was a bloodstain around his mouth that I'd have to assume had once been a rabbit and a wild look in his eyes that I'm sure Cygni would have considered to be quite charming.

Ildrit raised his hands. "Sorry, boss. Didn't know that the rabbits would . . ."

"Do you have any idea what you've done? The lives you've ruined? You think word of this isn't going to spread?" He stepped up to Ildrit and poked him in the chest. It was a ballsy move based entirely in having absolutely no idea who he was messing with. I'd seen Ildrit carve his way through ogres. This little chump would have lasted about three seconds. "The only way to keep this quiet is to kill or turn the whole village. And do you think I need all these peasants? You've damned the lot of them."

For his part, Ildrit managed to keep his temper in check by focusing more on what Stjepan was threatening. "You can't kill the villagers just because . . . tell them it was a gimp show. Eating live rabbits. Part of the act."

"Nobody is going to believe that!" Stjepan roared in Ildrit's face.

Ig was still standing aside, looking sheepish. It seemed that being a kobold exempted him from blame in the same way that yelling at a toddler probably wasn't going to result in them being disciplined so much as upset and confused.

I have been considering the problem of Stjepan since our encounter with his handiwork in the Badlands, and I believe that I have concocted a solution. Legend holds that silver can bypass a werewolf's intrinsic protections against magic. If we were to infuse a spell with that element . . .

Ildrit had now been seized by the front of his stylish yet practical black leather armor by the smaller man and dragged nose to nose with him. It was almost amusing to see the comparison between the pair: Ildrit with his years of real battle scars and Stjepan wearing his like it was a fashion accessory.

"You're the one that caused all this and you're going to be the one to fix it. Take that sword you carry everywhere and never use and put it to good work."

The ease with which the circus ringmaster jumped directly to mass murder was a little concerning. He had been roguish before, and criminal too, but I had not assumed that he'd be willing to make the leap all the way across into cartoonish villainy. Although I suppose that he didn't actually mean to kill all the people in this village; just force Ildrit to do it.

He set his shoulders. "I'm not doing it."

Stjepan pushed him again, but this time Ildrit didn't rock back on his heels like the little wolf had obviously expected him to. "You will do as you are told. You're part of this train, part of this pack, and that means you obey me. If I say heel, you come to heel. If I say jump, you ask 'How high?'. If I say kill, you ask 'How many?'"

"I'm not your dog."

A wiser man might have heard Ildrit's tone in that moment and shut their stupid mouth before it got them killed. Alas, Stjepan was not a wiser man. If he were, he likely wouldn't have gotten himself into this position to start with. The running-a-circus-of-werewolves position, not the nose-to-nose-with-a-savage-killer position. Well, either, really.

His eyes narrowed. "That's exactly what you are, Ildrit Elfbane. You think nobody knows that name anymore? You think nobody remembers what you did? You're a dog. A mad dog. And I'm finally taking off the muzzle."

"Up and down." Cygni's voice came from somewhere behind him, at about hip height.

It was unfortunate that dwarves are that much shorter than humans, because if Cygni had been as tall as Stjepan then that first swing of the sledgehammer they'd been using to knock in pegs and guy-lines would have hit him in the head, and that would have been the end of the gruesome display. Instead it took him in the side of the knee.

Magical resistance to harm or not, when your kneecap soars across the room like a hockey puck someone slammed, it has to hurt.

The noise coming out of Stjepan's mouth was not befitting of a wolf—certainly not the alpha big bad wolf that buffoon had claimed to be. It was distinctly sheeplike, in fact. A bleating. Not that I imagine I would have sounded particularly manly with my legs getting sledgehammered.

He fell to his knees—or rather to one knee and one bloody mulch—wailing all the way down. Cygni did not need any prompting to raise the hammer again.

"Up and down."

This time she landed what should have been a killing blow, slamming the weighty steel hunk at the end of the stick directly into the top of the bard's artfully draped hair. His skull caved in beneath the blow, yet he did not die. Here on display was that supernatural resilience that defined the werewolf, and here, I suspect, Stjepan regretted having such resilience.

Surviving is grand and all, but surviving with half your brains running out of your nose probably isn't all that worthwhile. Particularly when it prompts the little dwarf you were previously flirting with to raise her hammer a third time.

He was still twitching after that, so she hit him again.

On the fifth hit, she seemed satisfied that he wasn't going to get up again. But she still gave him two more for good measure.

Outside, all of the more animalistic screaming abruptly stopped. Similarly, our dear friend Ildrit seemed to wilt somewhat, as though a curse imbuing him with supernatural strength had just been lifted from him and he had been returned to humanity.

"Well, that works, I guess."

"Can't kill him with my magic sword." Cygni rolled her eyes at the man. "Idiot."

Ildrit was not accustomed to being insulted. Presumably a side effect of him being one of the most imposing and deadly swordsmen in all the world. So for a brief moment, I do not think that even he knew how he was going to react to that.

He burst out laughing. "Thanks for that."

She shook her head despairingly in answer. "Can't see the stone for the mines."

"Me not see mines neither," Ig offered Ildrit, as if being only as stupid as a kobold was some consolation.

CHAPTER SIXTEEN

A NIGHT TO FORGET

Given that the ringmaster of this particular circus had just been reduced to a red paste by a member of our party, my first inclination was for all of us to immediately flee into the night. Cygni, on the other hand, had laid down her hammer, crossed her arms, and scoffed at the very idea. "Probably blackmailing everyone else like Longshanks here."

Behind her, Ildrit mouthed, "Longshanks?"

"Ain't going to hear no complaints." She nodded smugly. "Just wait and see."

Despite himself, Ildrit conceded the point. "She isn't entirely wrong, I'm certain that a fair number of people in the caravan train have been enslaved the same way I was."

"They'll thank us," Cygni said, firmly.

Which just went to show that a degree of natural intelligence cannot hold a candle to a well-rounded education. History was not my area of expertise, beyond those places it happened to intersect with magical theory, and yet I was sufficiently well-versed to know what happens to saviors who overthrow the existing order. They are praised as heroes many years later by people standing on their graves.

Even the worst monsters had those loyal to them, and this dead bard had been far from the worst monster we'd encountered on our travels. With his wit and charm, Stjepan probably had half the circus ready to kill for him, half the werewolves convinced that he'd granted them some sort of gift with his bite.

Ig did his best to convey my train of thought to the others. "Me think they's going be angry."

The screaming outside of the tent had mostly stopped by now, though there was still the odd raised voice. Mostly people calling out to one another in the night after losing their way. At best we had a few minutes before the chaos was tracked back to its point of origination.

"*Might I strongly suggest that we depart with all haste?*"

Cygni seemed neutral on the subject of departure, and Ig had been born to run at the slightest provocation. The only one holding us up from my cunning plan to flee was Ildrit. Who rubbed at his chin and said, "I think we're better sticking it out."

The dwarf was right, he is an idiot.

"Why want stick?" Ig inquired, anxiety beginning to bleed into his voice.

Ildrit spread his hands as if it were obvious why we'd want to remain here and get hung. "Well, we're heading for Arpanpholigon, right?"

Indeed.

"Yep yep." Ig nodded.

"Can you think of any better way to sneak into the city than in a circus caravan?" He turned his eyes up to my physical form now instead of Ig's face. Looking at the hat part of me as though it were me. "When he's with the circus, people didn't even look at Ig twice. He was part of the show."

Cygni scoffed. "Nobody's going to bother the runt with both of us watching out for him."

"Well . . ." Ildrit rubbed the back of his neck. "I may have a little arrest warrant or two out in Arpanpholigon too."

The dwarf glared at me. Or Ig. It was hard to tell sometimes. "You consort with criminals, hat?"

"Oh yes, most assuredly. Even dwarvish ones. Lawbreakers galore." That shut her up.

Ig tried to get the conversation back on track. "Want stay circus, hide good?"

"I think it's the best option to get into the city. Tactically."

It does present a temptation, but how we are going to circumvent our current issue eludes me at present.

"We no have problems," Ig declared with a smile. "Me is everyone's friends."

I sincerely hoped that this was the case, because all of Ig's alleged friends began pouring into the burnt-out circle that had been the magic tent.

The freaks, geeks, clowns, jugglers, acrobats, and bearded lady came pouring in and encircled us, all silent and gawking at their dead ringmaster where he lay on the floor. I had expected tears from Angelina at least, but her expression was stiff and unreadable.

"What have you done?" whispered the fool.

Cygni opened her mouth, but Ildrit stepped in front of her and shouldered the blame like a champ. "What had to be done. How many of us were being kept here against our will? How many of us had felt that man's teeth?"

"You . . . killed him," Angelina whispered. It shouldn't have been so easy to catch, given how crowded the remains of this tent had become, but here we were, hearing her all the same.

"He wanted to bite everyone who saw what happened tonight. To kill them or make them his . . . pets." A shudder passed through the crowd at that. I would guess that there had been no secret amongst the carnival folk about just what their leader had been doing all this time. Which meant that they were complicit, and all the more likely to turn on us.

I really wish that we had run when we had the opportunity.

The rest of the circus had now arrived, queued up politely outside of the tent. Luckily for them, the tent covered about as much as a skirt by this point thanks to its slow disintegration into ashes. They'd have a full view of all these lovely people murdering us.

Public speaking has never been one of my favorite things to do. This may seem strange, given the position of power and authority that I once occupied, or considering that I often had to lecture to entire halls of students, but the truth of the matter is that I did my best work in solitude, far from the goggling eyes of the masses, and to be stared at by all of these people left me feeling . . . uncomfortable.

Ig did not share my reservations. He was one of the rare breed of wizard who thrived in a crowd. Indeed, the more people around him, the more comfortable and secure he felt. I put it down to him being an overgrown rodent, accustomed to nesting with a swarm. He trotted out in front of Ildrit and spread his arms wide. "Me friends!" he loudly declared, "We stomp stop bad man. All be good now."

The crowd, which had affixed Ildrit so readily with their murderous glares, softened when they looked at Ig.

I have something of a theory regarding this. The human mind is designed to seek out cuteness. Even the most hideous of creatures will have someone cooing over it. Back in the university, I knew wizards who kept familiars, and of those wizards, all would attest to the beauty and grace of whichever creature they held dearest to their heart, despite it looking to me like some sort of hideous abomination. Spiders and snakes, hounds and cats, no matter how bizarre looking they were, there would be someone who delighted in their appearance. Even those in the more mundane world who kept pets seemed to seek out the most deformed-looking versions of every animal. Dogs with faces folded in on themselves, or stretched out into pale puppet monstrosities, either one of which would give a wolf nightmares for life. These were the breeds most highly sought after and praised for their alleged cuteness.

In nature, nobody other than kobolds spent time with kobolds. Adventurers might encounter them in passing, but they weren't stopping to hang around. Typically a kobold and adventurer would only be together long enough for the former to be slaughtered by the latter and have its tail removed for bounty. But my dear Ig, he persisted.

Extremes of deformity when combined with ongoing proximity somehow transfigured into cuteness. I suspect that the same thing was happening with Ig as had happened with these ghastly beasts that some love. People keep hairless cats, which are essentially goblins without thumbs, so why shouldn't they come to appreciate the appearance of Ig, other than having the most basic standards of aesthetics? He was easily as malformed as a poogle or chihuahog, so why not?

Yet despite the way that they all looked on him with the kind of affection usually reserved for a beloved family pet, that did not mean that his words carried any weight with them. They may not have had flaming torches and pitchforks readily to hand, but they definitely had that "murderous mob" energy to them.

"Wolf man bad. Make work not want to. Make leave home. Tell lies. Bitey teeth. Lots peoples. We makes not. We free now!" He made a second attempt at the same speech, but I wasn't entirely sure that anyone could actually understand what he was trying to say. Worse yet, I could see that Ildrit's hand was beginning to drift up toward Widowtaker's hilt. If he drew that thing, there was going to be a bloodbath. A bloodbath that we might very well emerge from unscathed, because he was extremely good at acts of violence and there were now two people who could cast magic on our side.

Yet I could see from his hesitation that he did not want to do that. Perhaps it was because he had spent time with these people. Perhaps it was because he believed that they were, fundamentally, good people, undeserving of wholesale slaughter just because they'd been caught up in the machinations of a conniving song singer. When it came to matters of morality, Ildrit had a more practical concern than most of us. The nature of his curse ensured that he would suffer karmic punishment, which he had spent the latter part of his life frantically trying to avoid.

"I . . . I can't believe he's gone," sobbed the dead man's wife.

Cygni rolled her eyes. "Wasn't exactly a faithful spouse, was he? Tried it on with me earlier."

While her bluntness and directness had been an asset up until this point as we navigated dungeons, here in what passed for civilization, it was more of a hindrance. The crying woman had fallen to her knees by the corpse, and the rest of the gathered crowd, which had previously been ambivalent, now seemed outright angry on her behalf. Great.

"He was one of us," intoned a gimp with bloodstains around his mouth. Whether they were bunny blood and he had once been a werewolf, or it was the usual day-to-day chicken blood from his job, I could not have said.

"Forsooth," announced the fool. "Once filled with gaiety, he is now a grave man."

Thankfully that awful pun shifted the ire of the crowd onto him instead, at least briefly. There was widespread groaning.

Groaning that gave the next crowd time enough to arrive. There was a veritable swarm descending upon us. Farmers loping along on four legs and looking extremely confused, teenage peasants that shifted uncomfortably on two legs instead of four, clearly perplexed about their sudden shift from being dogs to being people, and in the midst of them, an old woman that I instantly recognized. The village elder from out in the Badlands.

"You!" she declared, pointing at Ig. "You did this!"

Ig opened his mouth to deny everything, but I jumped in before he could somehow make it worse. *"As promised, madam. I have broken the curse that ruined your lives and drove you beyond the edge of civilization. My only regret is that it took somewhat longer than intended."*

"You . . ." She was wheezing and out of breath. Apparently the switch from loping around on all fours as a perfectly healthy wolf to being a grizzled old hag was taking its toll on her. ". . . This was your plan? All along?"

"You must forgive my deception back in your village, but I knew that this was the only way." I forced Ig's head to bow a little before letting control of his body entirely return to him.

There are very few ways to dissolve an angry mob, and typically dumping an equally angry mob—one that had been chasing and tracking you for days, if not weeks—on top of that original mob was not the best of plans. However, in this particular instance, I had a suspicion that it was going to help.

If only because the original angry mob now had another ethical dilemma to tangle with. "Wait . . ." said one of the tumblers. "You guys got bit too?"

"Our whole village was cursed by that troubadour," declared one farmer.

"Ruined our lives," added a plump tavern wench who was currently trying to scratch behind her ear with her foot and wobbling erratically as a result.

The bearded lady, tears in her eyes, turned to them in horror. "He'd done this before?"

What we had right now was an opportunity. While the two factions of ex-werewolves chatted amongst themselves, our party could have quite easily beaten a hasty exit. It was not as though there was any tent left to keep us penned in, thanks to the still-simmering fire.

Alas, none of the others seemed to have noticed this opportunity, and Ig was not inclined to scarper without them. So he stepped up to speak once more. "We is stopping bad wolf hurt lots peoples."

It seemed that he had only the same moral argument to appeal to and was going to continue phrasing it in mildly different ways. There was a tension still hanging in the air. The ambivalence of the carnies pressed up against the shocked gratitude of the farmers. What we needed was an outlet for that tension. A release valve for that pressure.

Ig, you must cast the Golden Flames of Galgalagrin the Great.

"Weh?" he replied, as astute as ever.

You heard me, Ig. Cast the spell.

"But I is making . . ."

I am aware of your capabilities, my dear boy. Now do as you're told.

Shrugging his shoulders, Ig did as he was told. Raising his hands above his head, focusing on the element of Potassium, drawing markedly more

Quintessence than was really required because he wanted to show off. "*Fragor.*"

Outside of Arpanpholigon, it was rare to hear the language of the Arcane Archons being spoken, particularly by a kobold, so every head jerked around as Ig yelled out the spell, as though volume would make it more effective.

Then came an awful rain and thunder, except instead of thunder there was the echo of creation, as air was displaced by the creation of something that did not exist before, and instead of rain, there was bananas.

Of the elements that Ig had a tenuous grasp of, Potassium was the one that he had used in a practical spell the most often, and of those spells, almost every single one had failed to perform its desired function in exactly the same way. Yet this consistency of failure was precisely what my plan relied upon.

The bananas rained down in a spectacular non-sequitur, drawing all attention away from the dead werewolf and his killers, and directly to the funny-shaped yellow fruit.

There was a secret and ancient word, not of Archaic, but nonetheless taught to the students of Arpanpholigon—one that they thought that their tutors had long forgotten the power of. There was no situation that it could not alter for better or worse, and while there was a gamble afoot here, I could pretend to myself that Ig's presumed innocence was liable to protect us from the worst excesses of vengeance if the roll of the dice went against us.

"*Party!*"

The bananas rained down on everyone, sweet and ripe, the gathered farmers who'd suffered a lifetime as dogs let out a cheer, and for one long, awful moment it looked as though the fight we had been hoping to avoid was going to come to fruition as the faces of the carnies crumbled. But then someone somewhere started playing music, and all the people who had been kept prisoner seemed to realize that now they were free. A cheer shook the whole circus. Bottles of liquor seemed to spring from everywhere at once, and almost immediately, Ig was being hoisted onto shoulders and became a focal point of the cheering.

CHAPTER SEVENTEEN

GETTING THE SHOW ON THE ROAD

Later, as the evening drew on, he would be forced to produce more bananas from nowhere so that the daiquiris could continue to flow, but for the most part he was passed around from one guest to another, like a mascot or cat. Even when he did manage to wriggle free and escape, his scampering toward our allies was short-lived before he was intercepted by someone else complimenting his bravery.

Ig had too much to drink. Any amount of booze was probably going to be too much for someone with the constitution of a dehydrated ferret, but Ig seemed intent on matching Cygni drink for drink as she knocked the banana smoothie concoctions back. He lacked the emotional intelligence to know why he was trying to compete with Cygni, but I was intensely amused to realize that he was acting out of jealousy. She had been wearing his hat, the hat that had made him who he was, and Ig was not happy about that fact, even if he couldn't quite put a finger on why it bothered him so much.

Only once before in his life had Ig imbibed alcohol, and as a result of that one, he had spent almost an entire day feeling like his brain was leaking out his nose. This time was going to be worse. I knew this for several reasons. The first being that he insisted on telling everyone that he wasn't even drunk. The second, announcing repeatedly that he loved them all. The third, that he had lost count of how many daiquiris he had consumed early on. Perhaps most tellingly, his words were slurring so badly that he sounded like he was speaking like a normal person.

I personally did not have any blood, and as such, my blood-alcohol level could not hope to reach such lofty heights as Ig was attempting to achieve. However, I did get the joy of experiencing his ever-increasing inebriation as his senses began to fail. The world tilted sideways. The periphery of his vision became fuzzy and black until he was looking down a long tunnel, at the far end of which was revelry. His stomach, designed by nature for the consumption of partially decayed bugs, small rodents, and smaller lizards, along with a little grazing upon potentially noxious plants, should have provided some impediment to the poisons that he was so gleefully gulping down, but unfortunately there is a limit beyond which even natural resistances cannot overcome, particularly when one has consumed one's own body weight in rum, literally.

From that point everything became . . . hazy. Scenes presented themselves in no coherent order.

A trapeze artist dangling upside down from a strongman's arm, having liquor poured through a length of pipe into his mouth.

Standing face-to-face with the fool as he swayed from side to side, declaring, "I want an alligator sandwich, and make it . . ." before trailing off and collapsing under the weight of his own punchline.

A trained bear, or possibly a very hirsute druid, playing cards with an assortment of trained animals.

The bearded lady and Cygni, clinging to one another and sobbing.

The whole world turned upside down, a pile of banana peels beneath our feet.

Ildrit arm-wrestling with both Cygni and Ig at the same time, while I sat atop the head of some random passerby who had scooped me off the floor.

Ig being paraded around with a top hat on, atop a chair.

A blazing inferno, a bonfire, on which the accursed calliope had been cast and was now tootling and wheezing itself to a slow molten death.

The fool, now recovered, explaining to Ildrit, "No, it isn't like a cat, the bells aren't to scare birds away . . . they're . . ."

A whole circle of circus performers, all dancing around and around and around and I felt sick.

The ditch next to where latrines had been dug, where Ig was holding back Ildrit's hair as the man rid himself of some portion of the night's poison and also dinner.

The women of the circus and village trading stories and titters as the sun began to rise on the distant horizon. I was perched atop Cygni for that bit, I suspect. Or they thought Ig was a girl in need of love advice. Not impossible, but not likely.

When I did return to some semblance of linear time once more, I was dangling precariously off Cygni's bare foot, toes digging into my silk lining. Her legs were both pleasantly cool. sticking out from the edge of the bedcovers, bare for the first time in probably her entire life, and sunshine was streaming in through the stained glass of the caravan's window, bathing the whole space in beauty that she'd likely appreciate more without the hangover.

Despite the amount of booze she had consumed last night, it did not appear that she was much worse for wear, although I put that down to the fact that she was remaining in a fully horizontal position. In my limited experience, the hangover is less of a fact of life, and more of a presence, lurking just out of sight. More often than not, you can awake from a night of drunken debauchery and feel just fine, better than fine even, because you feel as though you have just cheated death. Then you attempt to sit up, and you raise your head into the storm cloud of hangover that was just waiting for you to make so foolish a move.

So long as Cygni remained lying down, with her eyes mostly shut, the hangover would remain lurking in a dark alley with several giant clubs lined up against the wall.

Good morning.

It was a gentle prompt to wake, especially compared to the veritable screaming it had taken to rouse her the morn before, but her eyes snapped open sharply, all the same.

"Hat."

I appear to be on your foot.

"How long you been there?" she asked with a degree of unexpected urgency.

I would assume that it is a recent development, as I don't recall much of what happened prior to this moment.

"Good, that's good." She started to sit up, and the hangover snatched up the first club and swung for her gut. Nausea swept through her, but as I've said many times before, dwarves are made of hardier stock than humans. She managed to swallow it back down rather than spraying me with stomach acid and liquor.

Much obliged.

She was briefly too queasy to speak, but that too was probably for the best, as the hangover had carefully lined up his next shot like a golf player and was now chipping a headache neatly into the back of her skull with one heavy swing of his club. If she had been able to speak, I imagine that it would have gone something along the lines of, "Aaaaauuuuuuuuuurghhh."

The third club that the hangover struck her with was perhaps the most insidious of them all. A symptom of drinking too much that most people entirely overlook, but which serves as a catalyst for much further misery. Giving the giant club a little spinning flourish, the hangover hammered it into her bladder.

The need to pee is hardly the greatest torment to ever befall a living being, but there is a sharp persistence to it that one cannot simply ignore. In normal circumstances, this is fine, but when the sword of Damocles is dangling above you, just waiting for you to make one false move and come into contact with the hovering misery that awaits you, it can be the worst thing imaginable.

Cygni was, like myself, a creature of inscrutable logic. Therefore, she carefully laid out a plan for herself, step by step.

One: slide sideways out of the bed and lower herself gently to the floor.

Two: crab-walk toward the doorway. It was already ajar, judging by the entirely-too-loudness of the outside world.

Three: sidle slowly into the sunlight, keeping her eyes averted, and make her way to the latrines.

Four: vomit copious amounts of liquor into said latrines after the pissing was done, thus removing at least some portion of the poison from her system.

Step one was intercepted by some sort of weight around her middle that seemed to tighten when she tried to slide to the side. Only when she reached down to untangle whatever blanket was holding her in place did she realize that it was not in fact a tangle, but rather an arm. A rather well-muscled arm. Of a man.

Her hand, which had been digging into the skin when she thought it was wool, now ran gently along the flesh, feeling the muscles beneath, and whosoever was lying in the bed beside her made a soft appreciative noise.

Who is that?

"Mind your business, hat."

If you're about to contract the horrible sexually transmitted disease that would render you entirely useless to me, I feel that it is important for me to know.

"What sort of horrible sexually . . ."

Babies.

That shot a spike of fear through her that I don't think had been matched since the dragon. Actually, the fear of the dragon had been fine compared to this. Entirely rational. Being burnt to a crisp was something you'd only have to deal with for a moment, but a baby, that was a problem that would persist for decades.

Images flashed through her head, the king on her throne, churning out an endless tide of baby dwarflings. An eternity trapped, fulfilling that same purpose. She would be a king then, or a queen if she chose the nomenclature, the head of her own dwarf hive, trapped for all time birthing generation after generation of workers.

I suppose that might be quite helpful in the long run, to have a whole dwarf colony available to do our bidding, but it would certainly have put a damper on things in the short-term. And the short-term was, unfortunately, where we currently were.

She pushed the terror from her mind, carefully lifted the arm off her, taking care not to wake whoever she'd bedded, and proceeded to the second half of step one. Sliding slowly across the sheets to the edge of the cot. She did not have far to go the beds in these caravans were hardly luxurious. One roll in the middle of the night would have had you kissing the wooden rim around it, presumably designed to stop such midnight dislodging. She continued to slide, despite the long cool length of wood digging into her back as she went, pausing only at the halfway point to whimper a little as that same ridge intersected with a matching dip in her rump and trapped her for a moment before she toppled over and out.

Her sleeping partner had ably pinned the blanket to himself, with the unconscious practice of someone who had shared bedclothes often enough to realize that tossing and turning could constitute an unconscious tug-of-war. As such, she fell to the floor without any protection from the elements. Groaning.

In all of the time that I had known her, Cygni had never removed her clothing. Not a single item of it. If anything, I think she would have been more comfortable with a few more layers on. Perhaps a full suit of gothic plate and a few slabs of lead added for good measure. The experience of her being nude was not one that I would willingly repeat.

That is not to say that she was hideous or anything of the sort, I'm sure as dwarves go her body was perfectly appealing, but the feelings that welled up in her when she was deprived of her clothes were so overwhelmingly negative that I could scarcely comprehend them. She herself was a dwarf, so shouldn't she have seen her body as attractive instead of something nauseating? It seemed that there were unplumbed depths of Cygni's psyche that I had not yet touched upon, bared only when her skin was likewise bared.

Step two was immediately changed: find her clothes.

She plucked me off her foot, plunging me into a brief moment of nonexistence, and when I came back, things were still a little fuzzy, my awareness of her and her sensations muted, as though our minds were not entirely in contact with one another. It was only when I felt a nipple drag across my rim that I realized I was being used as a modesty guard while she searched.

My first impulse was to be profoundly offended that my esteemed personage was being treated in such a blasé manner, then to be secondly offended that she perceived me so entirely as a piece of clothing rather than a man that it didn't even occur to her that such a thing was lewd. Yet for perhaps the first time in my life, when my life did not depend upon it, I chose not to be offended. Empathy is not the first and foremost talent cultivated in a wizard. To know an enemy's mind is a matter of plunging in and foraging for thoughts, carefully weighing the emotions of others and trying to live in harmony . . . that sounded like druid stuff. As such, choosing to put the feelings of another person before my own did not come naturally to me.

Yet here I was, feeling the turmoil and discomfort within dear Cygni, and finding I had no stomach to do anything that might make matters worse for her. It was a small indignity to endure for the comfort of a friend.

There is something resembling long johns dangling from the candelabra, which we must both be eternally grateful went unlit last night.

Cygni managed to muster a grumble as she tugged them down, setting the gilded apparatus swaying overhead.

Her boots were simple enough to find, as she managed to trip over them three times in her slow excursion around the tiny room. An impressive feat given that she only had two feet.

The trouble with her garb was not so much that she couldn't find it; there were bits and pieces of it strewn all about the room. The real trouble was that they needed to be reassembled in a specific order. The various layers on the outside were too coarse to have against skin, the various layers on the inside, which logically should have been found the closer to the bed that you came, were absent entirely so far as I could tell. Long johns aside.

Whoever lay in the bed was not snoring, which was a mild blessing given the knife edge of hangover headache that Cygni was tiptoeing along, but I did briefly wonder if he was perhaps dead, given the volume at which Cygni herself typically snork-mi-mi-mi'd.

He didn't stir as she dug under his belongings looking for her own, but as she untangled her rather rustic-looking brassiere from Widowtaker's crossguard, I finally pieced some elements of last evening's festivities together.

You and Ildrit?

"Shut up," she snapped, just loud enough that it sent a shot of pain through her forebrain.

No, that makes perfect sense. You like the bad-boy archetype, and it is hard to get more bad-boy than a man with a sword that murders innocent bystanders every time he swings it.

"Listen . . ."

She clearly thought I had more to say, and that her attempt to interrupt would fail, so her sentence ended there. Her poor poisoned mind was quite incapable of producing the remainder of the sentence. Even at crossbow point, I doubt she could have mumbled out whatever it was she had been trying to say to me. Thus we both lapsed into silence as she bent to pick up a pair of heavy woolen socks so crusty that I was fairly certain they could be used as boomerangs.

Perhaps we are missing the opportunity here. You are no longer dwelling beneath the earth; you are now a wizard in your own right. Surely it is time for you to acquire garments that more accurately reflect your new station in life.

That gave her brief pause. I am not going to attempt to joke about the idea that a woman was excited about new clothes, as I have scant enough experience with women not to know whether that stereotype is justified, but the dwarvish mind sought order in all things, and in uniforms in particular the dwarf could find solace. Every different job in the mine had a specific outfit, so that you could tell at a glance whether you were dealing with a surveyor, a digger, a rigger, a sapper, or whatever other highly specific but utterly boring profession the particular dwarf in front of you had damned themselves to.

There was some degree of hierarchy involved, of course, with each different profession convinced that every other was their inferior, but it was predominantly a matter of providing the king of the mine with an easily selectable tool set.

Regardless of the specific impulse, the idea of a new uniform befitting her new station was inherently appealing to her, and thus for the second time I had the opportunity to indoctrinate one of my apprentices into the fine art of wizard fashion.

The robe is traditionally worn by all wizards, embroidered with mystical symbols that inform the unwary of our puissance in the arcane so that we need not resort to demonstrations. Much like the bright coloration of a wasp.

"What's a wasp?"

Forget about wasps. Focus instead on the task at hand: let us assemble for you a set of robes befitting the greatest living dwarvish wizard.

"I'm the only . . ."

If they were better wizards, they'd still be alive. Now pick out a color.

With a gentle nudge, Cygni looked around the room until she settled on the rich burgundy drapery around the window. She pointed.

It was absolutely ideal, already enough cloth, so nothing would have to be fabricated from magic, and a decent thickness of material too. So she would not go cold.

Place me upon your head and seek the Scrynium you abandoned in the night.

"Cygnite."

She did put me on her head then, if only to free up her hands as she crawled around the room digging for her bag of holding, which, as it turned out, was sitting on some shelves above the bed. It was lying on its side, and the mouth of the bag was open. Slowly but surely the massive slab of Scrynium had been sliding its way out through that minute incline. Undisturbed for an hour or so longer, both Cygni and her new lover would have been crushed beneath it.

As it was, she was presented with an awkward situation. The only way to reach the bag on the shelf was to mount the bed, and to do so might very well wake Ildrit. Which was apparently something that she no longer wished to do. I was getting brief flashes through the hangover of the night before. Their teeth banging together as they kissed too fiercely. His hands on her body, prying away the leathers and grazing her skin. Untying the knot of his rope belt and unleashing . . .

And there was a mental image that was going to be seared into my mind for all eternity.

It would seem that Cygni was still reliving that memory, given the way that she was blushing. While I had observed it briefly before, now I learned it was in fact a full body experience. It was not only her face that flushed. Perhaps somewhere in prehistory, there had been some lobster in the dwarf genome. It would explain their hardiness, as well as the discoloration.

She hopped up onto the bundled rag mattress wearing naught but the long johns we'd retrieved, all else flapping in the wind as she reached out and averted disaster. If the stone had fallen, it would have been catastrophic, shattering man, bed, and wagon in one fell swoop. Instead, she tilted the mouth of the bag, the Scrynium slipped back inside, and the hardened battlefield reflexes of Ildrit finally kicked in. His eyes snapped open, staring up directly into Cygni's.

"Ah."

She opened her own mouth to give answer to this beautiful monologue. "Uh."

"Eh . . . ah," Ildrit elucidated her.

Not to be outdone, the poet Cygni responded with a cutting verse of, "Nnnnn."

Oh for the love of all creation, knock it off, the pair of you. Ig would be more eloquent.

That silenced their awkwardness for at least a moment, before finally Cygni managed to get words out. "Hat says you should have done Ig."

Ildrit choked on his own spittle. Armies could not lay this man low, yet a few carefully chosen words had destroyed him. Truly, Cygni was a wizard now.

That is not what I said.

Coughing his way back to breath, Ildrit managed to sputter out, "Not sure Ig's my type."

Cygni stared down at him from where she stood on the bed's frame. The sun at her back and her shadow cast over his prone form. "Ain't even giving him a chance. Shameful."

Now laughing loud enough that I feared we'd draw an audience, Ildrit reached up and took Cygni by the waist, pulling her back down into the bed. Their lips met, and I felt the heat spreading through the dwarf's body and . . .

TAKE OFF THE HAT.

Cygni mumbled against Ildrit's lips, "Better take off the hat."

"Better take everything off to be safe." Ildrit was still chuckling, but there was a heat to his voice that I'd never heard before and could quite happily never hear again for the rest of eternity. In fact, if I could devise some means to travel backwards through time and erase this event from my memory then that is precisely what I would have done.

Cygni fumbled at me, flapping her open hand at my rim to try and knock me off while she was otherwise occupied with a whole variety of sensory input that I was very deliberately not taking in. The long johns it had taken so bloody long to get were now on the floor again, and I was fairly confident that Cygni hadn't touched them at all. Ildrit truly had some sleight of hand in his repertoire of skills.

TAKE OFF THE HAT!

One of their flailing limbs collided with me and I was returned to the blessed darkness. But only oh so briefly. I could not truly judge, just as a ship cannot navigate without stars, but judging by how few thoughts flowed into me from Cygni's fingertips where they dug into my rim, it cannot have been long.

It seemed that vigorous physical activity involving a lot of jiggling was not ideal when you were as hungover and nauseous as she had been prior to falling back into bed with the swordsman. In fact, it seemed that they had scarcely begun the morning round of whatever perversity they were indulging in when last night's rum began to navigate northwards.

"Going to hurl," she managed to blurt out while seizing me off the floor.

Not in me you aren't!

There is a unique sensory hell of being both the sick bucket and the person being sick at the same time. As you feel the vomit burning up your throat and know that while soon, one part of you will feel better, not long later another part of you will be feeling infinitely worse.

I am dry-clean only! Don't you dare!

Up and up it burned, every part of her convulsing as the putrid mix rose toward its final, inevitable escape. The smell of it pervaded her nostrils long before the vile plume made it close to her mouth. Her nostrils and my mind. The sharp rankness of it, the smell that I would smell of for all of eternity.

In panic I seized control of her throat and stopped the involuntary motion of projectile banana mulch. She choked briefly before sprinting for the door of the caravan, clearly recognizing that it would be better not to share any more bodily fluids with someone in our social circle.

If she were entirely nude, then what followed would have been a rather unpleasant bout of sickness and embarrassment. But she was not. For while she had shorn her many layers of leathers and wool to reveal the skin beneath, and even toed off those mighty steel-toe-capped boots, the rings stuck on her fingers in haste still had not been pried from her. Two rings enchanted so that the smallest jump became a mighty leap. Not adding to one another's power but multiplying it.

She stumbled on the first step out of the wagon, stamped down too hard on the next step, and then pushed off with a panicked, frantic force born of desperation and impending retching.

A rainbow is a perfectly natural phenomenon caused by light beams curving through droplets of water. We cannot see the full circular curvature of such things because they typically manifest beyond the horizon, but they are most assuredly not simply arcs of colors across the sky. By contrast, the abomination that Cygni created as she soared across the heavens was a simple arc. A flash of pallid flesh followed by a slower rain of partially digested banana daiquiris.

A rainbow of regurgitation. A veritable volcanic vomit vector. A pouncing puke python.

All the villagers, both native to this land and brought here by their wolf halves, looked up in wonder at the unusual sight. All of the carnival folk that had already stirred caught a glimpse of what was falling toward them and remembered the time when the caravan had hauled rides around, the fast-spinning rides that had hoisted youngsters stuffed full of sweet things into the sky and blasted everyone below with the unfortunate results. They remembered, and they scrambled for shelter.

The rain of banana bile came down before Cygni had even landed. Her rational mind had entirely checked out, between the furious projectile vomiting, the overwhelming shame, and the hangover so severe that sudden exposure to sunlight risked her brain exploding. This left me more or less in charge of our survival. Luck had guided her last leap into something softish, but now she lacked the armor she had been wearing, or the wherewithal to twist and redirect herself in the air.

There was not enough Quintessence inside of her, or any living dwarf, to perform the kind of spell that might catch her as she plummeted to her doom. I reached first to her fingertips, which had so recently brushed against the Scrynium and managed to salvage from the dusty residue enough Quintessence to perform a simple act of magic.

I had no mouth with which to speak a spell, and Cygni's was entirely committed to the performance of its regurgitative duties, but I had my incredible mind and my will and I was damned if I was going to let this poor girl suffer any more.

The power flowed up through her fingers and into me, overwhelming me with the sheer volume of Quintessence now at my disposal. My will expanded out from Cygni's soaring body, far beyond the limits of her body or her spraying. The caravans had been set up to form a boardwalk around which they had assembled all of the fancies and distractions that they sold as their lifeblood. But back from that central line, there were other small streets formed of the varied caravans, sealed off from the outside world. A village on wheels. And between every caravan was strung a line, and upon each line were various items of clothing left out to dry. It took but a twitch to pull each line away and release it, letting the elasticity of the thing do my work for me. Then there was a flock of shirts and dresses in the air, shielding poor Cygni from the judgmental glares of strangers.

This may very well have seemed someone irrelevant given the impending death she was facing, but I meant for her to survive and to live afterwards as well. Something that would be difficult to achieve if shame were to explode her into flames every time that she tried to meet someone's eye.

No, I would have my friend alive and intact, insomuch as I could muster. So she was swaddled in the soaring cloth, padded with skirts and rugs and all the rest. Then, with all of that done and her eyes blinded to what was happening outside, I reached out with the last of the Quintessence, stretching out barely any distance at all, and I stopped her.

Powerful as the residue may have been, there was scarcely enough of it to empower low magic directly for more than a few moments. Low magic was the most inefficient use of Quintessence, exchanging forces directly instead of shaping the magic into something more robust and useful. One of those moments had been spent flinging clothes at Cygni, and I spent the last of it now.

Cocooned as she was, I had no means of seeing the world outside. I had no way of knowing when we were about to strike the earth except to turn my incredible mind to the task of calculating speeds and trajectories. What luck that mind was so incredible, really.

Cygni froze in her flight, her stomach blessedly emptied by the time that she was swaddled, so that she had only her aromas to deal with and not anything too chunky. She tried to speak, at last, mumbling, "What?"

Then my grip was lost as the last of my Quintessence burned away. Gravity took hold of her once more, dropping her the remaining three feet to hit the ground with a soft "Oof".

There, you have survived your jaunt through the sky unseen and unharmed, but might I please request that you remove the Jumping Rings as soon as possible?

"Okay," was all that she could muster in that moment.

Also, if you'd be so kind as to remove me from your foot before walking around again, it would be much appreciated.

"Sure."

And never attempt to use me as a sick bag again.

"Alright."

Good. I'm glad we're on the same page.

"Nobody saw?"

At the velocity you were traveling, you were a blur.

"Right. Good."

Although you may have to explain what happened to Ildrit, lest he thinks his bared form was so repulsive it led you to vomit and fly away.

"Ildrit." She groaned. "That's his name?"

I wasn't one to judge when it came to these matters. I'd be quite the hypocrite if I did, given that I couldn't have even remembered the faces of most of the people that had been wearing me on their various body parts last night.

That's the one. Ildrit of the Black Blade, the cursed swordsman striving to do good despite his fundamental nature being aligned with darkness. I hear that he has warrants out for his arrest across a great many civilized kingdoms. Arpanpholigon included.

To the untrained observer, it may have appeared that I was making that statement to dissuade our nude dwarf burrito from pursuing a relationship with the man, appealing to the parts of her that respected order, law, and goodness, but you forget that I had seen firsthand that the more of a bad boy any given person she encountered was, the more likely it was that she would immediately fling herself into their arms. Was it manipulative? Of course. One does not become the greatest living wizard without some degree of manipulation of one's enemies and allies. But was it done with malice? I think not. Neither Ildrit nor Cygni had known more than a fleeting moment's happiness in the time that I had known the two of them, but when they were together, before I was thankfully removed from Cygni's head, she had burned with a fierce joy that felt quite unlike her. A joy removed from her steady plodding thought processes and her careful planning. If I could help them to have that joy together, then I would have to be considerably more of a bastard than I actually am to deny them it.

Besides, we had little hold over Ildrit at present, beyond his blundering attempts to do the right thing, and it would have been nice if he had some reason to support my righteous cause beyond righteousness itself. Particularly when we may have been headed into somewhat morally ambiguous territory when we finally arrived in the city and I had my opportunity to wreak revenge upon whosoever murdered me resulting in my transubstantiation into a hat. Ig was entirely my creature through the bonds of friendship we had forged, Cygni had her own goals that were best served aligned with mine, but the swordsman was something of a wild card, and I did not like unknown variables.

Alright, so maybe I was being a bit of a bastard by shoving the two of them together, but honestly, if it stopped Cygni from attempting to mount every gentleman with a roguish demeanor between here and our goal then it was worth the price.

To my amazement, it was in fact Ildrit himself who came to Cygni's rescue, and considerably quicker than I would have expected, given the distance he had to traverse and the fact that he had to pull on trousers, boots, and apparently the baldric that held his sword so that the leather straps were pulled taut across the broad, muscled expanse of his chest.

Perhaps it would have been useful to enchant some sort of portable cold shower to deploy on Cygni when she was dealing with Ildrit. Just to keep things moving forward.

Luckily for all of us, Ildrit had not come alone, and but a moment after he'd torn open Cygni's cocoon, a little snoot protruded over the hemline. Ig, a creature so hideous and off-putting that he could serve as a prophylactic to everyone in his blast radius.

"Me brought clotheses!" he announced, dropping into the giant heap of clothes the most useless imaginable assortment of objects imaginable. To wit:

One left stocking—torn at the knee.

Two embroidered corsets—both made for a woman thrice Cygni's height and twice her voluptuousness.

One lace bonnet—of the sort that storytellers imagined all milkmaids wore.

One left sock, darned beyond all recognition.

One cape, silk lined and almost certainly pilfered from Stjepan's wardrobe sometime during the orgiastic delights of the evening past.

Three gloves of varying styles and materials, all for the left hand.

One length of cloth that at first appeared to be a patchwork skirt, and therefore actually useful, but which soon resolved itself into a collection of handkerchiefs that had been stitched together end to end. The fool later claimed this item, having lost it the eve before during a game of cards. Nobody could recall who had won it, and nobody actually wanted it but the fool, so it was all fine.

Wrapping a borrowed rug around herself for some dignity, Cygni found it tricky to walk—what luck then that the gallant Ildrit was ready to sweep her up in his arms.

She made a little noise in her throat somewhere between a hum and a growl, then her mind went entirely blank for a moment before flooding with heated glimpses of memory from the night before, mostly relating to how easy it was for a well-muscled human to throw her around when she wasn't resisting.

Might I please be passed to Ig, I'm not sure I can tolerate the mental images for much longer.

With an offensive lack of care, she knocked me off and let me drift down to the churned mud. Bless Ig for snatching me up before anything too grotesque could soak in. "My is wearing you agains now."

You certainly are, my diminutive friend. And what a relief it is to be back on the head of someone with absolutely no possibility of consummating a relationship.

"Weh?" Ig inquired.

Sex, Ig. They've been having sex and I don't want to hear about their lovemaking anymore.

"Not want hear about Ig's new wives and they big fat tails?"

I recoiled violently from the idea before realizing that the kobold was making a joke at my expense. Rather than indulge in the irritation that once would have followed such an event as my having been outwitted by the witless wonder, I instead changed the subject.

And what exactly did you get up to last night when you were not with the dwarf, the swordsman, or your wives, beyond producing a great many bananas for everyone?

Softly, and a little sadly, he informed me, "Me no actually have wives."

I am aware, Ig.

"Me, uh . . ." He strained a little trying to remember. Typically I would have put this down to his usual brain troubles, but there was a good degree of alcohol poisoning at work too. "Me had drinks. And me make friends. And me is ringmaster now."

I'm terribly sorry, did you say you were now the ringmaster of this circus?

He nodded, entirely too casually. "They votes."

The circus folk voted, and given the choice of every single one of their seasoned veterans or a kobold that they picked up off the side of the road a week ago, you were the first choice?

"Me make lots friends," Ig answered, as though that answered anything.

We plodded along beside the luminously blushing dwarf and Ildrit for a moment as I attempted to process all this.

Is it because they thought you were responsible for slaying the previous ringmaster?

"Weh?"

The werewolf. Did they believe that you were responsible for his destruction and their ensuing freedom to choose whether to go on with the circus rather than being bound to it by a curse?

Ig didn't quite grasp all of that. "They likes my banananananananas?"

Ildrit chuckled. "I'd say that everyone enjoyed their bananas last night."

Cygni's blush went thermonuclear. If you had cracked an egg on her it would have been fried in moments.

So it would be correct to say that you are now in charge of this entire circus, the one who could issue commands and see them done.

"Yes?" Ig replied with a degree of trepidation. As though after all this time he had finally realized that I sometimes asked him to do things that he didn't want to, and he somehow ended up doing them all the same.

Then might I suggest that we mobilize the caravans and head toward Arpanpholigon with all haste?

"Why hasty?"

Because it is only a matter of time before they realize what a bad idea it was to put you in charge, and I'd rather be markedly closer to our ultimate goal before they come to that realization.

"Me could be good top hat man." Ig seemed quite put out.

My dear Ig, you already have a hat that you must wear, and only one head.

"You has other heads you go on now." Ig did not pout, because he lacked the lips for such an act, but there was a definite petulantly aggrieved tone to his voice.

Ig. Circumstances forced me to take another apprentice; it was not by choice. Had I the option, I would have gone on through all the dark places of the world in your company, faced the monsters and dragons and traps from atop your head, fought off the dark god that was loosed beneath the . . .

"Me fine with you go other way," Ig announced as the litany of terrors continued to mount. "Sometimes need go different way. No bad."

To my surprise, I truly had missed Ig. Not just how easy he was to manipulate in comparison to Cygni, but the honesty of all his emotions. Admittedly, almost all of those emotions were blind terror, but he was entirely forthright about them being blind terror, and that was a breath of fresh air in comparison to the chronically repressed dwarf.

She giggled from in Ildrit's arms.

Repression only led to explosive outbursts of emotion down the line. Abrupt and foolish choices that could only end in heartbreak. Or marriage. Far better for it to leak out of my kobold companion gradually, staining every action he took, but not entirely overpowering his rational decision-making mind. And by rational decision-making mind, I of course refer to myself.

Sure, Ig was dumb as a rock and prone to wetting himself whenever there was a loud noise, but he was not willful. Not in the way that Cygni was. He had a few morals that he seemed to have developed entirely out of the blue, but even those could be circumvented with a little threat to his life or two. In short, he was the ideal host. When first we crossed paths, I had considered him to be a moron, a liability, the absolute worst thing that one could ever find oneself squatting atop, but the truth was that Ig had been exactly what I needed, when I needed it the most, and for that I would always be grateful to him.

As we made our way along the boulevard of dropped popcorn, I seized control of his throat. *"We're heading out at noon. Get it all packed up, folks."*

Given the severity of the hangovers on display in everyone that we met, this was not a popular announcement. There was a great deal of moaning, complaining, despairing, groaning, flatulence, and . . . well, a full list of all the reasons that I prefer not to interact with humankind as a general rule.

What luck that I was prepared for such an eventuality with the precise sort of plan that would ensure the loyalty of these entertainers forever. *"Just head along to the ashes of the magic tent if you have a hangover. I know the cure."*

Silence swept across the whole disheveled caravan at that announcement. For those who worked in customer service and entertainment, as the carnival folk did, a cure for a hangover was tantamount to the holy grail. I am not saying that every bard in the world had a drinking problem, or that every waiter was snorting ground-up unicorn horn in the bathroom during their shifts, but there were certain . . . trends. And among the carnival folk, there was no shortage of clowns whose noses were red and swollen without the assistance of prosthetics thanks to their copious consumption of booze.

In the rest of the world, if you had the cure for a plague, you would have received this sort of reception. If you had been able to cut loose the bonds of mortality, you might have received some portion of the reverence that Ig was in receipt of now.

It isn't even particularly complicated, as far as magic goes. Carbon to absorb the alcohol in the stomach, water to restore that which was lost and is causing the shrinkage of the brain, and a mild neurotoxin to numb all the senses.

Soft as a whimper, Ig told me, "Me no even understand most those words."

Fear not, dear Ig. I shall guide your hands as we make the potion.

That just seemed to spurn the poor kobold on even more. "Me is not preeminent kobold alchemist."

I had not expected him to recall any of the words of my earlier slights, let alone recall how to pronounce them. Truly Ig's mind was constantly growing better.

This is so, but luckily for you, this particular potion is one that I learned during my student days. And given that it is simple enough for an idiot to concoct while hungover, I do not think you shall have any troubles.

Things actually progressed surprisingly swiftly from that point on. Once the entire caravan had passed by the makeshift cauldron that we'd managed to liberate from the mess tent and gone through every stage of grief after tasting the potion, they were bright and sprightly, getting everything done with a well-practiced rapidity that would have put ants or dwarves to shame. I'd wager that the only two who did not take at least a sip of our hangover cure were Ildrit and Cygni, who had mysteriously vanished as we passed by his caravan. A caravan that I regret to add was rocking wildly from side to side as though traversing rough terrain from that moment on.

And lo and behold, it was still rocking thus when Ig latched it onto a donkey and we set off on our merry way toward Arpanpholigon. On foot, it would have been a week's travel. By cart, with the full supply train of the circus at our back and all the capering and nonsense that went along with it, we arrived there one day shy of a week.

Finally, I was home.

CHAPTER EIGHTEEN

THE CITY OF LIGHTS

And so our epic journey and my tale came to its end. Returning home to Arpanpholigon, it took no time at all for me to restore my physical form, rend the one who had slain me and fulfill all the promises that I'd made to my companions. Breaking Ildrit's curse so that he could act in accordance with his own desires instead of some abstract morality. Stripping Ig of his sentience so he could go back to living as a humble kobold in a hole. Developing magical treatments that allowed Cygni to expand her vestigial Quintessence channels and bring magic back to her people. Then I proceeded to live out many hundreds of years as the undisputed master of magics, expanding our knowledge to unseen heights and making the world a better place for everyone, as I'd always intended.

Nothing more to see here. Carry on with your lives. This tale is complete. Don't make me talk about the little details. Or the bad things that happened. Journey ended. Quest completed. Murder avenged. That's your lot.

Just look at it, Ig. Arpanpholigon, the City of Lights, the home of magic. A whole city founded on the principles of education and enlightenment.

No, there is no more story. We are done. You don't want to hear this next bit. Go and amuse yourselves with something else. I'm sure there are some bright colors somewhere for you to stare at. Go on. Shoo.

"It so big." He gawked.

Why are you still here, I told you to stop reading. I am Absalom Scryne, Archmage of Arpanpholigon, and I command you to depart!

Indeed, and its immense size is by far the least interesting part about it, for you see, though there are a great many people living in the city, their purpose is only to offer support and material to the university, and in turn they experience all the wonders that the High Art can provide. Their homes are free of vermin, their water is clean and refreshing, there is no crime to speak of, and not a one of them shall ever know hunger, so long as there are students in the university still studying the ancient art of conjuring food into existence from the aether.

Fine. You want to hear the rest. That's just fine. I'll tell you the rest, but let me tell you this first. You aren't going to like it. Until now our story has been joyful and uplifting, as I traversed dangers and adventures but always came out ahead. Admittedly some of the little people I met along the way may have died a bit, but ultimately, they were probably doomed to death anyway, so it should hardly be counted against me.

From here on, that is not entirely the case. So if you want everything to be perfect and happy, just take my word for it that things work out and go stare out the window or something.

No?

Fine.

The great wall that encircled the civilized world was nothing compared to the walls of Arpanpholigon. It may have been bigger and taller, but there was a beauty and grace to Arpanpholigon's walls that put it to shame. Beautiful vaulting and beams upheld the parapet, each enhanced with simple illusions to project flowers and birds so that the blander interstitial areas had something of interest for the eye to settle upon. Of particular delight to me were the birds of paradise that splayed awkwardly at an angle from the illusions of waterfalls, and the rainbows that those artificial sprinkles of water evoked in the air. Even before you set foot inside of the city, it was one of the most beautiful places you would ever have the joy of laying eyes upon.

"It so pretty!" Ig's running commentary would once have grated on my nerves, but in this case the simplicity of his description was apt. Arpanpholigon was indeed pretty.

Our caravans were making good time as we approached the gatehouse facing our direction of approach, slowing slightly to accommodate the other traffic, all the farmers bringing goods to markets and all the hopefuls streaming in with dreams of one day becoming wizards in their own right. The majority of them would be rejected, of course; there was only a limited number of slots for students in the university, despite how vast that university happened to be. Those unfortunates would filter out through the city. Some would settle into more mundane jobs, others would join the various lesser magicians' guilds that promised some degree of education, even though there was no possibility that they could match what could be learned in the Invisible College itself. Some even ended up as alchemists, healers, and . . . druids.

Of the world's population of able magic users, more than half lived here, and it showed in every part of the city. Where in other places children might run through the streets playing with toys, here they created illusions of spectral dragons in flight, chasing after one another through the sky and across the rooftops. They conjured lesser demons and set them to battling one another to settle arguments. Not a single child in the city would ever know a scraped knee for longer than the moment it took one of the others to cast, or for some kindly merchant to ply them with a free sample of a salve.

Ig's eyes were so wide I suspected that they'd been pinned open as he took it all in. We passed under the arch of the city gates and the protective magic woven through the stone itself washed over us, seeking out any that meant the city or its people harm. It was the sort of grandiose enchantment that I hoped to someday enact on a grander scale, encircling all the world in my protection, should I recover flesh and find the opportunity.

It made the little bristles of hair on Ig's body stand on end as it washed through us.

For a fearful moment, I could feel it begin to coalesce. Not around Ig, who meant no harm to anyone in the world, but around Ildrit. I could not say with certainty if the magic had been informed of the warrants out for his arrest, or only examined the motivations of those passing by. Technically, it probably should have prevented my passage into the city, what with my stated intention to murder someone when I learned the identity of my killer, but either my nature as an enchanted object or the fact that it was university business allowed it to wash over me harmlessly. Given that almost every faculty member of the Invisible College had at one time or another intended to destroy one of their rivals, I suppose that making this protective magic too sensitive would have precluded the majority of us from ever leaving town. Though given that an even greater majority of faculty barely even left their private libraries, labs, and chambers unless forced to by their teaching schedules, Too many of them traveling was unlikely, to say the least.

For a moment, Ildrit had a little glow about him, but it faded fast enough that none of the sparse guards around the gates took notice. By his side, Cygni had tensed, ready to leap to the defense of her new beau in the face of an entire city of markedly more competent magic wielders, and I supposed that was kind of sweet, if it wouldn't have instantly doomed us all. What luck then that we were able to proceed unimpeded.

Excitement rippled out through the city on our arrival. It had been many years since a circus had come to town, primarily because it was a city of magic that should have rendered any achievement that a performer could reach laughable, yet in spite of this there seemed to be genuine interest.

I suppose that it was as if someone had come to your town with a fish, promising that it could perform a samba. Everyone around you could perform a samba at any time, in fact it would be a relatively easy feat, given that they walked around on two feet. But to see a fish do a samba, that would be something special. To see a creature deprived of every natural advantage rising up onto its tail and beginning to dance, it would make the ease with which everyone else could perform a samba seem so much the sweeter.

Which is to say, sure, they could produce miracles the likes of which you'd never seen, but that didn't mean it wasn't fun to watch some idiot in a hat pretending to produce the same miracles using an elaborate series of mirrors and pulleys.

So those same children who could have blown the wheels off the caravan with a misspoken word bounded along beside us excitedly as we headed for one of the grassy squares near the middle of town, and Ig bounced up and down with an excitement to match theirs. "Look at towerses!" He gawked as we passed through the shadows of the immense spires that had until now been hidden from view by the lower slung buildings and city walls.

Just remember that all of these architectural marvels are trifles compared to the Invisible College itself.

"Where I see that?" Ig asked excitably.

It is . . . it is in the name, Ig.

"Is not just name?"

No, Ig. It is actually invisible. At least from down here.

"Where is?" He stood up in his seat and was almost immediately thrown into the crowd as the wheels slipped into a rut. Only the swift motion of Ildrit's hand snapping out to the scruff of his neck saved him. Still Ig gibbered on, "Me no see no big hill?"

Ildrit chuckled. "It's floating, Ig."

At that, Cygni's head snapped back too, both her and Ig peering up at the sky above, as though they might catch a glimpse of it through the layered spells of invisibility that kept it hidden from . . . wait a second. There was a faint ripple in the air at what was probably one of the corners, and once I could see that, it was simple enough to trace along where the lines led to make out where the outer walls of the college lay. You couldn't see the thing itself, of course, but where the clouds should have drifted on by undisturbed, they instead seemed to part. Their absence gave the thing form. That and the innumerable birds that had unfortunately splattered against the walls.

Standards were slipping; I had those walls hosed down twice a day when I was in charge. It was the reason people in the outer arrondissements all carried umbrellas when the city received no weather to speak of.

A little rain never hurt anyone, but a falling albatross would leave a mark.

"I think I can see . . ." Cygni trailed off.

Ig pointed. "Is that . . ."

We bumped out of the roadside rut and the two of them were flung bodily around. Only Ildrit seemed to have any sort of stability, so he ended up with the two snuggled up under his arm. At least until Cygni shoved Ig away just a little more forcefully than was really required.

She had a few days' worth of stubble grown in now, and seemed a lot more comfortable about her face, but even as she returned to the appearance she had fostered during her time in the mines, her attitude remained markedly different.

I had heard tales of love, and how it changed those that it infected, but I would never have predicted the ways in which it would warp my good friend

Cygni from the scowling and cynical voice of reason into the pouting, jealous creature that she had become. At first I had feared that she and Ig would fight over me, with the two of them so desiring the wisdom that I could impart, but it seemed she no longer had much interest in sharing her body with me now that she was sharing it with Ildrit at every opportunity.

In truth, it had been a very long time since I last descended to the city and explored its byways. Years at least. The streets were familiar to me, the structures and the buildings, but the faces were those of strangers. In the college itself, things would of course be better, in part because nothing ever changed behind its walls, but also because it was where I had cloistered myself for so long, never even contemplating the veritable kaleidoscope of experiences that might have been hidden just beneath me. It was so bizarre to me that I'd had to travel all the way across the Badlands and underworld before arriving here outside a little restaurant that I'd never even heard of in a city that might as well have been on the other side of the world for all the time I'd spent actually living in it.

Ildrit drew me from my reverie. "Where are we going exactly?"

"Continue straight over the vaulted bridge, then take a right and follow along the riverbank until you reach the fourth arrondissement acid pit. From there, go left." It took so little effort to commandeer Ig's mouth nowadays, it was becoming second nature to me.

Ildrit just nodded and carried on, but Cygni, from the region of his armpit, scowled at me, and Ig, by extension. "Acid pit?"

From above and around her, she felt Ildrit's chuckle vibrating more than she could have heard it. Clearly, he was familiar with the tale. That was good. It was good that other adventurers had learned about it. It would prevent similar accidents occurring in the future.

"Once upon a time, an adventurer came to town equipped with an unusual machine and some beans. They set up shop and began selling hot bean juice, which people quite enjoyed. Myself included." We crossed over the bridge as I spoke, trundling toward the site of this tale with surprisingly little traffic in our way. *"Sadly, those beans were an ingredient in the humble Stamina potion sold by purveyors of the alchemical arts. The guild of alchemists judged that the process involved in creating the bean juice constituted alchemy. Ergo there is now an endlessly roiling acid pit where the shop once stood."*

Cygni seemed to consider this for a moment, then nodded. "Scabs."

"I suspected that might be your position on the matter."

"I'm just glad it stopped before it got too far." Ildrit looked off into the middle distance, vaguely haunted in his expression. "That partner of hers was planning on opening more shops, all over the place."

The lost aspect of the story nagged at me. Perhaps part of my recollections lost to the creature in the darkness beneath the world. *"What was his name . . .*

the druid who was trapped in the form of a stag, but insisted on wearing a wizard's constellation-coated robes all the same?"

"Buggered if I can remember." Ildrit shrugged.

And so went the remainder of our journey through the City of Lights. With me or Ildrit pointing out some interesting local landmark and the other two showing as much interest in it as they had all of the rest, which is to say, not much. Their eyes were forever being dragged away from whatever historic event I was outlining to a fresh flash of color and excitement. I imagine that once upon a time, I had been just as excited to arrive in Arpanpholigon, to see the world through this new lens, realizing all of the wonders that it could hold. Though even stretching back to those earliest memories through the tattered lace of my shredded recollections, I simply did not feel it. Even as a child, being delivered from some farmer or merchant's cart after unexpectedly showing my puissance, I could recall no brightness in my heart or demeanor. Perhaps at heart I had always been a miserable old man. A bitter, joyless old . . . what is the masculine version of a hag? A wizard . . . perhaps.

The acid pit was considerably less exciting than the others might have hoped for. It had continued to slowly erode its way down, so it was mostly just a hole at this point. If you wanted to sightsee it properly then you would have had to jump in, and for some inexplicable reason none of us were tempted.

Except for the fool, who had to be intercepted and carried off by a strongman when he made a break for freedom from his awful existence.

Even as they dragged him off to put on his special straitjacket with bells on, he was cackling all the way, yelling at us, "Don't worry! Don't worry! I didn't mean it! Killing myself is the last thing I'd ever do!"

A few more of those and I might begin to be concerned about him.

"Weh?" Ig didn't seem to have noticed the events playing out by the pit, having instead been distracted by a butterfly fluttering by, and then transforming back into a seriously pissed-off-looking cat. Perhaps the fool's follies had been so frequent an event throughout their travels with the circus that it didn't even register anymore.

When we came to our allotted patch of green, the same magic that had broken down camp the other night sprang into action immediately. I'd personally have put it down to everyone being stir-crazy after being trapped in their little caravans for so long were it not for the joyful smiles. They say that if you love your job, you will never work a day in your life. With "they" in this circumstance being the people intending to underpay you drastically for the work you do on the basis that it is fine to do so since you are enjoying yourself. Nobody has to be paid to have a good time, after all.

Regardless, the carnival folk seemed to be genuinely delighted to go about their business, even when they were out of sight of the people that they derisively referred to as "townies".

The only person among their number that I had not seen since the party was the bearded lady, Angelina. She had kept entirely to herself since that night, or rather since consuming her hangover cure the morning after. She had not only been in hiding from Ig, the alleged killer of her husband, as I'd first assumed, but keeping entirely to her own company. Though the others brought meals to her caravan, I never once saw the door open, and when Ig did come close enough to investigate further, the fool had popped out from behind the caravan and threatened to speak until we fled.

So if she had or had not appeared as we began constructing our tents, it would have been equally unremarkable. What took every one of us by surprise was when she emerged in mourning dress, deprived of that feature that had granted her a livelihood in the circus. There was not even the hint of a five o'clock shadow upon her cheeks, and I must admit that I found her features markedly less interesting as a result. I am not by any means saying that the only women I find attractive are those with facial hair, but my life has been spent in a world where expansive beards are a marker of maturity, power, and influence, which were all things that I most assuredly did find attractive. You can understand why some mental wires may have gotten crossed.

She strolled across to Ig with a casualness so carefully acted that I fully expected an assassination attempt, but she simply waved up to him where he dangled from the loose guy-line he had been trying to pin down. "I'll be off now."

"You goes somewhere?" Ig asked.

She let out a huff of breath. "Too many bad memories here. Need to start over."

Without prompting, Ig was swift to ask, "You needing moneys to gets settled?"

The Ig that I knew had barely the vaguest concept of currency, so clearly Ildrit had been attempting to educate him in matters relevant to civilization.

Yet despite his near desperation to do something nice for the woman, Angelina shook her head. "Still got my little nest egg, from when . . . from before."

"Me is no likey watch go." Ig fumbled every word as per usual. "Even if you has ostrich to help."

The distance between what Ig understood of the world and the reality was always a vast chasm, but it was a distance that until now I had been able to traverse, using my own intellect as a bridge of sorts. Or at least as a springboard. Yet here I was looking down into this no-longer-bearded woman's face, feeling exactly the same level of perplexity as I could see upon it.

Ostrich baby?!

"From egg." Ig looked at Angelina intently, hoping that she understood.

Oh, for the love of . . .

"It's money, Ig." Angelina had already begun backing away. "Gold I saved."

"Ah." Ig nodded with some satisfaction. "Goods. Didn't know how ostrich helped."

I suspect that there are very few situations that are improved by the addition of a feral, flightless, terror-bird.

"Is why I want give her money instead." Ig rolled his eyes, as though it were obvious.

The tents had all been staked by the time that the sun went down and the crowds began to arrive. Angelina was long gone, Ildrit and Cygni had vanished somewhere private, again, even though they were meant to be standing guard at the doors of the various tents to ensure people paid their entry. As for Ig, his heart was hammering in his chest as hard as it had when he was being pursued by murderous ogres. Not the most uncommon of occurrences, given that he spent about 90 percent of his life in abject terror, but notable in this case because nothing could even be entirely misconstrued as trying to kill him. Rather, his nerviness was coming from performance anxiety.

It is all going to be fine. You've done this dozens of times, the only difference is that this time your magic is going to be markedly more impressive.

He let out an unintelligible squeak.

Yes, I will admit that the big top is going to be drawing in a larger crowd than your little burnt-out tent, but that does not mean that anything will be different.

Another whimper, akin to the noise of a deflating balloon.

I am aware that you are feeling some jitters despite your usual enjoyment of large crowds. But you must set them aside. Simply behave as though there is nobody else in the tent if that helps to ease your mind, or imagine that all of them are unrobed, I have heard that is effective too.

An unfortunate side effect of occupying the mind of Ig was that I was exposed to the imagination of Ig on those few moments that it sputtered to life. And while the imagination of Ig was not the most active, with the majority of its energies having been consumed by anxiety and turned over to randomly excreting new horrible ways that he might die in any given scenario, the viewpoint of Ig was at waist height when it came to the humans that surrounded him.

His stomach turned over. If I'd had a stomach, it would have been turning over too. He managed not to retch through a valiant effort.

Alright, so now we know what the absolute worst-case scenario during your performance would look like, I can guarantee that everything will definitely be better than that. Or at least less . . . flappy.

Ig managed to muster a little nervous smile. "Why I do this?"

Thankful to be back on more solid ground, I explained the plan to him for what must have been the hundredth time.

First and foremost, it was necessary for you to take over the role of ringmaster in the central tent as a result of Stjepan's untimely . . . departure. As you lack any musical talent, it made sense to tie together the different acts of the main ring through different performances of magic instead.

Ig was nodding, but I knew that he wasn't really paying attention, because I was in his brain. With horror, I came to the conclusion that he was using me as . . . a comfort. Listening to my voice in his head was soothing to him, somehow. I felt dirty.

It was working, however, so I continued automatically.

This decision also presents us with a unique opportunity, because while nobody from the college is liable to be in attendance at tonight's shows, the only people in the world who college attendees do interact with will be. As such, we will have the opportunity to attract their attention should we put on a sufficiently intriguing display and thereby secure an invitation to the Invisible College.

"How in-tree-ging we need be?" Ig carefully sounded out the larger word and surprised me by not meandering into introspection or entrapment. Even if, internally, he did truly believe I was saying that we had to perform from the boughs of an oak.

To be entirely honest, the moment that the people of Arpanpholigon recognize that you are a kobold capable of performing magic, it should draw sufficient attention, though I might suggest that you undertake some of those magics that are unique to you, if only to add a degree of spice to the performance.

"Spicy me spells," Ig replied, as though he had the faintest idea of what I meant.

For instance, your ability to direct magic in multiple directions at once, or your ability to draw Quintessence and cast simultaneously.

"Like knife thing?" he asked, with a degree of nervousness.

I was rather impressed that you came up with that particular trick, taking the focus that fear gave you and making it your strength. Genius, really.

That puffed up the kobold a little, though he did admit, "Me did first with rotten fruitses."

Had I the capacity I'm sure that would have drawn a chuckle from me as I imagined the scenario. More important than my amusement, of course, was that all of this mindless prattle was sufficient to keep Ig distracted as the first guests of the evening began to filter in.

The irony was that the presence of so many people actually helped to settle his nerves and make him feel more secure. When all of the bleachers were filled, all the benches stretching up almost to the roof of the big top itself, I could hear the echoing of the hundred or more voices surrounding poor Ig. Every one of them wondering why the hell there was a kobold in the middle of what was supposed to be a circus, and why one of the local pest exterminators hadn't already seen to it. They weren't to know, of course, and I imagine that had I been among them but a year or two ago, then my opinion would have been similar if not worse. To most people, a kobold was not a person at all, but a thing. Less than the lowest. Little did they know that they now stood in the presence of a creature that I'd be inclined to refer to as neither pest, monster, nor even human. I'd have called Ig a hero. Braver than any adventurer venturing into a dank cave that might be filled with monsters. He had strolled into this entirely hostile city where everyone wanted him gone in broad daylight without so much as a flinch. He had gone toe to toe with the most fearsome creatures of the Badlands and stood his ground when his very nature was screaming at him desperately to flee. I could not think of a more noble creature than this simple kobold. Though of course, I could never admit any of this to Ig, lest he develop an ego and become unmanageable.

Still, I think he must have felt my pride in him, even if I did not express it, because a new energy flooded through his quivering form. Confidence, or as close to it as a kobold was capable of coming. He clapped his little paws together, and to his—and my—amazement, the whole tent fell silent.

Clearing his throat like a waste disposal unit with glue in it, he announced, "Welcomes to the show!"

The silence continued for a moment, before some mild chuckles began. People who suspected that this was an act of ventriloquism, given that everyone knew kobolds were incapable of speech.

"Normal we is having music now, but bard was werewolf so me squishes him with big hammer." The chuckling at his absurd statement mounted now. The audience believed that this was a comedy act to warm them up. "But instead you is getting me. Me introduce self!"

Ig ambled around in a little circle until he found the little raised platform he had been looking for and scrabbled up, to yet more amusement from the crowd.

Another horrendous throat clearing, then Ig spread his arms wide. "Me is Ig! Me is first ever kobold wizard!"

What had been soft chuckles now developed into outbursts of laughter. This was going to be more difficult than I had expected. This all seemed farcical to them, not only farcical but very deliberately farcical, as though we were taking shots at their overhanging overlords in the college above. They thought this was subversive comedy.

"Me is doing magics for you tonight." He had to shout to be heard over the crowd's amusement. "But first me introduce friends!"

At that, the show began in earnest. Flipping tumblers came pouring out into the circle, trapeze artists leapt from where they were hidden up in the shadows to flip around overhead, everything was going exactly as a circus should. Everything except for the ringmaster being taken solemnly seriously.

Damnation.

"Weh?" Ig inquired.

They think you're a joke. They think that this is all an act.

"We is in circus." Ig gave credit where it was due to their reasoning.

This means that we shall have to escalate our display somewhat. Perform an act of magic so impressive that they'd seek out whosoever they believed was behind it, regardless of whether they were a kobold or not.

"How we do?" Ig chewed nervously on the already haggard end of his tail.

I suspect that our best course of action will be to do precisely what they are accusing us of.

Once more he graced me with his incomparable wit. "Weh?"

Seek the dwarf with all haste, pry her loose from Ildrit, and place me upon her head. It is time that she began earning her keep around this circus.

The thunderous applause that had accompanied the acrobatics was now slowing to a dull slapping, so before Ig could go forth and decouple the dwarf, he had to dash back out into the middle of the ring, looking as beleaguered as he felt and earning yet more laughter.

"Me is promising you big magics, but me in hurry now so . . ."

He whipped me off his head before I had the opportunity to prompt him with a simple spell.

From the torchlit dimness of the circus to complete and utter darkness I was thrust. Time's passage lost all meaning. All my power and wisdom were as naught in the face of that fathomless expanse of nothingness. The thing beneath the earth had been made of darkness such as this.

Then I was back and Ig was still holding the big white rabbit that he'd pulled out of me by the ears. The laughter was shot through with applause and cheers now that they'd seen him actually manage to do something. That was good, it meant the crowd was biddable and could be won over.

"Now me got get helper." He paused as he began scurrying toward the exit. "You alls be good now!"

This earned him more laughter and applause as the druid and his many tamed animals came ambling out into the center ring, unsure how they had been upstaged by the single white rabbit that was already there looking as perplexed as the druid himself.

CHAPTER NINETEEN

SHOW AND TELL

Time was most assuredly against my diminutive friend as he sought out my other, somewhat less diminutive friend. The next person that wore me was going to have to be a giraffe, to balance the books.

Our first port of call was the caravan in which they had allegedly been getting to know each other better, but as much as it still stank of them to Ig's somewhat more sensitive nose, they were entirely absent from the crunkled sheets. As were their clothes, blessedly.

Can you follow their scent?

Ig cocked his head to one side like a dog and sniffed. He took a few tremulous steps forward before he caught on to an aroma and then took off at a full sprint, with me flopping around on top of him for good measure. Ducking through the crowds and leaping the guy-ropes, he rounded a corner and came to an abrupt halt. There was the source of the scent. The popcorn stand.

You are exactly as smart as you look.

"Smell good," Ig replied, not in the least chastised.

Popcorn smells good. I believe you, but that is not particularly relevant to our hunt for the errant dwarf, is it?

He contemplated this for a moment before offering a counterpoint. "Maybe hunt better on full stomach?"

I am begging you to focus, Ig, please.

"Right," he said, staring longingly at the popcorn. "Find the popcorn."

The dwarf, Ig. Find Cygni.

With the fall of night in most places, darkness would have ensued, ensuring that it was remarkably difficult to see our companion wherever she lurked along the boardwalk, but even Ig's dim kobold vision could pick everything out here in Arpanpholigon. The City of Lights was not named in vain: there were glowing orbs drifting all over the place, illuminating the entire city all night long, preventing dastardly deeds being done in the dark and ensuring the strong sales of blackout curtains.

Yet even with that advantage on his side, Ig seemed to be struggling to spot her. In truth, I could see neither hide nor hair of her either.

Alright, Ig, I'm going to compose a seeking spell, and then I'm going to talk you through it step by step. It is going to require multiple elements being brought into play at the correct times, but it is my hope that I can directly share my knowledge of those elements with you rather than having to rely on your own grasp of . . . three.

Ig nodded.

Now let me think. Ideally we would need some object of Cygni's to serve as an anchor for the seeking spell, and what luck that she has formed so solid an emotional attachment to me that I can serve. Secondly, we will need to create some illusion or conjured marker that will act to translate the information that the spell has gathered into an easily parsed visual form. The soot cloud that you produced when trying to cast a multi-directional carbon blast should be sufficient for that. But next we must begin to delve into the other elements that will be required.

Once more Ig nodded, but it was in a somewhat halfhearted way, as he had wandered up to the popcorn stand and was chatting with the one-armed gentleman who was running it with a surprising degree of dexterity.

Ideally, we shall use one of the noble gases as our sniffer to seek her out, a some-what complex incantation compared to the single words that you are accustomed to, but one that I feel we can accomplish within our time frame, assuming that you can maintain your full focus throughout the process.

Ig nodded, shoveling popcorn into his mouth as he walked. It tasted nowhere near as good as it smelled, but given how good it had smelled, that was hardly surprising.

After our sniffer has located Cygni, it will have to trigger the second phase of the spell. While I know that you are not yet familiar with triggers, it is relatively simple to construct one with a few key words of Archaic and a specific event to set them off. In this case, we will likely use the dissipation of the noble gas and its natural replacement within the sphere of the spell with nitrogen as that trigger.

Every time that Ig nodded his little head, I became more and more certain that I was talking to myself.

Are you even listening to me?

He nodded his head.

So you can of course tell me how we're going to cast the seeking spell that will locate Cygni, a spell that we must perform within the next minute if we are to have any hope of successfully arriving back at the main tent prior to the current act's end?

"Me no listen," he said, somewhat begrudgingly.

Then I shall have to start over again with my explanation, if you do not even know how the spell is going to work then how do you expect to . . .

"Cygni!" Ig called out to the dwarf, and she turned away from the freak show tent where she'd finally started doing her job and selling tickets.

"Shortspout?" She was startled out of her argument with a man trying to pass off a teenager as a toddler by putting his shoes on his knees.

He reached up and seized me by the rim. "Me needs you come to big tent. Wear hat. Help spells. Hat explains."

There was a flutter of oblivion then I was perched atop Cygni's bullet head once more.

Ig had already turned tail and begun his capering run back toward the big top, but I had to know. "*Ig! How did you find her without the spell?*"

Despite his haste, Ig stopped to smirk. "Me ask popcorn man."

Aghast. That is the only word to describe my feelings in that moment. I was aghast at having been outwitted by a kobold. I had been so intent upon using my incredible knowledge of the world that I had entirely forgotten that others also had knowledge. And while it may not have been cosmic in scale or capable of remaking all reality to their will, sometimes the knowledge required was not anything grandiose, but simply what was relevant.

It seemed that I still had things to learn.

"Kobold outsmart you?" Cygni's grin was far more apparent now that she lacked the massive mustache that had concealed it through our travels together.

I don't know what you mean, we work together in perfect harmony.

"Yeah, he outsmarted you." She chortled, but at least she was wandering in the direction of the big top now.

Every teacher should hope to someday be surpassed by his students.

"Yeah, but . . . me, not the kobold?" She still had laughter in her voice, but it was tempered somewhat by bitterness.

My friend, you have been outsmarting me since the very moment that we met. I hardly think that you have anything to be jealous of when Ig uses his brain for once.

"Jealous?" She grunted, ducking under the arm of an already inebriated reveler. "You think I'm jealous of that runtling? It is just funny you spend all your time on his head because he needs all the extra help."

Have you missed my dulcet tones whispering in your frontal lobes, dear girl?

"No. Ain't like that." She fell silent and sullen as we trudged on along the boardwalk. "Didn't think I'd be so alone up here. With you around."

It was the kind of openhearted honesty that I'd never anticipated hearing from her, and it hit me like a blow to the gut. Here she was, separated from her people and all that she ever knew, and I'd abandoned her.

I am truly sorry. It was my impression that you wished to be alone in your own mind again. To have you feeling as though I'd . . . That was never my . . . No. No excuses. I am simply sorry. You deserve better, and I mean to give you better in the future.

She snorted again, trying to deflect any genuine show of emotion through humor. "Aye, you should have been on my head the whole time I was shacking up with Longshanks . . ."

If you had simply requested my presence, I'm sure that I could have given you both helpful pointers.

"Agh, no." She laughed, nauseously. "I can't think of anything worse."

Well, that shows a startling lack of imagination. Just think how much more terrible it would have been if I'd taken over for you because you weren't doing it right.

She was laughing so hard as we made our way into the big tent that it probably would have drawn the attention of the whole crowd, were their attention not already thoroughly captured by Ig, balancing atop one of the giant balls that the animal trainer had left behind, being slowly orbited by two more of the same balls and also a very confused-looking bear.

Very, very quietly, Cygni asked, "What am I doing here?"

It has occurred to us that many of those observing will believe that Ig's speech and magic are both tricks. Ventriloquism and the intervention of some lesser magic user to provide visual effects. To impress upon everyone that Ig himself is an impressive wizard in his own right, we need to cast something more impressive.

"Which Ig can't do, because he isn't impressive."

I mean, for a kobold he is downright remarkable, unique even.

"So you brought me to pretend my magic is his." She was trying not to grit her teeth, but I could feel the muscles in her jaw clenching.

One singular impressive, fully developed spell should be sufficient to convey to all and sundry that Ig is what he claims to be.

She let out a sigh. "What am I casting?"

With Cygni there were no limitations, not on the size and complexity of the working, not on the elements that she needed to know. She was essentially a fully fledged wizard in her own right by this point, and it would just be a matter of teaching her the correct correspondences of each Archaic word to each element, and the various gray areas that one could delve into between those elements, and the various subtle variations of tone that could shift the effects of words in Archaic, or the way that certain aspects of elements could be focused on to give them more bearing on the spell, or . . . She had the basics down. And I could work with that.

Phase One: Bromine, Antimony, Manganese, end phase. Phase Two: Livermorium, Krypton, Samarium, end phase. Phase Three: Bismuth, Rhodium, Calcium, end phase.

She nodded along as I spoke, and unlike Ig, I knew that she was actually listening. Memorizing the sequence, digging in the pouch at her belt for the Scrynium that would empower all her workings and drawing in breath to repeat whatever I told her to say.

"Crescere valde magna." She repeated it all quietly, so as to draw no eyes to her, word perfect, every inflection exactly as I'd said it in her mind.

Ig made a startled sound as the spell took hold, but he did not lose his mental grasp on the orbiting balls and bear; in fact, even as he slipped off the ball he'd been trying to stay steady on and it bounced around, it was added to the orbital decor.

Before our eyes, and those of the crowd, Ig began to grow. It was not the hideous malformation that you'd see in a druid's shapeshifting but the carefully measured and organized expansion that a wizard's magic could create. He grew and grew, surpassing first Cygni in height, then Ildrit, then everyone in the room regardless of their species of origin. He grew until his head was up among the dangling trapeze and his every confused wheeze echoed out of his cavernous mouth.

When he gasped out, "Weh?" those sitting in the back rows were almost blown off their seats by the impact of his voice.

This was an impressive act of magic in itself, probably enough to draw the attention of every guild in the city, but not enough to guarantee a call from the Invisible College.

"Circumfusa anulo ignis," Cygni hissed out through gritted teeth. The power flowing through her smoothly but straining against the restrictions of her limited Quintessence channels. Like trying to push a raw sausage through the eye of a needle.

If the bear in orbit had looked concerned before, now it was positively terrified, as before the magic fully came to life, sparks began to dance in concentric orbits around the now gigantic Ig. Thankfully, none of the purple flames that exploded into being intersected with the bear. Unfortunately, two of the balls did feel that fire's touch. It looked to the observer not like fire but like a solid band of purple light, but it burned like the flames of heck itself. Where the big bouncy balls touched on each line of purple, they burst instantly. Loud pops rocked through the whole tent as the tattered remains sputtered down to the ground.

Ig let the bear and ball that remained drop as the circles of purple light began to spin faster and faster around him before beginning to shrink.

Calling Ig a coward would be unfair. He was a member of a species that nature seemed to have designed exclusively to be prey, yet in spite of being entirely physically and mentally unimpressive in every way, he had still gone out into the world and faced that malignant world down at every turn. It would be rude to call him a coward now, just because impending and inescapable death was bearing down on him and he started screaming with his giant-sized lungs and nearly deafened everyone in the tent.

If he could have shrunk back down to his normal size then he might have outpaced the fire's approach, but he could not. The loops of lethal purple encircled and enclosed him, tightening closer and closer with every passing moment, and there was no escaping it. When he took a terrified, staggering step back, he remained the center of gravity around which the fires orbited. The rings followed after him.

"Cedere eum ad normalem et relinquere statuam retro."

It was not Ig that was screaming now, it was the audience. They thought from his horrified expression that something was going wrong, that the trick had gone awry and he was in danger. He wasn't, of course, but he was a terrible actor, so not informing him of what precisely was going on made for a far better show.

The purple fire struck and he was paralyzed in terror. The bands of blinding purple plasma washed over him, all over him, until his entire body was engulfed in the ghostly light. Then, as soon as it was there, it vanished. All that was left was Ig, still unmoving, still titanic, until suddenly, abruptly, he fell apart.

I do not mean that he had the emotional breakdown that you may have expected in this moment, but rather that he physically broke apart. The chalky remains of his massive body collapsed in on themselves under its own weight, square flakes of it tumbling away, drifting out over the crowd before splintering further into tiny little square snowflakes. Each time someone in the crowd reached out to touch them they shattered again, further and further shrinking until the whole vast edifice of Ig became dust and glitter. And there, down on the trampled dirt of the circus circle, Ig stood untouched, unharmed, shrunk back down to his usual height.

The applause was uproarious, deafening as Ig's gigantic scream. There was not a single seat that the buttocks had remained upon; everyone was up, giving that tiny little kobold a standing ovation.

Even at this distance I could see that he was shaking, but he did not hesitate to give the crowd a bow and a flourish of the top hat he'd replaced me with. "Me thank! Me thank!"

Cygni's smile wasn't just a reflection of my mood. She was proud of herself, what she had achieved, and strangely, she was proud of Ig too. The way that a sibling would be proud, begrudgingly, and unwilling to ever admit it.

Fatherhood was never something I'd contemplated in my mortal life, but here I was as a hat who had adopted a horny little dwarflet and a kobold. Wonderful. Excellent. Just how I planned to spend my afterlife.

We retrieved the beleaguered and staggering Ig from the edge of the ring as the next performers came pouring out. That would not just be a tough act to follow, it would be damned near impossible for anyone else to even be remembered tonight.

I would say that was a success, wouldn't you?

"Everyone's confused." Cygni chuckled. "Mission accomplished."

There will be some among the wizards quite capable of deciphering that spell, but they in turn will be mystified by the suggestion that it was performed by . . .

She reached down to pat Ig on his back awkwardly. He was still vibrating with terror too hard to speak. "A kobold?"

Someone who hasn't studied with them. It will be a challenge to the monopoly that they hold on wizardry, something that they most assuredly cannot tolerate. And so they will attempt to resolve the mystery to their own satisfaction, proving to themselves that only one of their alumni had performed the spell, even though that alumnus would of course then be hideously shamed for using the High Art for something so base as circus entertainment.

Her brows drew down at that. Intruding once more on my vision. "Ain't you shamed?"

Desperate times call for desperate measures. Besides, I am coming to believe that the snobbery with which magic and the common man are treated by the college is uncalled for.

"Hah." She snorted. "Going to be a union man now? For the workers, not the bosses?"

Well, let's not get carried away, I am merely stating that their isolationist self-aggrandizing pedantry is perhaps not conducive to the best relations with every-one else in the world. That a more inclusive approach might bring us . . .

"Up the workers." Cygni chuckled as she led Ig by the shoulder behind some tarpaulin and out of sight.

"How I do?" Ig asked.

"Very well, my friend." Cygni graciously loaned me the use of her vocal cords.

Ig shook his little head, less like he was announcing a negative and more like he was a wet dog. "No. How I do? How I go big and boom?"

Cygni stared at him in confusion at his confusion for a moment, then answered, "That was me, you nitwit."

Ig looked up at her with those big puppy eyes of his. Well, actually, they were rather small and beady, but the look definitely had sad-puppy energy to it. "You big boom me?"

"What did you think you were fetching me for?"

"Me no know?!"

"What did you think was going to happen?"

"Me no know!"

Please stop asking the kobold questions that he will never have an answer to. If you ever see him do something and wonder what he was thinking, he wasn't.

The snort that came out of Cygni was not entirely condescending, but her little laugh was tainted by that same twinge of irritation that persisted in her, that little niggling annoyance that I kept indulging Ig when she was clearly the superior student.

She nodded to the backstage area. "Come on, let's get you washed off."

Ig backed away out of reach. "No like wash."

"You can't go around covered in white." She was rolling her eyes, but even from the periphery I could see Ig darting from side to side as he looked for a means of escape.

"Me brush off." Ig spoke with the same nervous energy still carried over from his performance. Flight or fight and he didn't know how to fight.

Cygni scoffed. "It will not brush off. Just hold still."

She held her knowledge of hydrogen and oxygen in her mind and readied the right word of Archaic, but Ig was already running, and despite his legs being considerably shorter than hers, he was built for sprinting in a way that dwarves simply weren't. He shot out of sight faster than you could say, "*Purus.*"

"Stupid . . ." Cygni grumbled as she took off after him.

There could be no denying that Ig's actions were a little silly and impulsive, but given that he'd just had the latest in a long line of near-death experiences, I was inclined to forgive and forget. Cygni, on the other hand, felt that him running away from the hosing down she was about to give him was some sort of personal slight.

Slipping one of the jumping rings onto her pinkie finger as she ran, she gave chase.

Out in the crowd beyond the tarp, Ig should have been invisible. He was so short that the mere presence of other people should have kept him hidden from Cygni's view, more so given her own rather earthbound perspective. But this was why she had the ring. She sprang straight up into the air, catching on one of the guy-lines holding up the big top near where it was clipped to cloth.

There he went, scurrying. The crowd rippling out around him and chuckles emanating. As though this were all part of the show.

I suppose that if Ig and company were to continue with the circus then that was precisely what these kind of antics would be. A regular feature of Ig's traveling show. There would have been a time that I saw such a life as contemptable. Beneath contempt really; wasting your life on making others happy was such a squanderous use of time given all that a person could do with it. Now, seeing all the smiling faces, and feeling Cygni's heart beating with excitement, I struggled to remember why I'd thought that way.

She swung off the guy-line and rebounded off the ground hard into a great leap that cleared both the whole crowd and Ig's progress through it to land heavily in front of the fortune-teller's tent. Ig emerged from the crowd, bounding forward on all fours only to come face-to-face with her.

"Oh" was all he managed to squeak out before she cast *"Purus"* at last.

A sphere of water had gathered between her hands and now leapt toward the chalky kobold. He reared up on his hind legs, threw out his hands, and he caught the wave before it could wash over him. Adrenaline giving him the focus that he needed to hold it back with low magic.

That should have been impossible, of course. Water was not a solid object that you could hold, it was billions of tiny molecules all spread out, and catching just one of them with low magic was all that most people could accomplish. With nothing attaching that molecule to all the rest, the wave should have carried on unabated. But of course, Ig was too stupid to know that, so it worked.

With a heave of his little shoulders, he threw the water back at Cygni, and she was so startled by the turn of events that she didn't even have a moment to think about throwing up a shield. She was soaked to the bone in her lovely new red robes, and she was not happy about it.

"You little . . ." The word that she said next was in Dwarvish, and to fully understand it, you would need the context of several centuries of dwarven culture, and anatomy, and knowledge about the solvency of certain minerals when exposed to the natural acidity of certain regions of anatomy. It would have made a sailor blush, if they could have understood it in its entirety.

What luck that none of the bystanders spoke Dwarvish, or they likely would have burst into flames on hearing it.

Right, I believe that is quite enough foolishness for one evening. Our goal has been achieved, let us all just . . .

She readied another water spell, yelping out "***Fragor.***"

This time there was no moment for Ig to prepare as a fully formed blast of water crossed the distance between them in an instant, bursting over his dusty face like a bubble popping and completely drenching him too.

"Me no likey bath!" Ig squealed in dismay.

"Needed one anyway!" Cygni barked back, Scrynium still in hand in case she needed to defend herself against his counterattack.

The two of them were so caught up in their silliness that they didn't even feel the encroaching cold until it was already too late.

Frost had formed in the puddles of the ground around them as they yelled at one another, and now, with the spell completed, the ice rushed up to envelop them both, pinning the two of them in place in solid blocks that stretched up high enough to cover their mouths, but leaving Cygni's nose and Ig's snout still protruding so they could draw breath.

It was the kind of clever little trap I would have constructed if I came upon two foolish novices bickering in the college halls. I'd have frozen them and left them to defrost and let their tempers cool.

But the tutor who was instructing my two apprentices seemed to have no intention of giving them that time. The gathered crowds parted as Sabrinia the Blue, head of her own little department and fiefdom in the Invisible College, stepped forward to look upon us. "The archmage sensed a great magical working down here in the city and dispatched me to investigate. Imagine my surprise to find the two of you."

Ah good, Sabrinia, she is far from the most radical of my peers, I suspect that we shall have no trouble at all in convincing her to take us up to the college.

Cygni tried to reply, but couldn't, by virtue of the ice solidified over her mouth to stop her casting.

"A dwarf and a kobold, both species fundamentally incapable of wielding the High Art, yet I bore witness to both of you doing so." She stroked her chin, clearly wishing that she had an impressive beard like mine. "What an intriguing mystery."

I could not hear what Ig was trying to say with his snout sealed in a loop of ice, but Cygni's internal monologue was the sort of thing that you might have expected if a man had stubbed his toe on a coffee table in the middle of the night.

This is all going to work out just fine, simply a misunderstanding. As soon as she understands what we were hoping to achieve with our little display, I am certain that she can be talked around to our point of view.

"The archmage demanded that I put a halt to whatever you were doing down here, and that goal seems to have been achieved, yet I find that curiosity is getting the better of me. I should take you to the college, for further study."

Oh, that's perfect. We won't even have to walk anywhere, she's going to levitate us up. Problem solved. Steps three through seven of the plan can be abandoned. We are on our way!

Sabrinia raised her hands to cast and was interrupted by a boot in the lower back that sent her sprawling in the well-churned mud of the field. Ildrit stood over her, blade drawn, face emotionless. It was not that he was not feeling; I knew from my time with him that he felt deeply. Rather, it was that in battle, he allowed his face no leeway to give away his next movement. "Step away from my friends, wizard."

I don't believe that Sabrinia had ever been shoved in her life, and to find herself face down in the mud now was a real shock to the system that had left her stunned. She should have tried a month as a kobold; it did wonders for your sensitivity to indignity.

Well, that isn't ideal, but as soon as we can talk I'm sure that we'll be able to make peace.

Ildrit stepped over the fallen wizard, turning his back on her and lashing out with Widowtaker. For all his strength, I think we had forgotten just how graceful he could be in battle. It shattered the ice clinging to Cygni's face without coming anywhere near close enough to do her harm. She spat her own frozen spittle across to land in the mud beside Sabrinia. "What in the nine hecks was that about?"

Ig continued to wiggle in his frozen entombment, catching Ildrit's eye at exactly the wrong moment. As the swordsman turned to free the kobold, Sabrinia rose. **"Ori."**

The air around Ildrit thickened, pinning him in place as surely as the direct application of Quintessence would have, though much more efficiently in terms of expenditure of energy.

"You dare to lay hands upon a wizard of the Invisible College."

Of course he dared, what a useless waste of breath, if he hadn't dared we wouldn't have been having this conversation at all. Did she think that she was going to impress on him the mistake that he'd made? This was Ildrit; he'd cut down far more threatening foes than a single middling administrator with a talent for academic backstabbing.

"Technically, he laid a boot on you," Cygni piped up, still frozen up to the neck but none the less sassy for it. Even if she was starting to shiver.

The muscles of Ildrit's arms and back rippled as he strained against the spell that held him. He wouldn't be able to break through it. Not when it had been so competently cast.

Solvo is the word of archaic required to break the spell holding your lover. I suggest that you use it only when Sabrinia is within striking distance, lest she have an opportunity to counter him again.

"That is the sort of crime that is punished by transmogriphication in this city." Sabrinia had lost some of her dignity with the application of mud to her face, so she was overcompensating. She made her way over to where Cygni remained frozen. "Do you think that your owner would rather be a ferret or a lizard?"

Oh, I do wish she hadn't said that.

"Owner?" Cygni growled.

The smirk on Sabrinia's smug face just spread. "I assume that you two are his pets?"

Sulfur dominated Cygni's thoughts as she hissed, "**Ambustum.**"

The fire burst out of her, undirected by gestures of the hand or focus of the mind. It shot out wildly in every direction. The ice surrounding Cygni melted away in a wash and before Sabrinia had so much as thought of countering, the dwarf was on her. She didn't need magic to put some sneering bitch in her place. Her fist rose and fell, taking the wizard in the jaw as she rode her back down to the dirt.

Alas, Sabrinia was not some apprentice capable of working magic only in the moment. There were spells that she cast automatically upon rising each day to protect herself from those other faculty members who were envious of her position and not above a little skullduggery to see their own advancement. As pain shot through her, one of her contingencies activated a concussive blast that launched Cygni off into the crowd.

The dwarf landed heavily on her back and groaned, but nothing was broken yet, so she scrambled back to her feet. This added distance was ideal; it would give us time to formulate a plan of attack, to free our allies from their bindings and . . . Cygni leapt back into the fray.

She led with her fist, as though that cross-country haymaker couldn't be seen coming from miles away, and as though the very same protections that Sabrinia had set up wouldn't just launch her away again. What luck for all of us that she entirely missed. Instead coming down right in front of Sabrinia as the woman got back onto her feet yet again. Those sky-blue robes of hers had certainly seen better days.

Both women opened their mouths to cast, but Sabrinia was the swifter—that was what experience bought you, I suppose. Once more, she cast her curse of binding air, and once more, Cygni's progress ground to an abrupt halt.

"Did you really think that you could defeat me in a duel of magic? I am a wizard, dwarf. I have no clue as to what you might be."

Despite being pinned in place, she wasn't entirely muzzled. Cygni managed to growl out, "No."

Tittering, Sabrinia leaned in close so that she might hear what the dwarf had to say. "I beg your pardon?"

"No," Cygni snarled again. "Didn't think I could beat you."

"Then perhaps you are more intelligent than you first appeared . . ."

Cygni cut her off. "Thought he could."

The color drained from Sabrinia's face as she spun on her heel to face Ildrit. Who was still standing still as a statue. The wizard tossed back her head and laughed the affected laugh of someone who only really knows what laughing is by reading about it. Then she turned back to Cygni with a sneer. "Did you truly think that . . ."

Ig's spell blasted her off her feet and back into the mud. She started to rise only to be shoved back down again as if there were a giant hand descending from the heavens to crush her. Ig's low magic. The kind that everyone completely overlooked. He walked out of the parting crowd with his paw held out level in front of him. Gently patting down every time she struggled too hard to escape.

"You is not hurting me friends." He said it so softly that you shouldn't have even been able to hear him over the crowd, but all of us did. Sabrinia most of all.

She opened her mouth to cast, only to have her face ever so gently rammed back down into the mud. Ig sounded almost sad. "No more."

He was looking a little worse for wear after Cygni's outpouring of fire had melted the ice that held him, a little bit sooty, a little bit damp, rather like a cavy that had fallen in a bath. Yet despite that, there was a presence to the little kobold that I think would surprise those who did not know him so intimately.

This was not the little runt that I'd pulled wriggling and squealing from his hole out in the Badlands. This was a wizard, empowered by the same primal forces that made the stars turn and the world spin. He had faced down armies and ogres, necromancers, and heckfire. Despite his stature, he had earned his title and me as his hat.

From amidst the crowd came a soft clapping, soon picked up by the other fair-goers. Soon everyone was hooting and cheering to see one of those arrogant wizards brought down into the dirt with the rest of them.

The cheer was short-lived, however. A spell washed out over the crowd, silencing them, and a man mumbled, "That was meant to be a dramatic slow clap as I emerged to face my foe, you idiots. Don't you know anything about narrative structure?"

Danyeel the Dramatic, of the newly formed Department of Legendary Lexicology. Well, I say newly formed, it had been around for nigh on three decades by this point, but that still made it a toddler compared to the other branches of study. He stepped forward out of the crowd, cutting a sharp silhouette in his robe with massive shoulder pads. "I see you're a magician, kobold. But I don't think you can hope to defeat the both of us at once."

"Me no hope," Ig said. Ambiguously enough that it could be taken as a statement of absolute confidence rather than one of despair.

"Well, there is no need for any further conflict. The magical displays in this circus are at an end, and you are cordially invited to visit the Invisible College, so that we might discuss your future prospects. All three of you."

It's a trap, obviously. But it does get us where we need to be.

Ig looked askance to Ildrit, who was paralyzed, and then over to Cygni, who was also paralyzed. Neither of them were able to answer for them.

"Me is needing me hat first." Ig began to sidle my way, hand still held out, pressing Sabrinia none too gently into the mud.

"Your hat?" Danyeel asked, clearly thrown by this non-sequitur.

"Go on head." Ig explained what a hat was as he crept closer. "Keep brain warm."

"I'm familiar with the concept," Danyeel sneered. "But why do you need . . ."

Ig snatched me off Cygni's scalp, and after a flutter of darkness, I saw through his eyes once more. Cygni looked even more furious from the outside than she'd felt on the inside. No wonder Sabrinia had frozen her as quickly as possible. It was not the kind of face you'd like to encounter in a dark alley. Or a well-lit alley for that matter. Actually, well-lit might have been worse, because you could see the face better.

We should make our peace and go with him. We wanted an invitation to the college, and this is it. It may well be a trap, but it is a trap that will position us precisely where we wish to be if we happen to spring it. I'd suggest going with the flow.

"Go with flow," Ig repeated back.

"I beg your pardon?" Danyeel inquired with an imperiously raised eyebrow. As though he had been confronted by a poorly translated passage.

"We comes with you," Ig conceded generously. "Undo the freezy."

He released his hold on Sabrinia and she came up out of the mud gasping and spluttering, with a face full of what I could only hope was exclusively mud. She spat out a mouthful while her eyes raked around, then finally fixed on Ig. There was murder in those eyes. Easy to recognize now that I'd been on the murder-ee side of those glares enough time. Yet Ig stood his ground like the bravest little kobold of them all, and as she rose to her full height, drew in her breath, and readied to cast, he did nothing to stop her.

"**Solvo**," Sabrinia hissed through muddied teeth, and both Cygni and Ildrit immediately wilted from where they'd been trapped. Both of them coughed a bit as they became able to fully expand their lungs again, and Cygni looked up with that very same murder in her eyes as Sabrinia had. Oh good.

"*Be still, Cygni. Our new friend Danyeel has come to escort us to the Invisible College, and that is where we mean to go.*"

For a moment, Cygni's fury did not abate, but she was nothing if not rational. She folded up her wrath into a little envelope and filed it away for later. "Alright."

Ildrit, as the mass murderer with his sword out, was ironically the least dangerous moving part of all this. He glanced from Ig to Cygni, then nodded tersely.

Danyeel strolled alongside Ig and threw a well-tailored arm around his shoulders. This involved some degree of squatting. "That's a damned fine impression you did there. Sounded just like Old Scryne."

His words were like a lead weight in the pit of my stomach, except I didn't have a stomach. Old Scryne . . . So quickly my legacy had turned to mockery. Well, they'd all know what Old Scryne was about soon enough; I just needed to get into my library and laboratory and I'd have a new body grown in minutes. Then every one of these pedestrian propagandists would face the wrath of my rhetoric in turn. That and no small number of fireballs delivered to their rear ends.

"*Yes, I suppose that it would,*" I managed to say before returning control of the voice box to Ig.

Danyeel tossed his head back and laughed in just as fake a way as Sabrinia had, but with more theatrical flair. His long hair flicked back as he did it, shimmering in the torchlight. He'd learned to do that in front of a mirror, practicing, and for the first time he was doing it in front of an audience. "Come along then, my new friends."

CHAPTER TWENTY

THE DASTARDLY KILLER OF ABSALOM SCRYNE

One might have expected that there would be some teleportation at work bringing people up to the Invisible College where it hung in the sky. Other, more frivolous minds might have imagined that there were winged horses and fairy dragons saddled up and ready to carry the new students up to their glorious new life of academia. Alas, neither one was true.

At the center of the city of Arpanpholigon stood the gatehouse of the Invisible College, guarded by a vast, many-armed automaton known to the faculty as the Brass Titan of Arpanpholigon and to the students as Guardsman Steve. From the twelve eyes set around the construct's head shone that same spell-light that had illuminated the entrance to the city, searching the souls of all it gazed upon for any hint of malfeasance. It would find no evil in the heart of my companions, and luckily for me, I had no heart to probe, so any evil in the purely hypothetical version it was seeking was being overlooked entirely. We strolled on into the gatehouse without delay or being crushed by one of the many giant weapons held in Steve's many arms.

Before us lay the first challenge that every student of Arpanpholigon encountered, the one that did away with a solid quarter of the applicants before we had even begun. The stairs.

As it turns out, the type of bookish weirdos who want to pursue a career in wizardry don't tend to be the most athletic. They are almost exclusively what I have heard referred to as "indoor kids" and thus when confronted with a spiral staircase heading up into the clouds above, the majority of them have some difficulty with breathing. In recent years, accommodations had been made after it was pointed out to the admissions committee that they were deliberately excluding disabled people from applying.

Alongside the spiral staircase heading up at a sixty-degree angle, there was now a ramp. If you could push your wheelchair up that, then you'd be accepted just the same as anyone walking up the stairs. Complaints had been filed that this was still unfair, but by that point in time, the admissions committee had all ascended to a higher plane of existence through the use of guided meditation, copious amounts of hallucinogens, and some poisoned fruit punch, so the complaints were filed neatly in the fireplace.

Of course, as the archmage, I was aware of a dozen far less exhausting ways to enter the Invisible College. While general admission students had to make this climb, those who had someone on staff to vouch for them passed through the Nepotism Gate and were greeted by a cadre of nymphs with drink trays and carried up to their new lodgings on the feathered wings that they would sprout after enjoying those refreshing potions. Staff typically used the freight elevator because it was a bugger to get the feathers off everything.

Regardless, we were well on our way now, heading up and up into the sky, Cygni grumbling about her knees all the way. Ildrit did offer to carry her, but that had just earned him a scowl so foul I fear that it would have turned milk sour. As for Ig, though he was the least athletic of the trio, he also seemed the most devoid of complaint. I suppose that the close quarters of the stairwell may have reminded him of home, but mostly I suspect that he just didn't grasp the danger that we were walking into.

Whoever had the wherewithal and power to slay me lay at the top of this flight of stairs. The murderer that I had transcended death and traversed the Badlands to find. A puissant mage, whose wickedness knew no bounds. Yet Ig approached this challenge with the same indifference as everything else in his life. Not a single thought in that little head of his. I was startled to realize that I was jealous of the calm that ignorance bought him.

Everything since my death had brought me to this moment, but so too had everything in my life. Every choice that I'd made, every joy I'd denied myself in the pursuit of power and knowledge. Knowledge above all else. And here I was wishing that there wasn't a single thought in my head, because all that my knowledge was doing was making me unhappy.

Ig had been terrified when we first set out. Completely overwhelmed by everything in the world that he did not understand, but now he was fine. Well, not fine, he would be riddled with anxieties until the day he died because he had the brain of a prey item, but he was managing, while I was the one confronting the end of our journey and feeling as though I was losing all control. Our positions had reversed. My knowledge had become a burden, and his ignorance had become blissful.

There was time enough for many more profound and meaningful thoughts as we ascended that spiral staircase, but I shall not bother to list them here for fear of wearing my dear readers down as badly as poor Cygni was being worn down by the persistent cardiovascular exercise of the stairs. One might have thought all the extra practice she'd been putting in with Ildrit might have helped, but it seemed not.

Finally the spiral came to its end, and all five of us, six counting myself, arrived at the brass gates that marked entry into the college itself. This would have been a very important moment in the life of many a young wizard-to-be, but for us it was just a single brief stop on our journey deeper into the college with another attendant statue casting a prying spell at us, trying to discern our intentions.

You would have thought that two would have been sufficient, but no, it seems that they have so little faith in their magic working that they decided to take three swings instead of one. Though I suppose that being forced to climb all those stairs might have changed one's opinion on the college by the time that the top has been reached and made you entirely determined to destroy the place just to avoid walking back down.

Ig chuckled softly to himself, drawing the attention of both the college wizards, who had started to view him less as an oddity and more as a potential menace after the way that he'd thrown poor Sabrinia around. A kobold chuckling in any scenario was unlikely to be good news, but a kobold capable of magics the likes of which they had never seen chuckling was probably cause enough to sound an alarm bell ringing in both their heads.

What luck neither one of them had slain me and ascended to the position of archmage. I would have died all over again from the shame of having been bested by such pathetic examples of wizardry.

From the Gates of Knowledge—don't blame me, I didn't name every wing of the damned place—the new arrivals would typically proceed in the direction of the library, to be greeted in the Quint by their various tutors, mentors, and future rivals. The Quint was a five-sided grassy patch in between the various enclosed buildings of the college, typically used to play enchanted hacky sack, arcane frisbee, and to strum the lute aimlessly. Also for those rites and rituals that required a direct line of sight to the sky, which was more than one might have expected. The Quint needed to be booked several months in advance if one wanted an evening of stargazing for one's students, and even then you'd probably end up arguing over it with the assorted mixed couples attempting to get it on in the bushes.

We did not go to the Quint, which was something of a relief. I did not fancy retracing my childhood steps any more than I relished the thought of spending time there in that desolate patch of green. It had always felt like the sort of place that druids might like, and as such I had an intense and violent aversion to it.

Rather than following that well-trodden path, we instead looped back around to yet another staircase, this one ascending even farther into the heavens. Ildrit sighed. Ig sighed. Cygni made a noise somewhat similar to a washing machine with a brick in it.

It seemed that it was the wizards' plan to exhaust us before we came in sight of their ignoble leader, but I had a very simple solution. The moment we had all begun trudging up the steps to the archmage's solarium, I had Ig reach out, push a touch of Quintessence into a carved stone, and whisper, "***Sursum.***"

It wasn't really a spell as such, so none of the elements needed to be invoked. Rather, it was simply the activation of an ancient artifact, installed by one of the prior elderly archmagi who were similarly tired out.

Empowered with that tiny spark of Quintessence, the spell began to work. The steps beneath our feet began to shift, rotating their way up the stairwell at what could hardly be described as a breakneck pace, but would of course have been a breakneck pace if anyone were to topple over backwards due to the motion.

Both wizards accompanying us let out little scared sounds as the very stone lurched beneath them, but it was short-lived, with both recovering their composure just enough to shoot Ig a dirty look in tandem. We were escalated onwards and upwards with the gentle sound of grinding rocks. A noise that seemed to sooth Cygni considerably.

And then, finally we arrived. The moving stairs deposited us onto the landing outside of the archmage's study and all three of the mortal bodies I had once inhabited pulled themselves up to their full height. They knew that this was what they had been waiting for. What we had traversed all of this distance for. They knew that behind this rather charmingly carved cherrywood door sat the wizard who had murdered me and consigned me to a nightmarish afterlife trapped in an item of clothing. To say that they were tense would be something of an understatement. Of all the foes that they'd faced until now, with the possible exception of Cygni's dark god, there had been none nearly so dangerous as whosoever had been capable of killing me.

As the door was hauled open, each of them held their breath. Ig reached up and squeezed my rim, as though it would give me comfort rather than as though someone were contorting some part of my body out of its natural shape.

Whoever had stolen my office had changed nothing. The rugs were the same, the stained glass hadn't been recast, even all of my books were still on the shelves. The murderer had stolen my whole life, not just my job title.

And there the killer was, sitting behind the desk with their back to us. I could make out whisps of white hair trailing up and over the back of the seat, the subtle hint of a head.

With a creak, the chair turned, and Absalom Scryne looked at each of us in turn.

"So you are the three troublemakers who deigned to work a great act of magic beneath the very nose of the Invisible College of Arpanpholigon," he announced, before blinking in confusion and leaning forward to see us better and therefore stare us down more effectively. Then he blinked yet again as though convinced that his eyes were deceiving him. "I'm terribly sorry, but is that kobold wearing my hat?"

ABOUT THE AUTHORS

Luke Chmilenko is the author of the Ascend Online series, among others. He grew up in Mississauga, Ontario, and now lives in Burlington, Ontario, with his wife, daughter, and two cats. Visit his website at lukechmilenko.com.

G. D. Penman is the author of more books than you can shake a reasonable-size stick at. Before finally realizing that his guidance counselor had lied about one's not being able to make a living as an author, Penman worked as an editor, table-top game designer, and literally every awful demeaning job that you can think of in between. Nowadays, he can mostly be found smoking a pipe in the sunshine and pretending that deadlines aren't lurking behind him with a club. He lives in Dundee, Scotland, with his menagerie.